## About the author

Marco Vichi was born in Florence in 1957 and lives in the Chianti region of Tuscany. The author of twelve novels and two collections of short stories, he has also edited crime anthologies, written screenplays and music lyrics, and for Italian newspapers, magazines and radio. He has also collaborated on and directed various projects for humanitarian causes.

There are five novels and two short stories featuring Inspector Bordelli. *Death in Sardinia* was shortlisted for the Crime Writers' Association International Dagger 2013 in the UK, and *Death in Florence* won the Scerbanenco, Rieti, Camaiore and Azzeccagarbugli prizes in Italy.

Find out more at www.marcovichi.it

## About the translator

Stephen Sartarelli is an award-winning translator and the author of three books of poetry. He lives in France.

# MARCO VICHI

# DEATH
## IN THE
# TUSCAN HILLS

AN
INSPECTOR BORDELLI
MYSTERY

Originally published in Italian as *La Forza del Destino*
Translated by Stephen Sartarelli

HODDER

First published in Great Britain in 2016 by Hodder & Stoughton
An Hachette UK company

1

First published in paperback in 2017

A CIP catalogue record for this title is available from the British Library

Paperback ISBN 978 1 444 76122 1
Ebook ISBN 978 1 444 76123 8

Typeset in Plantin Light by Palimpsest Book Production Limited,
Falkirk, Stirlingshire

Printed and bound by Clays Ltd, St Ives plc

Hodder & Stoughton policy is to use papers that are natural, renewable
and recyclable products and made from wood grown in sustainable
forests. The logging and manufacturing processes are expected to
conform to the environmental regulations of the country of origin.

Hodder & Stoughton Ltd
Carmelite House
50 Victoria Embankment
London EC4Y 0DZ

www.hodder.co.uk

# DEATH
## IN THE
# TUSCAN HILLS

*La Nazione*, Monday, 20 February 1967
Page three

### HILLS OF HORROR
## SUICIDE IN THE WOODS
#### FLORENTINE BUTCHER, 44 YEARS OLD
#### SHOOTS SELF IN MOUTH AT CINTOIA ALTA
#### MOTHER AND DAUGHTER GRIEF-STRICKEN

Yesterday morning Livio Panerai, a butcher aged 44, killed himself by firing a shotgun into his mouth near the abbey of Monte Scalari. Shortly before 7 a.m., a hunter found the butcher's lifeless body in the woods, still holding the double-barrel rifle. Signora Cesira Batacchi Panerai, the victim's wife of nineteen years, had no explanation for her husband's extreme act. He had left early that morning before dawn to go hunting in the hills of Cintoia, as had long been his custom on Sundays. Livio Panerai had no apparent causes for anguish in his day-to-day existence. A hard worker, always cheerful and beloved of his customers, he led a transparent life. The inhabitants of La Panca, the site of the tragedy, now speak of 'hills of horror'. Not only was the area the scene of atrocious massacres by the Nazis at Pian d'Albero and nearby locations, but the horror hasn't let up since. The suicide victim was found not far from the spot where the lifeless body of Giacomo Pellissari, the young kidnapping victim who had been raped and murdered, was discovered a few months earlier. Pellissari's killer has never been apprehended.

The mortal remains of Livio Panerai have been transferred to the chapel of the hospital of . . .

Bordelli closed the newspaper and dropped it on to the table. He sat there without moving, staring into space, looking pensive. A dense cobweb hung from the ceiling, while beside it a huge, hairy spider waited for a victim to fall into its trap. The obsessive ticking of the clock on the wall was not enough to overcome the silence. Rather, it insinuated itself into one's thoughts like a worm into an apple. Life was strange sometimes. It surprised you when you least expected it. So the butcher had killed himself. Only Bordelli and Piras knew what kind of animal Livio Panerai really was. An unreconstructed Fascist, a child rapist, a killer . . .

He stood up, sighing. Tearing page three out of *La Nazione*, he crumpled it up and squeezed it into a ball, then went and tossed it between the andirons. Other pages met the same end: articles on the aftermath of the flood, the incalculable damage to artworks, the despair of those who'd lost everything, the families still living in makeshift lodgings, not to mention the polemics, the accidents, the films playing in town, the day's television listings, the Fiorentina football squad's loss at home, adverts for alcoholic beverages and headache pills . . .

Over the balls of newspaper he placed a small bundle of dry sticks, some larger branches, a few old pine cones with scales open, and then he crowned the stack with two small logs of oak. Striking a match, he lit the paper at several different points, then went and sat down on one of the two brick benches on either side of the enormous fireplace, right under the great hood of blackened stones, where peasants used to sit during the cold winter months.

I

Outside it was already night. He'd been living in the old farmhouse for a little over a month, and lighting the fire had become a pleasant ritual. He'd finally done it, after thinking about it for years. He'd managed to sell his flat in town and buy a place in the country, in the commune of Impruneta. It was a big two-storey farmhouse a few kilometres from town along an unpaved road full of holes and rocks where nobody ever passed. A secluded, wild spot . . . *Hic sunt leones.*

The water was brought up from a well with an autoclave, and for heating he had a cast-iron stove upstairs and the fireplace on the ground floor. To get a telephone connection he had to wait about three weeks. But with each day that went by he became more convinced that he'd made the right choice. Now that he was no longer spending his days tracking down killers, he had plenty of time on his hands. He'd even bought many books and sometimes spent whole afternoons reading in the armchair by the fire. The city was more distant than the moon, even though in reality it was barely a fifteen-minute drive away. When he thought of Florence the same things always came to mind: the dense, dirty band of heating oil still clinging to the façades of the churches and palazzi, the mud stagnating in basements, the gutted shops and businesses that hadn't reopened, the smell of car exhausts . . . But he also thought of the young people darting to and fro on their Vespas and Lambrettas and the girls who in summer wore miniskirts so short they left him in a daze.

When stuffing boxes and suitcases while moving out, he'd found a great many things he hadn't seen for years and had even forgotten he owned. Bundles of family photos, old letters, two pistols from the war, daggers from the San Marco Battalion still covered with blood, Nazi decorations stripped off the uniforms of the dead . . . He'd even found the piece of torpedo shrapnel, with bits of dry algae tangled in the crinkled metal, which had grazed his temple when he was stationed on a submarine. He'd put this in the drawer in his bedside table so he wouldn't lose it again.

Lighting his fifth cigarette of the day, he started watching the flames as they devoured the paper, sticks, cones and branches before enveloping the logs in reddish-golden tongues. Every so often the fire popped and a swarm of sparks rose in the air and vanished into the darkness of the hood.

He liked getting up every morning to find his bread and *La Nazione* hanging under the porch roof in a plastic bag. This was normal practice in the countryside. You had only to arrange it with the baker, who was so kind as to include the newspaper with the bread. The paper was indispensable for lighting the fire.

The *treccone*[1] came by once a week, but now instead of a bicycle he had a Fiat 500 Giardinetta with a boot full of every sort of thing imaginable. He didn't always succeed in selling or trading something, but he knew how to repair umbrellas and shutters that didn't close properly, how to sharpen knives and fodder-cutters, and he was always glad to accept a glass of wine and exchange a few words, bringing the latest news from house to house, perhaps embellishing things as he pleased.

Bordelli had done well to buy the house. Included in the price was a hectare of untilled land with a hundred or so neglected olive trees. It was in a magnificent location, *all in the sun and none in the shade*, as the local peasants said. The view stretched far into the background of a Leonardo painting. Rows of cypresses, vines, olive trees, expanses of red earth, soft hills with crests covered with black woods that turned violet at sunset, as in certain nineteenth-century landscapes.

And to think that in the end he still had several million lire[2] left over. After the flood, apartments from the third floor up had increased greatly in value. Whereas nobody wanted to live in the country any more. Country life was a horror. And not only for the children of peasants, who were fleeing to the city chasing a dream that led them on like a beautiful prostitute. Even the proprietors wanted to rid themselves of all those now worthless buildings before they went completely to ruin. They were in a hurry to sell them and didn't fuss much over the price. The owner who had sold him his house, a man of about sixty who looked like he'd never worked a day in his life, hadn't

3

even bothered to remove his own things. He'd left everything there, large antique armoires, cherrywood chests, cast-iron beds, terracotta stoves, a kneading-trough that smelled of wood and flour, tables, chairs, inlaid cupboards, and even two small, chipped panels of religious subjects, painted in oils in the sixteenth or seventeenth century. Nothing of great value, mind, but still quite pleasant to look at. He'd hung them in his bedroom, and at night, before turning out the lights, he would sometimes sit there studying them for a few minutes, trying to work out from which master the naïf painter had drawn his inspiration.

At night the silence was absolute, broken every so often by the call of some animal or the dull thudding of a herd of wild boar cantering through the olive trees, or the shifting of the logs in the fire downstairs. He'd loved the house from the moment he first saw it, the way he did sometimes with a woman he saw passing by on the street. He felt good inside those skewed walls, on those half-warped clay tiles. After living in a flat for so many years, he now enjoyed ascending a staircase or having to take a short walk to go into the kitchen or his bedroom. It was as if he felt younger in the country, except when he saw himself in the mirror.

Through a small door on the ground floor one entered the most rustic part of the house: a proper cellar with brick vaults, and a stall that still stank of animals, with old rabbit cages cobbled together by some peasant. There was even an old olive press with a big granite wheel and a pole to hitch to a donkey. Nowadays he stacked his firewood on it. Who knew, perhaps one day he would put those rooms in order and the house would get even bigger. He could live there with a woman and not see her during the day. He smiled, but it was a bitter smile. Whenever he thought of a woman he thought of Eleonora . . .

He heard the sound of an approaching car in the distance and looked at the clock on the wall. Half past seven. Punctual as ever, he thought. He tossed his cigarette butt into the fire, got up calmly and put a pot of water on the largest burner. He peered out of the kitchen window. A rusted lamp embedded in the outside wall scarcely illuminated the threshing floor, while the tops of the cypresses swayed in the wind in the darkened distance. The car pulled up in front of the house, the headlights went off, and a car door slammed. A shadow came up to the door, and Bordelli went to open it.

'Good evening, Inspector.'

'I'm not an inspector any more, Piras.'

'A leopard can't change its spots . . .' said the young policeman, shuddering with cold as he entered the house. A year and a half had passed since the shoot-out that had shattered his legs, and by now he walked almost normally. He had a strange air about him that evening, as if he wanted to know something badly and was having trouble holding himself back. He wrinkled his nose at the smell of cigarettes, but said nothing.

'Cold?' asked Bordelli.

'It's freezing out here, but it's a bit warmer in town.'

'Make yourself at home . . . Penne in tomato sauce all right with you?'

'Anything's fine with me,' said the Sardinian, sitting down inside the fireplace. He opened his hands and held them close to the fire. By now he knew that the former inspector didn't want any help in the kitchen. Ever since Bordelli's move they had talked often on the telephone, and he'd gone out to see him two or three times, always staying for dinner. Every time, he'd asked him how a human being could live in such isolation. He himself was born and raised in the country, but now he couldn't do without the chaos of the city.

'A glass of wine?' Bordelli asked, opening a can of tomatoes. The Sardinian nodded assent. Bordelli filled two glasses and brought one to Piras. It was a blood-red wine he bought by the demijohn from a local peasant. He would put it into flasks himself, pouring a few drops of oil on top to keep the air out.

They sat there in silence. The sound of the fire was relaxing. Bordelli started sauteeing some finely chopped onion in olive oil, let it sizzle for a spell and then poured the tomatoes on top of it.

'Have a pleasant day down at the station?'

'No murders, at least.'

'That's something . . .'

'And how was your day, Inspector?'

'I'm not an inspector any more . . .'

'It's okay, nobody can hear us,' said Piras. Bordelli dumped the pasta into the boiling water and, after stirring it for thirty seconds or so, took his glass and went and sat down in the fireplace opposite his young Sardinian friend. He was still waiting for him to blurt out the question that was burning his tongue. It was anybody's guess whether he would ask it directly or take a roundabout approach. In the distance a dog was barking wildly, and every so often they could hear the cry of an owl that must have been perched on the roof.

'How's your beautiful Sicilian girl?' Bordelli asked after a long pause.

'Everything's fine.'

'Why don't you bring her here with you some evening?'

'She's working on her thesis. She studies all day long and then goes to bed with the chickens,' Piras said with a smile of resignation.

'That girl knows what she wants.'

'I can't imagine her as a lawyer.'

'Are you kidding? People will be falling all over themselves to have her defend them,' said Bordelli.

Silence again. Piras was staring at the fire, every so often sipping his wine. His eternally serious face, which was a little like an ancient nuraghic stone, might mislead anyone who didn't know him. On the outside he might seem like a melancholy, gloomy lad, but he wasn't. He was actually light hearted, in his way, and when he wanted to he could joke around and have fun. But you couldn't tell, to look at him.

Bordelli finished his glass and got up to put another log on the fire. He went and tasted the pasta: it needed another two or three minutes. He'd set the table in grand fashion. White table-cloth, fine china plates and bowls, crystal tulip glasses, his grandmother's cutlery, clean napkins, a flask of wine, water, bread, oil and vinegar, salt and pepper, Parmesan cheese and grater . . .

All laid out in order. That, too, was a new and pleasant habit of his, whether he was alone or in company. When he still lived at San Frediano in Florence, on the rare occasions he ate at home he would sit on the couch with his plate on his lap. He would never again make such mistakes. Rosa, his friend and stand-in mum, would always say: *Eating is like making love; you have to do it right.* And to think it was a retired prostitute who said this.

He drained the pasta, served it in the bowls, and poured the hot tomato sauce over it. They sat down at the table, pleasantly famished. A smidgen of fresh oil, and plenty of Parmesan. They also added a bit of ground hot pepper. At his first forkful, Piras lightly raised his eyebrows in appreciation. Bordelli refilled their wine glasses.

'Your folks are doing all right?'

'Everything's fine.'

'What's your father been up to?'

'I spoke with him yesterday. He sends you his best.'

'One of these days I'll give him a ring,' said Bordelli. He and Gavino, Piras's father, had been comrades in the San Marco Battalion in the last year of the war. Gavino had returned to his village less one arm and gone back to the peasant's life.

'He said he might come to the mainland this spring to see me,' said Piras.

'Oh, good. So I'll finally get to meet your mum.'

'She definitely won't be coming.'

'Why not?'

'She's never left Bonarcado in her life; the mere idea of it frightens her.'

'Try to persuade her . . .'

'It'd be easier to get a brick to change its mind.'

'But are all you Sardinians like that?'

'Everyone is the way he is,' said Piras, cutting things short.

'Well, if Gavino wants to, he can come and stay here with me. I've got loads of room.'

'Thanks, I'll tell him that. But I don't think he'll really come . . . He's been saying that for years . . .'

They lapsed into silence again. They ate, drank, and exchanged long stares. The popping fire, the great kitchen and its cracked walls, the countryside immersed in darkness and peopled with animals out hunting in the woods under an indifferent moon . . . Bordelli, meanwhile, was still waiting for Piras's question, trying to imagine how he would phrase it.

In that silence, an old memory, for no reason, resurfaced from the depths of his mind . . . The corpse of a small child abandoned in the snow, riddled with bullets and hard as marble, eyes wide open and staring at the heavens. Its only crime was to have been Italian, an Italian traitor, a damned little traitor in a country occupied by the Nazis. He witnessed the child's burial again, when they broke apart the frozen earth with pickaxes, cursing and sweating like pigs in the cold of the wild. As they were covering the body with clods as hard as stones, he'd thought: If one day I found the man who shot this baby in front of me, what would I do? He'd pictured himself looking the man in the eye, glaring at him, and he'd realised with anger and terror that he would have found something familiar in that man's gaze, he would have found a man a lot like himself standing there before him . . . But he would have killed him just the same – indeed, he would have killed him for this very reason, because he was a man like him . . .

'Are you happy living out here, Inspector?' Piras's voice slid out on to the table like a wad of cotton, breaking the silence. But that wasn't the question Bordelli had been expecting.

'I'm not an inspector any more . . .'

'Don't you feel a bit isolated?'

'I don't think that's the right word for it.'

'What do you do all day long?'

'A whole lot of interesting things . . . I walk in the woods, read, chop wood, go shopping, light a fire, cook, eat, watch the telly, and soon I'll even have a kitchen garden to hoe.'

'Don't you get lonely?' Piras insisted.

'Depends what you mean.'

It was true that the seclusion and silence of the countryside tempted one to ruminate over everything and feed one's melancholy, but he loved this life more than he would have imagined. There was nothing he could do about it.

Piras refilled the wine glasses and took a long sip.

'Did you read this morning's *Nazione*?' he asked.

Bordelli smiled faintly. At last Piras had decided to broach the issue.

'You mean did I read about the butcher's suicide?'

'What do you think about it?'

'What do you mean?'

'Why do you think Panerai killed himself?'

'I don't know . . . Maybe he tried to shoot a sparrow and missed?'

'No, seriously. I can't figure it out . . .'

'He'd killed a little boy, Piras . . . You know that. You and I are the only ones who know it.'

'So, out of remorse?'

'Why not?'

'I just can't see someone like that shooting himself in the mouth.'

'Remorse can play some dirty tricks on you, Piras. It smoulders under the ashes, and when you least expect it . . .'

'Even a gorilla like Panerai?'

'Apparently . . .'

'What if he was murdered?' said the Sardinian, looking him straight in the eye.

'I really don't think so. But even if it were so, I have to confess that I wouldn't waste a single minute looking for the killer,' said Bordelli, peeling an apple. Piras kept brooding, casting long, interrogatory glances at Bordelli.

'I even thought that you . . . I wouldn't swear by it, of course . . . But the moment I heard the news, the first thing that came into my mind was . . . Seeing how things really are, it wouldn't even seem so unusual to me . . .'

'You think *I* did it?' asked Bordelli, saying it for him. Piras said nothing, but sat there waiting for the answer, gripping his wine glass. The inspector let him stew for a few moments, then shook his head.

'Well, I didn't, Piras. But I must say I certainly wasn't upset about it . . . Would you like an apple?'

'No, thanks.'

'One arsehole less in the world is still one arsehole less, Piras.'

'Of course . . . But . . . As I was saying . . .'

'Tell me in all sincerity . . . Do you have any suspicions? Have you been to the place where he killed himself? Did you see something that didn't look right?' asked Bordelli, chewing his apple.

'I went to the woods with Detective Silvis but didn't notice anything unusual. At a glance it did look like a suicide.'

'So what are you worried about?'

'The fact is . . . You said it yourself . . . I know that Panerai was an animal, whereas the others weren't . . .'

'You're right, Piras, absolutely right. Care for some grappa?' asked Bordelli, standing up.

'Four killers, two suicides . . .' muttered the Sardinian. Bordelli brought a bottle of grappa and two small glasses to the table and sat back down.

'I don't really feel like talking about this all evening, Piras . . .'

He poured the grappa and pushed a glass towards the young man. Piras took a sip, and had to make an effort not to cough. When he saw that Bordelli was about to light a cigarette, he got up and went and sat down beside the fire. He couldn't stand the smell of cigarettes and considered smoking the stupidest of vices.

'All right, then, we won't talk about it.' He sighed, staring at the flames. Bordelli took a few puffs and, as a favour to his young friend, quickly stubbed out the cigarette, which was still almost whole. He went and sat opposite him, on the same brick bench as before.

'Did you like fairy tales when you were a little boy, Piras?'

'Yes . . .'

'Why? Do you remember?'

'Well, I guess it was because the bad guy was always punished in the end, and good prevailed.'

'And do you think it's right that little children learn to believe in something that almost never happens in real life?'

'I don't know . . .'

'I think it is . . . In spite of everything, it's always best not to give up . . .'

'Are you trying to tell me something?'

'Never mind, Piras. Old men sometimes like to play the "wise grandfather", especially in front of a warm fire.'

After reading for about an hour, he turned out the light. Before getting under the covers he'd put a few logs in the cast-iron stove on the first floor, and the warmth filled the air, along with a strong scent of burning wood.

Piras had left about midnight. Over the course of the evening, Bordelli kept reading in his eyes a desire to reopen the discussion of the Panerai the butcher's suicide, but the Sardinian had asked no more questions.

He lay in the pitch darkness with his eyes wide open and, as used to happen when he was a little boy, saw bright kaleido-scope-like designs in the emptiness. He couldn't very well tell Piras the real situation. Not now, anyway. This was a war he had to fight alone. He had made a mistake, and he had to make up for it. He alone had to shoulder the burden. The regrets were already becoming hard to bear.

During the last days at his old flat in San Frediano, before falling asleep each night, he would think of all the things that had happened in that bed, not all of them pleasant. He couldn't help but remember the nights spent making love with Eleonora, her dark, luminous eyes, the lovely scent of her skin . . . But then he would see her between the sheets with her face swollen and her eyes empty, trembling in fear. Poor Eleonora. She'd been punished without having done anything wrong, brutally raped by a pair of goons for the sole purpose of sending a message to him, Bordelli, the ball-busting police inspector who'd been sticking his nose where he shouldn't. They'd broken into his home and waited for the beautiful girl, who'd wanted to surprise her knight between the sheets. But instead of her knight she'd found two thugs who forced her on to the bed to violate her in body and soul, for the sole purpose of advising her knight to stop making trouble for the king. And they'd even left him a piece of paper with a list of names on it: Rosa Stracuzzi, Dante Pedretti, Pietrino Piras, and so on. The message was as clear as a telegram: *If you don't desist, we'll kill every person you care about. Full stop.*

He'd been a damned fool. He'd threatened murderers, knowing he had no evidence to incriminate them. What had he expected to gain from it? Perhaps to scare them, make them feel in danger . . . But one of them was quite powerful and hadn't taken the joke too kindly. And Eleonora had paid the price for it . . . He couldn't forgive himself for this. And, as if that wasn't enough, she had left him.

And what about him? Had he done the right thing by quitting his job? But what else, really, could he have done? Could he have stayed on as chief inspector of police knowing he would never succeed in putting Giacomo's killers in jail? When you can't play by the rules of the game, it's best to stop playing. It was a little like the time when, many years ago, he'd won twenty-five months' worth of salary from a dear friend at poker. Obviously he'd declined to accept his winnings, but from that day on he'd never played poker again.

He turned on to his side and shut his eyes. Though he felt tired, his thoughts were preventing him falling asleep. He was a former police inspector, but he was also a former commander of the San Marco Battalion. There were certain things he simply couldn't tolerate. Nazism hadn't started with Hitler and hadn't ended with his suicide. Nazism by definition belonged to a specific moment in history, but its essence had always been in the air, everywhere around the world, imprisoning people and nations in its clutches . . .

Nice little thoughts for the middle of the night . . .

A nightbird's raucous cry split the silence and, imagining the abandoned countryside under the moonlight, he remembered a poem from his schooldays . . .

*The moon sets; the world loses colour;*
*the shadows vanish, and darkness*
*glooms the valley and hills . . .*[3]

He suddenly felt like going out into the night and wandering through the fields. He turned on the light, got out of bed feeling heavy-headed, and calmly got dressed. He put on a woollen sweater and a sports jacket and wrapped a scarf round his neck. Sticking a torch in his pocket he went out of the house, but there was no need to turn it on. The moon was almost full, the olive trees' black shadows stretching long across the faded ground. Great gusts of wind shook the foliage. He walked through the tall grass with his hands in his pockets, breathing in the cold air with pleasure. He'd always liked wind. It was a living force that made things move. Immobility was like death.

At the far end of the field a large white stone stood out from the darkness like the eye of a giant. Beyond the olive grove rose a wooded hill, while here and there the dark spikes of the cypresses poked through the round boughs of the Mediterranean pines. Reaching the edge of the woods, he heard at last the faint gurgling of the Fosso delle Acque Cadute – the 'Ditch of Fallen Waters' – a small stream that marked the end of his field. With each new blast of wind a tree trunk moaned.

He couldn't tell anyone his secret – at least not yet. By now he knew he would go all the way, and he preferred living this adventure alone. It wasn't some decision he'd made on the fly: the hand of fate had intervened.

Accompanied by his lunar shadow he started walking along a narrow path that cut through the grassy terrain parallel to the ditch, a trail almost certainly travelled by wild boar. The natural world immersed in the night made him shudder in a strange, animal kind of way. The call of the forest, you might say. Under his skin he felt a desire to tear off all his clothes and charge head down through the trees and shrubs, and maybe even howl at the moon . . . Obeying only instinct and the natural laws of survival, and turning his back on the filth and stupidity governing the human race . . .

There was no doubt about it: it was fate that had organised everything, in the simplest manner possible. Chance did not seem capable of as much. It could not have all been a banal coincidence . . .

Ever since he'd moved to the country he went often on walks through the woods, sometimes early in the morning, even at dawn. He would put a panino with prosciutto, a bottle of water and an apple in his backpack, get into his Volkswagen Beetle, drive up the dirt roads that led up into the hills, and finally park in some clearing by the side of the road. It was Botta who had first kindled this passion in him, when he'd taken him mushroom hunting on the Monte alle Croci some months before. And that was where he usually went nowadays as well. He would start the now familiar climb panting heavily, happy as a child to recognise the strangest-looking trees and the rocks jutting up from the ground. He would go farther each time, exploring new paths and descending steep slopes by grabbing on to the trunks of chestnuts to keep from falling. Often he was glad to lose his way, knowing he would later find it again. Little by little he was beginning to know the area and understand the network of trails. On those rare occasions when he crossed paths with a hunter, he would exchange a minimal nod of greeting and continue on his way. He didn't like hunting one bit.

The previous day, a Sunday, when he'd left the house, it was still dark outside, and as he began the climb up Poggio alla Croce he'd witnessed the sunrise. It was cold as hell, and he'd even worn gloves and a hat. Not five minutes would go by without him hearing at least one gunshot. He reached the three-way junction at Cappella dei Boschi in less than an hour and took the path that led from Monte Scalari abbey to Pian d'Albero. By now he knew these haunts rather well. He'd come the first time just before the flood, when the little boy's dead body was found hastily buried in these woods. He'd gone back several times in the days that followed, to inspect the area and look for clues. One morning a desperate squealing had caught his attention amid the shrubs, and he'd discovered Briciola, a kitten only a few days old with a damaged eye which he'd taken at once to Rosa's. Briciola could never have known, but it was thanks precisely to her mewing that he'd found the first tenuous lead that would later lead him all the way to Giacomo Pellissari's killers. He'd patiently managed to uncover everything, down to the last detail, but hadn't been able to arrest the culprits, because he didn't have enough proof . . . It had been a kind of checkmate for him . . . Then things came crashing down, and after Eleonora was raped he decided to quit the police force . . .

But he hadn't wanted to think about this that morning; he'd already worn himself out enough. He'd wanted only to take a long walk, forget about smoking, sit down on a rock and eat a panino in peace.

When he reached the huge oak that the Nazis had chosen to hang 'Italian traitors' from, he stopped to study its sturdy black branches, which through no fault of their own had served to kill innocent people. Who knew how many other things that powerful tree had seen over its centuries of life. If only it could talk . . .

He'd got back on the path to Pian d'Albero, never imagining that just a few minutes later . . . It had all happened so fast . . . Thinking back on it, he almost couldn't bring himself to believe that it had actually happened . . .

Round a bend he'd spotted a man crouching behind a hunter's blind at the top of a small hill and, though seeing him from behind, he'd recognised him at once. It was Panerai the butcher, one of the four men who'd raped young Giacomo and, more importantly, the one who had actually killed him, strangling him while reaching orgasm . . .

Without thinking twice he'd climbed up through the trees and come up behind him, silent as an Apache . . . He'd grabbed the rifle out of his hands and pointed it at him.

'Long time no see, Panerai.' The butcher struggled to his feet, shaking like a leaf on a tree. He could barely speak. His eyes flashed with hate and fear.

'How's the hunting? Kill any little birds?'

'No . . . not . . . yet . . .' Panerai muttered.

'Wasn't it around here that you buried that little boy?'

'No . . . I . . . didn't do anything . . .'

'Don't be so modest, man . . . Don't forget, you're a devotee of the Duce . . .'

All of a suddenly he realised he had to act fast.

'I . . . didn't . . . I . . .' the butcher kept stuttering.

'*Eia eia alalà!*'[4] Bordelli shouted, sticking the double barrels of the shotgun into Panerai's mouth so fast he hadn't time to react, and squeezing both triggers at once. The back of the butcher's head exploded in a burst of blood, and his flaccid body fell to the ground with a thud. The crack of the rifle echoed across the valleys, but it was normal to hear gunshots in the woods, especially on a Sunday.

The butcher had writhed in agony for a few seconds, kicking the fallen leaves between his feet, and after a final spasm stopped moving for ever. Bordelli had let the rifle fall to the ground and left the scene with his hat pulled down over his eyes. But he hadn't run. He wasn't worried. He felt that everything would turn out all right. And it had. Walking through the woods back to the car he hadn't run into anyone at all. It was as if he'd never left his house . . .

He'd had gloves on when he used the rifle, the leaf-strewn ground was so frozen and hard that he'd left no tracks, and the gunshot was just one of many that day. All the same, if he'd still been with the force he would never have done what he did . . . How could he not think it was fate? Even Diotivede, the old forensic pathologist and his friend, would never manage to uncover the truth about the butcher's death . . .

He stopped for a moment, eyes following the flight of a large nightbird passing silently overhead without moving its wings. Its white, moonlit feathers stood out in the darkness as though phosphorescent, as it disappeared, gliding softly, into the dense wood.

He started feeling cold, and began to head home. He'd once

read an interview with a writer who claimed he wasn't the one who wrote his novels . . . The stories simply unfolded before him as though they'd already happened, and he couldn't even bring himself to change the characters' personalities or words . . . That was more or less the way he, Bordelli, felt . . . As though he'd ended up in a story already written and could do nothing more than turn the pages. All he knew was that he would read the book all the way to the end . . .

The wind had picked up and was violently shaking the olive branches. It was a night for wolves. He quickened his pace, hair swirling over his head. Seeing his house from afar he imagined Eleonora waiting for him inside, under the covers, but this sweet thought did nothing but plunge him into despair.

The moment he set foot in his house he poured himself a small glass of grappa and knocked it back in one gulp. He went upstairs, legs feeling heavy, got undressed and crawled into bed. He turned off the light and curled up in the cold sheets like a little boy awaiting his goodnight kiss.

He was dreaming he was under a hail of German machine-gun fire, holed up with his mates in an abandoned farmhouse. A burst even fiercer than the rest woke him up . . . Someone was knocking at the door. He heard a voice call out and recognised it as Ennio's. He turned on the light and looked at the clock. Ten past eight. Dammit, he'd forgotten he had an appointment with him to start work on the garden . . .

'Coming! . . .' he cried in a hoarse voice. Getting out of bed with great effort, he got dressed with eyes still half shut. Botta kept on knocking. He staggered down the stairs, not yet having fully emerged from his dream, Nazi machine-guns still ringing in his ears. When he opened the door, Ennio Botta threw up his hands.

'Inspector, don't tell me you were still asleep . . .'

'I'm not an inspector any more, Ennio.'

'Inspectors are born, not made, and you, in all modesty, are one,' said Botta, stepping inside the house.

'Sorry. I went to bed late last night.'

'If you're going to be a farmer you have to get up with the sun.'

'Just let me have a coffee and I'll be ready. You want some?'

'I'd better make it myself.'

Botta got down to work, while Bordelli went upstairs to wash his face and pull himself together. When he returned to the kitchen, the coffee was ready.

'How many teaspoons of sugar, Inspector?'

'Just one, thanks.'

'Good . . .' Ennio spooned the sugar into the empty cups and poured the coffee over it, as he always did.

'Today we're going to prepare the ground for the tomatoes,' he said.

'I can hardly wait . . .'

'I still wonder whether you made the right decision, moving to the country.'

'No one will ever make me go back to the city, Ennio.'

They were sitting at the table, opposite each other. Botta's coffee was superb. And yet he'd used the same coffee pot and the same ground beans Bordelli used every day.

'You know, this whole story of you leaving your job doesn't really make sense to me, Inspector.'

'I did it for you, Ennio. Now you can tell me about all the crimes you committed without any worry.'

'Those weren't crimes, Inspector . . .'

'Then what were they?' asked Bordelli, curious to hear the answer.

'The art of survival.'

'There are people who work for a living . . .'

'So you want to pack Botta off to a factory to spend the day hammering slabs of metal? You want to kill me?'

'Weren't you going to open a restaurant?'

'Of course . . . If a certain deal goes well for me . . . I'm talking big stuff, mind . . . Something to set me up for life . . .'

'Just be sure you don't get caught, Ennio. It would make me too sad.'

'I've already told you, Inspector, I will never go back to jail. I've learned my lesson . . . I will never get caught again like some bleeding amateur. Nowadays I do things right. It's all scientific.'

'Like that deal in *Persons Unknown* . . .'[5] Bordelli said, smiling.

'Take a good look at me, Inspector. Do I look like the type to spend his life rotting behind bars?'

'If you get caught I'm going to start crying, Ennio.'

'It's not going to happen, I can promise you that.'

'So what's this *big deal* you keep talking about? Maybe I can give you some advice . . .' Bordelli said, turning serious.

Botta shook his head. 'I don't need any. It's all going swimmingly. Maybe I'll tell you about it when it's all done, over a bottle of wine . . . The way you like it.'

'As you wish.'

'Shall we get down to work, Inspector?' asked Botta, standing up.

'I'm not an inspector any more . . .'

'So what should I call you?'

'You know what, Ennio?'

'What?'

'I've only just now realised that I always speak to you in the familiar form and you always use the polite form with me . . .'

'So what?'

'Doesn't that seem strange to you?'

'I've never noticed.'

'So why don't we both cut the formalities?'

'I can't, Inspector.'

'Enough of this "inspector" stuff, Ennio. Call me Franco and scrap the formality.'

'Let's just leave things the way they are, Inspector . . . And now let's go and dig some holes for the tomato plants,' said Botta, heading for the door.

Bordelli stuck a cigarette between his lips and followed him. They went into the gardening room to get the tools left behind by the former owner, then out through a door that led behind the house, where they'd decided to put the garden. It was a beautiful day, with a sky that looked like the background to a Trecento Madonna.

'What are you going to do with *them*?' Ennio asked, referring to the abandoned olive grove in a tone of commiseration. 'Are you going to let them go or do you want to make oil?'

The boughs of the trees had been left to grow freely and now soared some fifteen to twenty feet in the air.

'I wouldn't mind making oil,' said Bordelli, scratching his head.

'Just at a glance I'd say nobody's touched these trees for at least ten years. You'd have to weed the whole grove, and then come April the trees should be drastically cut back, to reinvigorate them. If all went well, you might get your first oil by December of '69. Then you have to have them pruned every year, treat them with fungicide at least twice, and manure the ground . . . Then there's the harvest . . . the press . . . Actually, making oil's a lot of work.'

'You're making me change my mind . . .'

'If you want some advice, find someone whose does it for a living and would be happy to be paid with some of the oil.'

'Okay, I'll try . . . Thanks . . .'

'I think a kitchen garden's quite enough for someone like you.'

'I'm not sure if I should feel insulted,' said Bordelli, but Botta was already thinking about the tomato plants. He was studying the weed-infested future garden, rubbing his chin. One could see from his look that there was a great deal of work to be done.

'I'd say we should put them from here to down there – that should accommodate about thirty plants. Let's get busy.'

'Yes, sir!' said Bordelli, sketching a military salute.

'If you don't do things right, nothing will grow.'

'How's this soil seem to you?'

'Well, Impruneta is famous for its terracotta.'

'Meaning?'

'Meaning there's a lot of clay in the soil. The area's full of quarries and brickworks. Carrots won't grow here, and potatoes have a rough time of it, too, but cabbage'll come up like nobody's business.'

'So let's plant cabbage . . .'

'Not *now*, Inspector. Cabbage grows in winter. But anyway, it's not for you, believe me,' said Botta, shaking his head.

'Then what can we plant in spring?'

'A whole lot of things, but for now we'll start with tomatoes. If you manage to get a good crop, next year I'll give you a hand planting some cucumbers, aubergines, radishes and beans.'

'Sounds like a tall order to me . . .'

'Let's get down to work.'

They mowed the grass with billhooks and piled it up to one side. Then they started breaking up the ground, sweating under a blue sky that already hinted at spring. There was a blinding sun, but the soft, persistent wind got the better of the warm air.

Bordelli was thoughtful. Two days earlier he'd killed a child-strangler, and now he was working the land to create a kitchen garden for himself. He thought of the butcher's wife and daughter, who had done nothing wrong. Surely they were overwhelmed with grief, but wasn't a husband and father who died by his own hand better than a rapist and murderer? In essence he had spared those two creatures the pain of discovering something that would have ruined them for life . . .

'You know what you could plant? Hot peppers . . .' said Botta.

'Splendid.' Bordelli just loved hot peppers, even if he'd never dreamed he'd be growing them.

'They're easy, at least. You put the seeds in some nice big pots and then water them. They're beautiful plants, even to look at.'

'When can I start planting?'

'By next week.'

'Good . . .'

They finished turning the soil. Bordelli was exhausted, while Ennio, for his part, seemed as if he'd only played a round of bocce. Under Botta's direction they dug some holes almost a foot and a half deep. Three rows of twelve holes each.

'As in the time of Christ,' said Ennio, leaning on his spade.

'You'll have to help me plant the tomatoes, too.'

'You mean sow, not plant. If you want to be a farmer you have to use the right words.'

'I'll do my best. Where can I find the seeds?'

'You can try the cooperative in Impruneta, but I don't think they'll have any. You're better off asking some of the local peasants. And San Marzano seeds are best: they're good for making all kinds of things.'

'And then what?'

'You have to sow the seeds in a patch of well-turned earth and add a bit of compost . . . If you've got the patience, you can get some in the woods, otherwise just buy a sack or two of it at the co-op.'

'I'll just buy it, don't worry.'

'You could sow them here,' said Botta, pointing to a corner of the garden plot.

'Whatever you say.'

'After about a month, the plants will be about five inches tall, as long as the weather cooperates. If all goes well, you'll then carefully uproot them and plant them in the holes we've made. And get some peasant around here to give you some *pollina.*'

'What's that?'

'Chicken shit.'

'Splendid . . . And what am I supposed to do with it?'

'You must put it in a bucket full of water to mellow it, making sure to stir it with a stick every morning for about ten days. Three weeks after transplanting the small shoots, you can use it as fertiliser. Not before, however, or you'll burn the roots. It should be diluted with a lot of water, and you should use half a litre per plant every day for at least a month.'

'Anything else?'

'You thought that would be all? The first thing you must do is fence the whole area off, otherwise the boar will eat everything. Then you must cover the just-transplanted shoots with wooden crates, to protect them from the sun while they're putting down roots. You must water them daily – better yet, twice a day, early in the morning and at sunset. But not too much, just the right amount. When they start to grow you then have to plant poles beside them and fasten the plants for support. And obviously you need more and more water. By late June you'll need at least five or six litres of water per plant, twice a day . . .'

'I have to confess that by this point I'm thinking of going to the supermarket and stocking up on canned tomatoes,' said Bordelli, wiping the sweat from his brow with a handkerchief.

'You'll change your mind after you've tasted your own tomatoes,' Botta predicted.

'I can't wait . . .'

'Along the wall you could put some pots with aromatic herbs – basil, thyme, marjoram, chives, mint . . .'

'Right, I hadn't thought of that.'

'Don't waste your time looking for them. When the time comes I'll bring you some, already grown, so all you'll have to do is water them.'

'May God bless your soul . . .'

'It's not time for that yet.'

'Listen, it's almost one o'clock. What do you say we go and have a steak down at il Ferrone?'

'That's not a bad idea, Inspector . . .'

'I don't see any inspectors around here,' said Bordelli, propping his hoe against the wall.

They went into the kitchen to wash their hands and change as best they could. Climbing aboard Ennio's Lambretta scooter, they took the dirt road down to il Ferrone, a hamlet of a few houses, a little stream, a large modern church of stone and concrete, a memorial tablet with the words HE WHO DIES FOR HIS COUNTRY HAS LIVED WELL, and a simple, unpretentious trattoria.

They sat down at a table apart from the rest. There weren't many customers in the room, but the few there managed to make a great deal of noise just the same.

They ordered two grilled steaks with roast potatoes, and a salad to soothe their consciences. The wine arrived at once, and they started drinking.

'Come on, Ennio . . . tell me about this deal you're in on,' Bordelli said under his breath.

'Not now, Inspector . . .'

'Why? Don't you trust me?'

'No, no, it's not that . . . I'd just rather not say anything. I'm superstitious.'

'I won't deny that you've got me worried,' said Bordelli.

'It'll all go fine . . . I just need to borrow a car, because I have to drive a rather long way.'

'Tell you what, Ennio – and I'm going out on a limb, mind you – if you tell me what the job is, I'll drive you myself . . .'

'You don't know what you're saying, Inspector,' Botta said, smiling.

'I give you my word . . .' Bordelli said, all serious. He knew it was risky, but he didn't want Botta to get into trouble. Even if he was no longer active, a former police inspector might be able to save the day in certain situations. Ennio, too, turned serious and looked Bordelli in the eye.

'Are you sure you won't try to talk me out of it?'

'I promise I won't.'

'Well . . . Do you remember when, in the days before the flood . . .'

At that moment the steaks arrived, and Botta broke off. They started devouring their steaks like a pair of cavemen. Turning the soil certainly whetted one's appetite.

'So, you were saying?' Bordelli whispered after a long silence.

'Do you remember when, in early November, you couldn't find me?'

'Unfortunately, yes . . .' said Bordelli. He could scarcely forget that damned lock in Via Luna that he'd wanted Botta to pick, in hopes of finding evidence to incriminate Giacomo's killers . . . But then the Great Flood came and washed everything away.

'You know where I'd gone?'

Botta was beating about the bush, grinning with satisfaction.

'Where?'

'To Milan.'

'Go on . . .' Bordelli pressed him, anxious to know everything.

'And do you know what I'd gone to do there?'

'What?'

'To meet some people,' Botta said solemnly, as if he'd slain a dragon.

'Come on, Ennio, get to the point.'

'If this deal goes well for me, I'll be set up for life . . . No one can make me change my mind . . .'

'I won't try to change anything, Ennio. Every man chooses his own life.'

'Let's make a toast,' said Botta, raising his glass. Bordelli raised his own.

'To what?'

'You're asking me? To my prosperity . . .'

They clinked glasses and drank a long draught of Chianti.

'Get to the nitty-gritty, Ennio . . .' said Bordelli, increasingly impatient.

'We're getting there,' Botta whispered, and they both leaned forward over the table. Ennio cupped his hands over his mouth and, moving his lips while emitting no obvious sound, revealed his secret. Bordelli was speechless for a moment, then shook his head.

'That's another Totò film,' he said, discouraged.

'Gimme a break. Totò . . .'

'You should forget about this business, Ennio.'

'Inspector, you said you wouldn't try to talk me out of it.'

'You're right, I'm sorry. It was a moment of weakness,' said Bordelli, thinking that when something is done for a good reason . . . Hadn't he himself shot the butcher in the mouth? Did he feel like a murderer for it? Or rather . . .

'It'll all turn out the way it's supposed to,' said Ennio, and through gestures and whispers, like a Carbonaro,[6] he told him about the rest of the affair in detail. When he'd finished he wrote down some figures on a piece of paper, to show him how profitable the deal would be. Their steaks had been stripped to the bone, the potatoes were gone, the salads untouched.

'And what if something goes wrong?' Bordelli asked in spite of himself. He didn't want Ennio to end up back in jail.

'Don't play devil's advocate, Inspector . . . At any rate, you're not required to keep your promise,' Botta said as a kind of challenge.

'A San Marco sapper has only one word to give. I said I would take you there, and I will.'

This time it was he who raised his glass. Botta accepted the salute with a smile, and as they clinked their glasses they spilled some wine on to the tablecloth. Bordelli realised he was trapped, but lending Botta a hand was the only way to protect him. A wretch never gets rich, just as a rich man never goes to jail . . . Short of a miracle . . .

Country life was pleasant enough. The weather helped to regulate one's daily life, gaining an importance it didn't have in the city. The silence and slower rhythms invited one to meditate on everything, even when it seemed not worth the trouble. Sooner or later he would buy a record player, so he could listen to classical music and contemporary songs. But for now he would rather savour the silence.

The solitude and subtle melancholy that others might find disagreeable had become indispensable conditions for him. Even his customary walks in the hills might seem monotonous or tedious to some, but in fact they were profoundly different each time . . . The mood of the moment would merge with the colours and scents of the wood, which in turn changed with the seasons . . . There were always new things to see, and at every moment there was always the chance he might catch sight of an animal scampering away . . .

He got up very early that morning. After preparing his backpack, he drove off in the Beetle and went as far as La Panca. He'd decided to go for a long walk, by way of Celle, Ponte agli Stolli and Monte San Michele, all trails that until then he'd taken only in stages. The moment had come to put them all together in one great circuit.

The sky was overcast, and a pale bluish fog lingered between the trees. On the trail to Pian d'Albero he passed not far from the spot where the butcher had 'committed suicide', and again he had the feeling he'd set out on a difficult path with no way back. So, whose turn was it now? There were only two left . . . But how could he possibly . . . It was better to think things over calmly, perhaps let fate show the way.

Around midday he sat down to eat, leaning back against the wall of the tiny cemetery at Ponte agli Stolli, looking out over a broad valley and soft, tree-covered hills. Tossing the apple core aside in some bushes, he set out walking again, head full of thoughts. Thoughts were strange things. Past moments with no apparent connection to one another would stream by in succession like links in a chain . . . The face of a girl whose name he couldn't remember . . . the death of his mother . . . the hot focaccia sprinkled with nuggets of sea salt he used to eat on the sunny beaches of Marina di Massa, after a long swim . . . Images of Eleonora merged with others of the murdered boy, wartime memories he'd thought long gone and buried passed before his eyes . . . Not even the animals he saw scampering through the trees could halt that journey through the past . . .

He got back home around four in the afternoon, his legs a shambles. All told he must have walked close to twenty miles, not smoking a single cigarette the whole time. He'd purposely left the packet at home, so he wouldn't be tempted, but in reality he hadn't once felt the need to go for a smoke.

After a hot bath he lit a fire and started reading beside it in the armchair, in the dim light of the kitchen. His books he always bought at Seeber's shop, which with great effort had managed to reopen after the flood. The salesman was a young man not yet thirty, full of enthusiasm and with red pimples on his face. By now he always greeted Bordelli like a friend and gave him advice.

'Do you know Lermontov?'

'I'm afraid I don't . . .'

'You must read him, he's a genius. Died at the age of twenty-seven in a duel, for the same reasons that prompt the protagonist of his only novel to challenge a fellow-soldier. I have a beautiful BUR edition from 1950.'

'I'll take it.'

'You should also read his unfinished novels, they're unforgettable masterpieces that are hard to forget.'

'Give me those, too.'

'Do you like Dostoyevsky?'

'I think I've only read *Crime and Punishment* and *The Idiot*.'

'Did you like them?'

'A lot.'

'Did you know that part of *The Idiot* was actually written in
Florence? During one of the journeys he made to Italy to flee
his creditors. He was staying over by Palazzo Pitti . . . Have you
ever read *Notes from the Underground*?'

'No . . .'

'How about *The Eternal Husband*?'

'Neither.'

'You must read both. You can tell me afterwards whether you
agree with me.'

How had this kid managed to read all these books? Bordelli
wondered with admiration. Every book he'd bought on the
young man's advice had been a revelation.

So now he was reading *A Hero of Our Time*, by Lermontov,
while smoking his second cigarette of the day. After an initial
section told in the third person – very good but still nineteenth-
century in tone – came the surprise of the protagonist's
first-person diary, which read as if it had been written a
century later. The young Russian's ability to pull the reader
into the story was breathtaking, and Bordelli lost himself in
his daring adventures, which unfolded before him as in a
film. He felt as excited as he used to do in childhood when
listening to a fairy tale, and he actually forgot he had a book
in his hands . . .

After a short while he realised that the fire needed more
wood. Getting up with a groan he went and put another log
between the andirons. While pouring himself half a glass of
wine, he thought of something he should do. He wondered why
he hadn't done it already. He grabbed a pad and pen and sat
down at the kitchen table.

*Dear Eleonora, I have summoned the courage to write you this letter in the hope that . . .*

He stopped and reread these few words, tore the page out, crumpled it up and threw it into the fire. He had to find a better opening . . . At least something less trite . . .

*Dear Eleonora, Well, after such a long silence, here I am again . . .*

That page ended up in the fireplace as well. Maybe it was better to open with a sorrowful statement, so she might understand . . .

*Dear Eleonora, I cannot help but feel responsible for what . . .*

Dreadful. Another balled-up piece of paper in the fire.

*Dear Eleonora, It is not easy to find the words to . . .*

No, it certainly wasn't easy. Perhaps a lighter tone might be better, maybe even something a little playful? Something that left the past behind?

*Dear Eleonora, Who knows how many boyfriends you must have by now . . .*

No, no, no . . . Better start from the ugliest moment, just to get it out of the way.

*Dear Eleonora, I shall never forget that terrible night when . . .*

But what if she wanted never to hear any mention of it again?

*Dear Eleonora, I have never stopped thinking of you . . .*
*Dear Eleonora, I hope that your life has . . .*

*Dear Eleonora, Today my desire to write to you has become . . .*
*Dear Eleonora, After this long silence . . .*

But hadn't he already written that sentence? Tearing out this umpteenth page from his notepad to feed it to the flames, he realised that there were none left. So he tossed the pad into the fire as well and dropped the pen on the table. He would never manage it. If he wanted to see Eleonora again, he would have to find another way, or else wait until something happened on its own. This, too, perhaps, was part of fate's design. For now it was best to stop thinking about it.

He went over to the window to look out at the sky. It was clear and black and speckled with stars. The full moon was still low. At the top of the hill in front stood the silhouette of a castle with a high, slender tower, by now a familiar sight. As always, one of its windows was illuminated. Just one. Who knew who lived there . . . Maybe a beautiful woman who could help him forget the past. He fell back into the chair and resumed reading.

When he realised he was hungry he looked up and saw that it was already past eight o'clock. With the help of a fire-shovel he spread out a bed of hot coals in front of the fire, laid the cast-iron grill on top, and set two sausages and a pork chop down on it to cook. He'd bought them from the butcher in Impruneta, a glum old man who always smiled as he sliced meat and chopped bones. Even shopping had become fun for him. The shopowners seemed like characters out of the *commedia dell'arte*, and one always learned a great many things while awaiting one's turn . . . Tonio had cut himself with a brush-hook, Cesira had chased after a fox that had stolen a hen, Ginetta had quarrelled with her neighbour over a black cat that was killing her baby rabbits . . .

He washed four potatoes and a couple of onions and covered them with embers. The flask of wine was almost finished. He went down to the cellar to fetch some more, and patiently removed the oil with a piece of oakum. He set the table with great care, aligning the cutlery and folding his napkin with precision, a ritual that gave him a feeling of serenity. He turned on the television and, waiting for the second channel's evening news report, went and sat inside the fireplace. Every so often he turned the meat over with a carving fork like some Dantean devil frying the souls of the damned on the grill of repentance, thinking that for the first time in his life he had no choice but to believe in fate.

The news report began, but he followed it only distractedly . . . Government declarations, gloomy images of the USSR, other foreign policy news, ongoing polemics over the flooding of Florence . . .

By the time he sat down at the table the news report was almost over. He was hungry as a wolf. He ate with gusto and was forever refilling his glass, perhaps to forget the notepad that had ended up in the fire.

The *Carosello* adverts programme began. He enjoyed watching the little stories promoting biscuits, canned meats and toothpaste. The beautiful Virna Lisi didn't quite have the same effect on him that she used to. That must be because of Eleonora, who seemed even more beautiful to him than the movie star . . .

Being Tuesday, there were no films programmed, but the Nazionale was showing *The Count of Monte Cristo* at 9.30, which was in a few minutes. He finished what was on his plate and refilled his glass. After taking a long swig, he got up to get an apple, then changed channel and sat back down.

The serial began. He'd missed many of the prior episodes, and since he'd never read the book, he had trouble following the plot. He would rather have watched Lieutenant Sheridan with his gaunt face and white mackintosh . . . The man always managed to solve the most difficult cases in brilliant fashion . . . Sheridan had no need to resort to makeshift solutions to injustice, like certain police inspectors . . .

Leaving the television on, he cleared the table and washed up. He plopped into the armchair with a glass in one hand and a cigarette in the other. Bacchus and tobaccus . . . The only thing missing was Eleonora. She had become an obsession. But he'd been through worse, like the time in February of '44 in Monte Cassino, when he'd found himself face to face with . . .

The telephone rang and, with a shudder, he imagined it might actually be her, Eleonora . . . She was calling to ask him to come to her place at once, and he would dash into town to hold her in his arms again . . .

'Hello?'

'How are you, Inspector?' The booming voice of Dante Pedretti was unmistakable.

'Not bad, and yourself?'

He hadn't heard from him for a while. The last time Bordelli had spoken to him was probably when he called him to give him his new phone number. Dante lived in Mezzomonte, a few kilometres from Impruneta on the Via di Pozzolatico, in a large farmhouse surrounded by countryside. They were neighbours now.

'Have anything important to do tonight?' asked Dante.

'I had an invitation to the royal palace, but I declined.'

'You were right to. Are you alone?'

'Except for a few owls and wild boar . . .'

'Do you feel like displacing your bodily mass to come and have a drink at my place?'

'I'd love to . . .'

'So you, too, have converted to the country,' said Dante, cigar between his teeth and smoking, as he poured grappa into two small glasses. In the half-light of the vast underground laboratory illuminated only by candles, his gigantic shadow looked like a bear's, though there was something refined in his movements. The great work table was cluttered as usual with papers covered with designs and formulas, open books, alchemical alembics, tools of every kind and obscure objects that led one to imagine all sorts of fantastical adventures of the mind.

'I took your advice,' said Bordelli.

'Never follow the advice of a crazy old man, Inspector.'

Dante set his glass down and took a seat opposite Bordelli, his long, snow-white hair rising up over his head like a flame.

'I'm not an inspector any more . . .' said Bordelli.

'What does that matter? Words are mere air . . . *Flatus vocis* . . .'

'Sometimes they can kill, as the proverb says,' Bordelli muttered, thinking of the last words he heard Eleonora utter on the night of the rape . . . *Leave me alone, I'm fine* . . . She'd got out of the car and he never saw her again.

'If you were a character in a novel, at this moment it would read: *His face was the picture of melancholy* . . .'

'Do you believe in fate?' Bordelli asked, almost without thinking.

Dante started staring into space, pulling on his cigar a few times to keep it from going out. Clouds of dense smoke rose up towards the ceiling.

'I must admit in all humility that I've never got to the bottom of the question,' he said, bobbing his great white head around.

'Now and then I feel as if I believe in it,' Bordelli continued.

'Seeking an explanation for what happens is man's most ancient vice . . . A volcano erupts? The wrath of the gods. The plague mows down victims faster than a scythe? God's punishment. Fate is one of the infinite variants of this.'

'Can I change the subject?' asked Bordelli, spurred by the subtle desire to delve further into the wounds of his own conscience.

'You can even make Pindar your general, if you like,' said Dante, visibly pleased.

'Imagine you knew . . .' Realising he'd drunk all his grappa, he stopped. He stood up to get reinforcements himself. He refilled the glasses and remained standing.

'You were saying, Inspector?'

'Imagine a man who has committed some horrible crimes . . . Atrocious, unacceptable things . . . A vile, despicable man . . . But, lucky for him, nobody knows anything, and Justice is unable to make him pay for his acts.'

'Nothing unusual, in short . . .'

'Exactly. But now imagine you're the only person who knows the truth about this man, and who knows for certain that no court will ever be able to convict him . . . Unless he were to confess, which of course will never happen . . . In short, you're the only person in a position to settle accounts. You and no one else. Would you leave things as they are, or would you . . .'

'Would I what?'

'If you killed that man, would you feel like a murderer?' Bordelli concluded, staring him fixedly in the eye. Dante pulled on his now spent cigar, relit it, and blew the smoke upwards. He remained silent for a long time, looking inspired, and finally resolved to speak.

'The hypocritical answer would be: *I hope I never find myself in such a situation.* If you want a heroic answer: *I would kill him and bear the weight of my hallowed crime.* But if you prefer the straightforward approach, then: *I'd kill him like a dog with no regrets.* I'll spare you the rest. But the truth of the matter is that

I don't know what to say, and I must admit that this doesn't bother me . . .'

'What do you mean?'

'The older I get, the more I like not having any answers.'

'I'll have to think about that.'

'And now don't you want to tell me what's hiding behind this little story of yours?'

'Oh, never mind that, I was just curious.'

'Even my cigar doesn't believe you.'

'Pretend you just listened to a fairy tale . . .'

'Fairy tales always end with the unreal triumph of Good over Evil, but they always contain great truths as well. Snow White being revived by Prince Charming's kiss could never be true, but the Queen's envy is something we can see with our own eyes every day. No hunter will kill the wolf and save Little Red Riding Hood and her grandmother, but it's also true that if you're naïve the big bad wolf will indeed eat you up . . . So what is the truth behind your fairy tale? Who is this wicked man you're talking about?' asked Dante, slouching in his armchair like an indolent child.

Bordelli calmly sat back down and lit a cigarette. It was only his fourth of the day.

'During the war I personally killed twenty-seven Nazis, and each time I carved a notch in the butt of my machine gun so as not to lose track. I killed them in a variety of ways, with the machine gun, with a knife, a couple of times with my bare hands, looking them straight in the eye. I never once felt like a murderer. Unfortunately, in war, the uniform forces us to generalise . . . Once I happened to kill a very young German soldier, and to judge from what he'd written on his helmet, he seemed to have renounced Nazism . . . But I'd seen the SS ferociously massacre defenceless people, even babies, with my own eyes. All I wanted to do was to get rid of them. Some people are pardoned for their crimes . . . I'll never be so lucky, for some things . . .'

'And so this habit of yours has stuck with you . . .' Dante commented, putting a leg up on the arm of his chair.

'Let's just say I feel a strong need to respect the classic ending of the fairy tale, where the bad guy is defeated.'

'I find your eternally childish soul rather touching,' said Dante, erupting into powerful laughter. Even Bordelli couldn't suppress a smile.

'Unfortunately the rest of me has aged,' he said, downing his glass like a Russian.

'So what? Old age is nothing compared to death.'

'That makes me feel a lot better.'

'Another grappa?'

'Thanks . . .'

'Verily I say unto you, hold out your glass, and it shall be filled,' Dante declaimed. It was clear he was curious to know more about this 'fairy tale', but he was too discreet to insist any further.

They started talking about other things, jumping from old childhood memories to the effort of hoeing one's garden, ranging blithely from the magical beauty of the moon to the foundations of morality according to Schopenhauer . . .

'Compassion, dear Inspector, compassion . . . Hardly a groundless categorical imperative . . . Compassion is the prime root of morality . . . Nobody grasped this as well as friendly old Arthur . . .'

'One more round?'

'But of course . . . Let's drink to compassion . . . The sole force able to counter human egotism . . .'

Dante poured the grappa and they clinked glasses. They carried on chatting, drifting from subject to subject, free as the air tossed by the wind, paying no attention to the hourglass . . .

A little past three o'clock Bordelli got up to go home, staggering slightly. A faint alcoholic euphoria let him see the world as a little less gloomy.

'Sooner or later you'll have to come and see my dominions . . .'

'Whenever you like, Inspector . . . Have a good sleep . . .'

They said goodbye with a handshake, and Bordelli went back outside under the stars. A vast, round moon spread a violet cloak over the wooded hills. It was quite cold, and the Beetle's seat was freezing. Heading back to Impruneta, he started humming a song by the Lescano Trio, trying in vain to recall all the lyrics. He drove through the darkened village and continued on his way.

A large, frightened hare appeared on the dirt road that led to his house. Bordelli stopped the car and turned on the high beam, and the animal remained frozen in the middle of the path for almost a minute, staring spellbound at the headlights. Then it suddenly dashed off and vanished into the night. Bordelli put the car in gear and drove off, smiling. These small things were also what made living in the country agreeable.

He parked in the threshing area, and when he got out of the car, he turned to look up at the castle in the distance. The same window was still lit. A glowing rectangle that seemed to flicker slightly.

One minute later he was under the covers. He turned off the light and lay on his back. He was still thinking about the butcher, the shotgun blast that had blown out his head, the fat body falling down on to the leaves . . . And he decided this had to be the last time. In the darkness he traced the sign of the cross in the air with his hand, uttering the formula for absolution he'd learned at church as a child: *Ego te absolvo a peccatis tuis in nomine Patris* . . .

He woke up around nine, and between yawns he put the espresso pot on the fire. The sun was beaming forcefully through the window and probing the dusty corners. He could hear the wind rustling the leaves outside, and it made him think of the sea. The sea of his childhood, smooth and hot, glistening in the sunlight. The sea he used to look out upon from the deck of a ship or the tower of a submarine, a mysterious, fascinating sea that might conceal deadly ambushes . . . Every now and then he felt the need to see the sea, to let his eyes follow the flat horizon line . . .

Casting a distracted glance out the kitchen window, he was shocked to see a lady in a dark overcoat and black hat coming down the path. It was the first time he'd seen another human being walking along the little dirt road. He sat there and watched as she drew near. She must have been rather old, though she walked bolt upright. He didn't think he recognised her. He was expecting her to continue on past his house, but instead she crossed the threshing floor and knocked at his door. Overcome with surprise, he went to open.

'Good morning . . .'

'Please forgive the disturbance, I am Contessa Gori Roversi.'

'Pleased to meet you. Franco Bordelli.'

'I know your name already. May I come in?' She seemed anxious, but was trying to hide it.

'Please do,' he said.

'You're very kind,' she said, coming inside with stately bearing.

'Please excuse the mess; I haven't been living here for very long and haven't yet had time to—'

'Don't worry about it,' the woman cut him off.

'Actually, I was just making coffee. Would you like a cup?' He was trying to find the right words to use with a contessa, to put her at her ease.

'That's very kind of you, thank you.'

'Won't you sit down? I recommend the armchair, it's much more comfortable.'

'I prefer a chair, if you don't mind.'

'Please make yourself at home,' Bordelli said solicitously.

As the contessa sat down on one of the wicker kitchen chairs, he removed the sputtering espresso pot from the fire. He poured the coffee into two fine china demitasses he never used, which he'd inherited from an aunt of his father's, and put a silver sugar bowl, which he'd filled just then, on the table.

He sat down opposite the woman. Looking at her, he realised she wasn't that old after all, or not as old as he'd thought when he saw her from afar. She was probably only a few years older than him. It looked more as if her face had been aged prematurely by some sort of terrible suffering. The wrinkles were concentrated around her eyes, and on that skin, which must have once been like silk, they appeared sculpted in soft wood. Two magnificent pearl earrings hung from her little ears.

The contessa took no notice of the sugar, drank a tiny sip of coffee, and then set her little cup back down.

'I live in the castle you can see from here, on the hill.'

'I admire it every day,' said Bordelli, wondering what could ever have prompted the contessa to come knocking at his door.

'I don't want to waste your time . . . I heard in town that you are a police inspector.'

'Not any more. I was until a few months ago.' He sipped his coffee in as refined a manner as possible.

'You dealt in murder . . .'

'That's true.'

'I've come with a job for you.'

'I'd be glad to help, if I can . . . What is it?'

'You must find who killed my son,' said the contessa, suddenly authoritarian, as if she might bang her fist on the table at any moment. Bordelli sat there holding his espresso cup in midair for a second or two, then stood up.

'You'd do better to call the Florence police at once, Contessa.'

'Please sit down, Signor Bordelli,' said the woman, newly polite. Was she perhaps a bit mad?

'As I was saying, I'm no longer in service, and so there's no way I can . . .'

'Then please be so kind as to hear me out,' said the contessa, enjoining him again to sit back down with a slight nod of the head. Bordelli obeyed.

'Don't you think it would be better if—'

'My son was murdered fourteen years ago, on the night of June the sixth, 1953.'

'I'm sorry, I thought it had just happened . . .'

'No, *I'm* sorry, I acted a bit rashly,' said the woman, newly polite again.

'Please continue.'

By now he was genuinely curious. The contessa took another little sip of her coffee.

'I found my son hanging in his study. Everyone said it was a suicide, but I know that's not true.'

'Do you know it, or are you simply convinced of it? They're not the same thing.'

'I know it, and that's enough for me,' said the woman, hardening again.

'Can you tell me why?'

'My son would never have killed himself.'

'Forgive me, but . . . how can you be so sure?'

'I'm his mother, and I know it's true,' said the contessa, quaking in her chair.

Bordelli looked at her respectfully, thinking that perhaps it was best to humour her for the time being.

'Do you have any idea who might have killed him?'

'I have no idea. I just know that he was murdered. So you don't believe me either?'

43

'I didn't mean that. But I can't really form an opinion without knowing the details.'

Maybe she really was just a poor old madwoman.

'I'll pay whatever you want, but you must find out who killed my son.'

'Please tell me how it happened,' said Bordelli, steeling himself with patience. He felt very much like smoking a cigarette, but didn't want to be impolite. The contessa seemed to calm down. After a long, thoughtful silence she began to tell her story, not omitting certain details that had etched themselves for ever into her memory . . .

*Orlando was an only child. At that time he lived alone in the castle. Count Rodolfo had passed away two years earlier, and the contessa had moved into their villa at Castiglioncello. Mother and son spoke often by telephone, almost always late in the evening, sometimes even after midnight. Orlando got on well and wanted for nothing. On the night of Saturday, 6 June, the contessa rang him at around eleven o'clock, but there was no answer. She tried calling back every half-hour, each time letting the phone ring for a long time. Orlando might have gone to a party, since it was Saturday, or he might have stayed late at a friend's house or had a flat tyre . . . Or perhaps he'd simply fallen asleep and didn't hear the phone . . . Maybe he'd unplugged it, or the line was down . . . Then why did she feel so worried? She tried calling one last time at around 4 a.m., and finally decided to wake up her chauffeur and have him drive her to the castle in Impruneta. When they got there, day was already dawning. A faint light was filtering through the drawn curtains in her son's study. The contessa had the keys to the castle, but the main door was bolted shut. She knocked hard, pulled the bell-ring several times, but inside they heard nothing, aside from the ringing of the bell. And so she ordered her chauffeur to circle round the castle and call loudly to her son from outside, but Orlando didn't answer. At that point the only thing left to do was to go to the Carabinieri in Impruneta. The contessa rang and rang the bell outside the gate of the compound, and in the end a sleepy-eyed young carabiniere came out and told them that the marshal wasn't there. The contessa said she was very worried about her son. Something terrible had happened, she said. She could feel it. The lad seemed undecided as to what to do and tried to calm her down. She didn't give him any time to reach a decision, but immediately heaped insults on him and left in a rage to look for a telephone. She woke a friend who lived in a large villa just outside of town and asked her whether she would be so kind as to let her use her phone. She called the police and explained the situation in a few words. The officer put a young detective on the line, and she told him the reason for her concern. The detective also tried at first to downplay things, but when the woman kept insisting, he decided to accede to her wishes. The fire department was summoned, and to enter the castle while causing as little damage as possible, they had to break a few slats in a ground-floor shutter, cut the window-pane, and force the inside shutter. The contessa insisted that she be the only one to go inside, and they helped her climb through the window. She went up to the first floor with her heart in her throat, entered her son's study, and saw his lifeless body hanging in midair, his face livid and his tongue black and dangling . . . From the very start she'd thought what she still thought today . . .*

'He was murdered. That was no suicide,' the contessa concluded, jerking her head slightly and making her magnificent earrings quiver.

Bordelli tried to hide his perplexity, to avoid humiliating her.

'May I ask you a few questions?' he asked.

'Of course.'

'What kind of rope was it?'

'Whoever killed him had torn off the curtain cord.'

'And where did they . . . In short . . . What was the cord tied to?'

'There was a large wrought-iron chandelier in the middle of the room.

'Did your son leave a letter or note?'

'There was a sheet of stationery on the desk with only two words on it: *Forgive me*. Orlando would never have written anything of the sort. And the handwriting was strange . . .'

'It wasn't his own?'

'It looked like his, but there was also something strange about it.'

'In what way?'

'It wasn't as elegant as usual, a bit chaotic . . . Clearly somebody had forced him to write those words under duress.'

'Might it not have been simply the agitation he was experiencing at that moment?' Bordelli ventured.

'I will repeat it again, Inspector. My son was murdered.'

'Do you know of anyone who might have had anything against him, for any reason at all?'

'I have no idea, as I already said. Orlando never told me much about his private life,' the contessa said bitterly.

Bordelli felt a light tingling under the skin and realised he missed his job. That is to say, he was starting to take an interest in this story. By this point he knew that, in spite of everything, he would end up investigating this young man's death, even if the convictions of his grief-stricken mother were not to be taken seriously.

'If you want me to look into the matter you must tell me everything you can remember, even details that might at first glance seem of little importance to you . . .'

After lunch he got down to lightly hoeing the garden as Ennio had taught him, so he could sow – or, rather, plant – the artichokes. The thought of having an artichoke patch gave him a sense of satisfaction, even though Ennio had warned him that artichokes were strange plants. You had to find the right spot for planting them, otherwise they would dry up with the first cold snap; but if they took root they would grow strong and last for many years. It all depended on their exposure to the wind and the soil's ability to hold the right amount of moisture. Before anything else you had to ask a local farmer for some young artichoke shoots, which you would then plant in holes smaller than those for the tomatoes and hope the weather cooperated. Rosemary was another kettle of fish; it almost always took and grew strong no matter where you put it. You merely had to take some branches and stick them in the ground . . .

'If you want a nice little hedgerow around the garden, you can cut them from this plant,' Ennio had said, stroking the bristly ends of a large rosemary bush . . .

Unable to resist, he'd sprung into action. He cut off several branches of the rosemary and planted them in the ground along the garden's perimeter, continuing his botany lesson . . .

Sage, on the other hand, was capricious. You had to pick the small young plants that grew around the larger bush and stick them in the ground after working the soil a bit. Not all would take root, and in fact they might all dry up from first to last. It depended mostly on the moisture in the soil.

No profession, in short, was easy. Skill and passion were always required. He'd given his all to being a police inspector, and deep down he felt he hadn't done a bad job. Could flushing out killers be considered a passion?

He found a small dead bird at the base of a tree, its little feet stiff and its beak full of dirt. It had very short wings and must have fallen from the nest. He dug a hole in the ground, buried it, and put a rock on top. Poor little thing, it was born and died within a matter of days . . . without knowing why . . .

Wiping the sweat from his brow, he carried on hoeing, all the while thinking of what the Contessa Gori Roversi had told him. In talking about her son the woman's mood changed by the minute, going from nostalgia to vexation to jealousy to ill-concealed grief, even if the dominant feeling remained one of boundless admiration:

> *Orlando had taken a degree in law with the highest marks and at the right age, allowing him to continue his studies during the war. After university, he'd decided to practise the profession, even though there was no need. No Gori Roversi had ever earned money doing that sort of work, not even his father, Count Rodolfo. Managing the family's lands and real estate all over Italy had always been their sole occupation. He, on the other hand . . .*

'This accursed modern era had contaminated him with its stupid frenzy . . .'

> *Orlando wanted to show that the children of nobles could face life as well as anyone else. He used to say he couldn't stand being looked upon as a good-for-nothing, a mama's boy. It was almost as if he was ashamed of having illustrious origins. He got busy and before long he became the assistant of two elderly lawyers who had an office in the centre of Florence. Orlando used to say that he liked the work more and more, even though they paid him a pittance. The Manetti & Torrigiani firm had important clients, including industrialists and politicians, but mostly they administered the enormous estates of the city's*

*upper nobility. Orlando at the time had a girlfriend, a notary's daughter, a beautiful girl with a good head on her shoulders. He saw her often, especially evenings after supper at her parents' house. Sometimes, however, they would go out alone to see a movie or a play. Orlando worked a great deal, and in his spare time he liked to go riding, play tennis, and play the piano. He would also spend pleasant evenings with his friends . . . In short, he led an untroubled, rather satisfying life.*

After listening to the contessa's story, Bordelli had asked her for the names of the people to whom Orlando was closest at the time, and wrote these down in a notebook. There were of course Giulio Manetti, attorney; and Rolando Torrigiani, attorney; and Orlando's dearest friends, Gianfranco Cecconi Marini, and Neri Bargioni Tozzi. Finally, there was his old girlfriend, Ortensia Vannoni, who at that time lived with her parents in Via San Leonardo, one of the most beautiful streets in Florence.

The contessa had him write down her telephone number and told him he could call her at any hour of the day or night. She'd left after declining Bordelli's offer to give her a lift in his car, casting a disdainful glance at his Beetle as she went out. He'd watched her make her way back up the path with her confident gait, erect as a drill sergeant, and waited for her to vanish round the bend . . . Was she just a poor old madwoman? He would try to find out . . .

When the sky began to darken, he set down his hoe and went back inside. After a long hot bath, he lit a fire and sat down in the armchair with a book in hand. He went on reading for almost two hours, forgetting about everything.

At around seven o'clock he rang his former police headquarters.

'Hello, Mugnai . . .'

'Inspector, what a pleasure to hear from you! How are you? How come you never drop in for a visit?'

'What use would you have for an old pensioner? How are you?'

'I can't complain, Inspector. Even though there are two new arrivals here I don't like one bit. The airs they put on! Don't even say hello, they don't. But when you were here—'

'Forget about that, Mugnai. I'm a farmer now.'

'I still can't believe you're not in your office any more . . .'

'Today I dug holes for my artichokes,' Bordelli cut him off.

'It feels like the end of an era . . .'

'If you don't stop I'm going to start crying.'

'I mean it.'

'Me, too . . . Could you please get me Piras?'

'Straight away, sir. Stay in touch, eh?' said the guard, after which Bordelli heard only a great many rustling noises.

'Hello, Inspector,' Piras finally said.

'I need you to do me a favour, Piras.'

'Whatever you want, Inspector . . .'

'Could you find me a telephone directory? I still haven't received my copy.'

Then he asked him to do something a little more delicate: to look in police archives for the file on Orlando Gori Roversi's suicide and to take it out.

'I'll do what I can, Inspector,' said Piras, voice cracking with joy.

'Perhaps you could come to dinner here; you could bring it all then.'

'I can tell you're in a hurry. Have you already got a lead on a killer?' The idea that Bordelli was back investigating some violent crime excited him.

'Nothing concrete yet, Piras . . . I'll tell you later . . .'

'I knew you couldn't just sit there twiddling your thumbs.'

'Indeed, today I hoed my garden . . . So I'll expect you for supper?'

'I can't make it before nine.'

'Come whenever you like . . .'

He was awakened by two small birds quarrelling furiously outside his bedroom window, and he took advantage of this to get up. It was barely a quarter to eight. Bordelli staggered to the bathroom to wash his face, anxious to start the day. He'd supped with Piras the previous evening and told him about his meeting with the contessa. The Sardinian had brought the case file on Orlando's suicide and his own home telephone directory.

After taking coffee, he settled himself comfortably into the armchair and opened the file. There were only two documents. He read the very brief report, signed *Inspector Carlo Bacci*. It said the case was indeed a suicide, and presented a few details. Orlando had been found hanging from the sturdy chandelier in his study with the curtain cord round his neck. On the desk they'd found a note with the words *Forgive me*. The dynamics of the suicide were clear, but at the mother's insistence, after she'd stubbornly insisted that her son had been murdered, further verifications were conducted. The shoeprints left on the desktop were found without any doubt to be those of the dead man, and there were no factors that might lead one to conclude that anyone else had entered the room. The windows and doors, moreover, had been thoroughly inspected and found to have all been firmly locked from the inside: the main door and the one at the back were secured with massive bolts, the shutters and windows with deadbolts and crossbars impossible to reclose from the outside. No one could have left the castle after a hypothetical 'murder'. There was no doubt that Orlando had killed himself. The Forensic Pathology certificate attested that the cause of death was asphyxia and that it had occurred between

1 and 2 a.m. on the morning of Sunday, 7 June. There were no signs of a struggle, no indications of anything unusual. The death certificate was signed by Diotivede, therefore there was no reason to doubt it.

Bordelli closed the file and added Carlo Bacci's name to the list in his notebook. Then he opened the telephone directory. The office of Manetti & Torrigiani wasn't listed, but there was a number for Giulio Manetti, lawyer, in Viale Augusto Righi. There were several Torrigianis listed, but none by the name of Ronaldo. He nevertheless wrote down the numbers for all the different Torrigianis and continued his research. He found Gianfranco Cecconi Marini in Via Pian dei Giullari. He took down the number of the only two Bargioni Tozzis, who lived in Costa San Giorgio a little outside of town. He looked up the surname of Orlando's former girlfriend and to his relief found that there was only one Vannoni in Via San Leonardo. They all lived in areas that hadn't been touched by the flood. That left only Inspector Bacci, whom he would ask someone in police archives to track down.

He drank another demitasse of coffee and, standing at the telephone, started calling the numbers he'd written down in his notebook. He would lie and introduce himself as Inspector Bordelli.

He succeeded in tracking down an old cousin of solicitor Torrigiani, but the man had *absolutely* no idea where Ronaldo might be, and from the man's frosty tone it was clear that he wasn't keen to find out. Bordelli pressed him for a little more information, but the lawyer's cousin said only that Ronaldo had left Italy many years before and hadn't been heard from since. What country had he moved to? Nobody knew.

At Giulio Manetti's house, the lawyer's wife answered the phone and said in a whisper that her husband had passed away a few years earlier. Bordelli expressed his belated condolences and politely excused himself.

The two Bargioni Tozzis were relatives of Orlando's friend, and both said, in almost the same words, that Neri had gone to live in Paris some ten years ago.

He kept on phoning people, rediscovering the thrill of when he was still a police detective. He liked trying to unravel an enigma; he couldn't help it. Instead of an office at police head-quarters he now had a large country kitchen with a fireplace that had seen a lot of wood go up in smoke, but that was the only difference. Maybe Piras was right . . . A leopard can't change his spots . . . And in spite of everything he did not feel as if he was wasting his time, as might seem normal. Could it be just a desire to play at being a police inspector?

At Gianfranco Cecconi Marini's house it was the housekeeper who answered the phone, and she said in a haughty tone that the *signorino* would be home around seven that evening. So he'd finally found one.

He'd saved the call to the Vannoni home for last. Ortensia's mother answered the phone, but was at first so frightened at the idea of speaking with a police inspector that she very nearly lost her composure. Bordelli tried to calm her down, reassuring her that there was nothing to be worried about. After a long pause, in a faint voice from beyond the grave, the lady informed him that her daughter had married the architect Giampiero Falli in 1960. They lived in Fiesole, she added, and breathlessly gave him their phone number. Bordelli thanked her and politely said goodbye. As soon as he hung up, he dialled the architect's number.

After many rings, it was she, Ortensia, who answered. She had a sweet voice. She, too, seemed somewhat taken aback at first, and she got even more upset when she heard him mention Orlando. She lowered her voice, as though afraid someone might be listening. Bordelli asked whether she would be so kind as to meet with him, assuring her that he wouldn't take more than half an hour of her time. After some incomprehensible stam-mering, Ortensia asked him to leave her his phone number. She would call him back by late morning, or perhaps the following day. After muttering goodbye, she hung up.

Bordelli stretched his back, emitting a groan. He wasn't done phoning yet. He rang police headquarters, and Mugnai, after his customary nostalgic comments, told him that Piras had raced off in a squad car with the young junior inspector Anselmi.

'A murder?' Bordelli asked, curious. Mugnai said that as far as he knew a man had been found dead in his bathtub, electrocuted by an electric shaver still plugged in. The junior inspector had gone to the scene to verify.

Bordelli had him connect him with Porcinai, the fat fellow in charge of the archive. They exchanged some small talk, and then he asked him to look up the name of Carlo Bacci in the police department catalogues. After flipping pages for a few minutes, Porcinai told him that Bacci had been made full inspector and was now working at the commissariat of Verona. He also gave him the number. Bordelli thanked him and immediately rang Verona. Moments later, he'd managed to track down Bacci, who remembered Orlando's death quite well.

'I'm sorry to say, but the contessa isn't all there in the head. She kept repeating that her son had been murdered . . .'

'She still thinks so, apparently,' said Bordelli.

'She's insane, I tell you. I couldn't take her complaining any more, and so I took her and showed her every door and window in the castle . . . even on the first and second floors, just to eliminate all doubt. Deadbolts and latches everywhere. But she didn't want to hear about it and just carried on like a broken record, repeating that her son had been murdered. I realise that in a situation like that, a distraught mother might . . . but in the face of the evidence . . .'

'Did you talk to any neighbours, to see whether anyone had seen or heard anything? Just to be thorough . . .'

'Some people were questioned, again to make the crazy old woman happy, since she kept badgering us . . . But, I repeat, it was a suicide, I would bet the house on it.'

'All right, then. Thanks, Bacci.'

'Not at all . . . Cheerio.'

'Work well . . .'

Bordelli hung up and stood there for a moment staring at the wall. He was getting more and more drawn into this affair, but he didn't mind. For the sake of thoroughness, he decided to ring his friend in the SID, the Italian Secret Service, Admiral Agostinelli, known as Carnera for his massive physique.[7] Luckily this time he had no trouble getting through to him.

'My dear Franco, how nice to hear from you . . . Let me guess . . . you've finally decided to come and work for us . . .'

'I prefer the peasant's life, Pietro. I've moved to the country.'

'That's my point . . . Now that you've left the police, you could come and work with us . . .'

'Ah, so you already knew?'

'You're talking to the SID, after all . . .'

'Right.'

'But the real reason for your decision is something only you can tell me.'

'Let's just say that being a police inspector became incompatible with other concerns.'

'How mysterious . . .'

'Maybe I'll tell you one day, Pietro. First, however, I have to wait for the fairy tale to end with the sentence: *And they all lived happily ever after* . . .'

For whatever reason, he'd had something against fairy tales for some time now.

'I'll patiently wait until your grandmother has finished telling it to you,' said the admiral, though his tone was serious.

'My grandmother is very old. She speaks very slowly . . .'

'I've always been a very patient man, dear Franco.'

Agostinelli was dying of curiosity and didn't hide it, but he didn't insist.

'And how are things up your way?' asked Bordelli.

'Always on the razor's edge . . . You'd like it too, I assure you . . .'

'I doubt it, Pietro . . . Not my cup of tea. To each his own.'

'I think you'd fit right in,' Agostinelli said with conviction.

'I don't think so. It's a question of character . . . I can't see myself scheming in the shadows creating files on potential enemies of the state, possibly for even worse enemies . . .'

'Let's not exaggerate . . .'

'You know perfectly well I'm not exaggerating.'

'And yet when you need information on somebody, I'm the one you call . . .' The admiral laughed.

'I also go to the baker, since I don't know how to make bread.'

'In an emergency you'd work it out fast.'

'I'm sure I'd make a bloody mess of it . . . At any rate, Pietro, you guessed right. That's exactly why I called.'

'Haven't you stopped working as an inspector?'

'I have to say it's not easy stopping altogether. Sort of like smoking . . . And so I cracked at the first opportunity . . .'

'Anything to do with the fairy tale you mentioned?' the admiral prodded him.

'No, this is something else.'

'What do you want to know?'

'If you have any information on a lawyer named Rolando Torrigiani, who apparently hasn't lived in Italy for a while.'

'How soon do you need it?'

'I'm in no hurry,' said Bordelli, but he wasn't really being sincere. For whatever reason, this affair was pulling him in more and more.

'Give me your phone number. I'll give you a ring as soon as I know anything.'

'It's probably better if I call you. I'm often out and may not be here for your call.'

'As you wish. Try me late tomorrow morning. I'm not sure I can do anything today.'

'Listen, while you're at it, could you look and see if you've got anything on another laywer by the name of Giulio Manetti?'

'All right, I've written down the name.'

'Thanks, Pietro . . . Here's my phone number anyway, in case you feel like chatting some time . . .'

He gave him his new number, which in his area had only five digits. When he hung up it was almost eleven o'clock. Feeling the need to clear his head, he went out for a short walk in the vicinity, leaving his cigarettes at home.

He set out on the trail that led down to il Ferrone, skirting the olive groves and thickets of wood. When passing by a ramshackle farmhouse he saw an old peasant sitting on a chair under the portico and eyeing him.

'Good morning,' he said, approaching.

'Good morning, my arse . . .' the peasant muttered.

'Anything wrong?'

'And who would you be?'

'I live up the path a bit, just bought a house.'

'You'd do better to go back to where you came from, take it from me . . . People's nasty round here . . . Bloody communists . . . Think they own the world, they do . . . damn the mothers that brung 'em into the world . . . They're all a bunch of lice in disguise . . . Forget about it, or else . . . I know what I'm talkin' about, I do . . . Goddam it all . . . At any rate, good on you, sir . . . But nobody's gonna stick it up my bum, I can tell you that . . . I'm not some stinkin' peasant, you know . . . I worked with horses, I was a groom . . . Ten years in the Foreign Legion . . .'

As the groom kept talking, Bordelli looked up and saw a herring hanging from a rafter over the porch with a sign attached to its tail, saying: GUESTS STINK.

'If one of those shits dares come this way I'll shoot 'im in the bollocks, I tell you . . . And not with birdshot, mind, I use boarshot . . . Won't be a pretty picture, I can tell you that . . . An' I won't think twice about it . . . I'm not afraid, you know . . . I've killed a lot of lice in my day, one more or less won't matter . . . Bloody communists . . . They're the ones ought to be afraid . . .'

'Nice day today, don't you think?' Bordelli tried saying, but there was no stopping the old man's tirade.

'I don't talk much, I can tell you . . . In my house it's martial law . . . If a cat kills a chicken, he gets shot . . .'

'I'll be on my way . . .' said Bordelli, waving his hand. As he headed back towards his house, the peasant kept on grumbling, but after a while he could no longer hear him. There wasn't a cloud in the sky. It was less cold than the day before, and one could almost feel the first shudder of spring in the air.

His thoughts turned to the countess and her stubbornness . . . A madwoman, Inspector Bacci had said. Bordelli was tempted to think the same, but with a little compassion. For nearly fifteen years now the woman had obstinately persisted in thinking her son had been murdered; the desire to find the killer must have been her only way to survive her grief, the impetus that kept her going . . . And what if one day she finally discovered the truth, whatever it might be? Most likely her life would cease to have any meaning . . .

First, however, one had to get at that truth. He couldn't suppress a smile, but it was directed at himself. He'd let himself be willingly dragged into an adventure that wouldn't lead anywhere, and he already knew it . . . Then why did he have the feeling that he wasn't wasting his time?

At around nine o'clock that evening he got in the Beetle with an unlit cigarette between his lips. Driving along in leisurely fashion, he went through the village and then down the Imprunetana di Pozzolatico. He was still thinking about Orlando's suicide and his own childish and perhaps slightly unhealthy desire to play cop.

Earlier, at seven o'clock sharp, he'd rung the Cecconi Marini house, and the housekeeper had gone to fetch the *signorino*. Gianfranco had a shrill, almost feminine voice. After introducing himself, Bordelli more or less explained the reason for his call and asked him whether they could meet. After a moment of highly aristocratic perplexity, Gianfranco suggested they meet at noon on Monday, in the Salla Rossa at the Circolo Borghese. As Bordelli had no desire to tread on soft, precious carpets and sit in uncomfortable gilded chairs, he'd persuaded Signorino Gianfranco to have lunch with him at a trattoria near the Sant'Ambrogio market, assuring him that it would be a wonderful experience . . .

Upon hanging up he'd felt like a pathetic former inspector of almost sixty who couldn't resign himself to throwing in the towel . . . And he knew well that he wouldn't desist. Maybe it was just a way of staying in shape, in the hope of ageing more slowly. Whatever the case, he wanted to wait until he had a few more elements in hand before establishing once and for all that the contessa was an unlucky madwoman . . . Even though he already considered he would never get anywhere in this affair . . .

But weren't there sometimes instances where an apparently clear, straightforward case was undermined thanks to a detail that had remained buried for years? One had to be careful, however, not to be fooled by the desire to unveil a hidden truth at all costs . . . Just as it was best not to get so discouraged that one was afraid to fall into absurd conjectures, bearing in mind, of course, that intuition can sometimes prove to be an illusion . . . At any rate, it would be no easy matter to wriggle out of this affair, and that might well be why he refused to give up . . . Even if, in the final analysis . . .

He burst out laughing and shook his head. He was going round in circles like a bloody fool, jumping from one doubt to the next and congratulating himself on his own contorted arguments . . . He had to stop pussyfooting around. The wisest thing was to put everything off till tomorrow and try to have a quiet evening. A nice dinner at Cesare's trattoria, some good wine and coversation with Totò . . . Maybe afterwards he could drop in on Rosa and lie down on her sofa with his shoes off, as he used to when with the police . . .

At the crossroads at Poggio Imperiale, two youths on a Lambretta cut him off, and when he honked the horn they came up beside the Beetle cursing and pounding their fists on the window.

'What the fuck do you want, you old git!'

'Get out of the car, you piece of shit!'

Bordelli tried to ignore them. He had no desire to waste time on idiocies, but the two youths kept on threatening him and yelling at him to stop. They looked like scions of good families, with clean faces and longish hair. One was dark, the other blond. The kind of lads girls liked.

At Porta Romana Bordelli decided to pull over and got out of the car. The two put the scooter on its stand and came at him, not knowing that the old git had been a boxer for several years in Mazzinghi's gym. Bordelli dodged the blond youth's wild punch without any difficulty and dealt him a right jab to the stomach, knocking him breathless to the ground. The other one hesitated for a second, then rushed him, spewing insults. Bordelli dodged his punch as well and landed his own square in the lad's face, sending him rolling across the ground with blood pouring out of his nose.

'That'll teach you to respect the elderly . . .' he said, getting back into his car. He drove off, forging a path through the crowd of onlookers that had gathered. He didn't like coming to blows like that, but sometimes you had to, just to get by . . . Had he perhaps overreacted? Taken advantage of the situation to let off a little steam? Whatever the case, those two punks would henceforth think twice before strutting their stuff with an ageing pensioner . . .

He put the same cigarette back in his mouth, without lighting it. He would gladly have put the butcher and his friends out of his thoughts, but it wasn't easy. They formed a kind of grey fog that enveloped everything. He was anxious to dispel it.

Crossing the Ponte alla Vittoria, he encountered a bit of traffic on the Viali. Youngsters were darting every which way on their motorbikes, caps pulled down over their eyes and girls clinging to their backs, and he felt a slight pang of envy . . . Or perhaps just a bit of nostalgia for his lost youth.

He proceeded along Via Strozzi at a walking pace, and some, as usual, pointlessly honked their horns. He had been born in Florence and grown up there, but after just a few weeks of living in the country, he felt like an outsider come from afar. He'd already grown unaccustomed to the confusion; he felt that it wasn't for him. The knowledge that sooner or later he would go back to his quiet house reassured him . . . He would fill the stove and slip into bed under the duvet, which would warm up ever so slowly, and, as he read his book, he would hear an animal or two cry out in the night . . .

He parked in Viale Lavagnini outside the Trattoria da Cesare, and as he was getting out of the car he turned round for a moment and looked at the street that led to police headquarters. It was as though a thousand years had passed since the time when he used to take that street daily.

He went into the restaurant. After not showing his face there for over a month, he was welcomed like somebody back from the dead. He exchanged a few words with Cesare and the waiters, then slipped into the kitchen, where he customarily ate while seated on a stool. When the cook saw him, he let out an Apulian yell and ran to shake his hand.

'Where you been hiding, Inspector?'

'I'm not an inspector any more, Totò . . .'

'Down in my parts, whenever somebody disappears for more than two days, we think he's dead.'

'I may well be dead myself, but my ghost is very hungry,' said Bordelli. Totò immediately served him a glass of wine.

'What do you feel like eating, Inspector?'

'Something light . . .'

'The only light things we've got are the napkins and corks . . .'

'Would a simple dish of pasta with tomato sauce be possible?'

'Are you kidding, Inspector?' said Totò, returning to his burners. Carrying on the conversation while cooking for the restaurant's customers, he prepared an enormous bowl of 'simple' penne with tomato sauce for Bordelli . . . though it must be said that there were huge chunks of sausage floating in the sauce. Bordelli accepted the surprise with resignation and started eating heartily as Totò regaled him with lugubrious stories of his home town . . . Such as the time when a lad, to impress his friends with his bravery, decided one summer night to walk out to the cemetery alone, swearing that he would spend the night there, only to be found at dawn the following morning, wandering through the fields, hair having turned completely white . . . Or the young woman whom nobody knew, who was found drowned in a small, fast-flowing stream, completely naked, with a snake coiled round her neck, and some swore she was a witch . . . Or the rich landowner of about fifty who, after his wife died, lived all alone in a large apartment in the centre of town and one Sunday morning came to the window with a double-barrel shotgun in hand and started shooting at people coming out from mass. He killed three or four people before being shot down like a wild boar by the Carabinieri. Nobody could figure out what had happened to him, and when it was discovered that he'd left his vast estate to a beautiful girl of sixteen, a peasant's daughter, pandemonium broke out . . .

'The strangest things happen in your home town . . .' Bordelli commented. He'd finished his pasta with some effort, and after declining a dish of osso buco with beans he took a last sip of wine. The wisest thing was to leave before Totò pulled out the grappa. He stood up, wanting nothing more than to go to bed, and said goodbye to the cook, saying he'd be back soon. Totò tried to corrupt him with a slice of cream pie, but he managed to resist the temptation and left that place of perdition feeling proud of himself.

The cool night jolted him awake. Instead of getting in his car, he lit a cigarette and walked as far as police headquarters, to help digest his supper. Looking up at the building where he'd spent two decades of his life was like taking a leap back in time, even though, just a few months earlier . . .

'Need any help?' he said, sticking his head inside the door.

Mugnai gave a start, then smiled and made a vague military salute.

'Inspector! You scared me . . .'

'I can see you're busy,' said Bordelli, gesturing towards the *Settimana Enigmistica*, the weekly puzzle magazine.

'I've almost finished . . . I just need two or three more words . . .'

'Let me see . . . Five down . . . Five letters . . . *Foscolo's Jacopo* . . . The answer is: Ortis.'

'What?'

'Just write O, R, T, I, S.'

'You're right, it fits . . . Now there's four down . . . If I can get that, I'm almost done . . .'

'Let me see . . . Seven letters. *Killed Hector* . . . The answer is *Achilles*.'

A patrol car's tyres screeched as it sped out of the courtyard, and Bordelli managed just in time to salute the two officers inside, Rinaldi and Tapinassi, whom he knew well. A few seconds later the wail of the siren rose in the air. What could have happened? He felt more curious than an ageing auntie, and recalled the moments of emergency he used to experience until just a few months before, when, after days of total darkness, something totally unexpected would turn up . . .

'Inspector . . . Can you hear me?'

'Eh? Yeah, what is it?'

'Twelve across . . . *Talion law* . . . Eight letters . . . What's "talion" mean?'

'Vendetta,' said Bordelli, feeling a shudder at the back of his neck . . . And again he saw Panerai collapsing to the ground amid the rotting leaves, skull shattered by the shotgun blast.

'Okay, we're almost done,' said the guard, staring at the grid of words.

Bordelli stayed in the guard booth until they finished the crossword puzzle, then took his leave of Mugnai with a pat on the shoulder and headed off into the cold night, fidgeting with the matches in his pocket.

'There's a room just for you, with a nice big bed,' said Bordelli. He was lying on Rosa's sofa in the half-light of her little sitting room.

'I don't like the country, maybe because I was born there,' she said, caressing Briciola. The kitten was curled up at her feet, observing the world with its damaged eye. It had grown, but not much. One could tell it would remain a small cat. Gideon, on the other hand, looked bigger every time he saw him. He was dozing atop the back of an armchair, with one eye half open, keeping the situation under surveillance.

'Every man should have a little patch of earth,' said Bordelli, stretching to stub out his cigarette in the ashtray.

'Oh, we'll all have our little patch of earth . . . in the cemetery.'

'What a pleasant thought . . .' Bordelli muttered, imagining his own funeral for a moment. Would many people come? Or only a few with long faces? Rosa was frantically stroking Briciola's belly.

'Look how fat she is, the little piglet,' she said, rubbing her nose into the cat's head.

'Anyone would get fat in your hands,' said Bordelli, pulling himself up into a sitting position. He ran a finger over Briciola's head and got nipped for his effort. Rosa started laughing.

'You really have a way with women . . .'

'It's not always my fault,' Bordelli said in his own defence, thinking sadly of Eleonora. The night she was raped he'd spent the evening with Rosa getting his neck massaged . . . and when he entered the bedroom . . . Every time he thought of it he felt overwhelmed with guilt . . . If only he'd got home earlier that night . . . But maybe not, maybe it would have made no difference . . . But there was no point in thinking about it any more . . .

'Can you tell me now what happened with your pretty brunette?' asked Rosa, as if she'd read his mind.

'Let's talk about something else.'

'C'mon, ugly, you can tell me anything.'

'Not now, please . . .'

'You're so surly . . .'

'I'm just a little tired.'

'When you were chasing down killers you were tired, and now that you're no longer doing anything, you're still tired . . . Maybe you're just a big old lazybones.'

'Would you like to come and help me hoe the ground? Or maybe chop some wood?' said Bordelli, smiling as he imagined Rosa working the land in her spiked heels.

'That's nothing for a big strapping man like you . . .'

'It's harder than you think.'

'If you didn't feel like chopping wood you could have stayed in the city. They invented coal furnaces for that. It's called progress . . .' said Rosa, who started laughing like a fool. All at once Briciola jumped off her lap and ran away as though pursued by a monster.

'What's wrong with her?'

'She always does that, I think she's a bit dotty . . . A little more cognac?'

'Just a smidge, thanks,' said Bordelli, but he let Rosa fill his little glass to the brim.

'Chocolate?'

'You only live once . . .' said Bordelli, reaching out for the box.

Briciola was walking close to the wall, bobbing her head like a lioness and rearing up every so often as if fighting an invisible enemy. Maybe she really was crazy. Then she suddenly starting running round in circles, trying to chase her tail.

'At any rate, not too long ago I spent days shovelling mud,

don't you remember?' Rosa said suddenly, returning to the former subject.

'I can already see the marble plaque . . . *In November 1966, in these streets, Rosa Stracuzzi, championess of love, in a spirit of sacrifice and selflessness, undertook to remove several tons of mud with her own two little hands . . .'*

'That's too silly for comment,' said Rosa, laughing.

'I meant it in all seriousness . . .'

'Sometimes I can still smell the stink from the flood,' she said, sniffing the air.

'I think we'll be smelling it for a while.'

'Briciola! Leave the curtains alone!' Rosa shot to her feet and the cat ran off and hid under the sideboard.

'Did you know there's a castle on the hill in front of my house? A contessa lives there,' said Bordelli.

'How do you know?'

'She came and called on me.'

'I wish I'd been born a contessa . . .' Rosa said dreamily, dropping back down into the armchair.

'Contessina Rosa . . .[8] It has a nice ring to it.'

'Before the war, there was the daughter of a Sicilian baroness working at the *villino* on the Lungarno . . .'[9]

'Oh, really?'

'Pretty as a picture . . . And probably the biggest whore of us all . . .' said Rosa, chuckling.

'And now she's probably married to a prince.'

'So you said the contessa came to see you?' Rosa said, curious.

'About fifteen years ago, in that same castle, her only son hanged himself with a curtain sash . . .'

'Oh, the poor woman . . .'

'She's convinced he was murdered and wants me to find the killers.'

'What's this contessa's name?'

'Gori Roversi.'

'No!'

'Why? What is it?'

'I used to have a steady client by that name . . .'

'Was he called Rodolfo?'

'That's the one! A wonderful man. With enormous whiskers . . . A great nobleman. He used to bring me presents all the time.'

'A real gentleman . . .'

'In bed he was as sweet and cheeky as a child. And afterwards he would curl up beside me and tell me in a whisper about his beautiful wife and beloved son . . . I felt so sorry for the poor man . . . Briciola! That's enough now!'

By the time he left Rosa's building it was almost two o'clock. The dim street lamps in Via dei Neri struggled to overcome the darkness. A cold wind was blowing. Weather for wolves. There was nobody out on the street. Signs of the flood were still visible on the building façades and every so often one got a whiff of heating oil.

The front seat of the Beetle chilled his bottom. He started up the car and drove off sighing. He took the Lungarno, already knowing what he was about to do. Instead of turning on to the bridge he kept going straight, heart beating fast. He took Via Lungo l'Affrico and after the viaduct turned on to Via d'Annunzio. He pulled up outside Eleonora's building and leaned forward to get a better look at the façade. The light was on in a second-floor window . . . Might it actually be Eleonora's? What was she doing awake at that hour? Maybe she couldn't sleep . . . Or was writing a letter to her boyfriend . . .

He did a U-turn and drove off, feeling like an idiot. He lit a cigarette, swearing it would be his last. It wasn't the right moment yet to go looking for Eleonora. There were still a few things he had to take care of first. If he ever got up the nerve to knock on her door, he wanted to be able to tell her . . . At any rate, he had to wait . . .

Via Impruneta was deserted, the olive trees by the road visibly tossed about by violent gusts of wind. It occurred to him that Ortensia hadn't called back. He would wait another few days, then ring her back himself. Why did she sound so upset over the phone? He was very curious to find out, as curious as he was to discover whether or not the contessa was just a poor distraught mother who'd lost her mind. Or perhaps *curiosity* wasn't the right word. At this point he felt there was no turning back. He might come up empty handed, but he knew he had no choice but to get to the bottom of things . . . And again he wondered why. Maybe he was just ageing poorly.

Passing by the dirt road that led to Dante's farmhouse he was tempted to go and impose on him. Undoubtedly he would still be awake. Bordelli slowed down, but then changed his mind and continued straight ahead. He was too tired.

He drove through the town, and as he was going down the trail that led to his house, he again saw a hare in the middle of the road. He recognised it as the same one as before. There was no doubt about it. It had survived the hunters for another day. He waited for it to vanish into the darkness, then proceeded on towards home. The wind was gusting stronger and stronger, and the tops of the cypresses undulated like flames.

It was less cold upstairs. He heard a shutter slam and went and closed it. Shovelling a little ash out of the stove, he refilled it with wood with the ease of habit. He could never now give up this sense of peace, the way his thoughts could wander freely through the vast palace of memory. The cries of the animals outside, the creaky old furniture, the boughs of the trees rustling in the wind, only deepened the silence.

He went down to the kitchen to get a bottle of water for the night. He couldn't sleep without having water within reach. Sometimes he would wake up in the middle of the night with his throat parched and guzzle half the bottle.

He got into bed and started reading Lermontov. For a while now he'd been noticing that the letters on the page were slightly out of focus, and he had to hold the book farther away to read it. It was probably time to get some glasses, goddam it all. It was a thrilling story, and he didn't put the book down until he realised he'd been rereading the same line without understanding. It was past four o'clock. He turned off the light and buried his face in the pillow. When he was a child his final thoughts before drifting off to sleep were always confused and tumultuous; memories of the day just past would blend into fantasies of adventure. At times he would have trouble falling asleep, thinking he could see the silhouette of a werewolf or witch coming towards him out of the shadows. At other times as he was drifting off he would imagine himself as a giant as tall as a mountain and would lie down on top of the sky and gaze down upon Florence from above. He would curl up under the covers and lose himself in these adventures, seeing everything that happened in the streets, and he could intervene as he pleased. If a woman was assailed by a thief, his giant fingers would pop out of the clouds and carry the villain away. Or if he saw a man fall out of a top-storey window he would hold out his palm and catch him before he hit the ground. Other times he would put out a fire by sticking one finger in the Arno and letting it drip huge drops of water on to the blaze . . .

That night he indulged in the same fantasy and felt the same emotions as before. He turned into a giant and looked out over the city in darkness, his gaze following the deserted streets, the rows of street lamps along the avenues, pausing to take in the dark spots that were the parks and the gardens hidden in the courtyards of palazzi, trying to identify monuments, piazzas, his own childhood home. Then the moment he was waiting for arrived . . . From the black sky emerged an enormous hand that stretched over the city and with no effort at all tore the roof off a large villa on the hill of Marignolle. Two fingers reached down and picked one of Giacomo Pellissari's killers out of his bed and crushed him like a fly. A little red stain was all that remained between its fingertips. Now it was the turn of the fourth, the last, the worst of the lot. Stripping the roof of his villa in Viale Michelangelo, he saw him get up out of bed in terror. He lifted him delicately by one arm, hearing him scream, and after letting him hang in the air for a few moments, he dropped him slowly into the Arno, holding him under water for a few minutes. Then he pulled him back out and tossed him on to the hills of Cintoia, staying to watch the boar fight over his corpse.

After a walk in the woods behind the house, he collapsed into the armchair and started thumbing through *La Nazione*. In the city crime-news section there was a big headline in block letters: KILLS HUSBAND FOR INHERITANCE. The subhead read: *In teary confession, young wife admits to having a lover and setting up murder to look like accident.* The article told of the doubts that had arisen from the start, doubts that quickly turned into valid suspicions. They involved a faint mark left on the wall by a small bathroom table, which had apparently been moved from the other side of the sink and placed right beside the bathtub so that the electric shaver, still plugged in, would fall into the water. The wife was questioned at great length until she finally cracked and confessed.

Bordelli closed the newspaper, thinking that it was probably Piras who first noticed the mark left by the table. It was his style to notice small details, starting from the premise that appearances are deceptive and that what looks like an accident may in fact be covering up a murder . . .

He glanced at the clock: a few minutes after twelve. It was time to ring the SID offices. Agostinelli was in a meeting and called back almost an hour later. Bordelli was cooking and put the phone as close as possible to the stove.

'You'll have to forgive me, Franco, but the sky is falling in around here.'

'You guys must be used to that, no?'

'It's a big deal this time . . . I'm sure you'll be reading about it shortly in the newspapers.'

'Now you've aroused my curiosity, Pietro . . .' said Bordelli, stirring the chopped onions in the skillet with a wooden spoon.

'I can't tell you anything.'

'Nobody's listening . . . and if it's going to be in the papers I'm going to find out anyway.'

'Forget about it. It's just the usual Italian rot . . . What's that noise in the background?'

'Nothing, I'm just cooking . . .'

'You need a woman, Franco.'

'We'll talk about that another time . . . Have you found anything on those two people?'

'Nothing special . . .'

'I'm all ears.'

'I won't read you the whole thing . . . Rolando Torrigiani left Italy in 1955 and that's the last anyone's heard of him. It's presumed he's in Brazil, but nothing is certain. And he didn't leave empty handed. He took along a vast sum of money pilfered from the estates of the Florentine nobility he'd served as administrator.'

'I'm not sure whether to call him a thief or a hero of the Republic,' Bordelli said, smiling. With his own tomatoes still in the ground, he was opening a tin of canned tomatoes, holding the telephone between his chin and his shoulder.

'Actually the money preceded him over there. Before leaving, Torrigiani had transferred it to Brazil with a few skilful banking manoeuvres.'

'Nobody can touch the Italians in those sorts of things. They're the best.'

'A degeneration of the famous art of getting by . . .'

'Find anything on the other lawyer?'

'Hardly anything . . . He was Torrigiani's associate, in the shady dealings as well . . . An aficionado of art and ancient weapons . . . He died in February of '63. I've got nothing else of interest . . .'

'Thanks just the same.'

'Why did you want this information anyway? I'm a curious man myself, you know . . .'

'Tell you what. You tell me what you guys have got cooking up there, and I'll tell you what you want to know.'

'I don't think the two secrets are of equal weight, Franco . . . But actually you're right: in a few weeks you'll find out anyway . . . But you go first . . .'

'No, I don't trust the SID: you go first,' said Bordelli, stirring the tomatoes with his wooden spoon. Agostinelli sighed and resigned himself.

'In the summer of '64, before getting sick, President Segni set up a sort of *coup d'état* under the direction of General de Lorenzo. There are some people claiming it was merely a law-enforcement operation in anticipation of potential public unrest . . . You know, with the fall of the centre-left government . . . when some were clamouring for a technocratic government led by Merzagora . . .'

'And that's all?'

'And that's all.'

'The usual Italian stuff . . .'

'As I'd said. But now it's your turn.'

'There isn't much to tell you . . . *The authorities have no leads*, as the newspapers always say . . .'

'Tell me anyway, I'm curious.'

'Well, a contessa who lives on the hill opposite my house . . .'

In few words he told him the story, concluding by saying that Orlando, at the time, was working at the firm of Manetti & Torrigiani.

'What if the contessa's right?' asked Agostinelli.

'I doubt it, but at this point I want to see the thing through.'

'Torrigiani has vanished into thin air where nobody will ever find him, but now you have a motive. The lad discovered that the two lawyers were stealing money from their clients and so they killed him. It makes perfect sense . . .'

'That may well be, but don't forget that the castle was locked from the inside . . . The firemen had to break open a window.'

'My dear Franco, now that you're retired you have all the time in the world to devote yourself to mysteries.'

'I also have a vegetable garden to tend . . .'

'You want to have some fun? Try taking for granted that the

contessa's son was in fact murdered, and try to work out how it was possible in spite of all appearances. Almost every problem has a solution; take it from the SID.'

'I get it, you want to keep me from sleeping at night.'

'That's the method we normally use . . . If nothing else, it's a good workout for the mind and soul . . .'

'Ah, yes, a little gymnastics . . . Well, I have to go now, it's time to put the pasta in the water. Thanks, Pietro.'

'I'm on my way to lunch, too. Give my best to the chickens,' said the admiral.

Bordelli dumped a good handful of spaghetti into the boiling pot, and after stirring it for a minute or so, he started setting the table. Mentally he'd already accepted Agostinelli's challenge and was trying to imagine how it might be possible to kill someone at home by simulating the perfect suicide . . . Then he suddenly understood why he was so doggedly pursuing the mystery of Orlando's death . . . It now seemed as clear as day . . .

With a smile he thought back on his fantasy of the night before . . . Not so much the oneiric omnipotence as the desire concealed behind that fantasy. There were four people responsible for Giacomo Pellissari's death. One actually did commit suicide. The other committed suicide at the hands of a retired police inspector. That left two. He had to kill them. He couldn't help it. He had to. It was as though God himself had asked him to do it. *Ego te absolvo* . . .

He ran over to the boiling pasta water and tasted a strand of spaghetti. He'd made it just in time. Another minute and he would have had to throw it all away. He drained the pot, put the spaghetti into the bowl and poured the tomato sauce on to it. After pouring himself a glass of wine, he started eating.

He felt split in two. One side of him was the Franco he more or less knew, with his memories and obsessions . . . The other Franco was walking down a path already determined, which he had no choice but to follow. He would kill them; it was already written. But he couldn't very well hope to run into the lawyer

Moreno Beccaroni or Monsignor Sercambi in the woods, served up by fate on a silver platter, as had happened with the butcher. He had to get busy now. He needed another suicide. It was better to start with the lawyer Beccaroni, who seemed the more vulnerable of the two. And anyway, he would rather save the monsignor for last. He was sure of this, so it was Beccaroni's turn. But it absolutely had to look like a suicide. He couldn't afford for Monsignor Sercambi to get scared and unleash the secular arm of the masons again. Eleonora had already paid dearly for his mistakes, through no fault of her own. It must not happen again . . .

Whether the contessa's son killed himself or was murdered, probably nobody would ever know . . . But he would try to find out, if for no other reason than to convince himself that it was worth finding a solution to the mystery. The motive, as his spymaster friend had suggested to him, was possibly there. But that wasn't the point. If he could find out how to kill someone in their own home and somehow escape while leaving all windows and doors closed from the inside, he would have a model to use for setting up a suicide, one that would leave no room for doubt. This was the next move that fate was proposing to him. Now he understood . . . It had not, after all, been a waste of time getting involved with the old contessa's obsessions . . .

At eight o'clock the next morning he opened the bedroom window wide and went down to the kitchen to make coffee. He calmly prepared his backpack, still thinking about what his spymaster friend had said . . . *Try taking for granted* . . .

Half an hour later he parked his Beetle in La Panca and set out on the steep trail that led up Monte Scalari, thinking that these hills had seen every imaginable sort of thing, and not only during the war. The climb made him work up a sweat, and his heart was beating fast. Nowadays the only place where he seemed to feel right was in the woods. Walking through the trees allowed him to think more clearly. That morning the same question kept going round and round in his head . . . How do you kill someone and then escape while leaving all doors and windows locked from the inside? Was it true that there was a solution to every mystery? He wasn't entirely convinced. Not even the ape in the Poe story could pull it off.

As on every Sunday, reports of rifle shots through the hills were not wanting. A mere week had passed since his pleasant encounter with Panerai, and yet it seemed a distant memory. He decided to try to enjoy his walk without thinking about that nastiness, though it wasn't easy. The place had been fire-branded by events impossible to forget.

After passing the ancient abbey of Monte Scalari, he took the trail that led down to Celle. The backpack weighed heavy on his shoulders, as the shots rang out in the distance, breaking the silence . . . It brought back to mind another morning, on the fourth of August 1944, when news came that the bridges of Florence, with the exception of the Ponte Vecchio, had been blown up by the Germans. He'd tried to imagine the Arno without the Ponte alle Grazie, the Ponte Santa Trinita, the Ponte alla Carraia . . . but he couldn't. He'd seen the devastation a few months after the end of the war, when he went home. The Allied bombs had also unleashed their fury, razing whole neighbourhoods to the ground . . . He'd heard hundreds of stories from his parents and other people who'd stayed in the city during the fighting . . . The Carità gang . . . The torture in Villa Triste . . . The fear of informers . . . The German consul in Florence, who, thanks to a sort of conversion, had devoted himself to saving works of art and people of every kind, including Jews and partisan fighters, with the support of the Swiss consul . . . And the blasts of the German artillery in retreat, the Allied advance, the snipers firing from the rooftops . . . The partisans who'd come down from the hills, the endless bloody clashes in the streets . . .

His thoughts were interrupted by a spot of reddish fur up ahead on the path. It was clearly an animal, but it wasn't moving. As he drew near he realised it was a dead fox. Stopping in front of the carcass, he grazed it with his shoe, expecting the fox to leap to its feet and run off. It looked alive. It's eyes were still half open, and its sharp little teeth jutted out from its mouth. He prodded it a little harder with his foot and felt that it hadn't stiffened yet. Bending down, he put a hand on its soft fur. It was still warm. It must have died only a few mintues before. He turned it on its other side, but saw no trace of blood. It could not have been killed by gunshot. Apparently its time had come. He patted it on the head by way of goodbye and resumed his walk. Poor animal . . . Who knew whether it had had time to think its last thoughts before collapsing. He would never want to die suddenly, not even in his sleep. The very thought of it depressed him. He prayed heaven to allow him to savour the moment of his death in a state of full awareness, as had happened with some of his war comrades whose eyes he'd shut on the field of battle . . . Some, however, hadn't had time to realise what was happening as they were swallowed by darkness in an instant . . . What happened to their minds, their thoughts, the images that had filled their eyes until a second earlier?

After a long hike through the woods and some chaotic forays into his memory he returned to the car, pleasantly tired. As soon as he got home he made a nice fire and sat down in the armchair to read. He finished the Lermontov novel and sat staring at the flames with the book on his knees, thinking of the adventures of Officer Pechorin. He would never forget him. As happened every time he read a good novel, he felt as if he'd actually met the characters in the story. He knew that he would think back on them from time to time, confusing them with real people he'd met turing his lifetime. Don Abbondio, Raskolnikov, Emma Bovary, Hans Castorp, Gregor Samsa . . . Even Odysseus was part of his memory, just like his battle companions who'd been killed and the women they'd lost their heads over.

He felt like staying in Russia. Going upstairs, he put Lermontov back on the bedroom bookcase and took out a volume of Dostoyevsky. Back in the kitchen, he put a log on the fire and sat down again in the armchair. He opened *Notes from the Underground* and started reading, having no idea what kind of adventure awaited him . . . *I am a mean man, I am a sick man . . .*

The protagonist's thoughts fascinated him. Here was a man who penetrated the labyrinths of the mind with bitter satisfaction, falling into painful realisations, sinking into a disdain of mankind and especially himself, unable to live with any dignity because of his maniacal analysis of reality and his own conscience. At times Bordelli thought he recognised himself in the lucid confusion of the underground man's thoughts, and this helped him at last to unravel arguments and understand emotions that had been forever tangled in his mind. Every so often he would stop reading, and with his eyes on the fire he would sink into his own mental labyrinths, plumbing depths that until then he'd only imagined, digging like a worm into the earth . . .

At one point he heard a noise that sounded as if it came from the chimney flue, and after an avalanche of soot fell on to the fire, two small female feet, elegantly shod, appeared. A second later a young woman emerged whole from the chimney, standing on the fire. She was wearing a very white dress soiled with soot, and stared at him with two stern eyes. Bordelli looked back at her in wonder, trying to understand the reason for her visit. The woman slowly raised her arm and, casting him a menacing glance, she pointed an accusing finger at him, like the angel that banished Adam and Eve . . .

'You are mine,' she whispered.

'Who are you?' Bordelli asked, spellbound by her beauty.

Moments later she was enveloped by a great flame and disappeared . . . Bordelli opened his eyes, disappointed that it had only been a dream. He could still see the finger pointed at him . . . Who was that woman? Fate personified? Only now did he realise that she had Eleonora's face, and his desire to see her again became even keener.

It was almost eight o'clock. He picked up the book, which had fallen from his hands. He stuck the bookmark in it and got up to fetch the telephone directory. He looked up Eleonora's number, and with a shudder he read the six digits that stood between him and being able to talk to her. All he had to do was pick up the phone, turn the dial with one finger and . . . What would happen? What would Eleonora say to him? Would she be pleased or would she hang up?

The ring of the telephone startled him, and for a moment he imagined . . . What a fool. He had to stop imagining that every time the phone rang, it was . . . With the woman in white still in his eyes, he went to pick up.

'Hello?'

'Were you asleep?' asked Diotivede, who never missed anything.

'I was dozing by the fire.'

'That's how you discover you're old.'

'Has it ever happened to you?'

'Many years ago, when I was old like you.'

'You sound cheerful. Did you recently cut up a particularly nice corpse?'

'All corpses are nice because they can't talk rubbish,' said Diotivede.

'How's Marianna?'

Marianna was the forensic pathologist's pretty girlfriend, some thirty years younger than him.

'She's all right, thanks. Have any important engagements for dinner?'

'After frying an egg I thought I'd try to domesticate a spider.'

'Feel like coming down from the wilderness and into the civilised world?'

'I bet it's not your idea.'

'You're wrong. I had to quarrel with Marianna to invite you. She can't stand primitive men,' said the doctor. Bordelli could hear Marianna's voice in the background protesting, 'It's not true! . . . It's not true!'

'All women are liars,' said Diotivede.

'You wouldn't happen to be doing the cooking?' Bordelli asked.

'That's a loaded question . . .'

'I wouldn't want to find any human meat on my plate.'

'Now that you got that terribly witty quip out of your system, could you please tell me whether you're coming to dinner or staying at home to talk to your spider?'

'Don't worry, I'm coming . . . But only because Marianna's there.'

'What, no chicken?' asked Diotivede as Bordelli stepped into the house.

'I invited them all, but they declined.'

'If you can't even make it with chickens . . .'

'I do better with geese,' said Bordelli, taking his coat off. Marianna appeared, smiling and radiant, in the entrance hall, wearing a kitchen apron.

'Always talking about women, you two,' she said, shaking her guest's hand.

'He started it,' said Bordelli, like a bratty child.

'I bet you were always the first in school to snitch,' said the doctor, glaring at him from behind his spectacles.

They sat down in the living room, where a bottle of red wine and some small cubes of Parmesan cheese speared with tooth-picks awaited them. Marianna was a truly exceptional woman. She maintained her elegance no matter what she did, like a queen. She was full figured, like a Greek statue. Her dark eyes stood out like polished stones in her fine-featured, actress's face, the whole framed by long chestnut hair. Bordelli was utterly charmed. If he didn't still have Eleonora on his mind, he would be in danger of falling in love. Diotivede eyed him with an amused air, guessing what he was thinking. Suddenly he got up from the sofa and went to the door.

'I'm going to say goodnight to my granddaughter. I'm leaving you alone with my lady friend, so behave,' he said, bounding out of the room with a youthful step. The corpse-cutter wore his seventy-four years well. Bordelli drew near to Juno and lowered his voice.

'Let's run away, Marianna . . .' he said. She looked at him
for a moment in shock, then burst out laughing. Bordelli
pretended to be offended.

'I'm serious. I have a beautiful house in the country, and
soon I'll have a vegetable garden . . .' he whispered.

Marianna laughed again and got up and went to the kitchen,
followed by Bordelli's admiring gaze. A few minutes later the
doctor appeared in the doorway and looked at him
suspiciously.

'I can only guess what you said to her, to make her laugh
like that.'

'It was nothing of any concern to you . . .' said Bordelli. At
that moment Marianna came in and set a steaming soup tureen
down on the table.

'He said we should run away together,' she said, still smiling.

'Don't trust him, he says that to all the girls,' said the doctor.

'What's wrong with that?' she said, inviting the two rivals to
sit at the table in the small dining area.

She served the first course and they started eating. Aside
from being beautiful and intelligent, Marianna was a good cook.
A miracle of a woman. Bordelli didn't miss a chance to goad
Diotivede, expressing his unending astonishment at such an
unbalanced human pairing. The doctor laughed under his breath,
savouring the subtle envy that lay beneath Bordelli's needlings.

After supper they went back into the sitting room. Diotivede
served an excellent *vin santo* and sat down beside his woman.
His snow-white, close-cropped hair seemed to give off a light
of its own. Nobody spoke, and Bordelli sensed a slight tension
in the air. He noticed that Marianna and the doctor kept
exchanging meaningful glances, smiles playing on their lips.

'What's happening?' he asked, peering at them.

Diotivede shrugged. 'Nothing . . . We just wanted to tell you
we're getting married.'

'You're kidding, of course,' Bordelli muttered incredulously,
eyes flitting from one to the other.

'Not at all,' the doctor said serenely.

'Don't do it, Marianna . . . This man spends his days rifling through human entrails . . .' Bordelli said as though serious. She looked at her man with the sweetest of smiles.

'I know Peppino's a brute,' she said, stroking the back of his neck.

'Don't do it, Marianna. You can have any man you want, young, handsome . . . Just one glance and they'll fall at your feet. What are you going to do with an old corpse-cutter?' Bordelli continued, still as though serious. The doctor was leaning back on the sofa with legs crossed and an insolent look on his face.

'As I said, my dear, Franco is a true friend,' he said, serene as an emperor after a victorious battle. But Bordelli wasn't done yet.

'Just think it over, Marianna. It's a sacrilege . . . An aesthetic one, and even an ethical one.'

'Thank you,' she said without irony.

'Have I persuaded you?'

'No, actually, on the contrary, you've allowed me to give a higher meaning to my feelings.'

'Okay, I give up . . .' said Bordelli, throwing his hands up. Diotivede was grinning like an obnoxious child.

'Now that you've finished your comedy routine, can I ask you to be a witness at our wedding?'

'After what I just said?'

'For that very reason.'

'So this is revenge . . .'

'Call it what you will,' said the doctor, looking at him with compassion.

Marianna gave Bordelli a luminous smile. 'There's something else we have to tell you . . . My family knows nothing. We're getting married in secret.'

'Really . . .'

'I'd rather avoid pointless disputes.'

'So I'm not the only one who's against it . . .'

'I may announce it after it's done, or maybe not . . .' said Marianna.

'My relatives, on the other hand, will find out straight away,' said the doctor.

'I repeat. This marriage must not take place . . .'[10] Bordelli insisted. But it was no use.

'Do you have a reliable woman friend who could be my witness?' the future bride asked.

'I could ask Rosa.'

'What a nice name . . .'

'She's a very dear friend, but I should tell you straight away . . . Until the Merlin law was passed,[11] she worked in brothels.'

'That's not a problem for me at all,' said Marianna, looking over at Peppino.

'I'm actually glad,' said Diotivede.

'Good. When is the wedding?'

'July the fourteenth. The storming of the Bastille.'

'Yes, I know. I went to school, too.'

'One never can tell,' said the doctor.

'Does this date have some other hidden meaning?' asked Bordelli.

'As many as you like,' said Marianna, smiling.

'And where will this insane ceremony take place?'

'At the little church in Luiano,' said the doctor.

'And where's that?'

'Near your place.'

'Oh, really?'

'Along a sort of mule path that runs from il Ferrone to Mercatale.'

'And why did you happen to choose that church?'

'Because afterwards we'll come to your house to celebrate,' said Diotivede, as if it were obvious.

'Ah, I see . . .'

'It'll be your wedding present.'

'Sorry, I'd forgotten . . .'

'We don't need much – there won't be very many of us, maybe twenty people at the most. Three or four salamis, a leg of ham, two or three rounds of pecorino, a nice bit of fruit, and bread and wine in abundance. And if you feel like buying a few bottles of champagne . . .'

'Good thing it's not for another four months; that'll give me all the time I need to prepare myself spiritually to witness the biggest mistake ever made by a woman.'

'Don't start up again, you're likely to make a fool of yourself . . .' said Diotivede, as his future wife caressed his stubbly cheek. There was nothing to be done about it: they were like two adolescents in love for the first time. At around midnight Bordelli decided to leave the two lovebirds to themselves. He took elegant leave of Marianna, bowing and kissing her hand. Who knew what Marianna would have thought had she known that a week earlier her future husband's friend had shot a man in the mouth . . . After exchanging a nod of goodbye with Diotivede, he headed out on to the garden path.

'Don't do it, Marianna . . . There's still time . . .' he said in a loud voice. He heard them laugh, and then the door closed.

He got into his Beetle and drove down by way of the Erta Canina, slipping into the light fog enveloping the trees' black trunks.

While driving up the Imprunetana he thought he would never marry, not even were he to find the woman of his dreams. He couldn't say exactly why; he just knew he would never do it . . . even though he wasn't always consistent, and he didn't really mind the idea, deep down. It was the only way to be surprised in life. And at any rate, the important thing was to be consistent in the present, not over time . . . As a woman had once said to him, as she was leaving him.

As he drove through the central square of Impruneta, he cast a glance, as usual, at the basilica, where in all likelihood his funeral would be held one day . . . Bloody hell, why did he always have to think such cheerful things? Once he was outside the town he decided that if he saw the hare again that night, it would mean that fate was on his side . . . A silly game, but maybe not entirely . . .

Minutes later he turned on to the dirt road that led to his house, hoping to see destiny itself. He advanced slowly, at a walking pace, gaze fixed on the band of light from his high beam . . . And all at once he saw it and, shuddering, he stopped the car. It was still the same hare, he was sure of it. It had frozen in the middle of the road with its ears straight up and eyes wide open, blinded by the brights. It sat there without moving, for longer than usual, as if it knew . . . Then without warning it scampered away . . .

At one o'clock he was sitting alone in a trattoria in Via de' Macci, at the table farthest from the door. The other tables were occupied by carters and craftsmen from the neighbourhood. They were talking loudly of football, women, and every so often the flood that had reduced so many families to poverty . . .

Who knew whether Gianfranco Cecconi Marini knew where Via de' Macci was. Bordelli ordered half a litre of red, telling the waiter that another person would be coming. He'd spent the morning hiking along the paths near his home, avoiding the 'groom', and now had a painfully empty stomach.

Waiting for Signorino Gianfranco, he thought of Ortensia. If she didn't call by the following day, he would call her back himself. He was also curious to see what she looked like, and tried to picture her in his mind. She had a velvety voice over the phone, which led him to imagine a beautiful woman . . .

Gianfranco arrived twenty minutes late with both of his surnames and endless apologies. Tall, slender, well dressed, with watery green eyes that made one think of a lamb. He must have been about forty years old, but had a child's face. He pretended not to notice that everyone was looking at him. With graceful movements, he took off his Loden overcoat, folded it over the back of a chair, and laid his soft, white scarf on top of it. As he sat down he looked at the table settings with a lightly disgusted air, and at that moment the owner of the trattoria came up to the table.

'So, what can I bring you? Some nice steak, blood rare?'

'Good heavens, no . . .' said Gianfranco in a falsetto. The host looked at him askance, exchanging a glance with Bordelli.

'You got something against steak, golden boy?'

'I can't stand blood.'

'Then I'll make it well done . . .'

'No, please . . . No steak, no . . .'

'Sausage and spare ribs?'

'*Mamma mia!*' Gianfranco shrieked politely in distaste. He really seemed to be one of those types that Bordelli felt like slapping around. At last he found something that didn't turn his stomach: spaghetti with olive oil and a salad. As soon as the innkeeper left, Bordelli asked Gianfranco Cecconi Marini to tell him about his friend Orlando.

'Why do you want to know about Orlando? Has something happened?' Gianfranco asked, suspicious.

'I'd rather tell you later, if you don't mind.'

'All right, I can wait . . .'

'Were you close friends?'

'Very close,' said Gianfranco. They'd first met at the Liceo Dante, immediately bonded and remained friends for life. They saw each other almost every day. With the addition of Neri Bargioni Tozzi they became an inseparable threesome. When Orlando took his own life, he and Neri fell into despair . . .

'Did he ever confide to you that he was in danger, or perhaps afraid of someone?' Bordelli asked.

'No . . .'

'His job at the law firm was going all right?'

'He seemed rather happy with it.'

'Did he ever talk to you about the two law partners?'

'Now and then . . . He considered them a couple of pre-historic beasts,' said Gianfranco. He sniffed his wine without drinking it and, wrinkling his nose, put the glass as far away from him as possible.

Bordelli was observing him with curiosity. Against all expectation, he was starting to like the man.

'Do you remember the last time you saw him?'

'It was two days before the tragedy, a Thursday, I think . . .

89

The three of us got into my Jaguar and drove to Settignano, to a party of some friends.'

'Orlando seemed untroubled?'

'He was the way he always was.'

'Meaning?'

'Not very talkative, a bit gloomy . . .' said Gianfranco, searching for other words but not finding them. At the table beside them, a guy with a boxer's nose made a vulgar comment about women and burst out laughing, teeth covered with tomato sauce. Gianfranco looked at him with a combination of wonder and fear, as if he'd seen a great ape getting upset in a flimsy cage. Bordelli refilled his own glass.

'I know Orlando had a girlfriend. She didn't come with you to the party?'

'Ortensia never came to parties; her parents were against it. At any rate, they were no longer together at the time. She'd left him a few weeks before that . . .'

'How did Orlando take it?'

'Very badly, but he was able to joke about it. He wasn't the type to cry his eyes out over such things,' said Gianfranco, proud of his friend.

'Did you know Ortensia well?'

'I saw her only a few times . . .'

'Do you know why she left him?'

'Orlando didn't talk about it . . . I can only say that she seemed to be very jealous.'

The host arrived with the dishes, and before walking away he cast a glance of commiseration at the plate with spaghetti dressed in oil. Bordelli started devouring his filet like a wolf, accompanying it with a lot of bread. Gianfranco took a while to get acquainted with his spaghetti, but in the end he let himself go. He would raise the fork to his mouth ever so delicately, barely leaning forward. Bordelli decided to leave him in peace, but only for a few minutes.

'Getting back to that Thursday evening . . . Did Orlando seem normal? Did he say anything to you? Mention anything strange, express any bitterness . . . Anything at all . . . ?'

'I don't think so.'

'Did he seem to have fun? Did you see him dancing?'

'Orlando never danced. At parties he would just flit among the guests with a glass in his hand, watching the girls . . .'

'So nothing out of the ordinary . . .'

'All I remember from that evening was that he'd had a bit too much to drink and fell asleep in the car on the drive back to town.'

'Was that unusual?'

'It didn't happen very often.'

'Have you ever yourself wondered why he killed himself?'

'I still think about it sometimes, and I still can't understand it,' said Gianfranco, fork in midair.

'Couldn't he have done it over Ortensia?'

'I don't think so, it doesn't seem possible, but who knows? . . . Can you tell me now what's happened?'

'What if I were to tell you that Orlando was murdered?'

'Murdered?' Gianfranco said softly, upset.

'I'm just saying it hypothetically. Let's presume for a moment that it was murder . . . Who could have wanted him dead?'

'Nobody! He was a fabulous chap!' Gianfranco asserted, increasingly astonished.

'So he never got into trouble of any sort?'

'Not that I know of. But that wouldn't be like him.'

'Do you still see your friend Neri?'

'He's been living in Paris for years. We talk sometimes by telephone, and we meet two or three times a year.'

'Could you give me his number?'

'He'll tell you the same things I've just done.'

'I'd still like to have a little chat,' said Bordelli. He searched in his jacket pocket for a pen, then wrote down Neri's number on a matchbox.

They carried on talking about Orlando, but nothing of any importance came up. Gianfranco seemed glad to recount anecdotes of his deceased friend, and he even smiled sometimes.

Bordelli asked for the bill well after the other customers had cleared out. He insisted on paying, ignoring Gianfranco's polite protests. They went out to the street and shook hands.

'I really enjoyed talking about Orlando,' Gianfranco said, his eyes moist. He then headed in the direction of Santa Croce, stumbling on the uneven cobblestones of Via de' Macci. Bordelli stood there and watched him, thinking he would probably never see him again.

He didn't feel like going straight home, so he started walking towards the centre of town, forcing himself not to smoke. It was quite cold. The thick black band running along the building façades at various heights was now a familiar sight to Florentines, and nobody seemed to pay it any mind. But a variety of shops and craftmen's workshops still had no functioning metal shutters, as these had been destroyed by the waters, and it was anybody's guess whether they would ever reopen. Only the wealthiest shopowners had managed to come back to life . . .

Along the pavement he saw mostly young people, and so there was no lack of pretty girls, who seemed to have been created for the express purpose of tormenting him. On the streets, luxury cars and utility vehicles mingled with motorbikes and bicycles. The traffic seemed to be increasing yearly.

Eyeing the display windows of the few renovated shops he couldn't help but remember the first time he'd seen Eleonora, on a rainy morning a few days before the flood . . . Beautiful as the moon, raven-black hair, in her stockinged feet, as she was rearranging the clothing in a shop window in Via Pacinotti . . .

He slipped into a bar in Borgo San Lorenzo for a coffee. The market was winding up and carters were pulling their wares along the streets, making a great deal of noise. A woman with excessively blond hair and a fake mole over her lip came in. Bordelli cast her a quick glance, trying to guess how old she might be, and she immediately came over.

'Feeling lonely, handsome?' she asked with a fiendish smile.

'I like being alone . . .' Bordelli replied. The barman smiled.

'The usual glass of white, Fedora?'

93

'Thank you, Nanni – you, at least, are nice,' she said, sneering. Bordelli ignored the woman's insulted glare, paid for his coffee, and left.

He'd left the Beetle in Piazza Sant'Ambrogio, but when he reached the end of Via Sant' Egidio, he turned on to Via Verdi. He'd decided to pass by San Niccolò and pay a call on Don Baldesi, a parish priest. He'd met him at the time of the flood, when shovelling mud in hopes of getting closer to Eleonora, who lived in the neighbourhood. Don Baldesi had worked like a dog without ever losing his good humour, even occasionally telling jokes about priests or the Pope.

The statue of Dante in the middle of Piazza Santa Croce looked as if it had just emerged from the muck. Bordelli smiled, thinking the big-nosed old poet could hardly have expected otherwise from a city like Florence. He continued on to Via de' Benci, and while crossing the bridge looked out over the muddy Arno, which flowed swift and serene.

He arrived in San Niccolò, where on 4 November the water had reached a height of twenty feet. On the church's smooth façade, the thick black band that had marked half the city stood out even more conspicuously than elsewhere. The main portal was wide open, and Bordelli stuck his head inside. The church was empty. The benches had all been burnt in the days immediately following the flood and hadn't been replaced yet. The stench of mud and heating oil was still perceptible in the air.

He went out on to the parvis and rang the bell outside a small door in the corner. After an endless wait the sacristan, a very thin man with a trembling head, opened the door. Bordelli remembered seeing him wandering about the quarter in the days after the flood.

'Can I help you?'

'Is Don Baldesi at home? . . . In church, I mean?'

'Who shall I say wants him?'

'Inspector Bordelli . . .'

He used the title only so that the priest would remember

him, but in truth he himself had never really got used to being no longer in service.

'I'll let him know,' said the sacristan, who closed the door behind him.

Bordelli waited outside the church. After several minutes had passed, he was thinking of leaving when the door opened.

'Please come in,' said the trembling man. Bordelli followed him down a damp corridor that smelled of mildew and then up a staircase. They came to a large room with bookshelves full of ancient tomes and an immense desk covered with papers.

'Don Baldesi is on his way,' the sacristan muttered, and vanished behind a door, coughing. Bordelli started strolling about the room, thinking of the cigarette he would smoke when driving home. From the window one could see a courtyard full of children playing . . .

Hearing the door open, he turned round.

'Inspector! What a pleasure! . . .'

Don Baldesi approached and shook his hand, wearing his eternally ironic smile, the sort of smile one didn't often see on a priest's face.

'I was in the area and decided I'd . . .'

'You were right to do so. How are you? Everything all right?'

'I wouldn't go that far . . . And how are you?'

'Don't ask – in fact, it's better if we change the subject . . . Would you like a cup of tea?' Without waiting for an answer, Don Baldesi poked his head outside the door.

'Artimio, could you please make us some tea?' he called loudly, and a sort of grunt could be heard in the distance.

They both sat down. While awaiting the tea, they started reminiscing about the unending days they'd spent shovelling, the mountains of detritus piled up outside the shops . . . And the panini with prosciutto, which had never tasted so good as they did during those days.

The sacristan entered holding in both hands a tray that tinkled dangerously. He set it down on the table and went out without saying a word. Bordelli was distractedly studying the steam rising from the pot . . .

'Have you by any chance seen that dark-haired girl who used to live just across the square? I think her name was Elena or something similar . . .' he said, as though speaking of something of little importance.

'Eleonora . . .' said Don Baldesi, smiling, though his eyes had flashed dramatically for a split second.

'Ah, yes . . . Eleonora.'

'She came to see me just before Christmas.'

'Oh, really? And how was she?' Bordelli asked, trying to remain calm. Hearing someone talk about Eleonora upset him more than he would have imagined.

'She's a lovely girl,' the priest said vaguely.

'I've never doubted it . . .'

'Perhaps a bit too young for you.'

'What's that? No . . . Look, I . . .'

'But it's also true that love has no limits,' said Don Baldesi, pouring tea into the cups.

Bordelli looked the priest in the eye. 'You don't miss anything, do you?'

'Not the obvious things.'

'I haven't seen her since mid-November,' Bordelli muttered sadly.

Don Baldesi said nothing, only gazing at him with an air of understanding. Bordelli couldn't make up his mind. He didn't know whether he should keep asking after her or drop the subject. In the end he overcame his embarrassment.

'I just want to know if she's all right . . . She had a terrible experience, and—'

'She has a strong character,' Don Baldesi interrupted him, giving him to understand that he was aware of what the girl had been through. He had no way of knowing, of course, that the rapists had been sent by a minister of God, a monsignor of the Episcopal Curia, and Bordelli thought that, sooner or later, he might even tell him . . . But not before carrying out destiny's plan to the end. While sipping his tea, he imagined himself confessing to Don Baldesi that he'd murdered the butcher. What would happen? Would he grant him absolution, knowing he hadn't repented? Would he advise him to turn himself in?

'Well, if you happen to see her again, tell her that I . . . No, I'm sorry . . . Don't tell her anything . . .'

'If the seed is right, the plant will grow,' said Don Baldesi, tender as a child. Bordelli almost felt like kissing his forehead. He drank his tea and set down the cup.

'I don't want to take up any more of your time . . .' he said, standing up. The priest saw him to the door, and before Bordelli stepped out, he took him by the arm.

'Have you heard the one about the prostitute who goes to see the Pope?'

He opened his eyes wide after a long, restless half-sleep, realising that outside his window a great flock of small birds were twittering madly. He got slowly out of bed, rubbing his eyes. He went to open the window and look out. It was a beautiful sunny day. Hundreds of small birds were swirling round the tops of the cypresses, darting in and out of their dense boughs. Spring was advancing in fits and starts.

'That's enough!' he shouted, waving his arms. Silence fell, as the swarm of birds fluttered round the trees . . . Seconds later, however, the crazy creatures went right back where they'd been and started shrieking louder than before. Bordelli shook his head and smiled. He left the windows open and went down into the kitchen to make coffee, thinking that the silence of the countryside was only a figment of one's imagination.

His head was still full of the tortuous delirium of *Notes from the Underground*. Reading that book forced him to look inside himself . . . It was strange . . . In the final analysis he didn't think he was much like the protagonist, and yet the mean, sick man was talking about him just the same, compelling him to gain a deeper knowledge of himself . . .

He drank his coffee standing up and then went to get dressed. It was time to get serious about the garden. Just outside the door he found, as usual, a loaf of bread and *La Nazione*. He laid the small bag on the table and drove off in the Beetle.

At about eight o'clock the previous evening he'd called Paris and spoken to Neri Bargioni Tozzi, but as Gianfranco had predicted, nothing new had come of it. The only one left was Ortensia, and who knew whether she . . .

When he got to town he pulled up to the pavement and asked a small, wrinkled woman where the farmer's cooperative was.

'It's up there, opposite Manni's bakery.'

'I'm sorry, but where's Manni's bakery?'

'Do you know Troia?'

'Who?'

'The smith, no?'

'I'm sorry, I haven't been living here long,' Bordelli said patiently.

'Well, you go up that way and turn right, on to the street that leads to the Desco. You'll find it a little past that.'

'Thank you . . .'

Bordelli sighed and headed off, combing the little streets around the piazza until he found a glass door with the words FARMERS' COOPERATIVE on it. Parked along the pavement were a pair of Fiat Giardinetta station wagons and a 500, and there was even a tired-looking horse hitched to a cart.

He left the car a short way up the street and went into the cooperative, which was a vast room full of tools, with great balls of manure and some chickens in cages. Only ten kilometres away lay Florence with its fancy cafés and elegant women, its students full of lust for life, its craftsmen bent over their work-tables, the poor struggling to get by, the posh automobiles, the motorbikes, bicycles, thieves, whores . . . A faraway world, frenetic and noisy . . .

The guy running the cooperative was fat and placid and didn't talk much. After attending to a pair of peasants he turned and looked at the strange customer who seemed to have entered the store by accident.

'Can I help you with something?'

'I'm trying to make a vegetable garden,' said Bordelli, making the fat man smile.

He ended up buying four balls of soil, two rolls of screen fencing, some metal wire, a few wooden stakes, a watering can, a garden spade, and a small bag of hot pepper seeds. All he needed now were tomato seeds and some young artichoke shoots. He filled the boot and put the fencing on the back seat. The Beetle was packed as full as a truck.

At the brickworks in Via della Fonte he bought three large terracotta vases as heavy as boulders and managed to arrange them on the passenger seat. On his way home he pulled up outside a farmhouse. He got out of the car and called in a loud voice. Moments later an old woman with piercing eyes and wearing an oversized black overcoat appeared. The woman cupped her hands round her mouth, yelled something and walked away, muttering that she had to 'mind the little rabbits'. A few mintues later a hunched old man with a wrinkled face and a patched cap appeared.

'Did you want oil or wine?'

'Actually I was looking for *pollina* . . . Could you sell me a little?' asked Bordelli.

'Sell? You don't sell shit, man . . . Got a bucket with you?'

'No, unfortunately . . .' That was what he'd forgotten to buy.

'I'm afraid I can't help you . . . And you can't really carry it in your pocket . . .' said the old man. But then he went and fetched a rusty old pail and filled it a third of the way with that nectar of the gods.

'Here you go . . .'

'Would you also happen to have some tomato seeds? I've just moved to the area and don't know where to find them.'

'I can give you some, but if you've never grown 'em before it won't be easy.'

'I have a friend who's giving me a hand.'

'I can't give you very many . . .'

The man gave him a handful free of charge, wrapped in a sheet of yellow paper. Bordelli thanked him for his kindness, and asked him whether he knew anyone who might be interested in tending a hundred or so olive trees, adding that they'd been neglected for a number of years.

'I'll be happy with a little oil for myself, and whoever tends the grove can have the rest,' he said by way of conclusion.

The peasant thought about this for a moment. 'You know

who you could ask? Tonio . . . He's got some olives he tends for the owner.'

'Where does he live?'

'In that house down there, where you see those cypresses . . . But I have to go now . . . Take care of yourself . . .' said the old man, who then headed towards his field, arms dangling. Bordelli got back in his car and opened the windows because of the stink rising up from the pail of *pollina*.

He went and looked for Tonio at once, and found him chopping wood bare chested. He was a strapping man of about sixty with a long beard and fingers as big as carrots. Tonio brought him into the kitchen, a big, dark, shabby room where modernity had made its entry in the most unfortunate of ways: the traditional *madia* had been replaced by a blue Formica cupboard. The furniture sellers were always swindling the peasants, selling them mass-produced horrors and offering to throw away their old furniture, which they would then restore and sell dearly to Milanese *commendatori*. Peasants had always been known for being suspicious, but they'd fallen into that net like overripe pears . . .

'How many trees've you got?'

'A hundred or so.'

'Sounds good to me.'

A firm handshake and the deal was done. Tonio would look after the olive grove, the out-of-pocket expenses would all be charged to Bordelli, and in exchange he would get forty per cent of the oil. The simplest contract in history.

'We'll have to start the trees all over. I'll come by in late April to cut them back. I can't make it any sooner.'

'From now on, it's you who decides.'

'You won't see any oil for two or three years, and it won't be much.'

"That's all right, I can wait.'

'I know that farm. When there's no rain the ground is like stone, and when it rains it turns into quicksand.'

'I've noticed . . . Listen, you wouldn't also happen to have any artichoke shoots? I'm willing to pay.'

'No, sorry. I've already used them all myself.'

'Thanks just the same.'

They said goodbye, and Bordelli continued with his errands, having resolved the question of the olive trees. He went to a few other farms begging for alms. When he got home he had a wooden crate with some twenty artichoke shoots in it and a few clumps of sage.

He got down to work in the sunlight, trying to recall Ennio's instructions. He wanted to do things right. The first thing he did was fence off the garden, sweating more than he did when hoeing. He even managed to make a sort of little gate, by nailing some wooden boards together and using metal wire to close it. The results were acceptable. Five years of war hadn't been entirely useless. He put a bit of soil in the artichoke holes and then inserted the shoots. He scattered the tomato seeds in the patch of earth that he and Ennio had prepared, and then covered them up, spreading some soil over them with his hand. Following his own instincts, he planted the clumps of sage here and there, imagining the great bushes they would grow into. With the remaining soil he filled the vases and planted the chilli peppers. All that was left to do was to water all these small holes. He filled the watering can and let the water rain down into the holes, around the plants and in the vases. When he thought he'd finished his work for the day, he remembered there was still one thing left to do. He filled the pail of chicken droppings with water, stirred it with a stick, and set this down in a corner of the garden. Now he really was done, at least for that day. He was tired and sweaty, but content. He imagined the little roots beginning to move underground, the seeds awakening after a long sleep . . . Nature was already on the move, a perfect chemical mechanism on which every religion had tried to impose a meaning.

He was shocked to find that it was past two o'clock. Hungry as a wolf, he went into the house and washed his hands quite thoroughly, taking a long time to get the dirt out from under his fingernails. He put some water to boil for pasta and went upstairs to take a nice hot shower.

When he put the penne in the boiling pot, the afternoon news reports were already long over, so he didn't bother to turn on the telly. As he was setting the table, the telephone rang . . . To his great surprise, it was Ortensia.

At four o'clock in the afternoon on Thursday, he parked at the end of Via Martelli outside the Bar Motta, which the Florentines continued to call Il Bottegone. Stepping out of his Beetle, he cast a glance up at the Palazzo della Curia, imagining Monsignor Sercambi seated at his desk, with his piously bald head and his little gold-framed glasses resting on his nose. Fate would catch up to him, too, sooner or later . . .

He pushed open the door to the bar, where some soft music enveloped customers conversing amid little clouds of smoke. He looked around for a woman of about thirty-five and saw one sitting in the opposite corner of the room, beside an older woman. They were both staring at him anxiously, and he realised that the younger one was Ortensia. He approached their table and gave a slight bow. Ortensia shyly returned the greeting and hastened to introduce her mother, a common-looking woman dressed up as if she were rich, who held out a hand covered with brightly gleaming rings. Bordelli mimed the gesture of kissing her hand and sat down opposite the two women. Ortensia was blonde and pretty, slightly faded, with two sparkling, frightened fawn-eyes. A young boy dressed like a waiter appeared.

'Would you like to order something, sir?'

'A coffee, thank you.'

'Straight away, sir,' the well-trained boy said, and vanished at once.

Bordelli thanked Ortensia for agreeing to meet with him, and to save time he immediately asked her about Orlando. The woman blushed and turned towards her mother.

'Mamma, could you let us have a little time alone?' she whispered.

'What do you mean?'

'Please, Mamma... Just half an hour . . .' Ortensia begged her, touching her arm.

The woman screwed up her face, but in the end she obeyed and grabbed her handbag. Bordelli stood up with her and smiled politely, waiting for her to leave before sitting back down. Ortensia was about to speak, but the waiter arrived with the coffee and she immediately closed her mouth, seeming impatient.

'Did you want to tell me something?' Bordelli asked as soon as they were alone again.

'Forgive me for bringing my mother along . . . I didn't want . . . I have a very jealous husband . . . He knows nothing about my relationship with Orlando . . . And so I thought it best . . .'

'No need to worry,' Bordelli interrupted her. The woman gave him an embarrassed smile, then leaned slightly forward, looking him straight in the eye.

'I wouldn't be surprised if Orlando was murdered,' she whispered, immediately covering her mouth with her hand as though she'd said something outrageous. Bordelli felt a tingling at the back of his neck. In a fraction of a second a concatenation of thoughts flashed through his mind . . . If Ortensia was aware of some concrete motive on which to base a case for murder, then with a bit of luck he might be able to find . . . Maybe not proof that would stand up in court, but at least . . . In short, he would be compelled to try to discover the mechanism of a crime, and once he'd done this, he would have, on a silver platter, the solution for Beccaroni's 'suicide' . . .

'Please tell me everything you know.'

'Well . . . I . . . When Orlando passed away . . . we were no longer together . . .'

'I already knew that.'

'Ah . . .' said Ortensia, surprised and slightly alarmed.

'It was his friends from back then who told me, Neri and Gianfranco.'

'Quite a pair, those two . . .' said Ortensia, without malice.

'What do you mean?'

'All they ever thought about was having fun.'

'But you were saying, about Orlando . . .' Bordelli pressed her gently.

'But you . . . Why do you want to know these things?'

'Because I have the same suspicions as you about Orlando's death.'

'Well, I may be wrong, but . . .' She stopped.

'Please go on,' said Bordelli, putting his elbows on the table to get closer to her.

'As I was saying . . . We were no longer together . . .'

'Without being too indiscreet, may I ask why you left him?' Bordelli cut in.

'For a number of reasons . . .'

'Can you tell me which? Of course, you're under no obligation . . .'

'We saw things differently . . . At times it seemed like he was hiding something . . . And I wasn't sure I loved him any more . . .' said Ortensia, avoiding his gaze.

Bordelli smiled. Usually anyone who had *a number of reasons* for something was trying to hide just one, the real one. He sat there in silence, looking at her, and she blushed. She rummaged through her handbag until she found her gold cigarette case. Bordelli offered her a light, then took advantage to light up one of his own. Ortensia exhaled the smoke and shrugged faintly.

'I was convinced he had another woman,' she said, a bit of the old jealousy flashing in her eyes.

'Do you still think so?'

'I don't know . . . He always swore that it wasn't true.'

'Did you see each other at all after you broke up?'

'We still talked over the phone, and we often quarrelled . . . That is, I would quarrel with him . . . He would say he loved

me, and we should get back together . . . He said he would
marry me . . .'

'But you didn't believe him.'

'I admit I didn't . . . I was confused . . . There were certain
things I didn't understand . . .'

'Like what?'

'On the evening of the tragedy Orlando had phoned me a
little after nine . . . He was upset and kept asking if he could
see me . . . But not to talk about us . . . He had to tell me
something important that he couldn't put off . . . He didn't
want to say anything over the phone, but he swore that it was
something very, very serious. He asked me to forget my pride
for a moment . . . It wasn't an excuse to steal a kiss from me,
he said; he wouldn't even touch me, he promised . . .'

'And did you accept?'

'He seemed very troubled, and so in the end I let him talk
me into it. I asked my parents for permission, and then I told
Orlando he could come to my place . . . He showed up just
minutes later . . . He'd called from a bar not far from our
house . . . My parents welcomed him politely but were unable
to mask their embarrassment. They would have been very
pleased if I'd married him, and when I left him—'

'What did Orlando tell you?' Bordelli asked impatiently.

'Well, we went into the sitting room to be alone . . . He took
my hands in his and told me he'd discovered something
terrible . . . And he needed to get it off his chest . . . But it
might be dangerous, he said, and he made me swear not to tell
anyone what he was about to tell me . . .' Ortensia stopped and
looked around.

'Can you tell me now?' Bordelli whispered.

The woman squirmed nervously in her chair, as though
undecided. Then she stiffened, staring fixedly at something
behind Bordelli.

'Who is that man? What's he looking at?' she hissed with a
shudder. Bordelli turned round and saw a pale, thin young man
in glasses, who immediately looked away.

'You think it's strange when someone admires a pretty woman?' he said, smiling.

Despite the inappropriateness of the moment, Ortensia blushed at the flattery. She cast another furtive glance at the lad, and from her uneasiness Bordelli could tell that their eyes had met again. He, too, was staring at her, waiting for her to continue.

'Forgive me . . . I'm a little nervous . . .' She was batting her eyelashes, trying to recover her train of thought. She stubbed out her half-smoked cigarette in the ashtray.

'Take your time,' said Bordelli, to put her at ease.

The woman was biting her lips, but clearly she was about to start talking again. One just had to be patient. A long minute of silence passed, against a background of light music and laughter. Then Ortensia fixed her eyes on him and leaned forward.

'I've never told anyone what Orlando said to me.'

'Maybe that was a mistake.'

'He made me swear never to tell anyone . . . And when I found out that he had comm . . . I thought I'd go mad . . . I was desperate . . . I realised I still loved him . . . I remembered the look he had in his eye that evening . . . And I was afraid . . . I'm still afraid, even now . . .'

She looked over again at the bespectacled lad and immediately averted her glance.

'What did Orlando tell you?' Bordelli insisted.

'Do you swear you will never tell anyone what I am about to tell you?'

'You have my word,' Bordelli reassured her, hoping it really was something of great importance. Ortensia gave herself another moment of reflection, then made up her mind.

'Orlando had been working at the firm of two important lawyers for almost two years . . . and a few days earlier, he'd discovered, by accident, that the two partners were embezzling huge sums of money from estates they were administering . . .'

'That's no surprise,' said Bordelli, to avoid telling her that he already knew this.

Ortensia was worrying her wedding ring and seemed short of breath.

'He discovered another thing, too . . . Also by accident, he said . . . On the morning of the day before, he'd gone back to the law offices earlier than expected, after an assignment at the courts . . . He heard one of the lawyers talking rather heatedly over the phone, behind a closed door . . . It had only been a couple of weeks since he'd discovered that the two partners were cheating their richest clients, and he'd taken it upon himself to spy on them . . . He wanted to gather as much information as possible, and then turn them in . . . And so he went into his own office on tiptoe and picked up the receiver, trying not to make any noise . . . And he started listening in on their conversation . . . The solicitor was speaking with a man he kept calling "General" . . . He finally realised that part of the money was to be used to finance . . . a conspiracy against the government . . . or something like that . . .'

'Interesting . . .' said Bordelli, restraining the desire to start immediately connecting the dots. He'd finally discovered something he didn't already know. And apparently the SID didn't know it either, unless they were keeping it secret. But Ortensia hadn't finished yet.

'Then something happened, he said to me . . . I remember Orlando's story quite well, and the terrified look in his eyes . . . As he was listening in on the conversation, a coin fell out of his trouser pocket . . . The lawyer and general immediately stopped talking, and after a long silence they hung up without saying another word . . . Orlando quickly put the receiver back in its proper place, raced over to the bookcase and grabbed a copy of the Penal Code, which he pretended to be reading . . . He'd managed just in time . . . The door to his office opened slowly, and the lawyer looked at him with an icy smile . . . *Ah, so you're here? Did you need the phone?* Orlando said no, pretending to be surprised by the question . . . He'd just got back, he said, and wanted to review an article in the Code . . . *Which one?* the lawyer asked him in a calm tone that had nothing at all natural about it. As Orlando was stammering a reply, the lawyer approached the desk and bent down to pick up the coin . . . *You dropped fifty lire*, he said, smiling . . . He set the coin down on the desk and left without saying anything else . . . Orlando was afraid, but went about his work for the rest of the day as if nothing had happened . . . When it was time to go home the two lawyers invited him out to dinner . . . It was the first time they'd ever done so . . . They wanted to make him an offer, they said . . . They took him to a posh restaurant and kept filling his glass with wine . . . They were in fact too friendly, and they never stopped joking around . . . The time went by, but the lawyers still hadn't said anything of importance . . . Orlando forced himself to appear calm and even a little drunk, but he could actually hold his drink quite well and was perfectly lucid . . . At a certain point he asked what their offer was, and the two men said vaguely that he had a chance to earn a lot of money . . . He could even enter into a partnership with them, become a full member of the firm . . . One needed only to cheat the taxman a little . . . which everyone did anyway. But they would talk about it in greater detail on Monday . . . there was no hurry . . . Orlando said he couldn't wait to become a full partner, and proposed a toast . . . even though deep inside he was scared to death . . . The two lawyers were still smiling . . . Orlando pretended to be increasingly addled from the wine, but every so often he noticed them exchanging a meaningful glance . . . At last they left the restaurant . . . Outside on the pavement the two men alluded again to their forthcoming agreement, congratulated him, and said goodbye in a very friendly manner . . . Too friendly, according to Orlando . . . He confessed that he had a bad feeling and believed he was in danger . . . And that same night . . . he died . . . Do you see now why I'm afraid? I'm the only person he told these things to . . . I thought Orlando was murdered from the very start, but what could I do? When he revealed all this to me, he was scared, it's true, but I also thought he was playacting a little so that I would feel sorry for him . . . I didn't entirely believe him . . . I feel so guilty about that . . .'

Ortensia was squirming in her chair, trying to control herself, and for a moment seemed to regret having told him all this.

'Whatever the case, if it really was murder, you have nothing more to fear. One of the lawyers is dead, and the other fled abroad and hasn't been seen or heard from since.'

'Oh my God, are you serious?' She seemed a little relieved. Bordelli nodded, trying to appear reassuring.

'Did Orlando tell you anything else?'

'No . . .'

'Can you think of anything else that might be of use to me?'

'I don't know . . . He had a safe . . . Nobody knew about it, not even his mother . . . He only told me . . . All I know is that it's in his study . . . He said he'd hidden it very well . . .'

'I'll try to find it,' said Bordelli, still thinking about the phone conversation between the lawyer and the general . . . *A conspiracy against the government*. Might it have some connection with the affair Agostinelli had told him about? The business with President Segni and General de Lorenzo? Of course not, too many years had passed; this was a different plot . . . There certainly was no lack of them in Italy . . .

'I know the combination . . .' Ortensia said in a girlish tone.

'What's that?' said Bordelli, snapping out of his reverie.

'The combination to the safe . . . Are you interested?'

'Of course I am . . .'

'It's the last three letters of my name in reverse . . . A . . . I . . . S . . . , transformed into numbers . . .' Ortensia whispered, looking around to check whether anyone was eavesdropping.

Bordelli started calculating to himself . . . A . . . I . . . S . . . became 1 . . . 9 . . . 17 . . .

'Are you sure about that?'

'Unless he changed it after we broke up . . .' said Ortensia. She started stealing glances at the lad with the glasses again. Perhaps she liked him a little? Or was she simply so insecure that she couldn't do without men looking at her?

As soon as he got home he lit a fire, burning the newspaper of the day before, which he'd hardly glanced at. Nowadays he read only the headlines and the subheads, and every so often skimmed an article or two. Every line in the newspaper seemed like one less line he would read in a novel. He felt he got to know more profound things by reading Homer or Dostoyevsky rather than the dailies. The motivations that drove men to serve good or evil were the same today as they were a hundred years earlier, or in the sixteenth century, or in the age of Aeschylus. What had manifested over time and history were only variants thereof, different modalities of the very same things . . . In short, he would never burn the pages of a book to start a fire . . .

After waiting for the flames to gain strength, he laid a substantial log between the andirons. Lighting a cigarette, he leaned back in the armchair and started thinking again about Orlando's story. The whole thing seemed all too clear. Orlando had discovered something he wasn't supposed to discover, and they'd murdered him and faked a suicide. As easy as drinking a glass of water . . . But how they hell did they do it? And was that really what happened? The motive might even be real – actually it clearly was . . . But where was the evidence? Where was he going to find it, after all these years, assuming there was any? Not everyone who had a motive for murder actually committed it, otherwise the world would be a cemetery . . . That was why the courts existed, to evaluate evidence and pronounce sentences . . . Though he'd behaved a little differently with the butcher . . . No court, just a shotgun blast . . . *Ego te absolvo* . . .

After putting a pot of water on the fire, he rang the contessa.

He told her he'd been going ahead with the investigation and asked whether he could call on her at the castle the following morning, The contessa insistently wanted to know whether he'd already discovered something, but Bordelli politely asked her to be patient and said goodbye.

He started eating in front of the evening news report but paid no attention to it, and after amusing himself watching the skits on *Carosello*, he turned off the telly.

He spent the evening reading by the fire, hearing the cries of the owls in the distance. When he finished *Notes from the Underground*, he felt as if he'd sowed another tomato seed in the soil of his ignorance. In the end he was lucky: there were still a great many books for him to discover, and he even had the time to read them. He need only let the young salesmen at the Seeber bookshop guide him.

He sat there watching the fire with the book on his knees, still walking in the wet snow along the streets of St Petersburg, slipping into the brothels to talk to the young prostitutes . . .

A noise awoke him. He was surprised to have been asleep. What remained of the log had broken apart and fallen to both sides of the andirons. He scraped the embers together with the fire-shovel and went upstairs. After loading the stove he dragged himself into bed and immediately put out the light. He felt tired, but his brain didn't want to hear about falling asleep, as his thoughts kept going softly round and round like a merry-go-round. While owls big and small went about their amorous business in the night, he could hear Mussolini's voice croaking over the radio . . . He saw Ennio raise his glass for a toast . . . Eleonora's face appeared, covered with bruises . . . He stroked his dying mother's wrinkled hand . . . Imagined Orlando swaying under the wrought-iron chandelier . . .

He curled up under the covers, as he used to as a little boy when he heard a train in the distance, passing under the Pino viaduct, and a mysterious shudder would shake his feet.

The carousel gently began to slow down, and he sank into less chaotic thoughts . . . In a month it would be his birthday.

Not that he was really so keen on celebrating his fifty-seventh. Still, it might be an opportunity to organise a dinner with friends. He wanted to cook everything himself, and he thought of asking Ennio to write down some recipes for him. He would invite the usual crowd . . . Dante . . . Ennio . . . Piras . . . Diotivede . . . A quiet evening with the guys . . . And then, after the meal, over a bottle of grappa, each would tell a story, like the other times . . .

As he was falling asleep, a bird took up position on a tree outside his window and started singing. It had a thousand different calls, changing register every two or three seconds . . . *Cheep cheep* . . . *Tststststststs* . . . *Fiuuuuuu* . . . *Trrrrrr* . . . *Kew kew kew* . . . *Cheecheecheechee* . . . and other vocal about-faces that sounded like music . . . In his half-sleep he imagined the bird as his mother . . . She'd come to say hello . . . to tell him the living and the dead were not so far away from each other . . . The loving senses' correspondence . . .[12]

As he drifted into unconsciousness he started reviewing all the women he'd ever fallen in love with . . . Starting with Rachele, a beautiful little girl who, unbeknown to her, had made him lose a year of schooling . . .

He parked in front of the contessa's castle, next to an old black Mercedes. The moment he got out, the great door opened, and on the threshold appeared an elderly housekeeper with a feather duster in her hand. He went up to her, saying he had an appointment with the contessa. The old woman nodded without a word and gestured for him to come in. Bordelli found himself in a monumental entrance hall, with tapestries on the walls, ancient armour, precious vases, and mirrors with ornate gilt frames. An immense staircase in *pietra serena* led through the penumbra to the upper floors. The housekeeper motioned for him to follow her, and she hobbled her way down a long corridor that began to one side of the staircase. She opened a door for him and then closed it unceremoniously after he went in. While waiting, Bordelli started pacing across the room's carpets, looking around and sniffing the air, which smelled of ancient books. On the walls not covered with bookcases hung some large oil portraits, elderly men with monumental moustaches, portly women with generous eyes and a small animal in their arms, young men and young ladies looking fresh and haughty. At the back of the room was a great stone fireplace with the family crest, a two-headed wolf with a rather angry look, sculpted on it. Majestically placed here and there on various furnishings were a number of precious objects, bronze statuettes, fine candelabra, a magnificent table clock under a bell jar.

The large windows afforded a view of the hills, and Bordelli could make out his own house down below, which looked tiny. He peeked behind the inside shutters and, as he expected, found an iron crossbar hanging from an iron ring.

He went and sat down in a small, satin-covered armchair, and it creaked under his weight. He leaned forward and ran his fingers over the top of a lovely wooden table with an inlaid chessboard . . . At that moment the door opened and the contessa appeared in an elegant but sober house-dress. Bordelli stood up, and to put her at her ease, bowed as if to kiss her hand.

'Good morning, Contessa.'

'Can I get you anything?'

'Please don't bother.'

'Please make yourself at home.'

'Thank you . . .'

They sat down facing each other, and the contessa fixed her eyes on him as though trying to read his mind.

'Have you discovered anything?'

'You'll have to forgive me, but for the moment I'd rather not talk about it,' said Bordelli.

The contessa shuddered slightly.

'You said you wanted to visit the castle.'

'If it's not an inconvenience . . .'

'Come.'

They left the room and the contessa became his guide. Salons, sitting rooms, parlours, the billiards room, paintings with hunting scenes and mythological characters, a great cloakroom that smelled musty, the consummately dignified servants' quarters, a vast kitchen in which the housekeeper was already bustling about with pots and pans.

Bordelli repeatedly inspected the windows, and found them all to have massive inside shutters equipped with iron crossbars. Maybe the killer had escaped up the chimney, like Santa Claus?

Along one corridor the contessa indicated a closed door, saying that it couldn't be opened. She'd lost the key.

'What's in it?'

'It's empty.'

She stopped in front of a small door camouflaged to look like the rest of the wall and asked whether he wanted to see the cellars.

'There's no need, thanks.'

They went up to the first floor, which was thoroughly carpeted and more austerely furnished. A reading room lined with book-cases stuffed with books. A grand, empty salon with, on the wall, an enormous seventeenth-century painting depicting the conversion of St Paul on the road to Damascus. Other rooms with antique furniture and paintings from a variety of epochs ...

'And this is Orlando's study,' said the contessa, pushing open a door.

The room was dark, the window closed. When she turned on the light Bordelli immediately noticed the wrought-iron chan-delier and couldn't help but imagine Orlando with the cord round his neck. The desk was almost directly beneath the chan-delier. To hang himself, all he would have had to do was to climb up on it.

The study was not very big, and looked lived in. Yet another bookcase, stretching to the ceiling and packed with books. On the clay-tile floor, in the middle of the room, was a beautiful carpet in which the colour blue dominated. On Orlando's desk lay some files, scattered papers, an old, solid-black Olivetti typewriter, a packet of cigarettes, almost empty, a gold lighter, and a few other objects. A dark jacket hung on the back of the chair. It was anybody's guess where the safe was.

'I've left it the way it was. I only had the cord removed and had it tidied up a little. And I have it dusted once a week,' said the contessa, standing immobile beside the door. Orlando's study had become a temple of remembrance.

Bordelli circled round the desk and on it saw the note left by Orlando: *Forgive me.* Inspector Bacci must have been firmly convinced it was a suicide to have left the note here. Otherwise he would have had it catalogued and made available to a judge.

He looked around for another piece of paper with handwriting on it, to compare the two. The hand was indeed the same, even if it looked more indecisive on the suicide note. Was this due to nervous tension, or was Orlando, as the mother maintained, forced to write it under threat? He went and moved the curtain, noticing that the cord was still missing.

'I keep the cord upstairs. Would you like to see it?' asked the contessa, who'd intuited his thoughts.

'That won't be necessary, thank you.'

'I'll take you upstairs.'

'You're very kind . . .' Following the contessa through the doorway, Bordelli was still trying to imagine where the safe might be hidden.

On the second and third floors were the bedrooms, of varying dimensions and with different styles of furnishings. Canopy beds that had survived the centuries, time-worn wrought-iron bedsteads, monumental armoires and beds, marble-topped chests of drawers, and more paintings, carpets, and ceramics . . . Bordelli couldn't take any more. He felt as if he was in a museum. It was all very beautiful, but he could never live like that.

The contessa had saved Orlando's room for last. On the third floor, and occupying a small corner of the castle, it was the most austere and pleasant of them all. Not very large, with only a few elegant but simple furnishings. That room, too, had been left as it was fourteen years earlier.

'Every so often I have it dusted,' said the contessa.

Some clothes thrown over the back of an armchair, two pairs of shoes in a corner, old, yellowed newspapers on the table, books on the nightstand . . . From the window one could see the bell tower of Impruneta in the distance, and a little farther to the left, mounted high in the sky atop a pylon, the red star of the Casa del Popolo,[13] which would light up at night to remind the wretched of the earth that there was hope.

They went out into the hallway, and the contessa stopped at the bottom of a narrow wooden staircase that rose steeply and vanished into the shadows.

'Are you interested in seeing the attic?'

'I think that's enough for now, thank you.'

'If you want to visit the tower you'll have to go alone. The spiral staircase has seventy-two steps,' said the contessa, indicating a studded door.

'Perhaps another time . . .'

'And you have nothing else to tell me?' the contessa asked impatiently.

'Please give me a little more time.'

'Do you need anything else?'

'If you don't mind . . . I would like to be left alone in your son's study for a little while,' said Bordelli.

The contessa frowned, but for only a second. She led him down to the first floor and stopped outside the study.

'You can take your time.'

'Thank you . . .'

'If you need me, you can find me in the sitting room where you so patiently waited for me,' said the contessa, and she headed for the staircase.

Bordelli went into the study, wondering how Orlando had managed to live alone in that gloomy, enormous castle. It was probably even haunted . . .

He began inspecting the room inch by inch. He peeked behind the paintings, moved the lightest pieces of furniture, slid the books off their shelves and felt the wood-panel backing with his fingers, but found nothing. Did this safe really exist? He stuck an unlit cigarette between his lips and started inspecting the room all over again, more carefully this time. He got down on his kness and looked everywhere, checking every detail, even the clay-tile floor . . . And at last his perseverance paid off. Running his hand behind one foot of the bookcase, he discovered a small switch. As soon as he pressed it, he heard a low buzzing sound, and looking around he noticed the wooden backing of one shelf sliding off to one side, revealing a small safe built into the wall. Three numbered knobs . . . A . . . I . . . S . . . That is, 1 . . . 9 . . . 17 . . . From left to right or the reverse? He tried from left to right, and nothing happened. Reversing the order, he heard a click . . . The combination had not been changed. Opening the little door, he felt as if he were violating the intimacy of Orlando's secrets, but he was doing it for him, after all. For him and his mother. He took everything he found inside it and sat down at the desk. A small box, two envelopes, and a notebook. In the larger envelope were a number of photographs: a severe-looking man holding a little boy in his arms; other shots of the same boy at different ages; another of Ortensia, young and beautiful, posing in front of a fountain, smiling happily . . . On the back was the dedication: *To my beloved Orlando, your Ortensia*. In the other envelope, the smaller one, were some letters from Ortensia, spotted with mildew. Bordelli skimmed them quickly; they were love letters. In the little box he found some jewellery: a large gold ring with the family crest, a pair of antique earrings, a small pendant with the Madonna and a date inscribed on the back: *12-10-1928* . . . It must have been his date of birth. Apparently the safe was used to store mementoes . . .

He opened the notebook and started reading. On the first page was a poem . . .

27 *October 1951*

*To my father*

*I was unable*
*to hold your hand*
*in mine*
*as you were dying,*
*to feel from the grip*
*that you were leaving*
*to wait for me elsewhere.*

*I was unable*
*and would have liked*
*to feel inside me*
*the surge of blood,*
*the new movement,*
*to follow your veins*
*now motionless*
*and remember forever*
*your last breath of goodbye.*

# Death in the Tuscan Hills

*And I'll never know*
*if in that final second*
*you opened your eyes again*
*seeking*
*and not finding*
*inside you*
*the last drop of light for the journey.*

*Perhaps a stranger*
*seeing you there*
*and barely sighing*
*– dead, he too –*
*closed your eyes for you*
*depriving me*
*of one last look*
*at your gaze.*

*A few yards away*
*beyond two walls,*
*beyond the distance*
*of an injunction,*
*looking up at the sky*
*awaiting and hoping*
*your awaiting*
*imagining what follows*
*come what may.*

*You died alone*
*and I didn't see you*
*and you didn't see me.*
*In life at least*
*there's dream*
*which disregards distance*
*with never an injunction*
*and returns to our side*
*the beloved and the dead.*

Bordelli felt moved. He thought of his own father, who had died suddenly. And of his mother, at whose death he'd been present . . .

He kept thumbing through the notebook. Scattered thoughts, reflections on the great questions of life, a few muddled love sonnets to Ortensia. Then he found what he was looking for . . .

*5 June 1953*
*A few days ago, purely by chance, I discovered that the lawyers*
*Giulio Manetti and Rolando Torrigiani, proprietors of the law*
*firm where I work as an assistant, have taken advantage of*
*their role as estates' administrators to embezzle vast sums of*
*money by subtle, illegal means. Amounts embezzled in 1952:*
*7,200,000 lire from the Budini Gattai family; 12,800,000 lire*
*from the Magnolfi Bianchi Camaiani family; 5,700,000 from*
*the Baldovinetti della Torre family . . .*

Orlando had written everything down, in great detail. If not for the subject matter, it seemed like the diary of a little boy . . . He recounted his discovery of the swindles carried out by the legal partners, the phone call he'd secretly listened to, the financing intended for subversive activities, the mysterious offer they would make to him the following Monday . . . The last sentence certainly made an impression: *I fear for my life . . .* They didn't sound like the words of a man who had decided to hang himself, even though one never knew what sorts of things might be going through the mind of a suicide . . . On the following page there were only two lines of verse:

*Love, in your eyes my own time*
*becomes no time in God's eternity.*

All the other pages were blank. Apparently Ortensia was wrong; there was no other woman in her boyfriend's life.

He put everything back into the safe. Quite likely no one would ever find it again. He pressed the button behind the bookcase, and the wooden panel closed with the same hum as before. Putting his unsmoked cigarette back in its packet, he left the study and went to look for the contessa. He heard her authoritarian voice in the kitchen, and poked his head inside.

'I'm all done, thank you.'

'I invite you to stay for lunch,' said the contessa.

'Thank you so much, but I was thinking I—'

'I won't accept any excuses,' the contessa cut him off, and after whispering something to the lame housekeeper, she led the way. Bordelli followed her into the dining room, where a long table had already been set for two. Embroidered white tablecloth, silver cutlery, fine china and crystal goblets that sparkled under the chandelier. In the middle of the table were a bottle of red wine and a pitcher of water.

'Please sit down,' said the contessa, taking her place at the table.

Bordelli sat down at the other end, unable to refuse so peremptory an invitation. The contessa shook a small bell in the air, and a few seconds later a very thin man in livery appeared, with a long white face and a proud gaze that clashed with his role as servant. He greeted Bordelli with a slight bow of respect, went up to the contessa and served her an ever so noble bowl of vegetable soup. He also filled the guest's bowl, and after filling their goblets with wine and their glasses with water, he left the room with an elegant step.

They began eating in silence. The only sound was the ticking of the pendulum clock, which grew louder by the second. The soup was excellent, and Bordelli thought he would like to ask the lame housekeeper for the recipe.

Setting down her spoon, the contessa rested her hands on the velvet arms of her chair.

'If you tell me my son killed himself, I promise I will believe you.'

'May I ask why?' asked Bordelli, sincerely surprised.

'No.'

'Well, thank you for your confidence just the same . . .'

'I can read people's eyes,' the contessa said enigmatically.

As he was going back down the castle driveway in his Beetle, thoughts of the lunch he'd just had with the contessa filled his head. He'd felt a bit uneasy being served by a waiter in uniform with gilded buttons and white gloves, but the roast beef and potatoes were magnificent, the Barolo was worth centuries in Purgatory, and the pudding was peerless. For a lunch like that, he could put up with anything . . .

It was almost three, and he finally lit his first cigarette of the day. There were still a few things left to be done before he closed his private investigation. He pulled up outside the first farmhouse he saw, just a few hundred yards from the castle. There was the sound of a tractor in the distance. He knocked at the door, but nobody answered. Circling behind the house, he walked down a path that descended through the olive trees towards the tractor. For days he'd been thinking that the contessa was simply a poor old madwoman, and now he was starting to have doubts. Maybe the old madwoman was right. Whatever the case, he'd certainly unearthed more than enough motives for murdering Orlando . . .

He approached the field that was being ploughed and found an old peasant atop a Caterpillar tractor. He was one of the few. A great many still hitched the plough up to a couple of oxen, as in Fattori's paintings.

Bordelli waved to get the man's attention. After casting a glance in his direction, the old man turned off the motor and sat there eyeing the intruder. Bordelli approached.

'Could I speak with you for a moment?'
'About what?'

'Do you remember the tragedy that happened in the castle in '53? The contessa's son . . .'

'Of course I remember.'

'I wanted to ask you whether you saw anything that day . . . Anything . . . I don't know . . . unusual . . . Anything at all?'

'Why?'

'I'm trying to understand some things . . . Let's just say I'm working for the contessa.'

'Ah . . .'

'Did you see anything strange that day?'

'One sees so many things . . .'

'So you did see something?'

'What can I say? I don't think so . . .'

'Think hard . . . Did you see, say, a car you didn't recognise drive by, along the road to the castle?'

'I don't remember, but I would've noticed something like that.'

'So you saw nothing, in short,' Bordelli pressed, not having fully understood.

'Nothing . . .' said the old man, shrugging.

'Is this the contessa's land?'

'On this side it all belongs to the contessa, as far as the wood down there.'

It was a vast estate.

'Thank you, sorry to trouble you.'

'No trouble at all . . .' the peasant muttered, and after gesturing goodbye, he started up his motor again.

Bordelli went back up the path to his car. It wasn't as if he really hoped to find anything out from the local peasants, but he wanted to leave no stone unturned. Also because no investigation had been conducted at the time of the crime, and so even now, perhaps with a bit of luck . . .

He made the rounds of the other farms, even talking to the same peasants who had given him the chicken droppings and everything else, but nobody could recall having seen anything unusual on the day Orlando died. Only a toothless old hag mentioned a light she'd seen that night in the middle of the woods, though it wasn't on the night of the tragedy, but the following night. She remembered it well because for a moment she'd thought, with a shudder, *It's the soul of poor Count Orlando who can find no peace, poor dear* . . . But she knew well that it might be a boar hunter as well. In those days they often used to go around with torches, and they still did sometimes.

Bordelli got home feeling tired, as the sun was setting over the horizon. It was never quite so pleasant going back to his den when he lived in San Frediano.

After hastily watering the garden, he turned to the ritual of the fire. As he watched the flames climbing higher and higher, he wished he could reread the poem Orlando had written to his father. Why, indeed, hadn't he kept the notebook? Nobody was ever going to find that safe anyway . . .

Before sitting down in the armchair, he phoned the bar in Piazza Tasso.

'Ciao, Fosco . . . Is Ennio there by any chance?'

'He hasn't come in today, Inspector . . . He usually shows up around eight . . .'

'Could you ask him please to give me a ring?'

'Of course . . .'

'Don't forget – it's important.'

'Don't worry, Inspector.'

'Thanks, Fosco. 'Bye now,' said Bordelli, hanging up.

He got comfortable beside the fire, book in hand. He didn't feel like thinking about Orlando. It would be better to wait until tomorrow and start over with a clear head. And there was no point at all in thinking about Eleonora. He wanted only to find a little peace, get engrossed in the novel and free his mind of everything else . . . After ten pages, he closed his eyes and was already snoring . . .

The ringing of the phone woke him up, wrenching him out of an obsessive dream in which the same scene kept repeating over and over. For a few seconds he sat there in a daze, staring into the void, as the phone kept ringing. Finally he got up and staggered to pick up.

'Hello . . .'

'Back from the grave, Inspector?' asked Botta, against a background of voices and billiards.

'Hi, Ennio . . . I'd dozed off . . .'

'Fosco said you were looking for me.'

'Yes . . .'

'Has something happened? Need some locks picked?'

'Nothing like that, I'm sorry to say . . . I only wanted to ask if you would . . . I was thinking of having a dinner party for my birthday . . .'

'That's all?'

'It's an event of monumental importance.'

'When is your birthday?'

'The second of April.'

'Then there's time, Inspector . . .' said Botta, as though speaking to an impatient child.

'Of course, but I wanted to do the cooking . . . I'd like to practise a little . . . Think you could write down a few recipes for me?'

'Good God, are you sure about that?'

'Why?'

'You don't learn to cook by reading recipes, Inspector. It's a question of sensitivity.'

'I'm the most sensitive man in the world,' Bordelli said quite seriously.

'As you wish, Inspector . . . I'll bring you a few very simple recipes . . .'

'Don't underestimate me, Ennio. Even difficult dishes are okay; I think I can manage.'

'When do you need them by?' asked Botta, sighing.

'The sooner the better.'

'I'll see what I can do . . .'

'You'll be rewarded in heaven.'

'Will you be at home Sunday morning?'

'I think so.'

'By the way, Inspector . . . I'd almost forgotten . . .' Botta whispered into the receiver, which he'd brought closer to his mouth.

'What is it?'

'About that thing we discussed . . . Be ready . . . Unless you've changed your mind . . .'

'I said I'd do it and I will.'

'Good . . .'

'Milan?'

'Yes . . .'

'When?'

'I don't know yet.'

'As long as it's not the second of April. You're invited, too.'

'You wouldn't dare not invite me . . . Gotta go now, Inspector . . . Some punk from Ponte di Mezzo has challenged me at the billiards table . . .'

'Go and do your stuff.'

'I'm gonna make him cry and send him home in his knickers,' said Botta, before going off to take care of business.

It was almost nine. Bordelli turned on the telly and started cooking dinner, distractedly glancing at what remained of the evening news. Penne with tomato sauce, grilled pork chop, salad . . . Simple things anyone could make. But for his birthday he wanted a special menu, and he had confidence in Ennio's recipes. Who knew why he suddenly had this mania for cooking. Maybe eating in Totò's kitchen for years and watching him always at work had passed the sacred fire on to him . . . For no apparent reason he thought of Eleonora, but he quickly chased her from his thoughts . . .

Watching *Carosello* out of one eye, he continued his preparations, humming the refrain of a Rita Pavone song. After setting the table, he put the pasta in the water. While waiting for it to cook, he went outside and around the house to look at the darkened countryside. The sky was black and pierced with millions of stars. The hilltops were barely visible, and the dark silhouette of the castle seemed to undulate in the night. All at once the snarling frenzy of two boar fighting echoed in the distance . . . They sounded like devils . . .

He returned home in mid-afternoon, after a long walk through the hills of Cintoia. The temperature had increased, and he was sweating like a cyclist. He hadn't removed his jacket yet when the phone rang.

'Hello, you ugly gorilla.'

'I'm not ugly, Rosa.'

'Then, hello, gorilla . . . When are you going to come and see me?'

'Soon, Rosa . . .'

'Why not right now?'

'I'm a wreck, I've been out walking all day.'

'Come on, I feel depressed . . .' said Rosa in a little-girl voice.

'Why?'

'I don't know . . . Why don't you take me to the movies?'

'It's Saturday. It'll be too crowded . . .' said Bordelli, who couldn't wait to start reading by the fire.

'Then I'll wait for you; you're such a sweetheart . . . But don't take all day, okay?' said Rosa, hanging up before he could object.

Bordelli stood there with his mouth agape and the telephone in his hand . . . He started laughing . . . He'd been had, as usual.

He went to run a bath, and moments later immersed himself in the scalding hot water. He had no desire to go down to the city and trudge through the crowds, but he didn't want to disappoint Rosa. And, anyway, he liked a good movie as much as anyone. Since he had all the solitude he could ever want these days, seeing people every so often wasn't such a big deal, as he had the comfort of knowing that at the end of the day he would return to the quiet of his big country house.

Marco Vichi

He lingered in the tub less than usual, so as not to be late. As he was drying off he looked at himself in the mirror. He hadn't shaved that morning, and he didn't feel like doing so now, either. He kept looking at himself. It was one of those rare days when he thought he didn't look so bad. Despite his little afternoon naps and the wrinkles, he didn't feel like a poor old sod, the way he did when he lived in town. He no longer pictured himself living out his days drinking lukewarm broth with a blanket over his knees, or spending Sunday afternoons playing bingo at some club. Was it thanks to the country life? Or was it the spring, which had been quickening the blood of all living beings for millions of years?

He hummed while getting dressed, and then went down into the kitchen. The hot bath had revived him. He opened the copy of *La Nazione* on the table, and after a quick glance at the cinema programmes, he went out of the house.

It was a beautiful day, and there was still over an hour of sunlight left. Driving through the main square of Impruneta, he saw only some peasant folk, dressed in their Sunday best, chatting under the arches of the church, around the well and outside the bar. No women anywhere. And not a hint of any young people.

He entered Florence and parked in Via dei Neri with his wheels on the pavement. In that quarter the signs of the flood were still so much in evidence that it looked as if the Arno had burst its banks just the day before.

He rang the buzzer and went into the stairwell, to call up to Rosa that he would wait for her downstairs. Pacing outside the front door, he lit a cigarette, resigned to waiting who knew how long. Rosa surprised him, coming down after just a few minutes. She was made up and decked out in very showy fashion, tottering on her stilt-like heels, and emitting pungent clouds of perfume.

'I decided to dress up like a whore,' she said, smiling.

'That's not your style.'

'Silly . . .' said Rosa, taking his arm and trying to drag him away to the centre of town, but Bordelli dug in like a mule.

'At the Ideale they're showing *Action Man* with Jean Gabin . . . I like films about burglars.'

'Out of the question . . . You invited me, so I get to decide on the movie . . .'

'Actually . . .' Bordelli tried to say.

'We're going to the Gambrinus.'

'To see what?'

'*Barefoot in the Park* . . . And don't make that face . . . A friend of mine said it was very charming . . . And it has that handsome actor . . .'

'Handsome to you . . .'

'Jealous?'

'Of what? Nobody's more handsome than me.'

'Good God . . . Did you see that poor woman?' said Rosa indicating a woman passing by on the pavement opposite them.

'No, what did she do?'

'She ran into a pole, turning to look at you,' and she burst out laughing.

'That actually used to happen, way back when,' said Bordelli, staring into space nostalgically.

'You mean when everyone still rode horses?' She laughed again, hand over her mouth.

'Didn't you say you were feeling down?'

'I've been very down, but that's no reason not to have fun.'

'Is that why you're cackling like a chicken?' said Bordelli, prolonging the scuffle.

'But I *am* a chicken . . . Cackle-cackle, cluck-cluck . . .' And she kept on laughing, finally grabbing on to him to keep from falling off her spiked heels. People were turning around to look at them, and Bordelli amused himself pretending he was a pimp taking one of his girls out for a stroll . . .

'Well, don't complain . . . You've had more women than Casanova . . .' said Rosa, trying to pinch his nose.

'And every one of them left me.'

'There must be a reason . . .'

After looking at him sarcastically, she burst out laughing again.

They crossed Piazza della Signoria, swimming through a sea of people . . . Boisterous youths, little families from the provinces, couples of all ages. Rosa kept laughing; she seemed drunk.

'You're hands are a mess, you really seem like a peasant. *Hey, could you get me a bunch of onions?*'

More laughter.

'I fenced off my vegetable garden the other day,' said Bordelli, looking at his hands.

They got to the Gambrinus in time for the six o'clock show. People were streaming out of the cinema, next to the crowd queuing up to go in.

'Listen, Rosa, I hope you're not going to start laughing during the movie . . .' he whispered in her ear.

'Don't worry, I'll be okay in a minute,' said Rosa, trying to remain serious. At last they came to the ticket counter, where there was an enormous woman with long black hair that looked as if it was strangling her. Bordelli asked for two tickets, as Rosa tickled his ear with her long, painted fingernails. The cashier stared at them as though trying to work out who those two strange people were. If she did that with everyone, by the end of the day she must have been dead tired.

The cinema was already almost full, and they barely succeeded in finding two places in the gallery. Smoke rose slowly from the orchestra seats. The lights went off and the crowd fell silent. After an endless newsreel in black and white, the first credits appeared, and at last the film began . . .

It was in fact a rather amusing comedy . . . Bordelli would have preferred Gabin the Action Man, though Jane Fonda wasn't bad at all.

Rosa had stopped giggling. She followed the on-screen action with her lips half open and a charming smile in her eyes.

'See how cute he is? He's in love . . .' she said out of the blue, thinking she was speaking softly. Hisses of protest immediately rose up from the smoke-enveloped crowd.

'Rosa, you're not supposed to talk at the movies,' Bordelli whispered.

'I wasn't talking,' she practically yelled, and a cross voice told her to be quiet. Bordelli brought his mouth almost up against her ear.

'Stop talking, please. Let's watch the film.'

As the story got going, the dialogue became wittier and wittier. Whenever there was a close-up of Redford, he could sense the women in the theatre squirming in silence. Every so often Rosa squeezed his arm, but she kept her lips sealed tight, so he could see she wouldn't dare so much as breathe.

After the long-awaited happy ending, the lights came on as the closing credits rolled by on the screen. With an air of satisfaction, the crowd moved slowly through the clouds of smoke towards the exits, crossing paths with the incoming crowd in search of satisfaction.

They started strolling through the streets of downtown Florence, under a vast, black sky with few stars. The pavements were mobbed, cars and motorbikes streamed in every direction, and every so often one saw an old man on a bicycle. It was less cold than the previous days, but Rosa was shivering the whole time. She walked straight ahead in her spiked heels, hanging on Bordelli's arm, her blond hair shining in the light of the street lamps.

'It's strange to go into a movie theatre when it's light out and then to come back out when it's dark,' she said, innocent as a little girl.

'I've always liked that.'

'Look at that one there . . . If you ask me, that's one you could fall in love with . . .' she whispered, gesturing with her eyes in the direction of a dark brunette clicking her heels with great authority.

'Very pretty,' Bordelli admitted.

'You're old enough to be her father,' said Rosa, pinching his arm.

'You're the one who . . . Anyway, all I said was that she was pretty,' he said in his own defence, thinking the girl must be more or less the same age as Eleonora.

'And what about that blonde lady down there?'

'Certainly attractive, but not my type . . .'

'In my opinion they're all your type,' said Rosa, laughing.

She kept pointing out to him the pretty women passing by, elbowing him in the ribs. In the end he risked getting a stiff neck.

'You hungry?' Bordelli asked.

'Only if you invite me to a fancy restaurant.'

'Wouldn't a nice panino at the Porta Rossa tavern be better?'

'Ever the tightwad, I see . . .'

'That's not true . . . It's just that tonight I really don't feel like sitting for two hours chewing food in front of strangers,' Bordelli said to justify himself, pulling her in the direction of the tavern.

After a panino with prosciutto and a glass of Chianti, they continued their stroll through the crowded streets. While crossing the Ponte Vecchio, Bordelli looked up at the Vasari corridor,[14] as he always did, lingering on the four large windows, in the middle of the bridge, that interrupted the rhythm of the sixteenth-century 'portholes'. It was Mussolini who'd had those big windows made, in 1938, to afford Hitler a better view of the bridges over the Arno . . . Was that perhaps why the Führer had ordered his army not to bomb the Ponte Vecchio? Apparently he didn't know that there was another, even more beautiful bridge in Florence . . .

'Why don't we go dancing?' Rosa asked in a shrill voice.

'I'd rather box with Godzilla.'

'Why?'

'Are you coming to the stadium for the match tomorrow?'

'I'd rather die.'

'I'm the same way about dance halls,' said Bordelli, blowing smoke out of his mouth.

'But you're not going to the match.'

'It was just to make a point.'

'It would have been nice to see you dance . . .'

'Feel like solving a riddle?' Bordelli asked her in a serious tone.

'A riddle?'

'Listen carefully . . . You want to kill somebody, but you want it to look like a suicide . . .'

'What fun . . .'

'The person you want to kill lives in a castle . . .'

'I'd marry the guy, I wouldn't kill him.'

'Wait . . . Maybe I should tell it to you another way . . . A man is found hanging by a cord in his castle . . . All the doors and windows are locked from the inside, and everyone is convinced that it was a suicide . . . But you know for certain that the man was murdered . . .'

'How would I know?'

'That doesn't matter . . . The question is: how did they do it?' Bordelli concluded, feeling a bit silly.

'Wouldn't it be better to go dancing?' said Rosa.

'You see? You don't have an answer . . .'

'Look! There go two you're sure to like . . .' Rosa whispered, indicating two girls chatting and walking along the pavement across the street . . .

Bordelli stopped in his tracks. One of them looked exactly like Eleonora. She had short hair and was a little thin, but appeared to be her.

'Wait for me here . . .'

'Where are you going?'

'Don't move. I'll be right back . . .'

'What are you going to do?' asked Rosa, but Bordelli was already far away . . .

Was it really her? Or merely someone who looked like her? His heart was beating wildly, and he felt short of breath. He was following the two girls from the opposite pavement, gaining on them, and ready to hide if they turned round. When he was almost directly across from them, the one who looked like Eleonora turned round distractedly in his direction . . . Bordelli hid his face, blushing. But he'd managed to see her in time, and no longer had any doubts. It was her . . . Eleonora was there, just a few steps away from him, on the other side of the street . . .

What should he do? Go up to her and greet her? Was this not another sign from destiny? And what about her? Had she recognised him? Would she now wave her hand and call him over? He didn't know whether to be afraid or not . . .

He slowed down and pretended to look at a shop window, trying to find Eleonora in the reflection. He saw her walking serenely with her friend. When he finally turned round again, the girls were turning the corner. For a moment he thought of circling round the block from the other end and appearing suddenly in front of them, but after such an exploit he would certainly be out of breath and look upset. Better just give it up. He knew he would regret it, but he couldn't bring himself to step forward. He wasn't ready yet, as he'd already told himself so many times . . . He would try to see her again only after . . .

He walked back towards Rosa, who was waiting for him impatiently, scanning the pavements with her eyes. As soon as she saw him, she waved and came towards him.

'Would you please tell me what happened?'

'Nothing . . .'

He headed off down the pavement, with Rosa trailing him.

'What do you mean, "nothing"? I've never seen you act so strangely.'

'Forget about it, Rosa . . . Just pretend I saw a ghost . . .'

'A ghost? What fun . . .' she said, taking him by the arm again.

'I said "pretend".'

'I bet this is about a woman . . . You're incapable of thinking about anything else . . .'

'Can we change the subject?'

'I get it. It's that girl who left you . . .'

'I've already told you, Rosa, they all left me . . .'

'I meant the last one.'

'Feel like an ice cream?' asked Bordelli, to cut short the discussion.

Rosa shrugged, resigned to not knowing. 'I'd rather go home.'

'As you wish.'

'Now there's one you're sure to like . . .' she whispered, pulling him by the arm. She didn't miss a single one.

'Rosa, please . . . Don't you ever look at men?'

'Women are more beautiful.'

'That's for sure.'

'Why don't you get married?'

'Now that you mention it, I need you to be the witness for the bride at a friend of mine's wedding . . .'

'Are you joking?'

'No, I'm serious.'

'Who are these people?'

'He's a forensic pathologist . . . One of those doctors who cuts open corpses to find out why they died . . .'

'Nice . . .'

'She's a beautiful woman who's getting married in secret.'

'All right, then, I'll do it. I love clandestine love affairs!'

'They're getting married on July the fourteenth, so don't forget.'

'No, I won't . . . I'll write it down in my agenda.'

'You have an agenda? Even now that you're no longer working in funhouses?'

'You really know nothing about women . . .'

They kept talking until they got to Via dei Neri, then began the long climb up the stairs, legs tired from an evening out on the town. When Rosa opened the door, Briciola came running up to them meowing, her tail straight up in the air and vibrating. Her bad eye was all black, and smaller than the other.

'Hello, my pretty . . .' said Rosa.

Entering the living room, she tossed her spike-heeled shoes aside with a moan of relief. Gideon was sleeping placidly on an armchair.

'What's this mess I see? Not again!' cried Rosa, noticing the cigarette butts scattered all over the carpet. The culprit was Briciola, who liked to overturn ashtrays and play with the butts.

He opened his eyes, after a long, restful sleep. Without raising his head from the pillow, he peered out of the window, which he always left unobstructed, with the inside shutters open. A dazzling light was filtering through the slats of the blinds. It was a beautiful sunny morning, and in little more than a week it would be spring. It was one of those days that made him feel like driving out to Marina di Massa to see his friend Nessuno, the former partisan fighter who'd set up a trattoria specialising in fish. He could even ask Rosa to come with him.

He got up, drank a cup of coffee in haste, and went outside to water the garden. He couldn't wait to taste a tomato that he'd seen grow and ripen. For the artichokes, according to Ennio, he would have to wait at least a year. He stirred the bucket of *pollina*, turning his head away from the smell. It wasn't time yet to use it. He refilled the watering can, to give the seedlings and seeds a drink. City-dwellers had lost all sense of this magic . . . a little seed that comes into contact with the earth and is transformed into a plant or even a tree.

He thought again of Eleonora walking down the street, beautiful and smiling. Had she managed to forget the humiliation of that night? Would she be able to fall in love again? He really wished he could ask her these things, but it wasn't time yet . . .

As he was watering he heard some restless panting behind him. When he turned round he saw a big, pale-yellow, short-haired dog in front of him, wagging its tail outside the fence.

'And who are you?' he said, approaching the animal. The dog gave a slight whimper and let him pat his head. He was panting with his tongue hanging out one side of his mouth, as if he'd been running. Bordelli went outside the enclosure and got down on his knees to pet the dog some more. It was a male, had no collar, and seemed quite hungry.

'Come with me,' he said, heading for the front door, with the dog following placidly behind him. Bordelli let him into the house and put some bread and a cheese rind in an old pan, and served this to the dog, who devoured everything in a second, and then looked up at him.

'Still hungry? Let's see what we can give you to eat.'

He started making a soup of overcooked pasta, bread, cheese, bits of meat, and lettuce leaves. He stirred it all up in the pan with a large spoon as the dog waited patiently, sitting beside him.

When the soup cooled a little he set the pan down on the floor, and the dog stuffed his muzzle straight into it. He finished it in less than a minute, but he finally seemed sated.

'Now you must be thirsty.'

He found a plastic bowl and filled it with fresh water. The dog immediately started drinking, slowly wagging his tail and raising his head every so often to catch his breath. With his muzzle dripping he padded over to a corner of the kitchen and lay down on the floor. He yawned long and deep and seemed clearly about to take a nap.

'Let's go and look for your master.'

Bordelli had some trouble persuading the dog to get up, but then took him outside and put him in the back seat of the Beetle.

When he got to Impruneta he parked in Piazza Nova and started walking around the town with the dog beside him, asking everyone he met whether they knew to whom the big mutt might belong. But nobody had ever seen the animal before, and in the end he thought he might keep him for himself.

'You need a name,' he said to the dog, looking at him. It was Sunday, so there was nowhere to buy food for him. But he could manage that evening with what he had in the house. As he was walking back to the car, he decided he would call him Blisk, the name he'd given the enormous German Shepherd he'd brought home with him from the war.

'It's an important name, you must honour it . . .'

So now he was even talking to dogs. But he was really starting to like this odd sort of polar bear.

When he got home he noticed Ennio's Lambretta scooter parked on the threshing floor. He got out of the car, followed by the dog, and circled behind the house. Ennio was walking around in the vegetable garden, inspecting the work of the novice farmer.

'Not bad, Inspector, not bad at all . . .'

'I have a good teacher.'

'And who's that beast?' said Ennio, when the dog appeared.

'This is Blisk; he's my new tenant.'

'Where'd you find him?'

'He came knocking on my door.'

'He'll eat as much as a regiment . . . Look at that head . . .' said Botta, coming out of the enclosure.

'So what do you think of the fence I put up? And the gate?'

'One could do better.'

'You're never satisfied, Ennio.'

'There's always room for improvement,' said Botta, bending down to pat the dog.

'It's my first time,' Bordelli said by way of justification, looking at his work with satisfaction.

'Man, is he ever big . . . Are you a dog or a bear?'

The beast was rubbing against him, and if he'd been a cat he would have been purring.

'Blisk, that's no way to act with strangers . . . You're supposed to bark . . .' said Bordelli, tapping on the animal's head with his fingers.

They went into the house, and the white bear went and lay down in his corner. They sat down for a glass of wine.

'I brought you a few recipes, Inspector,' said Ennio, sliding a blue-covered notebook across the table.

'Oh, thanks . . .'

Bordelli started leafing through it and saw that it was filled with flowery handwriting, right up to the last page.

'That's a lot of work you've done, Ennio . . .'

'I hope it's not just time wasted.'

'You must have faith . . .'

'I hope you don't want me now to write you some recipes for the dog as well . . .'

'That would be very nice of you . . . Right, Blisk?'

But the dog was already asleep, and Bordelli kept thumbing through the notebook . . . *Zuppa lombarda . . . Peposo . . . Spezzatino 'mamma li turchi'* . . . The recipes weren't written the way they were in normal cookbooks; they had a storylike tone. It was as if he could hear Ennio talking.

'I don't know how to thank you.'

'Then wait; you might regret it,' said Botta, shrugging.

Bordelli, thinking again of Orlando's death, stood up.

'Feel like trying to solve a riddle, Ennio?'

'Sure, why not?'

'Listen carefully. A young man lives alone in a big castle, and one day he's found hanging from a curtain sash in his study . . .'

He explained the situation in detail, inviting Ennio to take it for granted that it was a murder. And then he gave him the riddle: How do you hang someone to make it look like a suicide, and then vanish into thin air, leaving all the doors and windows locked fast from the inside?

'Easy . . .' said Botta, without even thinking about it. Bordelli smiled, expecting some kind of witty quip.

'How?'

'You just don't leave the building.'

'Meaning?' said Bordelli, stumped. He couldn't work it out, though he felt close to the solution. Putting on a know-it-all expression, Botta began patiently explaining his theory . . .

'You hang whoever's supposed to hang, and you hide out in the house with emergency provisions . . . Didn't you say it's a castle? Then it really shouldn't be difficult. Sooner or later someone will break through a window and find the dead body, that much is certain. You wait patiently for the corpse to be removed, and as soon as it gets dark you leave right through the door, which can't be barred from the inside. And that's that.'

'Columbus's egg . . .' said Bordelli, mouth open.

'Botta's egg, if I may say so.'

'Have you ever heard of a situation like that before?'

'No, it just came to me.'

'You're a genius . . .'

'You've only just found out?'

'It was so easy . . .' said Bordelli, still a bit numb. He'd been pondering the question for a whole week, seeking the most complicated of solutions . . . But always with the idea that the killer had found a way to get out while leaving all the bolts locked from the inside. Whereas the whole thing was as simple as could be. You merely had to take a step back and let go of all your preconceptions.

'There's just one inconvenience,' said Botta, frowning.

'What?'

'There are usually two kinds of locks for the main doors of houses. The more modern kind – which you normally open from the inside by turning a knob – and the older kind, which have a key, and which require a key from both the outside and the inside . . .' said Botta, sounding like a professor giving a lecture.

'Go on . . .'

'In the first instance, even if the door has been double-locked with an extra turn of the knob, you can still get out without any problem . . . But obviously if you haven't got a key, you can't give the lock a double turn from the outside, unless you're a wizard with locks . . .'

'And in the second instance, you're screwed,' Bordelli concluded.

'You took the words straight out of my mouth.'

'So it's best to check first.'

'For you it would even be better if you had copies of the keys . . .'

'Who said anything about me? It was just a riddle.'

'I just meant it in a manner of speaking . . . But now I have to go, Inspector . . . I have a lot of things to do . . .' Botta said, standing up.

Bordelli walked him out to the threshing floor and patted him on the shoulder. 'Keep me posted about Milan.'

'It's any day now.' Botta kick-started his Lambretta, and after a nod of farewell he went up the dirt path, raising a big cloud of dust. Bordelli stood there watching him, with a smile of gratitude on his face. By this point the odds that Orlando had been murdered were almost a hundred to one. When Ennio vanished round the bend, Bordelli went back into the house, took out a pen, and wrote on the cover of the notebook of recipes: *The Gospel according to Ennio . . .*

'Forgive the intrusion,' said Bordelli, crossing the threshold and entering the castle. The contessa herself had opened the door for him, wearing a simple dressing-gown.

'Come in . . .' she said, closing the door behind him.

Bordelli caught a glimpse of the lock. It was the 'old-fashioned' kind, the one you could open only with a key, and if it was given an extra turn or two . . . But this wasn't necessarily a problem. Orlando's killer could have managed to get his hands on a copy . . .

They went into the sitting room and sat down in the exact same armchairs as two days earlier.

'Do you have anything important to tell me?'

'Not yet . . . I've come to ask you to tell me, as precisely as you can, everything that happened after the firemen broke through the window,' said Bordelli, hoping the contessa would bear with him.

'I remember everything as if I were seeing it now . . .' she said. After a long pause, she started telling her story, with a calmness that made one's blood run cold . . .

*Her son's body was taken away in an ambulance that same morning, and the firemen had reclosed the window as best they could, shuttering it with planks nailed together from the inside. Orlando's body was then washed, dressed, placed in a casket and then put on display in the* salle d'armes *of the church of Impruneta. The contessa had decided to remain alone with her son, keeping vigil for the entire day and night, and as she sat by the casket she vowed to discover who had killed him. The funeral was held on Monday morning, in the almost empty basilica. There were only a few relatives, a few of Orlando's friends, the two lawyers for whom he'd worked, and a few old women from the village, the kind who never miss a mass. The priest's homily was honeyed and rhetorical, with broad circumlocutions to conceal the sin of suicide behind a Catholic compassion. At the moment of farewells to the deceased, the contessa made a speech. Without a tear in her eye she said only that Orlando had not killed himself, but had been murdered, and throughout the church there was a gasp of surprise. The contessa added that after the service she would rather accompany her son to the cemetery alone. Her peremptory tone admitted no protest. At the end of the mass, everyone came out under the arched portico and watched the long black box as it pulled away. Orlando was buried in the Cimitero delle Sante Marie. A few days later the contessa went back to Castiglioncello, but stayed only as long as it took to settle some bureaucratic matters and pack her bags, after which she moved definitively to Impruneta, to be near her son . . .*

'Is there anything else you'd like to know?' the contessa asked, looking him straight in the eye. Bordelli had followed her account very attentively. Before ringing at the castle door he'd inspected the surroundings, discovering a number of paths that led into the woods.

'When did you return to the castle?'

'Late Monday morning, after burying my son.'

'Nobody else entered the castle before you did?'

'Nobody.'

'And where was your chauffeur during the wake?'

'He slept on a bench in the sacristy,' said the contessa.

Therefore nobody had gone back to the castle for an entire day, and if things went the way Ennio said . . . The killer, in short, could have hidden inside the castle and waited for night to fall to escape unmolested . . .

'Is your chauffeur the same man who served us lunch last Friday?' Bordelli asked, just out of curiosity.

'Mario has been with me for twenty-five years. He's also my chauffeur.'

'And the housekeeper?'

'Fedora is the same age as me; we used to play together when we were children. She stayed behind at Castiglioncello.'

'Is there anyone else in your employ?'

'No,' said the contessa, with a wrinkle in her brow. She didn't understand the reason for all these questions.

'There's one last favour I'd like to ask of you . . .' said Bordelli.

'Do tell.'

'I'd like to check your cellars and attic.'

'You can do that by yourself. By now you know the way.'

'Thank you . . .' said Bordelli, standing up. After making a slight bow, he went out of the sitting room, down the ground floor's long corridors, and opened the small door leading to the cellars. He pressed a button, and a small bulb hanging from a wire sticking out from the wall came on. He descended the stairs, taking care not to slip. When he got to the bottom he started poking around in the different rooms, lighting his way with matches. There were great barrels covered with cobwebs, terracotta pots green with mildew, old articles of furniture left to rot. The dampness entered one's bones, and it was almost impossible to hear any sounds coming from the first floor. It would not have made a good hiding place.

He went back up and took the staircase that led to the upper floors. He climbed up to the third floor without any trouble, thinking it was thanks to his long walks in the woods. Neither did he have any problem reaching the top of the steep wooden staircase to the attics. Opening the door wasn't easy, however, and it creaked on its hinges. He looked around for the light switch, and as soon as he turned it, a number of bulbs enveloped in dense spiderwebs lit up. He came to a huge space with a floor of rough mortar, a rather low ceiling, and some squat stone pillars from which the main truss-beams branched out.

He started walking along the walls. A few dusty old chests, enormous rolled-up carpets, old picture frames wrapped in now shredded cloth. From up here, if one left the door ajar, one could almost certainly hear sounds coming from below. It seemed like the ideal hiding place . . . The killer waited for the right moment to leave the castle, and escaped along one of those paths through the woods, perhaps with a shotgun on his shoulder so as not to look out of place.

Bordelli sat down on an old chest, trying to reconstruct the hypothetical murder in detail, to leave nothing unresolved. What about the keys to the great door? Maybe the killer had got his hands on a key, or was, like Ennio, well versed in matters of locks. Orlando's shoe-prints on his desk seemed to prove that he'd climbed up there alone to hang himself, but this detail, too, could easily have been part of the whole *mise en scène*: the killer could have strangled Orlando with the curtain cord, then put on his shoes and hung him from the chandelier, and then put his shoes back on the corpse to complete the picture . . . In the realm of hypothesis, at least, it all seemed quite clear . . .

He went down to the third floor. While he was at it, he opened the studded door and tackled the seventy-two steps of the spiral staircase. He reached the tower without stopping, but when he got to the top, he was out of breath. Pushing open a low door, he looked out on to the world. The panorama was magnificent; wherever one turned, one saw hilltops in succession under the open sky. He stayed there to enjoy the spectactle of the setting sun, smoking a cigarette. Was Orlando murdered? If so, it was a perfect crime. A suicide never risked stirring up a hornet's nest. Were the two lawyers the killers, or, as it were, the sponsors? One was now dead, the other had fled to the ends of the earth. It would be impossible to discover the truth at this point, unless Rolando Torrigiani decided to confess . . .

His investigation couldn't really go any further, but the upshot of his conclusions was enormous: thanks to this affair, he now knew exactly how to *arrange* things with the lawyer Beccaroni so as not to arouse any suspicion. A little luck would suffice.

Yes, it could work . . . How could he have any doubt? Hadn't it again been fate that had steered him on to the right path? If he hadn't moved out to the country . . . If he had never met that stubborn old contessa . . . If he hadn't played riddles with Botta . . . There were too many coincidences to think that it was mere chance . . .

Getting back down to the first floor was quite a journey. The contessa was waiting for him in the sitting room, calmly sipping tea. There was also a cup there for the guest, with a saucer over it. Bordelli came and sat down across from her in silence, and began to drink his now lukewarm tea. What should he tell the contessa? He'd completed his research; there was nothing left to learn . . . He'd already drawn his conclusions: one could not rule out that Orlando was murdered – indeed, it was quite likely he was. But there was no proof and there probably never would be. Too much time had passed. All one could do was make pointless conjectures . . . Should he tell the poor woman the truth? Or was it better to lie?

'Well, I've done my best, and I've come to the conclusion . . .'

He stopped to reflect a little more, and the contessa leaned forward in her armchair.

'Go on,' she said darkly.

Bordelli sighed. 'Your son took his own life.' He'd decided to lie.

'Oh . . .' she said. She looked lost, and with one hand she seemed to be grasping at something invisible. Fifteen years of hope, swept away by a single statement. But she was a strong woman, steeled by grief, and less than a minute later she seemed already calmer.

'I didn't find anything that might lead one to think otherwise,' Bordelli added.

'Are you absolutely certain?' the contessa asked, without much conviction.

'There is no doubt in my mind.'

What would be the point of telling her that in fact it looked as if . . . The poor woman would have pulled out all the stops to show everyone that she'd been right all along, encouraged by the conclusions of a former police detective. She would have come up against insurmountable obstacles and would have suffered even more by uselessly pursuing her obsession. She would have had no peace . . . It was too late. There was nothing anyone could do any more . . .

But Bordelli also knew he had his own personal reasons for lying . . . He wanted to make sure that no one ever knew the method he would use to kill Beccaroni . . .

He suddenly noticed that the contessa's eyes were glistening with tears, and that her gaze had softened a little . . . The suicide's mother was staring out of the window with an embroidered handkerchief between her fingers and letting the tears stream freely down her face.

'Thank you . . .' she whispered.

'No one can know the reasons behind certain decisions.'

'Don't say anything else, I beg you.'

'I'm sorry.'

'I'll see you to the door,' said the contessa, standing up.

Bordelli sprang to his feet and followed her out of the sitting room, watching those hunched shoulders that had borne years of sorrow. They were already at the door when they heard a sort of animal wail from the far end of a corridor. The contessa stopped to listen. There was no more sound.

'Come with me,' said the lady, and to Bordelli's great surprise, she took him gently by the hand. They stopped outside the door that could not be opened. The contessa slid a tiny window in the door to one side, and gestured to him to come and look. Bordelli went up to the little window and his jaw dropped. On a large bed with rumpled sheets, a human being hiding its face in its hands thrashed weakly, hunching over as though wanting to curl up into a ball. All one could see was a great mass of dark hair, crying sorrowfully.

'That's my daughter Isadora,' said the contessa, with more affection in her voice than he had ever heard before. She opened the door, went inside, and invited him to follow her, indicating there was nothing to fear. She, too, had lied. Orlando was not her only child . . .

A strong smell of urine, stale breath and sweaty skin hung in the air. The contessa sat down on the edge of the bed and started caressing the poor creature's back, little by little succeeding in calming her down. Bordelli stood motionless in the middle of the room and didn't dare say anything.

All at once the creature raised her head . . . She was frightening; her eyes looked like those of an aged little girl. She looked at her mother with a demented expression, grabbing on to her and starting to moan as she rubbed her face against the contessa's belly. Bordelli froze, not knowing what to say, and merely observed the heartbreaking scene, which seemed the very picture of pity.

At last the creature fell asleep, and her breathing grew calm. The contessa delicately eased her head down on to the pillow and pulled a blanket over her. They left the room without a sound. The contessa turned the key in the lock and led Bordelli back to the door.

'Don't tell anyone about Isadora,' she murmured.

Bordelli reassured her with a slight nod. 'My respects, Contessa.'

'Farewell, Inspector . . .'

When he opened his front door he was surprised not to see Blisk there waiting for him and wagging his tail. He went into the kitchen and saw him lying where he'd left him. The dog barely raised his head to greet him, then dropped it back down and fell asleep again.

'You could at least have washed the dishes,' said Bordelli, looking at the encumbered sink.

He calmly set about arranging some logs on top of the balled-up paper between the andirons. His investigation into Orlando's death was over, and he almost missed it already. After lighting the balls of paper, he remained standing in front of the fireplace, watching the flames gain strength. He could still see poor Isadora, and couldn't help but think that the life of the wealthy Contessa Gori Roversi had been one long ordeal . . . *Never call a man lucky until you've seen him dead . . .*

When the wood started to crackle he got down to washing the dishes and thinking about Beccaroni. He now knew how to go about it. He had only to organise the matter and choose the day. He was going to do it, and that was that . . . For young Giacomo raped and murdered, for his parents, and for himself as well . . . It might not be right, but he had to do it.

After washing the last little coffee cup, he prepared the dog's soup, sacrificing half a steak. When he set the bowl down beside him, Blisk opened his eyes, sniffed the air, and stood up with a yawn. He wolfed it all down in mere minutes, then went over to the front door and scratched at it with his paw.

'You don't talk much, but we get your message.'

Bordelli opened the door and went out with the dog. He

watched him saunter over towards the wood and vanish into the darkness. After waiting a few minutes, he whistled to call him back.

'Blisk!'

He kept on whistling for a spell, but there was no sign of the dog. He went back into the house to make supper, leaving the door ajar . . . What if Blisk never came back? Maybe he'd only dropped in on Bordelli to fill up his tummy and get a little rest before setting back out on his way, the way pilgrims used to do. Well, if so, too bad: he'd grown fond of the big white bear.

He opened the gospel according to Botta and started thumbing through it, searching for a simple recipe he could make with what he had at hand. After a great deal of reflection he decided to try *Spaghetti cacio e pepe*, spaghetti with cheese and pepper, a Roman dish. Ennio's directions were quite amusing: *This recipe can be a good solution when you have nothing in the fridge . . . The difficulty is all in the cooking of the pasta. The more complicated recipes have nothing on this one. Remember to set aside a glass of the hot pasta water before draining it (you'll need this later, to fold in the pecorino). If you're unlucky enough to forget this, you might do better to rename the dish 'spaghetti with cement'.*

He smiled as he started cooking with the telly on, distractedly following the news report. Now where had he put that pepper mill he'd just bought? He looked everywhere for it before finding it at the back of the cupboard. While waiting for the pasta to cook, he started looking out the window, elbows propped on the sill. The silhouette of the castle looked blacker than the night, and had the usual lone window shining in the darkness. The cool air wafted lightly into the room, carrying a vague scent of cypress and earth. As his mind wandered down tortuous, useless paths, the heartrending cry of an animal rang out in the silence, a sort of guttural wail that suddenly stopped, followed a second later by the same cry farther away. Then, again the same call and response. He couldn't tell what kind of nightbird it was. An intense, sorrowful dialogue began, and he realised that an animal was approaching very close by . . . Suddenly in the darkness he saw a large roebuck appear and stop about twenty yards from the house. Muzzle raised, it sniffed the air avidly, then gave another cry, eliciting an immediate reply. Nightbird, right . . . He'd had no idea that roebucks made those kinds of calls. After another guttural cry, immediately returned, the majestic lovesick beast dashed gracefully towards the wood, disappearing seconds later into the night. Who knew why it was so thrilling to see a wild animal like that . . . Perhaps it was the sense of freedom it elicited, or maybe it was because it forced one to imagine the mysterious existence of which one had managed to catch a moment's glimpse . . . Like when he saw Eleonora walking through the streets of Florence . . .

'The pasta!' he said out loud, closing the window. He drained it just in time; otherwise it risked coming out soggy . . . This was happening a lot lately. If he wanted to become a good cook, he had to be more careful.

When he sat down at the table, *Carosello* was just starting. It had become his favourite programme. The pasta wasn't bad at all; he had to remember to tell that pessimist Ennio.

The only reason he'd never cooked before was that he hadn't had the time. He'd always known he would be good at it. He was going to make a big impression on his birthday . . . He started laughing. Maybe this pride over his cooking was another sign that he was getting old. Like the desire to have a vegetable garden. But what could he do about it? Time didn't care what anyone thought . . .

He poured himself another glass of wine. At that moment he saw the door open and Blisk appeared, tongue dangling out of his mouth. Maybe he'd been chasing the lovesick buck . . .

'Is this any time to be coming home?' He got up to close the door. The dog looked at him with a perplexed expression, and Bordelli patted his head. Given how big the animal was, and with those teeth, he would frighten anyone, and yet he was gentle as a lamb. Who knew whether goodness and wickedness were innate qualities, or the result of the life one lived . . . It was probably both, maybe even for animals.

He sat back down to finish his pasta, watching the last skit on *Carosello*. Blisk was lying down by the fire, dozing and occasionally watching the flames. He certainly looked as if he felt at home.

Bordelli calmly cleared the table while smoking a cigarette, then went upstairs to get the two war pistols he'd found while moving house. A Beretta and a Guernica, nine-calibre both. He went back into the kitchen, spread some newspaper across the table and laid the two pistols down on it. They both looked in bad shape, but in fact it was nothing serious. He went down to the cellar to get a couple of screwdrivers and a can of gun oil the old owner had left there. Sitting down with a glass of wine beside him, he started dismantling the pistols. He methodically cleaned each part with an oil-soaked rag, rubbing them well. When he put them back together, they were as good as new. He grabbed one after the other, aiming them at the light bulb. He even remembered the sounds they made. The Beretta had a dry sort of cracking report, while the Guernica had a more powerful voice.

He wrapped the pistols in cloth and went and put them in a drawer in his bedroom. He returned to the kitchen with a box of old family photos. After stirring the fire with a poker, he sat down in the armchair and started looking at the photos. They were completely out of order, each image constituting a leap in time, sometimes to eras before his birth . . . His father in his *bersagliere* uniform before leaving to fight the Great War . . . His old aunts from Bologna sitting round a small table, dressed as in a nineteenth-century novel . . . His newborn mother, lying naked on a pillow . . . He himself at twelve, wearing shorts and the usual frown . . .

He continued his long journey through time, smiling and suffering at once, every so often finding in his hand a photograph he knew very well and being carried off to times long gone . . . An excursion to San Gimignano, a summer day on the wooden piers of Marina di Massa, a sad Sunday afternoon after a lunch with relatives . . . Photos were ruthless. They showed moments lost for ever, people long since dead. They were an attempt to cheat death, a painful illusion, and looking at them made one more aware than ever that time was a mystery.

After looking at them all one by one, he closed the box of memories with a sigh. Sitting down in the armchair with a cigarette between his lips, he started watching the fire without really seeing it. Every now and then Blisk would twitch in his sleep, whimpering like a frightened puppy. He was dreaming. Who knew where the big white beast had come from, where he'd lived before, why he'd decided to take to the road . . .

When his head fell to his chest a second time, Bordelli decided it was time to go to bed. He got up, heavy legged, wished the dog a good night with a pat on the head, and went up to his room. He climbed into bed and immediately turned off the light. With his eyes open in the dark, he started moving through the contessa's castle in his mind, opening doors, walking down corridors, going up and down stairs . . . The faraway cry of an owl ushered him into sleep . . .

He awoke with a start, feeling something touch his arm . . . and from the breath he felt on his face he realised it was the dog.

'Blisk . . . You're going to give me a heart attack . . .'

He turned on the light and saw that it was barely seven o'clock. He'd slept well and felt rested. If the weather was nice, he would do well to take advantage of it. It was Monday, the day for walking in the woods, as Ennio always said. Few hunters and no little families in search of adventure. He got up and went into the bathroom, the dog following behind. Looking out the window, he saw a clear sky.

'Today I'm taking you to the forest.'

He got dressed, put on his walking boots and went downstairs to make coffee. There was a pleasant smell of ash in the air. He readied his backpack, putting in some cheese rinds for the dog and a bowl for him to drink from.

When he went out to water the garden, he realised that it had rained during the night and so there was no need. The artichokes were looking good, even though they seemed not to have grown much. The pots where he'd planted the hot peppers still looked like the desert, but the tomato seedlings had finally sprung . . . It almost didn't seem possible.

Continuing his inspection, he tore out a couple of sage plantings that were already rotting. After the toil of farming, he could allow himself a walk. He put Prince Blisk in the Volkswagen and set off up the trail. He felt he needed to put his thoughts in some kind of order, and lately it was only in the woods that he found the serenity necessary to quiet reflection.

'When we start climbing, you'd better not expect me to carry you in my arms . . .' he said to the dog, who was lying in the back seat, taking up the whole space. Who knew whether the animal was capable of anything other than sleeping and eating . . .

They came to La Panca. The white bear got out of the car and started looking around and sniffing the air, then began jumping around as if he'd stuck his muzzle in a puddle of cold water. He ran up the hill, tail wagging, as though forgetting his indolence of the past few days. Bordelli clambered up after him, panting heavily, steam coming out of his mouth. After some twenty minutes of this, drenched in sweat, he got to the top of the hill, where the trail became relatively flat. All around him the expanse of naked, black chestnut trunks reminded him of a war cemetery.

Blisk kept scampering ahead of him, every so often smelling something and charging off through the trees, disappearing at the top of a hill or at the bottom of a steep slope.

Bordelli advanced slowly, with measured steps, contemplating his next move in the chess game he was playing: Beccaroni's suicide. He had to proceed calmly. He would have only one chance; he couldn't afford to fail. It was the only way for justice to be served. Then it would be the turn of monsignor, the most dangerous of all . . . Assuming all went smoothly . . .

He passed under the great boughs of the oak of the mass hanging, scattering the ghosts of war, and soon came to the ancient abbey. As on every other occasion, he thought he would like to live there. He imagined moving about those rooms, walking down the corridors, sitting in the cloister, reading . . . Who knew what sort of atmosphere one breathed behind those walls . . . Sooner or later he would have to work up the nerve to knock on their door and ask whether he could visit.

At the triple fork of the Cappella dei Boschi, he took the path for Pian d'Albero, which by now he knew better than his own garden. Meanwhile he kept thinking . . . Settling accounts with the butcher had been easy, but matters were now getting much more complicated. Was it merely a stupid and dangerous delusion to think he was being guided by fate? He'd never believed in destiny, after all. But now . . .

Blisk appeared on the path, happy as a puppy, but then dashed back down the slope, vanishing behind a big clump of brambles. At once Bordelli heard the devilish grunt of a boar, then the dog barking, then silence again.

'Blisk! . . . Bliiisk! . . .' he shouted, standing at the edge of the path. He called again, but the dog didn't come. Perhaps he'd gone off in pursuit of the boar . . .

Bordelli resumed walking, listening to the sounds of the wood and thinking still of Beccaroni. He had no choice but to take his dare all the way, trusting only in his instincts. He would not go and reconnoitre the lawyer's house, he would not study the man's routine . . . He wouldn't do anything . . . He merely had to choose the day . . . But maybe it was madness . . . Or just bloody stupid . . . But he felt like taking the risk . . . Anyway, all the precautions in the world wouldn't necessarily prevent things from taking a bad turn. He wondered again whether it was destiny or chance that ruled the world . . .

The white bear appeared out of nowhere and came towards him panting, tongue dripping. Bordelli realised the dog had a small red spot on his chest, searched through his fur and found that it was nothing serious. Perhaps the boar had charged him and grazed him with a tusk.

'You did all right . . .' he said, patting his big head. Blisk resumed his running about, but didn't stray as far as before. He seemed a little tired.

When they got to Pian d'Albero, it was a little past eleven o'clock. Too early to eat. He forged on down the trail, and about midday they came to the little cemetery at Ponte agli Stolli, which he'd never been inside. Pushing open the rusty gate, he began strolling through the crosses, reading the inscriptions on the tombstones: *Adalgisa Cencioni, 4 October 1845 – 7 December 1923* . . . He was thirteen and a half when she died . . . *Costante Baciocchi, 22 February 1862 – 24 July 1922* . . . Here was one who knew nothing about the March on Rome . . .[15] *Norina*

*Macelloni, 7 November 1912 – 28 February 1919* . . . Not even seven years, poor thing . . . She'd almost certainly died of the Spanish flu.

At one o'clock, he stopped and sat down on a rock to eat, along the trail that led to Celle. The dog gnawed at the cheese rinds, lying in front of Bordelli. The sun was giving its all, managing to warm the air a little.

After eating his apple, he searched his pocket for a one-hundred-lira piece, just to prod fate one more time. Before flipping it in the air, he established the terms of the wager: heads meant he would take care of Beccaroni on Tuesday, 21 March, the first day of spring; tails meant he would do it one day earlier, on Monday. The coin fluttered in the air and fell into his hand . . . Tails . . .

He'd just finished eating his lunch, watching the last minutes of the midday news broadcast on the National channel as the dog dozed on the floor. The telephone rang and as he went to pick up, he tried as usual to guess who it might be . . .

'Hello?'

'Inspector, this is Ortensia . . .'

'Hello, signora.' She was the last person he was expecting to hear from.

'I'm sorry to bother you . . .'

'Not at all, what can I do for you?'

'I wanted to ask you whether you'd discovered anything new . . . About Orlando, I mean . . .' she said in a hurried whisper.

'I've ended my investigation, and I've concluded that Orlando took his own life,' Bordelli lied, as he'd done with the contessa.

'Oh . . . I'm not sure what I was hoping for . . . I don't even want to think he did it because of me . . . But if Orlando had been murdered, I would never have forgiven myself for not having fully believed him . . . and not having been able to protect him . . .'

'There's nothing anybody could have done, believe me.'

'I confess I keep wondering whether Orlando had another woman, or even more than one . . . It makes me feel silly, but I can't help it . . .' said Ortensia, embarrassed by her own frankness.

Bordelli felt a shudder along his arms, remembering the last words in Orlando's notebook. He thought perhaps he should give Ortensia some true sorrow to cry over, by repeating the last two romantic lines her former lover had dedicated to her the very evening he died . . . *Love, in your eyes my own time/ becomes no time in God's eternity* . . .

After a long, tomb-like silence, Ortensia could no longer suppress a sob, then whimpered something incomprehensible, but clearly the inspector's words had lifted a weight from her heart. She muttered thanks and ended the phone call with a rather dramatic 'Farewell'.

Bordelli stood there for a few seconds with the receiver in his hand, imagining the terrible grief that would torment the poor woman that evening . . . He wasn't making light of her. Memory was a matter in perpetual motion, and transforming the past was always a painful affair. It forced you to level whole mountain chains and rebuild them with the stone of awareness. What would happen to him if he were to discover that the famous Mariella, with whom he'd fallen in love as a boy, to no avail, believing her to be inaccessible, had all along been madly in love with that surly boy who never stopped looking at her? Or if he found out that Anna, or Rosalba, or Matilde, had cheated on him? Or if he discovered that Eleonora . . .

'What do *you* think, Blisk?'

The dog opened one eye without moving and looked at him with what seemed to be compassion. Bordelli shook his head and went and made coffee. He drank it standing up, wanting to go out, into town, to be among people. Ortensia's phone call had made him melancholy.

'Hey, bear, coming with me?'

Blisk didn't move, not even when Bordelli called him again from the doorway.

'As you wish.'

He let the dog stay, and locked the door behind him. Getting into the Beetle, he drove up the rock-strewn path and lit his first cigarette of the day. The sky was a flat grey slate, and a light drizzle fell on the deserted fields.

He drove slowly, blowing his smoke towards the open vent. At the top of the uphill dirt path, he saw a Fiat 500 parked at the side of the road, just outside a nearly concealed shrine between the cypresses that contained a terracotta statuette of the Madonna. Passing by it, he noticed, through the trees, right in front of the shrine, an attractive young woman looking up at the sky, hands joined in prayer and in a position of supplication. Was she praying for help with an exam? For her infirm grandmother? Or was it only a matter of the heart?

'At any rate, I hope the Blessed Virgin answers your prayers,' he said aloud, in a scratchy voice.

Damned cigarettes. Maybe it really was time to put an end to the stupid habit. It would certainly please Piras, who hated smoke as much as old maids hated married women. After three long drags, he threw the butt out the window and made a major decision. From that moment forward, he would try to smoke only five a day, abstaining in the morning and not smoking his first until mid-afternoon . . . Word of honour of a San Marco Battalion commander.

When he got into town he parked in the San Frediano quarter, where he'd lived for almost twenty years. It hadn't rained in Florence, and the clouds seemed to be dispersing. Walking through the narrow streets he stopped every so often to say hello to the shopkeepers and craftsmen who'd managed to reopen their shops after their visit from the Arno, and all of them asked what had become of him . . .

*I've moved to the country*, he replied to them all, and they all reacted the same way . . .

'I can't believe it . . .'

'I'd go to jail first . . .'

'Why go and live up the world's arse?'

'Have you been to see a doctor, Inspector?'

'I'm not an inspector any more . . .'

He found himself outside the bar in Piazza Tasso, where Ennio often went to play billiards. He went in and said hello to Fosco, a colossus who had spent more time at the Murate prison than at home.

'Somethin' to drink, Inspector?'

'No, thanks . . . Seen Ennio around?'

'He normally shows up late in the afternoon, Inspector. For a few rounds of pool.'

'I'll come by again later, Fosco . . . And, by the way, I'm not an inspector any more . . .'

'Then I guess there's a cure for everything,' said the colossus, with a sneer that in his own mind must have passed for a smile.

'Not for bollock-brains, Fosco. You take those with you to the grave,' said Bordelli, waving goodbye and going out.

He crossed the Arno and walked to the posh part of downtown, where the gloomy stone palazzi seemed to absorb the sunlight. The cars and motorbikes rolled through the streets, trailing clouds of bitter smoke behing them. Smartly dressed women, out of the corner of their eyes, checked the effects of their charm on the men passing by . . .

Ever since he'd moved to the country, coming into Florence for a stroll had become almost pleasant. The inner-city confusion was merely a break from routine. His big bed amid the rustic silence remained ever present in his thoughts . . . An empty bed, warmed only by memories . . . All that was missing was a contorted little poem on solitude, written late at night by a dying fire . . .

He walked the streets for a good while, turning round to look at haughty ladies and miniskirted girls alike, and in the end he sat down at Gilli's for a coffee. It might well have been the first time in his life he'd gone into the pricey establishment, but by now he felt like a tourist in the city of his birth.

Through the picture window he distractedly watched the people passing by in unsightly Piazza della Repubblica, which was born of the demolition of one of the poorest, most ancient quarters of Florence. Men sporting ties and carrying briefcases, ladies on their way to spend their husbands' money with the seriousness of ambassadors, young men following pretty girls, mothers holding toddlers' hands, tourists with their noses in the air and wearing a fortune in shoes . . . In a hundred years, all that remained of all the people passing by at that moment would be a pile of bones . . . Same for the children, and even the pretty girls, who added colour to the world . . .

'Franco!'

An attractive woman of about forty had sat down just opposite him. Dark, well dressed, fashionably short-haired, eyes black as coals. It took him a few seconds to recognise her.

'Adele . . .'

'I was just walking by and I saw you here . . . How are you?'

'I can't complain, and you?'

'I'm fine, really . . . But how long has it been? How many years? You haven't changed at all . . .'

'Normally, it's only men who tell those kinds of lies.'

'Thanks a lot! Do you find me aged?'

'I find you beautiful.'

'Now I don't believe you any more,' said Adele, pleased with the compliment.

Bordelli tried to remember . . . When was it? In '50? '51? Adele was the daughter of a carpenter from San Frediano, and she was twenty years younger than him . . . Why was he always falling in love with women so young? He'd taken such a shine to her he couldn't sleep, and when he saw her in the street, he would awkwardly try to get her to see that he . . . But she would slip away like an eel . . .

'You're even more beautiful than before,' said Bordelli, suppressing the desire to take her hand. She truly was beautiful, with luminous eyes full of life.

She looked away for a moment, smiling in embarrassment.

'Enough lies . . .' she said. 'Tell me about yourself . . . What have you been doing all these years? Did you get married? Do you have children?'

'No, unfortunately. No children . . . Whereas I bet you did get married . . .'

'Yes, unfortunately. I thought I'd found the great love of my life, but then after three children he ran off with a twenty-year-old slut . . . I'm sorry, I said a bad word . . .'

'Unforgivable . . .'

'At any rate, it's water under the bridge. At least the bastard left me the house and slips me a lot of money for the kids,' said Adele, smiling.

'So he's not such a monster . . .'

'Of course not! I'd run away with a twenty-year-old, too!' Adele said, laughing.

'You could have stabbed me instead,' said Bordelli, feigning offence. 'That would have hurt less.'

She laughed.

'Oh, go on . . .'

'Women are cruel.'

He also laughed. Meanwhile he thought of the one time he'd succeeded in inviting Adele to dinner, taking her to a fine restaurant in Fiesole, a century ago. She'd lied to her parents, making up some story about going to study at a girlfriend's house. She let him woo her all evening, but managed to keep her distance. Nothing happened, not even a kiss. So why did he now feel as if he was looking at a former girlfriend?

'So, are you with anyone now?' Adele asked out of the blue.

'Not at the moment.'

'Sometimes it's nice just to be alone . . .'

'Can I invite you to dinner, one of these evenings?' Bordelli asked, point blank, trying to smile to mask his desire to see her again.

'Absolutely,' she said, pleased.

'What about your kids?'

'I'll leave them with my mother, which is where they are now. Every now and then I need to be alone . . . But I have to go now, unfortunately.'

She stood up, and Bordelli shot to his feet.

'How will I find you?'

'In the phone book . . . Goffredo Bini . . . That's my husband's name.'

'What time of day can I call?'

'Whenever you like, but you'll be sure to find me at lunchtime.'

'All right . . .'

'Don't keep me waiting,' said Adele, without insinuation, and a moment later she vanished into a cloud of smoke.

Bordelli sat back down, feeling a little numb. He'd had a terrible crush on her, and seeing her again had the same effect as a punch in the face . . . Was she perhaps the woman who would . . . ? He remembered the words of Amelia, Rosa's fortune-teller friend who had read his tarot. After informing him of a forthcoming love affair with *a beautiful, dark young woman* – that was Eleonora – which would end quickly and badly, as indeed happened, she'd made a final prediction: *In a few years . . . A beautiful woman, a foreigner . . . very rich . . . divorced . . . with two children* . . . Could it be Adele? She didn't really correspond in full with the prediction of the cards, though. She was beautiful, separated from her husband . . . But she had three children, was probably not very rich and, most of all, she wasn't foreign. Maybe even the tarot got a few things wrong every now and then . . .

These thoughts made him feel almost guilty about Eleonora, which meant that Adele had made her mark. He paid for his coffee and headed back towards San Frediano, still thinking about his old flame. He couldn't get her out of his head.

Late that afternoon he went into the bar in Piazza Tasso, exchanged a nod of greeting with Fosco and slipped into the billiards room. Botta had his back to him and was challenging some skinny kid with a pimply face to a round. Six or seven people watched the match, commenting on the contestants' shots. Bordelli kept his distance, to avoid ruining the players' concentration. As soon as Ennio noticed him he came forward.

'Inspector, I was looking for you myself . . .'

If this had happened in any other neighbourhood, the room would have fallen silent at the sound of the word 'inspector'. But everyone in San Frediano knew him and greeted him without any worry. Only the pimply lad didn't know who he was and looked around in surprise.

'Can I get you a drink, Ennio?'

'Give me just one minute, I need to finish teaching this poor kid a lesson, then I'm all yours,' Botta said loudly.

The carbuncular lad gave him a dirty look, ignoring the laughter of everyone present. Ennio made good on his promise. He won the game in little time and pocketed the money, giving the loser a pat on the back.

'You humiliated him,' said Bordelli, sitting down at the same bench as Botta.

'In my own way I'm actually teaching him about life's adversities . . .'

'Could we have a couple of reds, Fosco?'

The ex-con grabbed the neck of a flask and filled two glasses to the brim. Ennio waited for the barman to walk away.

'It's all set, Inspector . . .' he whispered, more conspiratorial than ever.

'Milan?'

'Shhh . . . Speak softly . . . Nobody must know . . . It's all set for Thursday, midnight . . .'

'At what time do we leave?' asked Bordelli, eliminating that Thursday in his mind from the possible days for inviting Adele to dinner.

'I'd say mid-afternoon . . . Better not take any chances . . .'

'Whatever you say. You're the gang leader,' Bordelli said smiling. He would never have imagined himself in this sort of situation, but he'd given his word and wouldn't back out.

'Shall we go in your car, or do I need to look for one?'

'Don't look for anything,' said Bordelli, who already had an idea of how to make their journey worry-free.

'Thanks, Inspector. With this job, you'll change the life of the great Ennio Bottarini,' said Ennio, hiding his sincere emotion with irony.

'I'm hoping with all my heart . . .'

'You shouldn't hope: you must believe.'

'We mustn't underestimate the obstacles.'

'There won't be any,' said Botta, clinking his glass against Bordelli's.

'I need to ask you for a favour myself,' said Bordelli, thinking of his appointment with destiny on Monday.

'Whatever you want, Inspector.'

'Do you think you could look after my dog for a couple of days, maybe even three?'

'When?'

'Next Monday.'

'No problem . . .'

'Thanks. I'll leave you a set of keys,' said Bordelli, searching in his pocket.

'I don't need any, you ought to know that by now.'

'Ah, I forgot . . .'

'A romantic tryst, Inspector?' asked Botta, winking.

'Unfortunately not.'

'Then where are you going? Can you say?'

'Maybe one day I'll tell you.'

'As you wish. But for a peasant, you certainly are mysterious,' said Botta, who was as nosy as a concierge.

'All in due time, as my grandfather used to say.'

'I always give in to grandfathers . . . Another round?'

'Why not?'

They drank another glass of red, discussing the final details of their trip to Milan. They arranged to meet on Thursday, outside Fosco's bar, and after a meaningful handshake, Bordelli left.

The moment he turned the Beetle on to the Imprunetana, the city already seemed far away. He thought about Botta's Milanese job while smoking a cigarette. Fake money in exchange for a small percentage in real money. And if all went well . . . But this was no time for worrying . . .

He could hardly wait to light the fire and eat a dish of pasta in front of the telly. After dinner he would read a few pages, reclining in the armchair . . . A late-night excursion into the surroundings with Blisk, and then beddy-bye. He could invite Adele for Friday night . . . or maybe Saturday . . .

After lunch he went out on foot with the dog, not bringing his cigarettes, and they climbed up the dirt road. He wanted to go as far as the contessa's castle. The previous night, for the first time, he hadn't seen the window under the tower lit up. He was simply curious to know whether anything had happened. Blisk scampered off ahead, stopping every so often to wait for him.

It took him over half an hour to reach the castle. The Mercedes wasn't there, and the shutters were all bolted tight. He pulled the doorbell ring, but nobody came to the door. Could the contessa have gone away?

On his way back to the house he ran into one of the old peasants who worked on the castle farm, and asked him about the contessa.

'Cut and run, she did . . .' said the old man, bobbing his head.

'Oh, so she left?'

'Her car was stuffed to the gills, even on top.'

'Know where she went?'

'She said down to Puglia. 'Parently she's got a castle down there twice the size o' this one.'

'And she's not coming back?'

'Ah, I really can't say, sir . . . It's not as though she comes and tells me things . . .'

The peasant shrugged his shoulders and continued on his way. Bordelli resumed his descent down the trail, with the dog now trotting beside him. So the contessa had gone away, left for Puglia immediately after 'learning' that her son had not been murdered. It could hardly have been a coincidence.

When he came to the crossroads, instead of going home he

took the road leading into town. Past the football field he took a small, steep track that led to the cemetery of the Sante Marie, without slowing his pace. He was out of breath when he got to the top.

'You wait for me here . . .' he said to the dog, and he ducked into the cemetery, closing the little gate behind him. He started walking through the alleys of graves until he found Orlando's. There was a small, glass-encased oval photo of him on the tombstone. A dark-haired lad, good looking, with the troubled gaze of a *poète maudit*. He looked like neither a count nor a lawyer. Just a lad. Under the portrait, inscribed in the marble, were only two words: *My son.*

Coming out of the cemetery, he began the descent with Blisk at his side, trying to imagine the kind of words he would like on his own gravestone. Surely nothing like: *Here lies . . .* Nor: *He devoted his life to . . .* Perhaps something silly, like: *Who would have thought . . .* Or: *Who have we here?* . . . Or even: *I wish I could have stayed . . .*

He'd always been thinking of death, every second of his life, ever since he was a little boy. He'd always been trying to imagine the nothingness that follows death . . . Was it a conscious nothingness or an absolute nothingness? He wished he could meet a ghost, so he could chat and ask some questions. He remembered something that had happened to him some ten years earlier . . .

*One morning the wife of Gilberto, a good friend of his, called him on the phone. Gilberto had been very sick and bedridden for months at home, awaiting death.*

*'Franco, you must come at once . . . Gilberto wants to see you . . .'*

*She sounded upset.*

*'Has something happened?'*

*'He just said he wants to see you at once.'*

*'I'm on my way . . .'*

*He got into his car and drove across the city. When he entered his friend's room, he found him sitting up in the middle of the bed, looking dazed but serene. His wife had left the room at Gilberto's request.*

*'I have to tell you something, Franco.'*

*'I'm listening . . .'*

*He'd remained standing at the foot of the bed, trying to imagine what might have happened. Gilberto waited for a few moments before speaking . . .*

*'I'm dead,' he said in the most natural way imaginable.*

*'What's that?'*

*'I'm dead . . . Look here, read this . . .' He handed him the doctor's certificate, which declared him deceased.*

*'I don't understand . . .'*

*'The doctor left here an hour ago, and he thinks I'm dead . . . And he's right, actually . . . I really did die . . .'*

*'Please, Gilberto . . .'*

*'You've got to believe me . . . I died, and I came back . . . I saw a blinding, amazing light . . . I knew I was dead . . . I have no doubt whatsoever . . . I was happy . . . And now that I know what awaits me, I'm no longer the least bit afraid . . . I'm going to die soon, I know that . . . Maybe even in the next half-hour . . . But I'm no longer afraid . . . Actually now I can't wait to get to the other side . . . I wanted to tell you this . . . I wanted to tell someone, and I thought of you . . .'*

*Gilberto died that night, once and for all. During the funeral mass Bordelli couldn't stop thinking of his round-trip journey to the beyond, trying to imagine it. Could it really be true? What if it was only . . .*

*The coffin was lowered into the grave and covered with earth, as friends and family looked on. Before leaving, Bordelli approached the priest, Don Serafino, and took him aside to tell him about Gilberto's brief excursion in the afterlife. The priest grabbed his wrist.*

*'Did he really say that? It gives one hope . . .'*

*'But don't priests already have faith?'*

*'One never knows . . .' said Don Serafino, shrugging.*

As Bordelli was cooking, Blisk got up and went over to the door, looking defensive, as if he'd just smelled an animal.

'What is it?'

Seconds later, he heard the sound of a car pulling up on the threshing floor.

'Calm down, it's a friend.'

He went and opened the door for Piras. When the Sardinian saw the dog, he stopped short.

'Who's that?'

'That's Blisk.'

'Does he bite?'

'I haven't known him for very long, but so far he hasn't killed anyone,' said Bordelli.

Piras entered the house apprehensively, holding a bottle of wine by the neck. The dog sniffed him long and carefully, then returned to his corner and lay back down.

'Couldn't you have picked a smaller dog?'

'I didn't pick him; fate did . . . Put another log on the fire, would you?'

Bordelli filled two glasses with wine and continued cooking, following the instructions for pork chops '*my way*' in the gospel according to Ennio . . . : *Now you can take the griddle off the fire, but you must follow one last rule: before bringing the chops to the table, you must cover them with a lid and wait for a couple of minutes, even three . . . You may not believe it, Inspector, but there's one hell of a difference . . .*

During the meal Bordelli asked Piras to tell him in detail about the bloke who got zapped in his bathtub, even though

173

he'd read about it in the paper. The Sardinian didn't really want to talk about it, but at Bordelli's insistence he finally gave in. As soon as he'd entered the bathroom where the corpse was, he'd noticed a horizontal mark on the wall to the right of the sink, a sign typical of a table left in the same place for years. But now the table was mysteriously on the left-hand side, and this detail explained why the electric shaver had fallen straight into the tub. He'd spoken about it with Anselmi, who'd said he was right. The following day the widow was called in for questioning. He and the inspector had conducted the sensitive yet intensive interrogation together, until the woman finally broke down and confessed. She had a lover and didn't have a cent to her name, and so she'd hoped to inherit from her wealthy husband . . .

'As old as the hills, Inspector . . .' Piras concluded.

By now Bordelli had stopped reminding people that he *wasn't an inspector any more*. It was useless.

'I need to ask a favour of you, Piras,' he said out of the blue.

'Go ahead . . .'

'I want you to bring me a squad car tomorrow.'

'What do you need it for?' asked the Sardinian, shocked.

'Don't ask.'

'All right, Inspector. I'm sure it's for a good deed.'

'Thanks for trusting me.'

'I imagine nobody must know . . .'

'Precisely.'

'I'll try and pull the wool over the mechanic's eyes. What time do you want it?'

'After lunch would be fine. And I'll leave you the Beetle, of course.'

'How long do you need it for?'

'Just one night. You'll have to come up here and get it the next morning . . . Oh, and don't forget that on the second of April you're coming here to dinner. It's my birthday.'

'Okay, thanks, Inspector.'

'It'll be a dinner among men, my apologies to Sonia.'

'Don't worry about that. Lately she's only got time for her studies.'

'Give her a kiss for me. You should come here together some time, perhaps on a Sunday. I'll take you walking through the woods, and then we'll eat some nice grilled steak . . .'

'It's not easy for me to see you retired, Inspector.'

'It's not easy for me, either, Pietrino . . . But what can you do?'

'You haven't told me anything else about the contessa . . .'

'There isn't much to tell. I didn't find anything that pointed to a murder.'

'But I bet you enjoyed investigating just the same,' said Piras, and Bordelli smiled.

After dinner they sat in the armchairs beside the fire, glasses in hand, as the white bear kept sleeping. The flames lovingly enveloped the logs, making them pop every so often.

'Maybe you're right, Piras. I miss my work.'

'Then why did you quit?' asked the Sardinian. It was the first time he'd asked, and you could see in his eyes that he was dying to find out. Bordelli took a sip of wine. He'd decided reluctantly to forgo a cigarette, so as not to offend Piras's olfactory organs.

'When a general loses a crucial war, it's time to retire.'

'Giacomo Pellissari?'

'Right . . .'

'We know who the killers are, Inspector.'

'But we can't do anything . . .'

'Except hope they kill themselves one by one, tormented by their guilt,' Piras said suggestively.

'I see no other solution.' Bordelli smiled. He wished he could tell Piras the way things really were, but it wasn't time yet. First he had to *take care of business*, alone. He wanted to be the only one to risk his neck . . .

'So the next to commit suicide will be the lawyer Beccaroni?'

Piras was no longer merely making suggestions; he already seemed to know everything. Bordelli had always thought the kid was someone with his eyes wide open. He would go far in law enforcement.

'The ways of the Lord are infinite . . .' said Bordelli, certain that Piras would understand.

'Well, if you need me, I'm with you,' the Sardinian declared, and it was clear he wasn't joking.

'At the moment I don't.'

'As you wish, Inspector.'

'So how's your dad doing? When's he coming?' asked Bordelli, to change the subject.

'He's not coming any more.'

'Why not?'

'He said he has to look after his field . . .'

'Leave me his number. One of these days I'll give him a ring.'

After topping up the petrol tank, at one minute to five he pulled up outside Fosco's bar in an Alfa Romeo Giulia of the police, to the curious and suspicious stares of the locals. In case of need, he'd brought along one of his pistols, the Beretta, carrying it in a holster under his armpit. This was unusual for him. When on duty he almost always left his gun in a drawer in his office.

At five o'clock sharp Ennio came out of the bar holding a leather bag, and upon seeing the squad car, he stopped dead in his tracks. Bordelli tooted the horn to alert him that he was inside . . . Botta ran a hand over his face to recover from the fright.

'You gave me such a scare, Inspector,' he said, opening the car door.

'Apparently you have a guilty conscience . . . Come on, get in.'

'I must admit, however: you're a genius.'

Ennio got into the car and put the bag between his feet, as though afraid someone might steal it.

'This way no one will bother us,' said Bordelli, driving off.

'It's the first time I've ever ridden in one of these as a free citizen,' said Ennio, pleased with his quip.

They went as far as the Certosa and then took the Autostrada del Sole, under a dark sky that threatened rain. The Alfa was a souped-up model and chewed up the miles without effort.

They crossed the Apennine chain, speeding past dozens of lorries struggling up the inclines, and talking of women and swindles, politics and cookery . . . And naturally they ended up talking about the recipes Bordelli was considering for his birthday party. Ennio's scepticism was downright obnoxious. He kept advising the novice cook to stick to simple dishes, whereas Bordelli wanted to throw himself into elaborate preparations . . .

'The menu's already been decided . . . *Crostini di fegatini, Zuppa lombarda, Peposo all fornacina, "Conigliolo" alla Tex*, and an apple tart to finish . . . What do you think?'

'Listen to me, Inspector . . . A nice little pasta in tomato sauce and you'll do fine . . . I say that also for my own sake, since I'll be there, too . . .'

'Have faith, Ennio, it'll be an unforgettable meal . . . If I'm able to host it.'

'What do you mean?'

'Tonight we may both end up in jail,' said Bordelli, looking down at the bag with the counterfeit money in it.

'Don't say that even in jest, Inspector. Everything will go just fine, and for your birthday I'll bring you a case of champagne.'

'I can't imagine you rich, Ennio . . . What will you do with all that money?'

'I've already told you. I'm going to open a trattoria.'

'I can't imagine you all day in the kitchen, either.'

'Why not?'

'You're accustomed to a life of adventure and risk . . . It's not that easy to give up certain thrills . . .' said Bordelli, thinking also of himself.

'Well, I'm going to give it a go. If I don't succeed, I'll sell everything and spend the money on cars and women.'

'Brilliant. That way you'll spend it all and have to abandon the straight and narrow path yet again.'

'You're just like my grandmother, Inspector . . . Regardless of the situation, she would run through all the possible ways it could go wrong, and obviously every so often she was right on the money.'

'I'm only trying to review all the possibilities.'

'Only the bad ones, if you ask me.'

'It must be a bad habit of mine . . .'

'Things don't always go bad, Inspector. There are, sometimes, pleasant surprises.'

'Amen . . .'

Along the straight road that stretched across the cultivated plains after Bologna, each drifted off into his own thoughts. Early that morning Bordelli had phoned Gavino Piras, and after some emotional greetings they started reminiscing about the war, the real war, the one after 8 September.[16] The call was cut off several times, but the thread of memory remained intact . . . Comrades blown up by mines, fierce battles with the Germans, the bombing of Cassino . . . They hadn't seen each other since May of '45, so it was inevitable they would end up talking about the war. In spite of everything, they felt a twinge of nostalgia for those years, and not only because they weren't young any more. Extreme situations always leave their mark. It was good that it had all come to an end, but it was also good to remember that they had experienced certain things . . .

At around lunchtime he'd phoned Adele, and she was happy to hear from him. He invited her to dinner on Friday. Adele had joked about it being a Friday the seventeenth,[17] to which Bordelli had replied that the number had always brought him good luck. They decided to meet at eight o'clock, outside her block of flats in Viale Don Minzoni. What would happen? He couldn't imagine, but whenever he thought of Eleonora he felt the same emotions he always had . . . And above all he continued to feel guilty, as if he were somehow cheating on her . . . But why? They certainly weren't together any more. Other questions naturally arose . . . Was Eleonora with someone? Was she in love? Had she forgotten him, or did she still think of him? What if he paid her a call? She might just slam the door in his face . . . Or, worse yet, she might stroke his cheek and wish him a good life . . .

'Twenty miles to go,' said Botta, shaking Bordelli out of the skein of thoughts he'd become entangled in.

'We've got all the time we need to go and have dinner.'

'It's better if we go first and locate the place where we have our appointment, and then we can go and eat,' said Ennio, who was starting to feel nervous.

'How much money is in the bag?'

'Sixty million lire,' Botta whispered, as if somebody might hear him.

'Not bad . . .' said Bordelli.

In exchange, Botta would receive twenty per cent in real cash. Twelve million.[18] A fortune, especially for someone like him. He'd been working on this deal for months, and said he'd worked it out down to the finest details . . . But sometimes the best-laid plans . . .

'*O mia bela Madunina, fai che vada tutto bene,*'[19] Ennio chanted, with hands folded in prayer.

'Have I sparked a little pessimism in your heart, Ennio?'

'No, it's just that one never knows.'

'If anyone had ever told me that one day I'd be doing this kind of thing . . .'

'You're just lending a friend a hand,' Ennio minimised.

'Try saying that to a prosecutor . . .' said Bordelli, while thinking that Botta really did deserve to have at last a little money in his pocket. A few extra counterfeit bills certainly wouldn't bankrupt Italy, and justice would be served, if not in the most orthodox of fashions . . . An eternal pauper would become rich . . . Perhaps . . .

They got to Milan just before nine o'clock, and following the directions that Botta had written down on a piece of paper they managed to find the right address. An ugly building, on an ugly street in an ugly area. The real Milan was far away.

Now that they knew where they were to meet, they could go and have dinner. They went towards the centre of town and ducked into a fancy restaurant. Botta kept his leather bag between his legs, eyeing other customers for potential threats. But there were only bald *commendatori* with their mistresses and young couples gazing into each other's eyes.

'Shall we dine *alla milanese*, Inspector?'

'Whatever you prefer.'

'Tonight it's on me . . .'

'You have every right.'

'But you'll have to front me the cash . . . I'll give it back soon . . .'

'What about the money from your last scam? The phony Guttuso . . . Have you already spent it all?'

'No . . . I mean . . . I lent some to a friend . . . And he hasn't paid me back yet,' Botta said to justify himself.

'You may never see it again.'

'I should do like my grandad used to do. Whenever anyone asked him to lend them money, he'd say: *I won't do it, you're too good a friend . . .*'

'They should write a book of sayings by grandads . . .'

'Today's kids don't give a damn about their grandparents. They just want a Vespa under their bums, a pretty girl and a bit of music . . .'

'You think there's something wrong with that?'

'And beware of ever talking about the war with those airheads . . . *What a bloody bore,* they'll say, *you and your war! That was a hundred years ago . . .* They just want to have fun.'

'Deep down I understand them. Why should they bear the burden of the war if they didn't live through it themselves? It's good for them to feel light hearted . . .'

'I really can't agree, Inspector. Those kids can afford to have fun because somebody died for them . . . That, at least, they should never forget . . .' said Ennio, signalling to the waiter.

It was already half past ten. They ordered saffron rice, Milanese cutlets, fried potatoes and a bottle of Barolo. Ennio was nervous, though he tried not to let it show. He ate as though forcing himself, but left almost everything on his plate, excusing himself to the waiter. Bordelli's plate, on the other hand, had been thoroughly cleaned. The bottle they'd split evenly, each drinking half, and Botta's eyes were glazed.

After coffee, Bordelli paid the bill, as Ennio kept mumbling about how he would pay him back *very soon*. They got into the Alfa, and without a word they headed back to the area of the meeting. They left the squad car on a side street about a block away and continued on foot. The neighbourhood was poorly lit, and from the closed windows the sound of televisions came in waves. Ennio was carrying his bag slung over his shoulder, keeping it close to him with one arm. They were early, and they could take their time. Every so often they saw another person on the pavement, and Botta would mutter something between his teeth.

When they stopped outside the appointed door, it was three minutes to midnight. They found the right buzzer, and before ringing, Botta raised one hand.

'It's better if I go alone . . .'

'I didn't come two hundred miles just to wait here outside, Ennio.'

'I don't want to get you into trouble.'

'I'm already in trouble, as far as that goes . . . Don't you think?'

'We'd said only the journey . . .'

'If you're going to do someone a favour, you must do it all the way,' said Bordelli, opening his jacket to show him his handgun.

'Good God, I hope there's no need of that!'

'Go on, ring the bell.'

'They'll think we're Swiss,' said Botta, looking at his watch. When he pushed the buzzer it was twelve o'clock sharp. Seconds later the electrical lock clicked open, and they slipped into the building.

'What floor?' Bordelli whispered, as they began to climb the stairs.

'Third.'

'Can these guys be trusted or might they try to get cute?'

'Well, we're not exactly on a pilgrimage to a Carmelite shrine . . .'

'Whatever happens, try to stay calm.'

'I'm perfectly calm . . . I just feel a little like throwing up.'

'It'll pass.'

'Of course.'

'I just hope my policing instincts don't get the better of me and I end up arresting the lot of you.'

'Please, Inspector . . .'

'Come on, I was just kidding.'

'Here we are.'

On the third-floor landing there was a door ajar, and one

could see an eye in the crack. As soon as they approached, the door opened, and a shabbily dressed-up, pudgy man with a cheerful face appeared. The exact opposite of the sort of person they were expecting.

'Follow me,' said the man, in a strong southern accent. Sicilian? Calabrian? His self-assured air made clear that it didn't even enter his mind that he might be cheated, or than anyone would be crazy enough to try. He didn't even need a bodyguard. He led them down a smelly corridor, unconcerned about turning his back on the two strangers. They entered a room with only a table and four half-broken chairs.

It was the simplest exchange in the history of the world. In total silence Botta laid the leather bag on the table, the guy took the counterfeit notes out of it, and after checking the quality of the manufacture, he counted the sixty stacks of one million each. Nodding with satisfaction, he looked the two Florentines in the eye, and with a half-smile he left the room. He returned moments later with a packet of paper bundled with string, opened it and put the money on the table. Ennio pulled out two or three notes at random and with hands trembling held them up against the light. He exchanged a glance with Bordelli, to let him know everything was all right, then counted the twelve stacks and put them in the bag.

'We've never met,' the man said, showing them out and bidding them farewell with a nod in the doorway. As soon as the Florentines headed down the stairs, the door reclosed without a sound. Botta could hardly contain himself.

'I can't believe it . . .' he kept muttering, clutching the bag to his chest.

'Now comes the hardest part,' said Bordelli.

'What do you mean?'

'Maybe we'll find two gorillas waiting for us outside the door, who'll politely ask us to give the money back.'

'Nobody's going to take this bag from me,' said Ennio, ready for anything.

'Well, if anything happens, leave it to me,' said Bordelli,

taking the pistol from its holster and putting it in his jacket pocket, without letting go of it. Before leaving the building, they opened the front door a crack to check the street in front. There wasn't a soul about. In the distance they could hear a baby crying.

'Let's go . . .'

'The car's this way, right?' asked Ennio, tenser than ever.

'I think so . . .' Bordelli joked, just to rib him. They walked briskly, and a few minutes later they sighted the Alfa at the end of the street. It seemed very far away.

'We'll be home by four,' said Ennio, short of breath.

'We can have another coffee on the motorway,' Bordelli whispered, putting the pistol back in its holster. When they were about twenty yards from their Alfa, a Milan Police Fiat started approaching at a walking pace . . .

'Fuck . . .' said Botta.

'Just stay calm.'

When the Fiat pulled up beside them, Bordelli was inserting the key into the door of the Alfa. He gave an almost imperceptible nod of acknowledgement, and after exchanging a military salute, the two police officers drove away.

'Jesus Christ . . .' said Botta, collapsing into the passenger seat. Bordelli started up the car and calmly drove off.

'All thanks to the Alfa.'

'I'd marry this Alfa if I could . . .'

'At any rate, I'm going to have to get used to the idea that you're rich now, Ennio.'

'I've never seen that much money all at once, for Chrissakes!'

'You'll have to build up resistance.'

'I still can't believe it . . . And if you hadn't been there . . . Man, I'm still sweating . . .' said Botta, wiping his brow with his hand.

'We were lucky.'

A miracle seemed to have occurred: a poor man had got rich. It didn't matter how – it was still good news . . .

'Inspector, you deserve a cut,' said Ennio and, opening the

bag, he pulled out a stack worth a million lire and set it down on Bordelli's lap.

'Don't push it, Ennio. I'm still trying to digest the fact that I was your accomplice.'

'But you earned it . . .'

'Put this stuff away or I'll arrest you,' said Bordelli, giving him back the money.

'Take ten thousand lire at least, for the petrol and the dinner.'

'Just so you won't be offended.'

'Here you go . . .' said Botta, handing him a note. Bordelli put it in his pocket, knowing he would never spend it. He wanted to keep it as a souvenir and write the date on it.

'So what'll you do now?'

'What do you mean?'

'You can't very well go to a bank with twelve million lire in a bag and say you want to open an account, with the kind of record you've got.'

'That's not a problem. I've already worked it all out,' said Ennio, with a particularly criminal smile.

'Oh yeah? And how's that?'

'The daughter of a close friend of mine has married a bloke who works in a bank.'

'So you've taken care of everything . . .'

'Isn't that what I said?'

'If you ask me, the first thing you'll do is buy a Porsche.'

'I know what I'm doing, Inspector.'

They turned on to the autostrada and Bordelli stepped on the gas. At that hour there were mostly long queues of lorries on the road, and luckily it wasn't raining. Ennio kept muttering to himself, eyes beaming for joy. He simply couldn't believe that it had all gone well. It wasn't just a question of filthy lucre; it felt more like a genuine victory over life. Bordelli listened to him distractedly, thoughts turning every so often to his dinner with Adele . . .

When he opened his eyes the following morning he remembered what he'd done the night before. He could hardly believe it. His ears were ringing. He'd driven four hundred miles in just a few hours, and when he finally got under the covers it was past 4 a.m. It had all been very easy. A walk in the park . . . But what if something had gone wrong? He could imagine the notices for *La Nazione*:

### FORMER POLICE INSPECTOR ARRESTED
#### ESCORTED COUNTERFEITER TO MILAN
#### IN FLORENTINE SQUAD CAR

He'd done it for a friend, of course, to minimise the risks, to keep a dream from dying . . . Very touching, but between tears the judge would have sentenced him to ten years. Who knew what Diotivede would have said, had he known . . . Rosa would probably have got a chuckle out if it, but what about Adele? Or Eleonora? It was best to stop thinking about it. In fact, that night never happened . . .

It was almost eleven o'clock. He'd closed his bedroom door to avoid getting woken up by Blisk at seven. A greyish light filtered through the shutters, and he realised the sky was overcast. He wondered whether Ennio would change, now that he had all that money . . . Would he lose his head and squander everything in a short time? Or would he squirrel it away? Bordelli got out of bed, and when he opened his bedroom door he found the dog lying on the floor outside it.

'If anybody asks, I did not leave the house last night . . . Don't forget . . .'

He remembered the ten-thousand-lira note he had in his pocket. Taking it out, he wrote the date on it, *16/03/1967*, and put it in the drawer of his nightstand. For the ages . . .

He went into the kitchen to make coffee and, looking out of the window, was pleased to see that Piras had already come and exchanged the cars. In the place of the Alfa squad car was his Volkswagen Beetle. Everything was back to normal. With just a little effort, the memory of that night would become pure fantasy. He'd never gone to Milan, he hadn't taken part in the trade-off, it was all just a dream . . . Then he smiled to himself . . . He was worried about a few counterfeit banknotes, when he himself . . .

He drank down a whole cup of coffee in a single gulp. After a long hot shower he went out the back door to water the garden and found a surprise: a number of small vases with herbs in them were lined up along the wall. He'd forgotten all about them, but Ennio, as usual, had kept his word. He went and smelled them one by one, tearing off some little leaves and rubbing them under his nose. He couldn't wait to try them. A true cook couldn't do without such things.

Entering the vegetable garden, he noticed that the tomato seedlings had grown another good bit, pointing proudly skywards. The chilli peppers, however, hadn't come up yet, but according to Ennio there was nothing to worry about; sometimes they took three weeks to appear.

The dog hung around outside the fence, head down. He seemed almost offended that Bordelli wouldn't let him inside, and every now and then he scratched at the wire fencing with his paw. Bordelli continued watering, thinking that in just a few hours he would be dining with Adele . . . But he was also thinking about Eleonora . . . The whole business was getting very complicated in his head . . .

He tried to imagine what he would do if Eleonora phoned to invite him to dinner that same evening. Would he accept?

Would he make up an excuse to cancel his date with Adele? Or would he tell Eleonora he already had an engagement? If Aladdin's genie appeared before him, he would ask it to make a double of him, so he could dine with both women at once . . .

He laughed to himself, but not without a twinge of bitterness. He was fantasising uncontrollably, chasing daydreams just for pleasure, so he could feel like an interesting person . . . Not only would Eleonora not seek him out, but Adele probably wanted nothing more than to spend a pleasant evening with an old friend . . . But it was nice to dream just the same; it was good for one's health . . . And so he continued to do so . . .

The morning went by quickly. After lunch he went out for a short walk with the dog, to digest. After many days of sun, the sky now looked like a dirty mattress. But it didn't feel like rain.

His mood kept changing. It swung from melancholy to sudden bursts of adolescent euphoria, from indifference towards everything to a kind of ill-defined hope. It must be spring. He went into the woods, following Blisk's wanderings through the trees. When he was a little boy, there were moments in spring-time when voices took on a sort of echoing sound, as when one breathes very deeply, and he would get these sorts of shudders in his belly. The new, late-March light would put him in a state of exhilaration that he couldn't understand. Adolescence was a difficult, painful time for him, his first frightened plunge into solitude. He discovered his own uniqueness and aloneness, and while this condition would later become a strong point, at that moment it only made him feel lost . . . Why was he thinking about these things? Perhaps because he felt now the way he did then? Unable to steer the ship?

He was back at home by mid-afternoon, and making an effort of will he decided to repair one shutter that didn't close properly. Blisk followed his labours with a questioning air. It took him little more than half an hour, and gave him great satisfaction. Living in the country also meant knowing how to use one's hands. As his father would have said, he'd just now saved the two or three thousand lire he would have paid to the carpenter . . .

He lit a fire and sat down in the armchair with a book in his hand. It was now Bulgakov's turn. He enjoyed reading more and more, perhaps because he had more time now. Since finishing *Notes from the Underground* he hadn't felt like the same person. Though he couldn't exactly say how or why, his view of things had changed. Sensation was more pleasurable. Nothing kept still for ever; change always lurked round the corner . . . After a while he realised he was counting the minutes till his dinner with Adele . . . Was Adele also a *change*? Was he going out to meet his destiny that evening? He kept thinking about Eleonora as well, remembering the best moments he'd spent with her . . . And in spite of everything he kept right on reading, getting lost in the story, experiencing the characters' feelings from within his own skin . . .

'Were you really so in love with me?' Adele asked with a hint of a smile, as Bordelli poured her a third glass of wine. They'd opted for a small restaurant on a narrow street in the centre of town and were lucky to grab the last available table. Fortunately no one was talking too loudly, and the general buzz merely lent their conversation a more intimate tone.

'Are you asking just to make sport of me, as you did then?' asked Bordelli.

'I never laughed at you.'

'Your nose just grew longer . . .'

'You want to know the truth?' said Adele, feeling a little euphoric from the wine.

'I'm ready.'

'You scared me . . .'

'Scared you?'

'I was almost twenty years old, but I was still a little girl . . . I didn't . . . Actually, I . . . I hadn't yet had sex with anyone.'

'Ah . . .' said Bordelli, feeling embarrassed.

'What's wrong?'

'I'm sorry, I wasn't expecting such frankness.'

'What's wrong with that?'

'Nothing. On the contrary . . .' He didn't have the courage to tell her he felt slightly shocked.

'So, anyway, I was really afraid of you . . . I saw you as *a man* . . . You were my father's age . . .'

'I still am, as far as that goes.'

'You know perfectly well that it's not the same thing now,' said Adele, smiling. She had a beautiful smile.

'At any rate, you certainly didn't seem like a frightened girl,' said Bordelli, remembering how awkward he felt in the face of her carefree, natural manner.

'I swear I was terrified.'

He could see in her eyes that she wasn't lying. The waiter approached the table, and as he was taking their plates away he asked whether they wanted any dessert. Bordelli raised a hand.

'Not for me, thanks.'

'What have you got?' asked Adele, in a flirtatious manner that made Bordelli feel jealous. The waiter began to enumerate the desserts, while unsheathing an odious Don Juanesque look in his eye. He was in fact a good-looking lad and may even have thought that he was dealing with a father and his beautiful daughter. Bordelli would have gladly arrested him at that moment.

'I'll have the *torta della nonna*,' said Adele, and Don Juan finally left.

'If you keep acting that way, you'll kill him,' Bordelli muttered, forcing a smile.

'Oh, he'll survive,' said Adele, pleased with the compliment.

'There's no guarantee . . .'

'You're such a sweetheart, you want me to feel pretty.'

'You know perfectly well you're very pretty, I can see it in your eyes.'

At that moment it suddenly occurred to him that there were only three days left before his 'appointment' with Beccaroni the lawyer. Who knew what Adele would think if she had any idea that on Monday . . .

'Well, you're pretty handsome yourself . . . And don't make that face. I mean it. And if you really want to know, you look younger now than you did back then.'

'No kidding . . .' said Bordelli.

The waiter reappeared, smiling, and delicately laid a slice of tart in front of the old man's beautiful daughter. She returned the smile, and the lad walked away with a gunslinger's swagger.

'He's cute . . .' she said, still looking at him.

'You wouldn't like him, I'm sure of it.'

'I know. I only said he was cute . . . Are you jealous?' she said, sketching a Mona Lisa smile on her lips.

'I admit I am, but it's just vanity,' said Bordelli, charmed by Adele's smile.

'For me to like somebody, it's not enough for them just to be cute,' she said, and, putting a piece of tart in her mouth, she closed her eyes and moaned with pleasure.

'Now you're killing me . . .'

'Why? What did I do?'

'Nothing . . .'

'It's just delicious . . . Want a taste?'

She brought the spoon to his mouth, and he let himself be fed like a baby. The tart really was good, but that wasn't the important thing. She had no problem letting him eat from her spoon. Maybe she would even settle for brushing her teeth with his toothbrush . . .

Adele finished her dessert, and after two small glasses of *vin santo*, Bordelli asked for the bill. He left a nice tip for the 'cute' waiter, happy to leave him behind. After helping her with her overcoat, he led her out of the restaurant with nineteenth-century chivalry.

'Shall we have a little walk?' she suggested.

'I couldn't ask for more . . .'

On the streets in the centre of town they saw some couples walking hand in hand, a few solitary old men smoking, noisy groups of university students . . .

'I can't stay out very late,' Adele said with a note of sadness. 'Cinderella's will be done.'

'I like talking to you. I feel free.'

'That makes me happy.'

'I feel I could tell you everything about me, even the most intimate things.'

'You shouldn't trust strangers . . .'

They carried on chatting on the razor's edge, smiles on their lips. They walked close to each other, with their elbows occasionally touching. And what if they crossed paths with Eleonora? Bordelli prayed this wouldn't happen . . .

Round about midnight Adele said that her evening, unfortunately, was over. They walked back to the Beetle, and Bordelli drove her slowly home.

'I've had a wonderful evening,' she said, looking him in the eye.

'Me, too,' he said. How original.

'And now you'll drop me off and go to see another woman . . .'

'Actually I've got three waiting for me . . . A dog, my bed and a book,' Bordelli said disconsolately.

They got out of the car together, and Bordelli escorted her to the door. She already had her keys in her hand. Time to say goodbye. Bordelli drew near, took her face in his hands and grazed her lips with the lightest of kisses. It came very naturally to both, with no embarrassment at all . . . As if deep down it really meant nothing.

'Sleep well, young mother . . .' he whispered.

'Pleasant dreams,' Adele said with a smile, more beautiful than ever, before vanishing behind the great door. Only then did Bordelli notice all the traffic on the boulevard. Getting back into the Beetle, he lit his first cigarette of the evening. As he drove home he felt handsome, even young . . . Only women could perform miracles like that . . .

He was coming down the Imprunetana, headed for Florence with Blisk asleep on the back seat. The sun had returned at last. At noon he'd phoned Rosa to invite her to the seashore, and she'd shrieked for joy.

He'd woken up early with a feeling of disgust that he knew well, a sort of rejection of Adele, which meant that he really did like her a lot. This always happened, when he first started falling in love. And yet if anyone had asked him whether he was still in love with Eleonora, he would have had no trouble answering yes. It was the first time anything like this had happened to him, except, of course, during the confusion of his youth . . .

He drove through the centre of town and parked in Via dei Neri, just outside Rosa's building. He rang the buzzer three times, so she would know it was him. While waiting he let the dog out of the car, so he could leave his mark on the world. Who knew whether the white bear liked the sea . . .

He thought of Botta. He hadn't thanked him yet for the little pots of herbs he'd brought him. He tried to imagine him all dressed up, in suit and tie . . . Had he bought a sports car yet? Maybe even a motorcycle? Would he move to a penthouse apartment somewhere in the centre of town? Would he eat out in posh restaurants with one woman after another? Perhaps one evening he would end up dining at a table next to one of the judges who had sentenced him in the past, and he would acknowledge him with a smile . . .

Rosa came down five minutes early with respect to her usual half-hour lateness, confidently striding on her spiked heels, dressed in rosemary-flower blue, her blond hair fluttering in waves around her heavily made-up face, with lipstick so red it seemed to radiate light. Upon seeing the dog she opened her mouth in surprised delight, like a little girl seeing her first elephant.

'He's gorgeous! . . . Is he yours?'

'Actually, I'm his.'

'How sweet . . .'

She bent down and took Blisk's enormous head in her hands, and in gratitude the dog licked her face.

'Now you have to make yourself up all over again,' said Bordelli.

'He's so cute . . . He likes me . . . Right, Meatball?'

'His name is Blisk.'

'What kind of name is that? . . . No, his name is Meatball . . . Right, Meatball?'

The dog wagged its tail, rubbing against Rosa with such force he nearly knocked her to the ground.

'We'd better get going, it's almost noon,' said Bordelli.

'Are you taking me to that nice friend of yours' restaurant?'

'He's married, you know . . .'

'Oh, there are plenty of married men in my life,' said Rosa, chuckling. The three of them got into the car and drove off.

On the motorway Rosa took her shoes off and put her feet up on the dashboard. She started singing a song by Mina, butchering it as only she could. Every now and then she turned round to pat Meatball, and the bear returned the affection by licking her hand.

'I smell a woman,' she said suddenly.

'What are you talking about?'

'I know you too well, monkey. When you have that eternally lovesick look on your face, it means you're thinking of a woman.'

'You're wrong . . .'

'I'm never wrong, you ought to know that by now.'

'This time you're wrong . . . I'm thinking of two women . . .' Bordelli blurted out.

'You're such a pig!'

'It's not what you think . . .'

'You men always say that, even when you're caught in your lover's arms . . . Or between her legs . . .' she said, laughing.

'No legs, for now. Just thoughts.'

'Come on, let's hear about it . . . Who are the unlucky girls?'

'Some other time, Rosa . . .' He already regretted saying too much.

'No, no, no, you're going to tell me everything, now.'

'I wouldn't know what to tell you. I'm a little confused.'

'You're always confused . . . Because you're always in love . . .'

'Don't exaggerate.'

'All you ever think of is women . . .'

'Are there other things in the world?'

'Women aren't *things* . . .'

'Prove to me otherwise.'

They kept goading each other like silly children until they reached Migliarino. Along the seaside promenade Rosa opened her window and sang another song with the wind blowing in her hair. She was so off key that she created new melodies.

They got to Marina di Massa, where Bordelli had spent his summers as a child, adolescent and young adult. Every villa, every area of pines, every street brought back some memory. He knew the silhouette of the Apuan Alps by heart, and had often gone walking along their trails . . .

The holiday season was still a long way away, and the beaches were empty, with no umbrellas or cabins. You could see the sea from the beach . . . But Bordelli saw only women on deckchairs, in striped bathing suits that came down to the knee . . . children playing at the water's edge, under the watchful eyes of their parents . . . groups of boys and girls frolicking in the water . . . and him there, with his frowning face, among those kids, trying to have fun like the others but not succeeding . . .

'What's with the long face?' said Rosa.

'Sorry, I was a little distracted.'

'The sea's so beautiful . . . Right, Meatball?'

Bordelli parked amid a great many other cars in the car park beside the trattoria run by his friend Nessuno. It was a Saturday, so naturally the place was packed. Meatball reluctantly got out, promptly raised a hind leg at a pot of plants, and then trotted behind them. Before going in, Rosa pointed to the sign.

'Riccà means Riccardo, I guess . . .'

'Rosa, you're a genius.'

'Oh, stuff it. It wasn't a question,' she said, elbowing him.

The restaurant was full of hungry customers, the room echoing with shouts and laughter. At first glance there seemed to be no free tables. Bordelli poked his head into the kitchen, and upon seeing him Riccà shouted in greeting. Turning his pans over to a fellow cook, he wiped his hands on his apron and came over to welcome his old friend. He was a big ox of a man, wider than he was tall, with penetrating blue eyes and two demonic eyebrows, though his gaze was as gentle as a fawn's.

'Long time no see . . .' he said in dialect, crushing Bordelli's hand in a handshake.

'You'll be seeing me more often now. I quit the police force.'

'I can't see you retired and feeding chickens . . .' He greeted Rosa and crushed her hand as well. 'A beautiful woman . . . What's she doing with this guy here?'

'They're going to make me a saint,' Rosa chuckled, coquettish as ever.

'Well, you'd better be careful with this one here . . . he's dangerous . . .' said Riccà, winking. His wife emerged from the smoke of the kitchen and, after a hasty welcome, she went back to the stove. It was a hellish moment, with waiters ceaselessly rushing back and forth.

'Today there are three of us,' Bordelli informed him, indicating Meatball.

'Here, everyone eats!' said Riccà, stroking the bear's head.

'It looks to me like you're all full . . . Should we come back a little later?'

'Give me just a minute and I'll take care of you.'

Riccà made his way round the room, greeting customers, and

noticed a table that was about to become available. He went back to Bordelli and told him they had to wait only a few minutes.

'I'm going into the kitchen, and as soon as you're seated I'll come to you.'

'See you soon,' said Rosa, waving her blindingly red fingernails in the air.

They went over into a corner to be out of the way, and the dog plopped on to the floor with such force that everyone laughed. As soon as the table was available, they went and sat down, without waiting for the waiter to clear it. The dog waddled between them and lay down half under the table. Bordelli was quite hungry, peeking at the plates on the table next to theirs with a touch of envy. There was a delicious scent of fish in the air, puncuated every so often by the smell of cigarette smoke.

'I could eat a horse,' said Rosa, eyes smiling.

'Sorry, they only serve fish here.'

'Silly . . .'

'The last person who said that to me is now resting under three feet of cold earth,' said Bordelli, trying to look tough.

'You couldn't frighten even a chicken . . .'

'The last chicken that dared say that to me was forced to change its mind, and now it no longer lays eggs.'

'Does this game last very long, Einstein?'

'The last person who said that to me is now eating only broths and purées . . .'

He felt like making an ass of himself, just to lighten things up. For the moment he wanted to forget Eleonora and Adele, not to mention his appointment on Monday with Beccaroni . . .

He imagined himself saying to Rosa: *On Monday I'm going to kill one of those gentlemen who raped Giacomo.* What would she do? Would her jaw drop? Would she clap her hands? Or would she simply smile, thinking it was another bitter attempt at wit?

The waiter arrived with a smile, quickly cleared the table, changed the tablecloth, and brought some clean cutlery. He was a tall, thin lad with eyes popping out of their sockets and buck teeth. As nice as was necessary, never pushy . . . The perfect waiter.

Moments later Riccà came across the room, steam rising from his apron, and stopped at their table. He'd brought a bowl for the dog, a tempting fish soup. Meatball sniffed the air, raised his head and, without bothering to stand up, started eating.

'So, Tuscans, what'll you have?'

'You Massese are also Tuscan, according to the map,' Bordelli pointed out.

'That stuff means nothing . . .'

'So you're Ligurian,' said Rosa.

'Better dead than Ligurian . . . We're Massese, and that's enough.'

'If you ask me, you're all pirates,' said Bordelli.

'How romantic . . .' Rosa sighed, lips puckered, forming a heart.

Riccà cast her a sidelong glance, pretending to be offended.

'So, what can I get you? A nice dish of spaghetti with clam sauce . . . A mixed fry of calamari, shrimp and little fish . . . and a carafe of Candia . . . Excellent choices, congratulations . . .'

And he left without waiting for their confirmation.

'He picked everything himself,' said Bordelli.

'He's not a sluggard like you.'

'The last time a woman dared to—'

'No, I beg you! If you say that one more time, I'm leaving!'

'The last time a woman—'

'Oh my god! You're not usually such an idiot!'

'Okay, I'll stop.'

'Praise be to God . . .' said Rosa, folding her hands.

The bug-eyed waiter brought the wine to the table, and while waiting they began to drink.

Fifteen minutes later the spaghetti finally arrived, before quickly vanishing from their plates. Almost immediately afterwards the mixed fry arrived, and another bottle of wine had to be opened.

'When will we be driving back?' asked Rosa, glass in hand and looking a little tipsy.

'You're worse than a spoilt child . . .'

'Why?'

'Can't we just enjoy the moment without thinking of what pleasures lie ahead?'

'Oh, you and your complicated arguments! I hate them . . .'

'Complicated?'

'The last man who said that to me . . . went to sleep and never woke up,' said Rosa, laughing so loudly that for a moment everyone in the room fell silent. Even the dog raised his head, then lowered it again.

'You're drunk . . .'

'So what if I am? I feel fine . . . And you look like a mummy . . .'

She kept on laughing without stopping, but it wouldn't last much longer. Bordelli was very familiar with the effects of white wine on Rosa. After the good cheer and laughter would come the melancholy, and then, to finish things up, a good little cry to wash it all away. Once the cycle was completed, everything would return to normal.

At around three o'clock customers began to get up from their tables. Rosa was already at the melancholy stage, remembering old stories about her family with a quaver in her voice.

'Zia Bettina died all of a sudden . . . and I didn't manage in time to . . .' And right on schedule came the tears, only a few, punctuated by a sob that sounded almost like a burst of laughter.

'Would you like a dessert?' Bordelli asked her, as though nothing was wrong.

'I can't. I've eaten like a horse,' she said, sniffling. Wiping her face with a pink handkerchief, she flashed a smile. She was drifting back into cheerfulness. Her eyes were just a little red. Bordelli lit a cigarette, blowing the smoke towards the ceiling. He looked at Rosa with affection, thinking he'd never met a woman as innocent as her.

When the room was completely empty, Riccà came and sat at their table, managing not to step on the dog, and he filled a glass with Candia.

'To women . . .' he said, raising the glass, and he savoured a big gulp of wine.

'To women? I don't see why . . .' said Bordelli, which earned him a kick from Rosa under the table. Riccà turned round.

'Domenico, bring us three coffees,' he shouted.

Less than a minute later, a dark kid with blue eyes brought out a tray with the coffees. Behind him appeared a beautiful little girl with the same colour eyes as her brother. They were Riccà's children. And Bordelli started thinking bitterly that it was sad to grow old without any children . . .

'When are we going home?' asked the little girl, looking bored.

'I'll be along in a minute . . . Go to your ma . . .'

'Ouf!' said the girl, walking away with her brother as Riccà gazed at them fondly. After knocking back his coffee, he started telling them about a lifeguard friend of his, Azelio, who a couple of days earlier had very nearly drowned in rough waters, owing to bad disgestion . . .

Bordelli looked at his friend Nessuno, former partisan of the Divisione Garibaldi, and it made him think of the war . . . This placid man, who now cooked fish for dozens of people daily, had gone up into the mountains after 8 September . . .

*The Germans launched their attack on La Brugiana on 2 December 1944, and immediately the partisan divisions took up defensive positions between Monte Penna and Bergiola Foscalina. A bit like everyone else, Nessuno had a model 91 rifle, with only one charger. Within his division, he formed a trio with his brother, known as 'Torero', and Alessandro Rocca, known as 'Viper'.*

*When they suddenly spotted a column of German soldiers in single file, the shooting began. They mostly heard the crackling of the Germans' automatic weapons. Fearing encirclement, the partisans fell back. The Nazis continued firing wildly, and Nessuno was hit in the shoulder. The bullet was headed straight for his chest, but was deflected by a German torch he kept in his jacket pocket. Gushing blood, he managed to follow his comrades as far as the Gioia Quarries, where they encountered other partisans and a group of evacuees. They all took shelter in the quarry, but nobody knew what to do. News from the outside kept accumulating. Were they surrounded? Was it better to leave the quarry? Meanwhile, down below, at Poggio Piastrone, the shooting went on ceaselessly.*

*Luckily the Germans did not come up as far as the quarry and slowly began to withdraw. Nessuno's wound kept leaking blood, and only around sunset was his brother able to head off on foot for Carrara, with Viper, to look for a doctor. They didn't return until late that night, and when the medic saw the wound, he told Nessuno he'd been very lucky. If the bullet hadn't been deflected by the torch, it would have punctured a lung. Which, in a situation like that, would have meant certain death . . . Amen.*

At midnight they passed the roadhouse at Montecatini, in an entirely unexpected drizzle. The dog was dozing on the back seat while Rosa slept, her blond head propped against the window. Bordelli thought of Nessuno and the bullet that could have killed him. He, too, had had several brushes with death during the war, and each time he'd felt as if someone on high was looking out for him . . .

It had been a long, pleasant day. After lunch they'd taken a long, slow walk along the beach, shoes in hand, in front of a steel-grey sea, while Meatball kept diving into the water, as happy as when running through the woods. They'd all watched in silence as the sun dipped below the horizon, with Bordelli recalling all the times he'd witnessed the same spectacle from the deck of a ship. Under a Leopardian moon that appeared in the sky out of nothing, ghostly and indifferent, he thought of the long summers of his youth, the blinding sun setting over an expanse of sea ablaze, the gulls diving into the water, his first crushes, which had the mysterious power of keeping him from sleeping . . . Once, as a child, he'd nearly drowned, dragged out to sea by the undercurrent on a stormy day while playing at the water's edge, before his father saved him, fishing him out of the water half conscious and making him throw up all the water he'd swallowed . . . It felt like a thousand years ago . . .

While walking barefoot across the sand, a profound melancholy had come over him, and he slowly slipped into a sort of strange resentment of time itself for transforming everything . . .

Without realising it, they'd walked all the way to Ronchi. Given the hour, they'd decided to stay for dinner, turned round and walked slowly back the way they'd come. Just before eight they returned to Riccà's trattoria and sat down at the same table. The restaurant was still half empty, but was sure to fill up quickly.

After dinner they'd lingered for a long time, chatting with Nessuno over a bottle of wine. They didn't just talk about the war but amused themselves with lighter subjects as well. Rosa kept downing glasses of Candia and laughing, getting more and more drunk, throwing her head back in laughter till she was out of breath and her eyes full of tears. When she got into the car she'd started crying, handkerchief pressed to her nose, then fell asleep.

'Rosa! We're here,' said Bordelli, turning on to Via dei Neri. Rosa answered with a sort of childish grunt. When the car came to a halt, she half opened her eyes without bothering to raise her head.

'Where are we?' she mumbled, then closed her eyes again.

'Rosa . . . hey, Rosa . . .' said Bordelli, gently shaking her shoulder.

'Sleep . . .' she moaned, followed by a long yawn.

'Do I have to carry you over my shoulder?'

Rosa didn't answer. She'd fallen back asleep. Bordelli stroked her cheek, to push the hair out of her eyes, but was unable to wake her. He gave up. At least it wasn't raining. Sighing, he got out of the car, opened the door on Rosa's side, and after several attempts succeeded in standing her up before Meatball's sleepy eyes.

'Where are you taking me?' she asked, sounding still drunk. She was about to collapse on the ground when Bordelli put an arm round her waist. Grabbing her bag, he searched about for the keys. With an acrobatic contortion he even managed to grab Rosa's red shoes, wondering how one could ever walk in such heels. He left the dog in the car, to avoid any scuffles with Rosa's cats, and they went into the building. He started dragging Rosa up the stairs as she mumbled incomprehensibly and occasionally giggled. She was hardly a slip of a girl, and reaching the top floor was no joke. As soon as Bordelli opened the door, he found Briciola in front of him, meowing desperately. The more dignified Gideon watched them from a distance.

'I'll get to you two in a minute . . .'

Tossing aside Rosa's bag and shoes, he took her in his arms and carried her to the bedroom, laying her down on the bed. He started to undress her, remembering how nice it was when his mother used to take his clothes off to get him ready for bed, without him having to lift a finger.

'What are you doing to me?' Rosa muttered with a dazed smile, not bothering to open her eyes.

'If I wasn't a gentleman, I would know what to do . . .'

'You're a brute . . . a brute . . .'

She seemed to be dreaming. Bordelli removed her bra as well, noting that she hadn't lost all the freshness from her brothel days and, raising her legs, he managed to tuck her under the covers.

'Sweet dreams, Queen of Candia.'

He turned the light off and went into the kitchen to feed the cats. Briciola attacked her bowl, devouring the meat like a starving lioness, while the gigantic Gideon observed her from a distance, patiently awaiting his turn.

Bordelli left, feeling sleepy. On the drive home he allowed himself a cigarette, blowing the smoke out the window. Still thinking about the past, he let himself be coddled by his melancholy . . . When he was a little boy, he had no idea what his life would be like . . . He didn't know he'd go off to war and end up shooting at Nazis.[20] He had no way of knowing he would end up in law enforcement, and that one fine day he would throw his badge down on the commissioner's desk . . . Nor did he know that fate would drive him to kill as a way of settling accounts with child-murderers . . .

Early next morning he was already in the Cintoia woods with his backpack, blowing steam out of his mouth as Blisk amused himself as usual, running through the trees. He took a steep path scattered with large reddish stones that led up to the crest before descending softly down to La Panca. The humid air smelled of moss and wild grasses. It was Sunday, and gunshots rang out periodically. The hunters normally avoided the main trails and penetrated deeper into the woods, and with any luck he wouldn't run into any. The chestnut trees were still naked, aside from their now swollen, life-filled buds waiting to burst open. He also saw new shoots on the plants in the underbrush, and the birds seemed more restless than ever.

Every so often a shudder of emotion passed through his belly without warning, reminding him that the start of spring was only two days away. But perhaps it wasn't just the spring . . . Adele . . . Eleonora . . . But not only . . . He had an important appointment the following day. Would everything go well? He asked himself for the umpteenth time whether it wasn't utter folly to have embarked on this adventure, trusting only in some hypothetical design of destiny . . . But by now he knew he would go through with it. He hadn't organised anything specific, aware that sometimes even the most carefully studied plans came to naught owing to unforeseen events. It wasn't human will that governed things; he would do well to remember that . . .

He knew only a few more or less important things, which had come out during the investigation into the boy's murder: Beccaroni lived alone, was separated from his wife, had a daughter, kept two Dobermanns in his garden, and normally came home around half past eight. That should be enough for him. At quarter past eight on Monday he would take up position somewhere near the lawyer's villa and wait until he came home from work . . .

During his solitary walks in the woods he noticed that his thoughts now unfolded differently, following slower rhythms, and at this point he could no longer live without that feeling. *Mutatis mutandis*, it was a little like the experience of a painter he'd known shortly before the war, whose name he couldn't recall . . . One evening, over a bottle of wine, the artist had admitted the reason why he painted . . . He wasn't interested in the final result, even though he did what he had to do to exhibit and sell his works. What he really sought when he confronted a canvas was the feeling he experienced whenever he had a paintbrush in his hand, the mental space that would open up before him, the long, aimless journeys that invited him to lose himself in unknown worlds. If he'd never experienced this, he said, he would never have wasted his time painting . . .

Instead of paintbrushes, Bordelli had the woods. It wasn't just a question of moving his legs; you could almost say it was a spiritual activity . . . He smiled at the thought of this . . . Maybe it really was just his age, which kept advancing inexorably.

After roving through his memories, not stopping at any single one in particular, he found himself making a mental list of the things he had to bring to pull off the business with Beccaroni. A pair of leather gloves, the ski mask he'd used during the war, the two handguns, and an electric torch. Food for how many days? Two? Three? Maybe even four? And what if a month went by before anyone came looking for the lawyer? No, impossible . . . Beccaroni had an eighteen-year-old daughter; they might even talk every day . . . And certainly his secretary would grow suspicious, not seeing him come into work . . . There might even be a cleaning lady who had the house keys . . . Some concerned relatives . . . His ex-wife, looking for him to ask for more money . . .

Bordelli sighed, imagining that with any luck he wouldn't have to wait more than three days. Six panini, six apples, two tablets of chocolate, and a lot of shelled almonds should suffice.

If worse came to worst, he could rummage through Beccaroni's kitchen. One bottle of water could suffice, and as he finished it he could refill it with tap water. He would also bring along a book, so as not to get too bored while waiting. Ennio would look after Blisk, as agreed. Everything seemed taken care of.

He got to La Panca, crossed the road, and continued hiking along the path he knew best . . . The great oak with the shrine . . . Monte Scalari Abbey . . . The triple fork at Cappella dei Boschi . . . He passed again the small plateau where he'd helped the butcher kill himself, and felt nothing.

At around midday he stopped at Pian d'Albero, in front of the farmhouse where the Nazis had committed a massacre, and sat down on a flat boulder looking out over the Figline valley. As hoped, he hadn't encountered a single hunter. Lunchtime was approaching, and the sound of gunshots had diminished. The hunters were going home to their wives and children, to stuff themselves with pasta and roast meats.

Blisk had been gone for a while now, and Bordelli started calling him, shouting his name repeatedly. In the end he got tired of this and pulled his panino out of his backpack. He barely had time to take two bites before the dog came running. He started circling round, panting. Bordelli realised that to make him come he shouldn't call him but ignore him. The same was true in matters of love, according to the cliché, but he'd never really believed it. Whatever the case, he'd never liked using strategies with women; he felt more comfortable acting spontaneously . . . Come what may . . .

'Are you hungry?' he asked Blisk, offering him a piece of bread. The white bear took it delicately between his lips and swallowed it in an instant. Bordelli gave him the cheese rinds he'd brought along for him, then the rest of the panino as a bonus, before biting into the apple.

He decided to play another game with destiny, just for fun. He grabbed a one-hundred-lira coin and, squeezing it in his hand, thought: tails, Eleonora; heads, Adele. He flipped the coin into the air and caught it on the fly. Heads. He felt a twinge of regret. Must he now forget Eleonora? And if it had come up 'tails', would he not also have suffered at having to give up the beautiful Adele? He felt silly, but it was amusing just the same. One had only to refuse to believe the coin's verdict . . .

Despite his scepticism, he got ready to flip the coin again, this time for something other than love. Tails, the business with Beccaroni would go well. Heads, it would go badly. With some apprehension, he tossed the coin into the air, let it fall into his palm and then closed his hand into a fist. He didn't believe even remotely in this sort of thing, but he knew that if it came up 'heads', he would feel uncomfortable. No more than an impression, but still he would prefer not to have to carry it around with him. He stared at his fist, opened it suddenly, and felt a shudder pass through his chest: tails. So the stupid coin was on his side, too . . . But if he gave credence to this prediction, he should also believe the verdict on Eleonora, and again he felt a pang in his midsection. And yet he liked Adele, more than a little. What would he do if he were forced to decide? If one fine day the two of them together put him on the spot and demanded that he choose between them? He didn't know . . . Damn it all, he didn't know. He tossed the apple core into the bushes, shaking his head . . . He kept on fantasising, like a little kid, imagining himself as a bone of contention between two dogs and enjoying the thrill of it.

Blisk had disappeared again, but every so often he heard him running through the shrubs nearby. A large lizard popped out at the edge of a crag, and after stopping for an instant to look at Bordelli, its head almost vertical, it fearlessly continued its course, coming straight at him. Taken by surprise, Bordelli shot to his feet and stood aside, letting the lizard climb the boulder and disappear into the tall grass overrunning the courtyard of the farmhouse. He sat back down, smiling. In a way he admired the little reptile brave enough to challenge a living being a thousand times bigger than him. It was as if a man were to start running straight at King Kong, convinced he would frighten him . . . But wasn't everything like that, in life?

Mid-morning he started packing his bag. He'd already been in town to do the shopping, and had put three panini with prosciutto and three with salami, well wrapped, in the fridge. Along with the things he'd decided to bring he added a towel, which he would spread out on the floor of the attic of Beccaroni's villa, to catch any crumbs he might leave. Had Orlando's assassins done likewise? It was the first time he found himself trying to think like a killer, and it wasn't a very nice feeling. Normally he sent killers to jail, or tried to, at least. And indeed, in his investigations he'd always succeeded in getting to the bottom of things – except once, in '52. A woman was found murdered in the woods, completely naked, with dozens of stab wounds. No clues, no witnesses, not even any documents that might lead to the victim's identity, not a soul coming forward to declare her missing. The case was shelved after three weeks. Every so often Bordelli would think about this mystery, imagining that one day he might come across something that would lead him to the killer . . . Apparently by chance . . .

The bag was now ready. It was as though the gears of some complex mechanism were turning and could no longer be stopped . . . He could think and reflect, but he couldn't change things. He was unable to keep things he'd thought over many times from continuing to pass through his head: the most important thing was for people to think, beyond the shadow of a doubt, that Beccaroni had committed suicide . . . Nobody must investigate . . . It must all be as clear as sunshine from the very first glance . . . Otherwise there was always the risk that something would turn up. This must not happen. If anything went wrong, the deadly wrath of Monsignor Sercambi might make itself felt . . . This time the prelate of the Curia might even go beyond rape and order the murder of a friend of the hard-headed ex-inspector. One selected at random, perhaps followed by all the rest . . . No, this must not happen. He could never forgive himself if it did. The half-hour of hell that Eleonora had lived through must remain the only wound. It must never happen again. Everything must work to perfection . . .

Was it perhaps better to take care of Monsignor Sercambi first? He seemed to be the more dangerous one, but he was also the hardest to strike. Bordelli shook his head, thinking things were fine as they were. Beccaroni might even be a freemason, in which case the problem would remain the same. So it was better to start with him . . . Who knew what the respectable lawyer was doing at that moment. Was he at court, upholding the cause of Justice, engaging in a spirited harangue full of quotations from ancient philosophers and Latin maxims? Was he studying a case file, comfortably seated in an armchair at his desk? Or perhaps penning an astronomical bill for some industrialist he'd just rescued from fraud charges? Whatever he was doing, he was unaware of his fate. He had no idea that in just a few hours . . .

Bordelli went out of the house, with the dog following behind, and as he passed the vegetable garden, he cast a glance at his labours. The tomato plants were growing, the artichoke shoots had sprouted new leaves, and the first chilli pepper seedlings had finally appeared. It was terribly satisfying to watch plants grow. Who knew what it might be like with a son or daughter . . .

He started walking through the olive grove. A cold wind carried away the sun's warmth on the skin. All of a sudden a doubt came over him. It was the first time. Might there not be some other way to settle accounts with Beccaroni? Force him to write a confession, for example? Life imprisonment would do just fine. A nice confession in which he also named the upright monsignor of the Curia . . . But what was a confession extorted at gunpoint worth? Beccaroni would immediately renegotiate, perhaps passing the poor inspector off as a madman who never got over his failure to solve a terrible murder. He was a lawyer; he knew how to manage these things. The only result would be to anger Monsignor Sercambi . . . No, he had no choice. So even this last doubt had come to nothing. There were no more obstacles in his mind. Full speed ahead . . .

For lunch he cooked himself a dish of spaghetti according to the gospel of Botta, and ate it while watching the midday news and drinking only half a glass of wine. As usual, the most boring news stories were the ones on politics. The Moro government was still standing, but for how long?

After his coffee he went and sat down beside the fire to read Bulgakov, smoking a little and having a great deal of fun. At moments he even laughed out loud. The phone rang several times, but he didn't. He needed solitude and silence. He kept turning the pages, engrossed in the plot, oblivious to the time passing.

When he instinctively looked up at the clock, it was ten minutes to six. It was time to get moving. He closed the book and got up. After letting Blisk out, he warmed some stew for him and changed the water in his bowl. He checked his bag again. It was all there . . . Gloves, chocolate, book, torch, ski mask, almonds . . . He added the panini, apples and bottle of water. He tried lifting it, and was amazed to find how heavy it was.

He went to change his clothes, choosing old articles he hadn't worn for years. He slipped the pistols into two holsters fastened to his sides, and buttoned up his jacket. He put his grandad's spectacles in his pocket, took an elegant old hat out of the wardrobe, and went back into the kitchen. The dog was already scratching at the door, and as soon as he entered he went straight for the stew, sniffing the air. He seemed a little astonished to find dinner ready so early, but after a moment's hesitation, he plunged his muzzle into the bowl. Bordelli ran his hand over the animal's big head.

'Tomorrow morning Ennio's going to come to let you out

and give you din-din, and I'll see you again in a couple of days.'

The dog turned round to look at him, barely moving his tail, then resumed eating. Bordelli grabbed his bag, locked the door behind him, and got into his car with a sigh. The sun had set half an hour earlier, and despite the fact that night had descended on earth, the sky was still veiled with a fading light.

When he parked in Viale Petrarca it was ten minutes to eight. Before getting out of his car he disguised himself as best he could. He put the hat on his head and donned his grandfather's glasses, keeping them down at the end of his nose to avoid looking through the corrective lenses. It was just a minimal device to make him look a little different, should anything go wrong. Anyone who might see him prowling around Beccaroni's villa would remember a bloke with glasses and a hat.

At that hour many were returning home after a day's work, and the boulevard was buzzing with cars and motorbikes. The pavements were teeming as well, though nobody seemed to notice the anonymous-looking man with a bag in his hand. When he got to Porta Romana, he continued at a leisurely pace along Via Senese. He'd decided to leave his cigarettes at home. He had no way of knowing how long he would remain shut up inside the lawyer's house, and he didn't want to risk giving in to the temptation to smoke. It would be hard, he knew that, but he couldn't afford to leave that kind of trace behind.

A hundred or so yards later, he began the steep climb of Via Sant'Ilario, in the wan light of a few rare street lamps. By this time he was used to hiking in the woods, so it was pretty effortless for him. He had a clear sense in his mind of what he wanted to do, but it all depended on one thing: that Beccaroni came home at the usual hour, and came alone, with no one waiting for him, either outside the gate or inside the villa. Again Bordelli put his trust in destiny, and swore to himself that if, that evening, for whatever reason, he was unable to carry out his mission, he would give it up once and for all. In other words, if fate was not on his side, as he believed, it was best to drop everything.

He turned down Via delle Campora, which was darker than ever, and, seeing a car approach, he buried his face in the collar of his jacket. He'd spent a good deal of time in this area a few years back, when investigating the murder of several little girls, and, turning round, he saw the killer's villa, immersed in darkness, in the distance. He remembered when, with Piras's help, he'd succeeded in cracking the case. After his arrest, the killer was found mysteriously hanged in his cell . . . Another fake suicide – and a rather crude one at that. He had to do better . . .

By this point in his life, every street in Florence brought back one memory or another. And not just murders . . . Women, too, passionate kisses, old love stories, desperate moments of rejection, and many other things . . . A forest of memories from which he would never break free . . .

The moment he turned on to Via di Marignolle, he looked at his watch in the yellow light of a street lamp. 8.14. Normally he would have said 8.15, but in that situation he paid attention even to the seconds. The villa was still some three to four hundred yards away. If, before getting there and before having time to take up position, Beccaroni's Jaguar were to pass, or if, when looking in through the gate, he noticed that the lawyer was already at home, there would be nothing more to do, and he would give the whole thing up. The following morning he would go to the Trespiano cemetery and apologise to Giacomo, telling him that one can only do certain things if one has destiny on one's side; otherwise there's no point, and one risks doing more harm. Would Giacomo understand?

The street sped by under his feet, the seconds passed, the villa loomed ahead . . . He crossed paths with a long-haired youth walking with his hands thrust deep in his pockets and not deigning to cast a glance at the elderly gentleman with the glasses and hat. A couple of cars passed, but he'd spotted the beam from their headlights enough in advance to hide in the shadows of a gate. The fewer people noticed him, the better.

At twenty-one minutes past eight, he was outside the villa. He stopped at the gate and looked into the garden. A wall lamp at one corner of the house cast a lunar glow on flowers and gravel. There was no light filtering through the locked shutters. Suddenly he saw two low shadows in the garden come silently towards him, and the two Dobermanns appeared. They stopped a short distance away without barking, but growling softly. They must have been trained.

He kept walking, in search of a good spot to lie in wait. Some twenty yards down, the road curved softly, lined by two high stone walls. That was what he needed. With his back to the wall he could comfortably watch for the Jaguar approaching, without being seen by the driver. This was a first sign from destiny. If the road had been straight, he would not have been able to count on the element of surprise, and everything would have been much more difficult.

Time now seemed to stand still. The least he could have done was bring along one cigarette, damn it all . . . 8.23 . . . He put on his gloves, keeping the ski mask ready in his jacket pocket . . . 8.24 . . . He heard a car approach from behind him and pretended to be walking normally, until he saw it disappear round the bend. He quickly turned back and resumed his position behind the bend . . . 8.26 . . . 8.27 . . . 8 . . .

Out of the darkness at the far end of the road he saw the white beam of two headlights approach. That's him, he thought. He was certain it was Beccaroni. He quickly removed his glasses and hat and put on the ski mask. Flattened against the wall, he heard a powerful engine downshifting. As soon as he saw the car stop with its nose outside the villa's gate, he grabbed the Beretta. He had to hope that no one passed by in the next two minutes. That would be the second 'sign'. Scanning the street, he saw Beccaroni's shadow get out of the Jaguar and thought: *Now!* He nearly ran and came up behind the lawyer just as he was about to open the gate . . .

'Keep calm and everything'll be all right,' he whispered, pressing the gun to Beccaroni's neck. The lawyer raised his hands, trembling like a leaf.

'Please don't kill me . . .'

The dogs had approached and were growling more loudly.

'Put your hands down and do not at any moment raise your voice.'

'I'll do whatever you want,' the lawyer whispered.

'At the proper time . . .'

'Yes . . .'

'Send the dogs away and open the gate.'

'Yes . . . Yes . . . Adolfo! Benito! . . . Go to your bed!' Beccaroni whispered at them, again revealing his nostalgia for the good old days. The dogs withdrew immediately.

'Open the gate and get in the car,' said Bordelli, still in a whisper, to avoid the danger of being recognised from his voice. The lawyer opened the gate wide, glancing at the pistol pointed at his head. They got into the car, with Beccaroni at the wheel and Bordelli in the back seat. They pulled into the driveway. Before getting out of the car, Bordelli warned him, 'If I see the dogs appear, I'll shoot you first and kill them second.'

'They won't come . . . I swear . . . And if they do . . . I'll send them away . . .' He had trouble speaking, as he was breathless with fear.

'Let's go.'

They went back together to close the gate and then headed towards the villa, still side by side. Bordelli studied the darkness for unpleasant surprises, ready to shoot, but the dogs were nowhere to be seen. The lawyer's hands were trembling, and only after several tries did he manage to get the key into the lock. At last they entered the house. Beccaroni turned on the light switch, and a number of wall lamps in the spacious vestibule came on. Bordelli quickly shut the front door, sliding two large bolts to secure it, then looked around. Fancy furniture from a variety of epochs but well matched, a magnificent floor of red and black hexagonal tiles in alternating diagonal rows. It was a beautiful house, tastefully furnished, sumptuous but welcoming. If he'd seen it without knowing Beccaroni, he would have thought it was the creation of a refined sensibility.

'Let's go into your study.'

'Yes . . . it's over here . . .' the lawyer muttered, heading down the corridor. He seemed more and more terrified, continually running his hands over his face to wipe away the sweat.

They went into a large room, furnished in the Classical style, with shelves full of books and a beautiful antique desk of burnished wood. A vast carpet covered most of the floor, allowing just a glimpse along the edges of the antique terracotta tiles. In one corner lay a tiger's skin with an embalmed head and eyes of glass.

'Where do you keep your gun?' asked Bordelli, bluffing.

'In the left-hand drawer . . .'

The lawyer looked at the stranger with the ski mask over his head, clearly wondering who the hell he could be and what he could want. Bordelli laid his bag down on the carpet and circled round behind the desk. He opened the drawer and found a pistol, a Browning 7.65 with a full cartridge clip. Another fateful sign, he thought, putting it in his pocket. If Beccaroni hadn't had a gun, he would have had to sacrifice one of his own.

'Sit down at the desk and keep your hands visible at all times,' he ordered him.

The lawyer obeyed without a word. Bordelli sat down in front him, pistol still pointed at him, and took off his ski mask.

'You . . .' said Beccaroni, stunned. He even couldn't suppress a sort of smile. It wasn't clear whether the discovery frightened him even more or made him feel less in danger.

'I'm here to remind you of your sins,' said Bordelli.

'What sins?' Beccaroni stammered, pretending not to understand.

'I'm your conscience now, since it seems you've lost your own.'

'Please explain what you mean . . .'

'I know everything, you're perfectly aware of that.'

'Everything about what?'

He was a pretty good actor, like all lawyers. Bordelli shook his head slowly, showing disapproval.

'If you act that way, I'm going to have to get angry, and when I get angry, I become rather wicked,' he said very calmly.

Beccaroni, despair in eyes, searched for the right thing to say. 'It's not what you think . . . Just give me time to explain . . .' he finally managed to say.

'Allow me to explain something to *you* . . . If five demons tore your clothes off and took turns having their way with you, you might get a vague sense of what Giacomo Pellissari went through, when you and your friends raped him in that basement . . .'

'I am endlessly repentant,' the lawyer was quick to reply, hand over his heart, using the same church-inspired language as Bordelli.

'All right, then, take a pen and a sheet of paper and write me a nice confession.'

'Let me explain first . . .'

'Let's hear it.'

'What happened—'

The ringing of the telephone made him jump in his chair, and Bordelli signalled to him not to answer. After ten interminable rings, silence at last returned.

'You were saying?'

'It was a terrible accident . . . A tragedy . . . Nobody wanted that to happen . . .'

'I'm really moved, I assure you,' said Bordelli, smiling.

'I swear . . . We had no intention of . . .'

'You just wanted to have a little fun, is that it?'

'We didn't realise . . . It was as if we'd lost our minds . . .'

'He was twelve years old . . .'

'Anyway, I wasn't the one who—'

'I know, it was Panerai who strangled him . . . But wasn't what you all did to him a way of killing him just the same?'

'Well . . . I . . .' Beccaroni tried to speak, and when Bordelli slammed his hand down on the desk, he gave a start.

'Enough chit-chat! Take that pen and paper and write me a confession.'

'All right . . . Yes . . .' He looked for a pen, took a blank sheet of paper, and laid it down in front of him.

'Start it like this, in your own words: *I am endlessly repentant for the crime I committed* . . . Come on, write . . .'

He pointed the gun between Beccaroni's eyes, and the man began to write. Completing the phrase, he raised his head, awaiting further instructions.

'*I can never forgive myself. My conscience gives me no rest* . . . Write . . .'

'Yes . . .'

'*I trust in God's forgiveness* . . .'

Bordelli got up and went and stood behind him. He noticed that although Beccaroni held the pen in his right hand, he couldn't rule out that the man might be left handed. Maybe he'd been forced in elementary school not to use the hand of the devil. It was a detail not to be ignored. He waited for the lawyer to finish writing, then took the sheet from him and read it. The sentences were correct, written in a very tidy hand. He compared it with some of the other papers scattered on the desk, and found that the handwriting was the same.

'It's not good enough. Let's start over,' he said, laying the sheet down on the desk.

'What should I write?' asked Beccaroni, docile as a lamb. He seemed a little calmer, perhaps because he knew that a confession of that sort would be worthless.

'Recount what happened in that basement in Via Luna, on the night of the murder. Make it a proper document, I mean it. You're a lawyer, you know what I mean . . .'

'Yes . . .'

'And I advise you not to lie. Signorini told me all the details. If you write anything different . . .'

'No . . .'

'Good. Be sure to include the names of your friends . . . Livio Panerai, Italo Signorini, and Monsignor Sercambi . . .'

'Signorini and Panerai . . . are no longer around . . .' the lawyer timidly pointed out.

'As you can see, every so often, conscience bears fruit. Now get busy,' Bordelli concluded, pressing the barrel of the gun against Beccaroni's neck. He waited for the lawyer to find the inspiration for the opening and, still standing behind him, started reading:

*20 March 1967*
*I, the undersigned, Moreno Beccaroni, born in Florence 9 July*
*1922, confess to the following: on the night of 11 October 1966,*
*Livio Panerai, Italo Signorini and Monsignor Sercambi, of the*
*Episcopal Curia of Florence, and I . . .*

Beccaroni stopped, panting softly, as though the word that followed cost him great effort.

*. . . raped a young boy, Giacomo Pellissari, who had been*
*kidnapped and drugged by Signorini. Most unfortunately, in*
*the agitation of the moment, Panerai strangled the boy. It was*
*a terrible accident; none of us wanted that to happen. Our*
*intention was to release him that same night. We were desperate*
*and didn't know what to do. Panerai suggested a solution, and*
*we all agreed to it. We put the body in the refrigerator, to slow*
*down the process of decay, and a few days later, on a Saturday,*
*taking advantage of the fact that the National station was*
*broadcasting* Studio Uno, *Panerai and Signorini loaded the*
*body into Panerai's car and . . .*

By this point Beccaroni was well on his way and progressed without any difficulty, calling things by their proper names. Bordelli let him write and started pacing up and down the carpet, never once letting him out of his sight.

The lawyer now seemed almost calm. But it certainly wasn't due to the opportunity to get these things off his conscience. By now he must have been convinced that his life was no longer in danger, and he was probably already thinking of the moment when he would retract his confession . . .

Having reached the bottom of the page, he grabbed another and kept on writing. He jutted his lips out slightly, like a schoolboy writing his theme in composition class. His golden fountain pen raced across the page without stopping. In the silence of the room the only sound was the scratching of the tip against the paper, accompanied by the slow tick-tock of the tall pendulum clock that elegantly occupied one corner of the study. Bordelli felt sorry as he watched him, newly prey to doubt . . . Was he right to do what he was about to do? Was it really the only possible solution? He bit his lip and banished these thoughts . . .

Beccaroni finished covering a second page and raised his head.

'I'm done,' he said, setting the pen down.

Bordelli went over and picked up the pages and, still pacing back and forth, read the entire confession. The account matched the more detailed one that young Italo Signorini had given him orally before throwing himself out of the window. At the bottom of the second page was Beccaroni's signature.

'Very good . . .'

'What will you do now?' Beccaroni ventured to ask him, beginning to sweat again.

'There's no hurry.'

'You may not believe it, but I'm happy to pay for my crime.'

'You could have done so earlier, of your own accord.'

'I know, I know . . . You're absolutely right . . . But it's not easy . . . It was you who . . .' And he stopped, tears in his eyes.

'Well, you ought to thank me for giving you the opportunity to fulfil your wish to atone.'

'Yes . . . Quite right . . . I'm infinitely grateful to you . . . You've no idea how grateful . . .'

There was a slight quaver in his voice, as if he were about to start crying. He actually seemed sincere. Bordelli folded the pages and put them in his pocket. He now had to check something very important. He took a pencil out of the pen-holder and threw it at Beccaroni, who tried to catch it on the fly. With his left hand. He was left handed. So to kill himself he would have to hold the pistol in his left hand. The lawyer did not grasp the reason behind that strange act, and smiled obtusely.

Bordelli decided that the time had come. Pacing slowly, seeming absorbed in thought, he circled behind the desk again and stopped behind Beccaroni's chair.

'Don't look at me,' he said.

'What is happening?' asked the lawyer, turning his head.

'Don't worry . . .'

Without Beccaroni seeing him, Bordelli put the Beretta in the holster and grabbed the Browning. For a moment he thought of telling Beccaroni that his friend the butcher hadn't committed suicide, but then decided against it. It would have served no purpose, other than to upset him even more. He took the first page the lawyer had written under dictation, and put it in front of him.

'What do you want me to do?' asked Beccaroni, eyes scanning the page.

'Nothing . . .' said Bordelli.

Taking him by surprise, he managed to make him practically grab the pistol in his left hand, then fired it point blank into his temple. The lawyer's head jerked slightly to one side and then fell hard on to the desk, directly on top of his first, very brief confession. The dogs outside started barking. A stream of blood trickled out of the entrance wound, and the dead man's eyes retained an astonished expression. His left hand hung down, lightly touching the rug. Bordelli raised it, wrapped the lawyer's fingers around the butt of the Browning, then let the hand fall back down. He was wearing gloves, so he would leave no finger-prints, and if it occurred to anyone to test for paraffin on a suicide, the result would confirm the facts . . .

At that moment the doorbell rang, and Bordelli held his breath. It was 10.27. Time had flown. It rang again, more insistently this time. The two Dobermanns had stopped barking.

Making no sound, he went and took the torch out of his bag and, covering the light, moved out of the study and up to the first floor as the doorbell kept ringing. Slipping into a room that gave on to the street, he peered out through the slats in the outdoor blinds. He could see the silhouette of a person looking in towards the house, behind the bars of the entrance gate . . . Was it the nightwatchman on his first round? Beccaroni's daughter? Or perhaps a neighbour who'd heard the shot?

Every so often the silhouette stepped away from the gate to ring the bell again, then went back to watch the house. The person stayed there for another couple of minutes, then disappeared, and moments later a car's headlights could be seen moving away down the road.

Bordelli went down to the ground floor with the help of the torch, to make sure that all the windows were shut tight and to see whether there were any other doors. He discovered two large drawing rooms and a number of smaller ones, nicely furnished and welcoming, like everything else. The inside shutters were locked and bolted, and the back door was locked not only with a bar but also a deadbolt. The exact same situation as in the contessa's castle, when Orlando was hanged . . .

He continued his little tour of the premises, never once turning on any lights. He went back up to the first floor and poked his head into all the rooms. Canopy beds, large, dark armoires, a few paintings from various epochs, sometimes by great painters, hung in the right places. One of the most beautiful villas he'd ever seen. It seemed impossible to him that such refinement could coexist with perversion, but history was full of similar examples. There were some very cultured men among the Nazi and Fascist ranks, aficionados of the arts and letters who could speak six or seven languages fluently, learnedly discuss philosophy, music, the Italian Renaissance . . . And as they savoured fine foods and sipped prized wines, their thoughts and actions produced violence and death.

At the end of the corridor he opened a door narrower than the rest and found himself looking at a long staircase that led upstairs to the attics. He went all the way up, pushed open another small door and cast the beam of the torch into a large, almost empty space. Aside from the spiderwebs hanging from the rafters, there were only a pair of old armoires and a dismantled bed. The whole place smelled of dust and centuries past. A forgotten place, perfect for hiding at the proper moment. But for now he had no desire to shut himself up in there.

He went back down to the ground floor, into the 'suicide's' study, and dropped into a chair opposite the dead man. If he'd had his cigarettes with him, he would have lit one immediately. All he could do now was wait . . .

Looking at Beccaroni's goggled eyes, he recalled the man's desperate words . . . Had he really repented? Would he have been willing to confess in front of a judge? And even to drag Monsignor Sercambi into court? At one point he'd even seemed sincere, as if he'd suddenly realised the gravity of what he'd done . . . Was Bordelli right to have killed him? It was too late to turn back now . . .

He studied the spines of the hundreds of volumes lining the shelves. None of these books had been able to prevent Beccaroni from becoming what he was. Could men ever change? Could they transform themselves the way the grub becomes a butterfly? During one grappa-fuelled night, Dante had once said that Plato did not think so: one is necessarily born the way one is, and the only way to be different is to be born 'someone else' . . . Was it really so? Was there no such thing as guilt? Or merit? Were St Francis and Hitler the way they were because fate had decided so, or did they have a choice? At that moment it was easy to be overcome with doubt . . .

The ringing of the telephone shattered his thoughts, filling the silence of the great house with its anxious sound. He imagined it must be the same person who'd been ringing at the gate. The phone wouldn't stop ringing, and began to seem downright hysterical. Then it suddenly stopped, only to start again a few seconds later, for longer than the first time around. And again it stopped, then resumed, several times over, as though angry . . . At last it stopped in the middle of a ring, and the house fell silent. Now what?

He realised he was very thirsty. He went and got the bottle of water from his bag and drank almost half, with the feeling that, little by little, every cell in his body was getting its proper dose of fluid. He wasn't the least bit hungry, but it was better, just the same, to chew on something. Without removing his gloves, he opened a slab of chocolate and ate a few squares, letting it melt against his palate. He took out his book and started reading, clumsily turning the pages with his gloved fingers.

Half an hour later he heard a car pull up outside the villa. Actually it sounded as if there were two. Grabbing his bag, he went out of the study, and as he was climbing the stairs he heard the doorbell ring. He went and peered out of the same shutter as before. One of the cars was a police car, with its light flashing. Visible behind the bars of the gate, sporadically illuminated by the revolving blue light, were two officers and another man in uniform, no doubt the night guard who'd heard the gunshot. The doorbell rang again, then once more. The third time it lasted for almost a whole minute, then silence returned at last . . .

At half past three in the morning, he pulled up on the threshing floor in the Beetle, and as he turned the engine off he felt all his muscles relax. While driving up the Imprunetana he'd eaten a panino and drunk a little water. Before entering his house, he turned round to look at the dark mass of the castle, which for some time now had shown no lights in its windows. In his mind he sent a final word of thanks to Orlando and the contessa, who, without knowing . . .

Opening the door he immediately found Blisk, all waggy tailed and bleary eyed, and stroked his muzzle.

'There was a change of plan . . . I've come home early . . .'

He went and put the remaining panini in the fridge, then went over to the fireplace, where he set fire to Beccaroni's full confession. He'd only wanted it to compare it with Signorini's. He scattered the ash with the little shovel, to get rid of all trace. Grabbing a pack of Nazionali cigarettes, he went outside with the dog for a stroll through the olive grove. He smoked one cigarette after another, blowing the smoke up to the star-filled sky. He had a faint sense of oppression, of something lightly weighing on his conscience . . . but it would soon pass. It was probably mostly fatigue. Whatever the case, everything had gone better than expected.

The private guard had stopped to leave his ticket in the mailbox at the exact moment he'd fired the Browning, which set all the machinery in motion . . . Wasn't that, too, a sign of destiny?

The guard had rung the bell, tried to phone, and in the end had gone to the police. A squad car came to the scene, and half an hour later the fire department also showed up, accompanied by two more police cars. He'd kept spying through the slats in the first-floor shutters, and the floodlight pointed into the garden allowed him to recognise Piras. This discovery had almost made him smile. The Sardinian knew all about Beccaroni and company, and was probably presently racking his brain with questions . . . He was sure to ring his former boss the following day in the hope of finding out what had happened.

The firemen succeeded in snaring the dogs and then locking them up in their own enclosure at the back of the garden. Bordelli had observed the difficult operation through the shutters of several different rooms. He even saw a couple of journalists arrive with cameras. When the officers gave the order to break through one of the windows, he fled up into the attic, keeping the small door ajar in order to listen. He heard some crashing sounds, then the voices of the people coming in. It was impossible to understand what they were saying, but he could nevertheless tell at what moment they discovered the dead Beccaroni with his head on the desk . . .

The whole thing went pretty quickly, considering the circumstances. Just a little over forty minutes passed between the moment they broke through the window and the moment the corpse was loaded into the ambulance. It took another half-hour to nail the window shut from the inside, and to iron out the last bureaucratic details. Finally they all left, and silence returned . . . Shortly thereafter, he'd suddenly remembered something that made him break out in a cold sweat. He realised he'd completely forgotten an extremely important detail. Had the front door of the villa been simply pulled shut, automatically locking it, or had they taken the trouble to find the keys and give the lock an extra turn or two? He hadn't even checked to see whether the lock opened from the inside with a handle, or whether you needed the keys. What a stupid shit he'd been! With his heart in his throat, he quickly went downstairs to check, thinking inevitably of fate. He was biting his lips as he approached the door, but then heaved a sigh of relief . . . It was a modern lock, one of those with a handle, and on top of this, nobody had bothered to give it a turn of the key. He could walk out unmolested, leaving no trace whatsoever of his having been there. But he didn't want to spoil everything in his haste to leave, and he waited nearly another hour, sitting on the staircase.

Time seemed to have stood still, and he went on a sort of journey through his memory. An incoherent but relaxing journey through the different stages of his life . . . He even remembered a freezing-cold night in February of '44, in Cassino, when to distract himself in his insomnia he'd fashioned a knuckleduster from part of an aluminium propeller blade from a British plane that had been shot down. At the end of the war he'd taken it home with him as a souvenir, but one morning his mother had secretly thrown it out with the rubbish. For him it was as if a part of his life had been thrown away, but he managed not to get angry, so as not to humiliate the poor woman, who'd already been through so much . . .

At half past two, he'd decided it was time to leave. He opened the front door a crack and peered out into the darkened garden faintly illuminated by the dim glow of the outdoor lamp. The two Dobermanns had been left in their pen, and he could hear them jumping against the wire fence. No doubt someone would come and take them away the following day, with the requisite stamps from the courts.

He'd closed the door behind him, quietly crossed the garden, pressed the button to unlock the small service gate, and found himself out on the street. The dogs hadn't even barked. With the hat on his head and the glasses on his nose, he'd headed off at a leisurely pace along the same path he'd taken to get there. All the way to Via Senese he hadn't seen a living soul, either on foot or in a car. He'd made it to his Beetle and driven home feeling as though he'd just emerged from a bad dream.

With Blisk at his side, he went back into the house and got into bed. He turned out the light, too tired to read anything.

Everything had gone the way it was supposed to, without the slightest hitch. A textbook suicide. No one would ever suspect otherwise, not even Monsignor Sercambi. As he was falling asleep the same scene kept replaying in his mind, of Beccaroni's head falling hard on to the desk . . .

A beautiful woman . . . black hair in the wind, love in her eyes . . . came towards him gently smiling, lips slightly open, looking him straight in the eye . . . She took his head in her hands . . . At that moment he woke up with a start, with the sensation that he'd just heard a noise downstairs. He turned the light on and sat up, holding his breath. He clearly heard footsteps coming up the stairs . . .

'Where are you? I'm gonna take you for nice little ride in the country,' said a male voice, and Bordelli dropped back down in bed with a smile, having recognised Botta, who hadn't forgotten his promise to look after the dog.

'Ciao, Ennio . . .' he said in a loud voice.

After a second of absolute silence, the door opened a crack, and Botta's bug-eyes appeared in the gap.

'Do you want to scare me to death, Inspector? Especially now that I'm a rich man?'

'Didn't you see my car outside?'

'So what? You could have gone away in somebody else's car . . .'

'You're right, I'm sorry . . . I forgot to warn you . . .'

'You certainly did . . .' said Ennio, still a bit shaken. The dog had come over to the bed and was resting its muzzle on the mattress.

'In the end I never made that journey.'

'*La donna è mobile* . . .' Botta sang, smiling ironically.

Bordelli didn't catch the provocation. He got out of bed and dressed as best he could. It was barely nine o'clock, and he'd slept about five hours, more or less, but he didn't feel too tired.

'Shall we have some coffee?' he asked, rubbing his eyes. They all headed downstairs, dog included.

'So, what's happening?' asked Botta.

'Nothing is happening . . .'

'Weren't you supposed to be away for a few days?'

'I changed my mind.'

'Or maybe some *woman* changed her mind . . .'

'Maybe . . .'

'Still want to carry on with the mystery, Inspector?'

'What mystery? . . . Oh, I still haven't thanked you for the pots with the herbs . . .'

'You're very welcome, Inspector,' said Botta, resigned to not having his curiosity satisfied.

'Now I have everything I need to become a proper cook.'

'I found the bread hanging on the door, Inspector, so I put it on the table.'

The day's edition of *La Nazione* was sticking out of the bag with the bread. Bordelli was curious to read the city crime-news section, but didn't want to appear too anxious to do so, and instead he started rinsing the coffee pot. Botta practically snatched it out of his hands.

'Here, let me do that.'

'*Ubi major* . . .'[21] Bordelli admitted. He went and opened the door to let Blisk out, as Ennio fiddled with the coffee while mumbling a tune by Rita Pavone.

'Care for a panino, Ennio?'

He was hungry and remembered the panini he hadn't eaten.

'Maybe later . . .' said Botta, still humming.

Bordelli grabbed a panino from the fridge and went and sat down. He spread the newspaper out on the table and turned the pages slowly, pretending to be in no hurry . . . At last he found what he was looking for . . .

## Leaves Confession and Kills Himself
FLORENCE LAWYER WRITES MYSTERIOUS CONFESSION
AND SHOOTS HIMSELF IN THE HEAD
Distraught Family: 'He was a wonderful man.'

At half past ten yesterday evening, when night patrolman Lorenzo Degl'Innocenti stopped outside the gate of the villa belonging to the lawyer Moreno Beccaroni, he heard a . . .

Bordelli read the article quickly, distractedly chatting with Botta all the while. It told how the scene had unfolded from the moment the security guard heard the shot until he and the others found the body. It also mentioned the two Dobermanns, which would be kept at the municipal kennel until a relative of the owner came to get them. As he'd hoped, there was no mention of any doubts as to what had happened. In short, a suicide by the book.

Finishing his panino, he crumpled some paper and threw it into the cold fireplace, on top of the ashes of Beccaroni's confession. He imagined Monsignor Sercambi opening *La Nazione* and finding a picture of another of his fellow adventurers. Would he tremble at the sight of the word 'confession'? Or would he remain impassive, confident of his own power? The most important thing was that he should suspect nothing . . . But how could he? There was no reason to. It was entirely plausible that remorse over participating in the murder of a little boy could nag at someone's conscience until it pushed him to that final act. And perhaps Monsignor wasn't even displeased to be the last remaining keeper of the obscene, abominable secret. But he had his own rendezvous with destiny . . . In due time . . .

'It's spring today,' said Botta, bringing the cups to the table. Bordelli closed the newspaper and yawned.

'Funny, you don't look like a millionaire . . .'

'What were you expecting, for me to come in coat and tie and driving a Porsche?' said Ennio, sitting down. The coffee spread its scent of serenity through the air.

'When you buy your Porsche, will you let me take it for a spin?'

'Forget about the Porsche, Inspector . . . I'm going to squirrel everything away, like you said . . . Nobody must know . . .'

'But I know everything. I've got you in the palm of my hand.'

'I'm more worried about your birthday . . . Don't you think it's better if I do the cooking?'

'Now I've got your gospel, I'm not worried.'

'Here's hoping . . .'

'You're not the only one in the world who knows how to cook, Ennio, you'll have to accept that . . .'

'A lot of people know how to drive, but racecar drivers are rare.'

'Thus spake Zarathustra . . .'

'No, I said that . . .'

They finished their coffee and Bordelli got up and put the cups in the sink.

'Have you seen the vegetable garden? It's coming along quite nicely.'

'I'll be the one to judge . . .'

'You'll fall to your knees . . .'

At that moment the telephone rang and, as Bordelli expected, it was Piras.

'Good morning, Inspector.'

'I know what you're thinking . . . I've just seen the paper . . .'

'One suicide after another . . .'

'Remorse is unforgiving, Piras.'

'Of course it is, Inspector. But one day you'll tell me how you did it.'

'I'm sorry, I don't follow . . .'

'I'm on your side, Inspector . . . Don't forget that . . .'

'Well, thanks . . .'

'Now I have to go.'

''Bye, Piras.'

He smiled as he put down the phone, then went outside with Botta to have a look at the magic garden. Little blue flowers had appeared at the tips of the rosemary branches, the sage shoots had taken root, and by this point all the chilli pepper seedlings had sprouted.

Ennio was not as impressed at this monumental achievement as he should have been, but it was merely a question of character. Bordelli did not get discouraged.

'So, what do you think, maestro?'

'It will all depend on the weather, Inspector . . . At any rate the fence could have been a little nicer.'

'Everything can always be a little better, Ennio. That's the good thing about life.'

'Thus spake Bordellustra . . .'

'When should I transplant the tomatoes?'

'In a couple of weeks, but it's probably best if I come and lend you a hand.'

'No, I can do it alone. It's fun.'

'Anyone can turn the soil a little, but making plants grow is no joke.'

'I'll manage . . . Feel like taking a little walk?'

'Even a long one, as far as that goes,' said Ennio.

They headed off through the olive grove, under a sun that was starting to heat up. It hadn't rained in earnest for a while now, and the clayey earth was beginning to crack.

It occurred to Bordelli that if he'd been less lucky he might still be shut up inside Beccaroni's villa, eating panini and waiting.

'I've decided to ask you for my share in the Milan caper, Ennio.'

'Ah, how much do you want?'

'I don't want any money . . . But if you open a trattoria, I want free meals.'

'Is that all? I would have done it anyway.'

'I almost feel like crying . . .'

'Speaking of which . . . Tomorrow I have to go and look at a property in Borgo dei Greci. If I like it I'll take it.'

'What are you going to call your trattoria?'

'I was thinking, *Botta e risposta* . . . What do you say?'

'How about . . . *Un Botta e via* . . . ?'

'*Botta da orbi* . . .'

'*Dallo Sbotta* . . .'[22]

Spouting their silly puns they entered the woods, where the sun barely filtered through the branches. The vegetation quivered with life, ready to burst forth.

When he was in the fifth form of primary school, those were the days when Mussolini and his *squadristi* were setting fire to communist and socialist meeting houses, with the tacit approval of the bourgeoisie and even the government. He was still a frightened little boy, crushed by his own shyness. When the schoolteacher called the roll, he was one of the first named: Adorno, Bini, Bordelli . . . Every time he heard his name called he would raise his hand and blush as if he were standing naked in the middle of the road. He didn't like being in the classroom with the other children. He could never wait to go home. He felt much better holed up in his bedroom playing with the cloth puppets his mother had made for him, dreaming up fantastic stories he would repeat each time with a few minor variations. The best story of all was when he managed to save his mother from an evil man who wanted to hurt her. He would swell with pride over his feats, and he went to bed at night feeling like a hero.

One morning at school he was looking out the window. It was the start of spring, the sun was out, and being in class was a bore. The swallows were darting around in the sky as though crazed. He wished he could fly with them, instead of being shut up within four walls. As usual he was sitting alone on the last bench, trying to hide. The schoolmistress was telling the story of a Carbonaro who'd given his life for his country, fighting the foreign enemy. He felt bored and started fiddling with his penknife, used for sharpening pencils. Every so often he cast a glance around the classroom, like a cat looking for an escape route. He saw the yellowed walls, the crucifix hanging over the photographs of the king and the Duce, the backs of his school-mates' necks, the glass door of the bathroom at the back of the room, the black-enamelled benches, the great map of Italy on the wall, the grit floor . . . He was thoroughly familiar with it all, down to the last detail . . .

At a certain point his hand slipped and the penknife's sharp blade punctured his thumb. The blood began to bubble up and drip down on to the bench; he was worried he would die. It was the first time he'd ever seen so much blood. In a panic he stood up and managed to slip into the bathroom. He leaned back against the wall, facing the pane of glass separating him from the classroom, as the blood now dripped down his arm. His breathing became laboured, he felt faint . . . His classmates slowly turned into a sea of little black dots, and the teacher's voice reached his ears with an echo as in a bad dream. A few seconds more, and he would be dead. He was sure of it . . . At that moment, at the centre of the wall of black dots, he saw a darker silhouette coming forward, and heard the sound of the bathroom door opening.

'Bordelli . . . elli . . . elli . . . Are you sick . . . ick . . . ick . . . ? What have you done . . . one . . . one . . . ? What's all this blood . . . ood . . . ood . . . ood . . . ?'

Through the fog the teacher turned on the tap, muttering words he couldn't understand . . . He thought he would collapse on the floor, but in fact he started slowly to recover . . . Now the voices sounded normal again, the black dust-cloud dispersed, and the schoolmistress reappeared, a comforting smile on her face . . .

'It's nothing, just a little cut . . . Just go and sit down and keep your hand raised . . . I'll see if I can find a bandage . . . The rest of you, go back to your places . . .' said the teacher, chasing away his schoolmates, who had gathered in the bathroom doorway.

He slid down against the wall and sat on the floor. Obeying the teacher, he then raised his hand over his head, not under-standing the reason.

A few minutes later he was again sitting on his bench, feeling embarrassed, with a bandage over his thumb, trying to ignore the looks of the other children, who kept glancing at him furtively. He felt inescapably different and, with an unpleasant sense of satisfaction, a vague malaise. If it had been up to him, he would never have set foot in school again . . .

Two years later, also in spring, another thing happened to him that he would never forget. But it wasn't anything you could see on the outside; it was an intimate thing, all his own. He'd never told anyone about it, and in any case would not have known what to say . . . It happened one Sunday afternoon, when his parents were in the living room chatting with friends who'd come to lunch. He was playing with his puppets and was in the middle of a thrilling adventure. And all of a sudden he thought: 'It's no longer any fun playing with puppets . . .' And, combined with a slight feeling of sadness, he'd felt for the first time a fear of the unknown . . .

'It'll be so nice to see where you live,' said Adele, happy as a little girl.

They were on their way up the Imprunetana, after dining at the same resturant and the same table as the last time. It was a few minutes past ten. They'd drunk some good wine, and she was joyously tipsy. The skirt she was wearing wasn't too long, and every so often Bordelli cast a glance at her round knees, which stood out faintly pale in the darkness.

'Don't be shocked by the mess,' he said after a long silence.

Good thing he'd spent the afternoon cleaning up, dusting the furniture and sweeping clumps of fluff and dog hair from the floor. He hadn't done it for Adele's sake; at the time he still didn't know whether she would ask to see his house. It was only a way to channel the agitation he felt while waiting for evening.

'If you had a woman, she could keep your house in order,' Adele said suggestively. The scent of her perfume was reminiscent of fruit hot with sunlight, and it filled the air with a sweet sense of tension. There were long pauses between their exchanges, but neither seemed to feel any embarrassment about this.

'I've known some very disorderly women,' said Bordelli.

They fell silent again. The olive trees and cypresses sped by, alternating silver with dark green. Bordelli thought of the last time he was in a car with Eleonora, when he'd taken her home to her parents on the night of the rape. They'd driven through a Florence devastated by the flood, and the silence in the car seemed to bode a last goodbye. He would never forget it. Eleonora was sitting right there beside him, where Adele now was. Then she'd got out of the car, seeming absent, and a moment later vanished behind the front door.

'Who knows how many you've had . . .'

'How many what?'

'Women.'

'Oh . . .'

'State secret?'

'I don't think I've ever bothered to count.'

'A true gentleman . . .' she whispered, smiling.

'Don't be fooled by appearances; I'm much worse than I seem,' said Bordelli, thinking of what he'd done just the night before.

More silence. Beautiful, serene silence. Adele was lightly shaking one of her knees slightly, gazing distractedly out the window at the countryside.

'Today's the first day of spring,' she said, looking at the shining slice of moon that cut through the black sky like a fingernail.

They drove through the main square of Impruneta, which was dark and deserted, along one side of the basilica, continuing up the provincial road. Shortly thereafter they turned on to the dirt road, and as they slowly proceeded they saw a hare freeze in the glare of the headlights, ears pricked straight up. It was the same one. Bordelli stopped, as Adele smiled like a child who's just unwrapped a beautiful present.

'How cute . . .'

'I see it here often; by now we're friends.'

They waited for the animal to run away, then continued down the road to the house.

'And here's my cave.'

'It's huge.'

'Are you afraid of white bears?' asked Bordelli, turning the key in the lock. As soon as he opened the door, Blisk came out, looking bigger than ever, and after sniffing Adele he rubbed his big head against her thighs.

'He's so sweet . . . Maybe he takes after you . . .' she said, smoothing his fur with her hand.

They went into the house, leaving the dog on his own outside in the dark. Adele wanted to see all the rooms, and in the bedroom she looked around with a faint smile on her lips. Bordelli also showed her the tool room, the cellar and the old olive press.

'So, what do you think? Do you like it?'

'I don't know if I could live here alone . . . It's a bit scary . . .' she said with a shudder, shrugging her shoulders. They went back into the kitchen, and Adele dropped into the armchair.

'Would you like something to drink?' asked Bordelli, lighting a cigarette.

'What've you got that's good?'

'Just red wine . . .'

'Then I'll have a nice glass of red wine.'

'Shall I light a fire?'

'You mean for me? How chivalrous . . .'

'It'll take me a couple of minutes, princess.'

And like a medieval knight he poured the wine into two goblets, offered one to Adele and set about making a fire with great diligence. After arranging the logs and lighting the crumpled newspaper beneath them, he went and sat down beside her. Adele was truly beautiful. Three children, a lost husband and twenty years had not managed to wilt her freshness. Bordelli could still remember when she used to pass by on the streets of San Frediano, wild and fascinating, attracting everyone's gaze.

'So, here we are, just the two of us,' she said, turning the glass in her hand.

As Bordelli looked at her he thought again of the butcher and Beccaroni. In his mind he kept hearing the words: *Now it's Sercambi's turn*. But he couldn't very well make it a topic of conversation . . .

'Who's looking after the kids?'

'My mother's sleeping at my place tonight.'

'What a saintly woman . . .'

'I told her I was going out with a friend.'

'Women are all liars.'

'If she knew where I was, she would call me a tart.'

'For so little?'

'The night's not over yet,' said Adele, looking him in the eye.

Bordelli felt his face go hot, and realised that the night had yet to begin. He tossed his cigarette butt into the fire, wondering to himself whether he would have preferred Eleonora to Adele at that moment . . . But he had no answer. He set his goblet down on the floor and stood up. Going over to Adele, he bent down and kissed her on the mouth. It started as a faint touching of the lips, but then Adele also stood up, put a hand behind his neck and pulled him towards her . . . The long kiss left them both out of breath.

'You're a barbarian . . .' Adele whispered, smiling. Then she took his hand and led him like a child into the bedroom. She didn't turn on any lights, letting the lamp in the hallway cast a faint glow into the room. She took off her shoes and fell back on the bed. Bordelli lay down beside her.

'There's still time for you to change your mind,' he whispered into her ear. They hugged each other tight, still kissing all the while. Moments later they were under the covers, naked as the day they were born . . .

He dreamt he was in the Beetle with his father driving and paying close attention to the road, while he, a little boy, was lying on the back seat, happy to be taken somewhere without knowing where. His father wasn't talking, as though he had too much on his mind. All he knew was that it would be a very long journey, and this filled him with joy . . . He was so happy he felt like crying . . . In fact he started sobbing, but his father didn't hear him and kept on driving . . . The road was full of bends, and he could see only the tops of the trees . . . Then he slowly awoke and realised that it was Adele who was crying. He felt her body shake in the bed. He embraced her affectionately and ran his hand over her cheeks wet with tears.

'Adele . . .' he whispered.

'I'm sorry . . .' she said, trying to stop crying but not succeeding.

'What's wrong?'

'Nothing . . . I'm fine . . . I've never felt so good . . .'

And she embraced him in turn and smothered him with kisses. Passionate kisses, but also sweet, and also desperate. Wonderful kisses that would have left any man astounded. Then she suddenly burst into laughter, but quickly stopped and started crying again. Bordelli hugged her tight.

'You're going to drive me crazy,' he said.

'No . . .'

'You're a wounded woman – easy prey for men . . . And that's what makes you dangerous. At some point you'll realise that all you needed was to feel desired, and you'll toss me aside like a used dishrag . . .'

'What do you care? All you men want to do is add another notch to your pistol butt, and you're happy,' said Adele, whimpering and laughing.

'It's true, I am happy . . . I've been dreaming of this night for twenty years . . .'

'And tomorrow you can go to the bar and tell your friends you screwed me.'

'Absolutely. And in great detail . . .'

'Me, too . . . I'm going to call up all my girlfriends . . .'

'But you must tell them I'm twenty years old . . .'

'I wouldn't know what to do with a twenty-year-old.'

'Thirty-five?'

'I'll tell them the truth . . . That you're an old fogey . . .'

She'd stopped crying and now intertwined her legs with Bordelli's.

'I haven't turned fifty-seven yet,' said Bordelli, thinking of his birthday in two weeks' time.

'Kiss me . . .'

And it started all over again, even better, more fun than the first time. In bed with her, Bordelli felt the same lightness he had with Eleonora . . . But it really wasn't the right time to be thinking of her . . .

Afterwards, they remained embraced, staring into the darkness and panting. Again Bordelli thought of Eleonora . . . Who knew what she was doing at that moment? Had she, too, just finished making love? Or was she tossing and turning in bed, thinking of someone? Maybe she was simply sleeping . . .

He realised she now seemed farther away, more unreachable than ever . . . Like some mythological figure . . .

'What are you thinking about?' Adele whispered.

'A woman.'

He didn't feel like lying, not at his age. Old age was revolting, but at least it had allowed him to discover how nice it was not to hide oneself.

'Did you cheat on her by sleeping with me?' she asked, mildly anxious.

'We haven't been together for a long time, but I do still think of her.'

'She left you?'

'It's sort of a complicated story . . .' At the moment he didn't feel like telling it.

'What's she like? Pretty?'

'I'd say so . . .'

'Prettier than me? . . . No, don't tell me . . .'

'You're absolutely beautiful, don't pretend you don't know.'

'Don't change the subject . . . How old is she?'

'A little younger than you . . .'

'Thirty-five?'

'Younger . . .'

'Thirty?'

'Come on, let's forget about it . . .'

'Less than thirty?' she said, almost offended.

'Sort of . . . Twenty-five . . .'

'I don't believe it . . . What could a beautiful girl of twenty-five possibly see in a pot-bellied lug like you?' said Adele, punching his chest.

'Ouch . . . I wondered the same thing myself.'

'So, in short, you're still in love with her . . .'

'Maybe . . .'

'And what about me? Are you in love with me? . . . No, don't tell me . . .'

'You stopped me just in time.'

'No, on second thought, I want to know . . . Tell me . . . Are you in love with me?'

'Seeing the way things have turned out . . . and judging from the witnesses' testimonies . . . and considering the extenuating circumstances . . . it would seem I am . . . While maintaining the option of a contingent suspension of the sentence . . .'

'Well, that's such an exciting declaration of love I might just die here and now . . .'

'You have to forgive me . . . Words fail me in such matters . . .'

'Oh, I don't know about that,' she said, laughing.

'I'd love to meet your children.'

'Ohmygod, I wonder what time it is . . .'

'I think you turned into a pumpkin a good while back,' said Bordelli, concerned.

She turned on the light and looked at the clock. 'It's almost two . . . My mother's going to have a fit . . .'

'Why don't you just tell her the naked truth?'

'That's all I need,' said Adele, getting out of bed.

She started getting dressed in a hurry, looking for her clothes scattered about the room. Bordelli sat back and enjoyed the show. Watching a woman get dressed was almost more beautiful than watching her strip.

'You're not bad, you know . . .'

'Silly . . . Come on, get dressed . . .'

'Yes, sir.'

Less than a minute later he was ready, while Adele was still fussing with her stockings.

'But did you leave your dog outside?'

'Damn . . .' said Bordelli. He went downstairs and opened the door. Blisk was lying on the threshing floor. He rose to his feet, looking offended, and waddled into the house.

'Come on, try and understand . . .' said Bordelli, following behind him. The dog drank some water and went and lay down in his corner beside the fire. He sighed rhetorically and then closed his eyes, ignoring Bordelli's apologies.

Adele descended the stairs, trying to fix her hair a little with her hands. She had a sweet, soft look in her eye, dreamy and afraid, like that of a little girl who had just goofed up yet again.

They went out of the house and got into the Beetle. She shivered with cold, and Bordelli turned on the heat. Going down the Imprunetana, he realised that Adele's anxiousness was starting to affect him, too . . . He felt guilty, the way he used to do when as a lad he would come home late at night and find his father waiting up for him.

The glow of his high beam lit up the stone walls and silvery olive boughs along the road, under a clear, remote sky.

'So, in short, you're in love with two women . . .' said Adele, with just a touch of jealousy.

'Let's just say I'm a little confused.'

'What's her name?'

'Eleonora.'

'Why don't you introduce me to her? That way we could become friends and decide together what to do about you,' said Adele, swatting him on the knee. She was trying to make light of the whole thing, but there was a note of agitation in her voice.

'Maybe you could roll the dice for me,' said Bordelli.

'That would be fun . . .'

But her tone didn't sound at all like fun.

'I would win either way,' said Bordelli, trying to recover some lightness.

Adele had folded her arms across her chest. 'How can anyone be in love with two people at once?'

'I don't know . . . It hadn't ever happened to me before . . .'

'If you ask me, you prefer her.'

'Adele, please . . . I haven't seen her for months . . . Something really terrible happened . . .'

'Why don't you tell me about it?'

'Some other time.'

'I don't want to suffer any more,' said Adele, caressing his hand and forcing herself to smile. They both remained silent. Every so often they looked at each other and exchanged a smile. Neither said a word for the rest of the ride.

Bordelli pulled up outside Adele's building, and after he turned off the engine, they kissed. Adele's lips were soft and nervous. When they got out of the car, she already had her keys in her hand. They kissed again outside the door, more hurriedly this time.

'When can I see you again?' asked Bordelli, squeezing her wrist.

'I don't know . . . I'll ring you . . .' she whispered, as if afraid to wake up everyone in the building.

'Sleep well, my little princess.'

'I'll do my best . . .'

She put her key in the lock, waved her small hand, and vanished behind the door.

Was Adele real? Had she ever existed?

For two days he did nothing but walk in the woods with his dog, tend the garden and read by the fire, trying not to wait for Adele to call. He was unable to keep from thinking of her, but that didn't mean he'd forgotten about Eleonora, who by this point was like Venus emerging from the seas, a Renaissance fresco serving as backdrop to all his thoughts.

On Friday morning he awoke with a sense of foreboding, as though something unpleasant were about to happen, though he tried to ignore it. It was probably just his mood, though he was unable to work out exactly what the problem was. Loneliness had nothing to do with it, nor the fact of living completely alone in a large house. That was actually pleasant, far more than he would ever have imagined.

He got out of bed with his back in knots, and when he opened his bedroom door, as usual he found the white bear waiting for him, tongue hanging out.

'Why couldn't you be a beautiful woman?' he said, squeezing the animal's muzzle.

Together they went downstairs to the kitchen, and Bordelli opened the front door to let him out. Blisk stopped for a moment on the threshold and turned around to look at him, sad eyed, then barked a couple of times and ran off. He'd never done this before, and at that moment Bordelli was afraid he might never come back. He went out on the threshing floor and watched him. Blisk was galloping towards the woods without turning round, and when he disappeared through the trees it was as though a light had gone out. Bordelli felt a twist in his gut, then shrugged and shook his head . . . As if a gluttonous beast like

Blisk could ever . . . Where was he ever going to find soups like the ones he ate at Bordelli's house?

He made coffee and sat down at the table to drink it, staring into the void. It was a strange day. He could feel it. All at once he realised that Eleonora and Adele resembled each other . . . Black hair, dark eyes, at once lunar and solar, ironic, modern, but also sweet, capable of tenderness, of throwing themselves without shame into a man's arms . . .

Was he really in love with both? If they ever did force him to choose, he knew that whatever decision he made, he would stew with regret afterwards. For the moment, however, the question didn't arise, and he wasn't the one to resolve it, anyway. It would really have been too much of a good thing, in spite of everything. At the moment only Adele was a concrete reality; Eleonora was sort of a dream.

He finished his coffee and went out to water the garden, as every morning. But the monotony of the daily ritual was not accompanied by any inner monotony on his part. On the contrary, it always felt as if he was doing something new, perhaps because his thoughts were different each time. The days passed, his life changed . . . Surprises, discoveries . . . Confused dreams blending with equally muddled hopes . . . So much for the wisdom of old age . . . Around women he still felt like a bumbling little boy, at the mercy of the feminine elements . . .

The seedlings were coming up nicely, despite Botta's doubts. Bordelli finished watering, and after stacking a good bit of firewood in one corner of the kitchen, he went for a short walk in the woods behind the house. Every so often he saw a yellow or white butterfly flutter by like a hallucination and disappear into the broom and juniper shrubs . . .

At one point he very nearly stepped on a viper that was sunning itself on the footpath, then followed the reptile with his gaze as it slithered slowly away over the rotten leaves. It looked harmless enough . . . But wasn't it man's own fault that he was condemned to suffer? A snake, an apple, a woman . . . Foolish man was innocent; he'd done nothing wrong, other than being simple minded. He'd obeyed the woman and given in to her urgings. He hadn't decided anything himself . . . It was always women who decided, right from the start . . .

He called to Blisk in a loud voice, expecting to see him appear through the shrubs. But there was no sign of the dog. He crossed paths with a game warden with a double-barrel shotgun on his shoulder, and asked him whether he'd seen a big dog that looked like a white bear. The game warden stopped and shook his head. The man was short and stout, with a deformed nose covered with little red veins, typical of inveterate drinkers.

'I haven't seen anyone.'

'Thanks just the same.'

'You're welcome . . .' said the man, taking his leave and walking slowly away.

The guy's even got a flask of red in his jacket pocket, thought Bordelli as he ventured farther into the woods, every so often calling the dog's name . . . But maybe Blisk was already back at the house, waiting for him.

Round about midday he headed back home. He hadn't yet smoked any cigarettes, and had no intention of doing so until after lunch. Who knew whether Adele would call . . . He wanted to see her again, talk to her, kiss her, take her into his bed . . .

At the house there was no sign of Blisk, and so Bordelli went back into the woods to look for him. He started shouting his name, hands cupped round his mouth, and realised that there was a note of desperation in his cry . . . As if he were calling out a woman's name . . .

Was it possible Blisk had simply left just like that, the same way he'd come? What kind of call had he heard? What was he looking for? Maybe he'd just strayed a little farther afield than usual, chasing a pack of boar or a stag, and would be back soon.

He called to him again, voice cracking with disappointment,

hoping to see a spot of white through the underbrush . . . But it was pointless to keep looking for him. Blisk knew his way home. If he'd decided to leave, there must be a reason. His choice must be respected, however painful . . . Wasn't that the way it was with women, too, when they left you? What point was there in trying to make them stay? It was wiser to say goodbye to them with a kiss on the forehead and wish them a happy life. But it was never so simple . . . In fact on most such occasions he'd reacted instinctively, swinging between bitterness and pleading, and the mere memory of it made him feel ashamed.

He stopped calling the dog and headed back home with a lump in his throat, thinking of the premonition he'd had upon waking that morning. Wasn't that another sign that fate existed? *The Book* had already been written, and every now and then someone happened to catch a glimpse of one of the pages beforehand.

As he drew near to his house he heard the phone ringing and broke into a run. He unlocked the door and rushed to answer.

'Hello?'

'It's me . . . Are you all right?'

'Hi, Adele . . .'

'You're out of breath . . .'

'Sorry . . . I was outside and ran to get the phone.'

He could hear a little girl chattering in the background.

'I wanted to tell you something . . .'

'Okay . . .'

'I've thought a lot about this . . . It's better if we don't see each other any more . . .' she whispered, her voice cracking.

'What do you mean?'

'You're in love with that other woman . . . And sooner or later . . . You know how these things go . . .'

'Adele . . .'

'I have no desire to compete with a twenty-five-year-old . . .'

'What do you mean?'

'I don't want to suffer any more . . . I just can't do it . . . I need to be alone . . .'

'Don't leave me . . .'

'Please . . . Please . . . Don't come looking for me any more . . .'

She burst into tears, stifling her sobs, and hung up before Bordelli could find anything to say.

So another had left, just like the white bear. He put the phone down and stood there staring into space. Now it was clear that his premonition had been right on the money, more than ever . . .

He'd managed to react not too badly, not to insist on seeing her again, and to respect her wishes, he would never call on her again. This, at least, he could be proud of. If, on the other hand, she herself one day . . .

He mustn't let the ways of the world get him down, not at his age. He took a deep breath and began making lunch, though he wasn't very hungry. He felt dazed, but didn't want to think. It was better to put off all speculation for the moment. Every so often his eyes fell on Blisk's bowl, and he decided he would leave it where it was.

He ate his pasta without bothering to turn on the telly, washing it down with half a flask of wine. After the coffee, he went and sat down in front of the cold fireplace, book in hand. He didn't have the strength to make a fire. He tried to read but was unable. Dropping the book into his lap, he started staring at the ceiling rafters. The silence penetrated all the way into his bones. Had he been wrong to be frank with Adele? In spite of everything, he was convinced it was the right thing to do . . .

His gaze fell on the dog's bowl again, and he couldn't help but remember Adele's last words: *Please . . . Don't come looking for me any more . . .* And he immediately remembered Eleonora's last words: *Leave me alone, I'm fine . . .* The meaning was essentially the same . . .

He wished he could cry, but couldn't. He hadn't wept even when his mother died while listening to her son whispering some lines of D'Annunzio:

## Death in the Tuscan Hills

*Hear it? The rain falls*
*on the lonely*
*greenery,*
*a persistent hiss*
*in air varying*
*through fronds thick and thin.*
*Listen. The falling*
*tears elicit*
*the cicadas' call . . .*

On Saturday and Sunday the weather was gorgeous and sun-drenched. Bordelli spent them hiking in the woods above Cintoia, between hunters' gunshots and fleeing quarry, expecting to see a large mass of white fur appear at any moment through the brush. It was a childish hope, like wishing he would find Adele waiting for him at the house when he returned.

By now he was used to seeing Blisk scampering through the trees like a wolf in search of prey, and travelling the trails without him was a sad affair. But the mysterious dog had taught him something that should already have been obvious to him at his age: that life was governed by illusion. *That* was what groped its way towards the future. You thought what you had today you'd still have tomorrow, even though no deity had promised you this. Equally true was that it was hard to live without illusions; you could only hope to be conscious of them and to gain some advantage from that awareness. To enjoy your dreams and be ready for disappointment, that was the way to do it . . .

He spent the rest of the week in similarly hermit-like fashion. Solitary walks, vegetable garden, books and fireplace. The cold weather had pretty much ended, but the habit of lighting a fire died hard.

Every so often the phone would ring, and he would run to answer. He succeeded in not giving in to Rosa's insistent invi-tations, resisting her childish desires . . . He really didn't feel like going into the city and seeing all those people.

At one point he had a chat with Piras that was full of insinuations as to Beccaroni's suicide, and to dodge the elephant in the room he made sure to remind him of his upcoming birthday dinner and asked him not to bring any presents. Come hell or high water, he really wanted to pull off that dinner party.

Even Diotivede called once, caustic as usual, to announce the great event for the second of April, rigorously without presents.

Botta had already known for a while about the birthday party and would certainly not forget. He was probably very curious to see whether his gospel could convert an inspector into a cook.

Friday evening after supper Bordelli rang Dante and invited him to the birthday party. Dante was pleased to accept and asked him whether he felt like a grappa at that moment. Bordelli hadn't seen a living soul for days, and going to Mezzomonte certainly wasn't the same as diving head first into the crowds of Florence . . .

He got in his car and fifteen minutes later was reclining in an armchair in the penumbra of Dante's laboratory, with a glass in one hand and a cigarette in the other. The church-like light of the candelabra was intimate and relaxing. It felt like a faraway world in which pain and sorrow were only memories.

Dante sat opposite him, puffing on his cigar. Plumes of dense smoke rose up to the ceiling. After a few minutes of this, Bordelli broke the silence.

'Why is the world so ugly?' he asked, smiling at the triteness of his question. But he knew that a phrase like that would trigger Dante's reasoning processes . . .

'If the world wasn't ugly, Jesus Christ would not have had any success,' said Dante in one of his typical syntheses, before he burst out laughing.

'I'll have to think about that . . .'

'We could also justifiably add that if the world were all peaches and cream, there would be no art. Every work of art is a little like Jesus Christ . . . It tries to create a bridge between what is and what should be . . . It is an attempt to put things in their proper places . . . The link between Good and Evil . . .'

'I get it but I don't get it . . .'

'Try to imagine a world with no Leonardo, no Schubert, no Van Gogh . . . no Homer . . . no Leopardi . . . no Shakespeare . . . no Aeschylus . . . no Dostoyevsky . . . no Pontormo . . . no Bach . . . I could go on all night.'

'It would be hard.'

'They are all the other face of horror . . . All war, all abuse of power, all injustice, all horror drives the soul of certain men to create immortal works . . . Without them really even knowing it. They are simply tools, instruments of history, who by mysterious means have the power to steal fragments of truth from the world beyond the heavens, where the Universals reside.'

'I must admit I'd never thought of that before.'

'The world must be seen as a whole . . . It is like a great anthill teeming with activity aimed at survival, in equipoise between life and death. Without horror, there would be no art, but if there were no art, life would be hell. It's nature herself that finds the remedies – or, perhaps more accurately, tries to patch things up. And yet Good never gets discouraged and keeps opposing Evil. It's possible the Manichaeans were right; they saw the eternal struggle between Good and Evil, between light and darkness, in every aspect of existence.'

Dante got up to refill the glasses and remained standing in front of Bordelli, a cloud of smoke enveloping his head. His eyes sparkled with goodness and intelligence, like the eyes of certain dogs. He smiled and continued expounding upon his vision of things, as though thinking aloud.

'If we take all of humanity as a single organism, we can see its illnesses as well as the cures that keep it alive. Individuals are of no importance in all this, and yet each person nevertheless pursues his or her minuscule desires, which in comparison to the Universal Project are less than fly-shit in the wind . . . All the same, I must admit that for the moment just what the Universal Project is, exactly, eludes me. But I have no right to complain: no single individual can grasp Being in its totality. We have our own little universe to administer, and we can't do otherwise.'

'Well, after that speech I feel like a real nothing, but it's sort of nice,' said Bordelli.

He felt better now. He wished he never had to leave that great room in candlelit shadow, where one discussed profound things without resolution. He didn't want to think about going back to a house without Adele, without Eleonora, without Blisk . . .

'Did you know you have a beautiful voice, Bordelli?' asked Dante, sitting back down.

'This is a night full of revelations . . .'

'The voice is supremely important. Try looking at someone and imagining what kind of person he is, without ever having heard his voice. As soon as you hear him speak, nine times out of ten you'll change your opinion.'

'You're right; that's happened to me before,' said Bordelli, pleasantly surprised.

'Whereas your voice corresponds perfectly with what your appearance expresses.'

'Should I be happy about that?'

'I'll leave you to decide,' Dante said with a smile, downing his glass in a single gulp.

The moment he awoke he went down into the kitchen and opened the front door, but there was no white bear lying on the threshing floor. Blisk really had left, and Adele, too, had run very far away, both on the same morning . . . A day he should mark on the calendar. It didn't seem possible he would never see them again.

The previous night, when he got home he cast a glance, as usual, up at the castle's dark silhouette against the sky. He might never see the contessa again, either, and the tower window would remain dark for eternity.

He made coffee and sat down at the table with paper and pen, but it wasn't to write a letter to a woman. Ignoring his melancholy, he compiled a careful list of things to buy the following day, in accordance with the gospel according to Botta. It was the first time he'd ever organised a dinner that he would cook entirely himself, and he wanted to be equal to the task.

He quickly shaved, got dressed, and went into town. The church square was filled with the livestock market, and he had to park in Piazza Nova. He amused himself as always, queueing up with the old peasant women and hearing their discussions of things about town. At the La Romana store he bought a white tablecloth and a kitchen scale, the old-fashioned kind, with two dishes and weights.

When he got home he arranged his purchases in the fridge. It wasn't yet ten o'clock, so he had a long, lonely day ahead of him. He went and carefully watered the garden, observing his creatures' progress. The chilli peppers by now seemed to be growing before his very eyes, and the leaves of the tomato plants gave off a pleasant scent. The sage and rosemary had visibly straightened themselves up . . . to say nothing of the artichokes. He finished watering, got back in his car, and descended at a leisurely pace towards Florence.

When he got to Viale Michelangelo he parked at the bottom of the stairs to his favourite church, the basilica of San Miniato, the headless saint who, after being decapitated by the Romans, picked up his head and climbed up that very hill.

He went into the cemetery of the Porte Sante, the Holy Gates, for a short stroll. It had been a long time since he'd last entered. He'd always enjoyed walking among the graves, amid the silent, sleeping multitude.

*Through sublime sacrifices to God and Family . . .*

*He devoted his good and humble life . . .*

*She offered her life to God and Family with humility and abnegation . . .*

*He passed away to the peace of Christ . . .*

*A loving husband and father . . . Prudent and hard-working . . .*

He looked at the photos of the deceased enclosed in their oval frames, scanned their poetic epitaphs, read the dates and calculated how long they'd lived, and sometimes tried to imagine their lives, their homes, the moment of their death . . .

*Remembered by his colleagues for his brilliant studies . . .*

*Eternal peace to his inviolate soul . . .*

*Great esteem and endless love were his lot . . .*

*An angelic vision of uncorrupted purity and resigned
sorrow . . .*

*Gentle and pious . . . She devoted her life unselfishly to her
family . . .*

He remembered an old story, one he'd looked into some ten
years earlier, a mystery that had started right there, as he was
walking in this same cemetery. He'd discovered that the grave
of a certain Antonio Samsa was identical to one in the Jewish
cemetery of Via di Caciolle, with even the same birthdate. How
was it possible to die twice? He'd taken it upon himself to get
to the bottom of the mystery and uncovered a sordid tale of
betrayal and money at the time of the Nazi occupation. No
matter where you scratched, you found only filth. Who knew
how many other similar stories were buried under the dust of
the past? Sometimes things came together to bring the truth to
light, as happened for Antonio Samsa. Was it all only a matter
of chance? Or was fate itself the Great Architect?

*Torn from his parents' loving arms . . .*

*A charitable minister . . . Precious font of domestic
virtues . . .*

*Hard-working, honest citizen . . . Master of his art . . .*

*She shunned the worldly vanities, and in heaven helps her
loved ones . . .*

*Taken up too young by cruel death into the light of the
angels . . .*

Still strolling through the chapels and family vaults, he started
thinking seriously of the sort of inscription he would want on
his own gravestone, but he couldn't decide. A touching state-

ment? Something solemn? How about a poem? Or a tercet from the *Inferno*? Or something light or silly . . .

*At last a little silence . . .*

*From now on, no more clichés . . .*

*I've finally gone on a diet . . .*

The silliest thing was worrying about matters that would no longer concern him after his death . . . But maybe they would concern him, more than he could ever imagine . . . A person's life did not end with his death, but left behind a trail of slime, as snails did.

He went out of the cemetery, but felt like seeing the church again rather than going back to his car. When he came to the front of the building, he looked up at the marble geometries of the ancient façade, which loomed over all of Florence with graceful power. Atop the central gable, where most churches customarily had a cross, stood a golden eagle with a roll of fabric in its talons, symbol of the Arte della Lana, the wool guild that had paid for the construction almost a thousand years earlier . . . Money was more powerful than religion . . .

Crossing the portal was like leaving the world behind. Faith, imagination, lightness and magnificence combined harmoniously in the rhythm of the columns, the great mosaic of Christ Pantocrator, the decorated truss beams, and again in the perfect geometry of the polychrome marble.

The church was empty. He had it all to himself. He started walking about, studying every detail, accompanied only by the shuffling of his feet. Climbing the staircase that led to the choir, he slipped into the sacristy to see the trecento frescoes of the life of St Benedict. The images succinctly presented the main episodes of the saint's life, as in a film, in a way that the illiterates of the time could fully grasp . . .

Suddenly a door opened and a tall, elegant friar came out.

Bordelli had the impression he'd met him before, but, try as he might, he couldn't remember. The friar stopped in front of him and smiled.

'Welcome back.'

'Good morning, Father . . . I'm sorry, but I can't remember in what circumstances we met . . . My memory doesn't go back much farther than last Wednesday . . .'

'I'm Father Lenti. Ten years ago you brought me a suitcase full of dollars.'

'Ah, yes, now I remember . . .'

The whole strange affair of the dollars he'd donated to the monastery of San Miniato came back to him. He'd turned the money over to this particular friar.

'I promise you they were well spent,' said Father Lenti.

'That's not why I'm here . . .'

'I should hope not . . .'

'I've always liked this church.'

'Even the faithless like it,' said the friar, pointing two dark, penetrating eyes at him.

'Can I ask you something?'

'Would you like to confess?'

'I'd like to ask you a question, if you have a minute to spare.'

'I hope I can answer it.'

'It's just something I'm curious about.'

'Go right ahead.'

'Well . . . If someone took justice into his own hands and killed some murderers, and then came and confessed to you . . . How would you respond?'

'The only justice is God's Justice, which man cannot replace.'

'Of course . . . But imagine that it's 1944, and you see a Nazi about to slaughter a group of children . . . You have a machine gun in your hand and you can prevent a massacre . . . What would you do?'

'Well, in that case, I'd shoot . . .' said Father Lenti, smiling, after which he made a slight bow and left.

Alone in the dark kitchen, he waited by the fire for half past one to strike, at which point he ever so slightly raised his glass of wine, toasting himself on his fifty-seventh birthday. His mother had always told him he was born at that hour of the night, during a windstorm. Maybe that was why he'd always liked wind.

That afternoon he'd gone alone to the Aurora to see *The Graduate*, a film everybody was talking about. The theatre was full, and as usual it wasn't easy finding a seat in the balcony. He was able to follow the story without distractions, even though just opposite the cinema was the women's clothing shop where he'd seen Eleonora for the first time. In spite of everything, he managed to smoke only one cigarette. He found the film's ending quite touching and, feeling a little silly, imagined himself doing the same thing with Eleonora . . . or maybe Adele . . .

Drinking one glass after another, he finished the remaining half-flask, enveloped in the twilight of the kitchen. The only source of light was the fire in the hearth, as the shadows trembled on the walls. He lit his last cigarette, the fifth of the day. In spite of everything, he felt good. The lake of sadness surrounding him was familiar to him; he swam in it like a fish. His mind flooded with childhood memories, and he languished in melancholy. He would have given his right arm to go back to those days, when the world was a perpetual surprise – though, truth be told, there was no lack of surprises in his present life as well. But that was different. When he was a little boy, the world could change before his eyes at any moment. Now it was a little like looking into a kaleidoscope, where the little pieces of coloured glass would change their positions but were always the same pieces . . .

He tossed his cigarette butt into the fire and went to bed. He didn't even try to read, feeling too tired. He switched off the light and turned on to his side, keeping his eyes closed in the hope that he would fall asleep quickly. A stream of confused thoughts and memories flowed through his brain, and he let the current carry him away like a boat adrift . . .

He dreamt of Blisk, the first Blisk, the big Nazi German Shepherd he'd taken home with him at the end of the war, after nursing a nasty wound the animal had . . . and he relived an episode that had actually happened. He'd come home a few weeks earlier, after five years of bombs, torpedoes and machine-gun fire. He was still living with his parents, in Viale Volta, while waiting to find his own accommodation. Blisk woke him up in the dead of night, pulling the covers off him with his teeth, soundlessly, and continually going over to the door as if trying to tell him something. Bordelli pricked up his ears and heard some sounds. Rushing into the dining room with a pistol in hand, he found two petty burglars rifling through the drawers. He managed just in time to stop Blisk, who was about to attack them. He turned on the light to get a better look at them. Two sorry wretches, with faces gaunt from privation. They were paralysed with fear and shaking, afraid to run away because of the dog, which had sat down and was still growling. Bordelli took him out of the room and closed the door, then gave the burglars some loose change and told them they could leave. The two looked at him as though he was mad and, after a moment's hesitation, high-tailed it out of there. He went and patted Blisk, to let him know he'd done a good job . . . But in the dream he found the big white bear's head in front of him . . .

When he woke the following morning, he realised that the sheet and blanket had ended up on the floor. Apparently Blisk – or rather, both Blisks, the Shepherd and the bear – had pulled them off. He pulled them up and stayed in bed for another half-hour, just to warm up a little.

It was almost nine when he got out of bed. After a cup of coffee and the customary sprinkling of the garden, he went for a long walk in the woods behind the house. Just a few months earlier, at that hour he was already in his office at police headquarters, hunting killers. Now he was no longer a working man, and yet he was still doing more or less the same thing. In the present instance he wasn't arresting the killers, however, but resorting to different methods. But it wasn't he who'd decided this . . . You simply couldn't let a crime like that go unpunished. A little boy kidnapped, drugged, raped, strangled to increase the pleasure of orgasm, and then shoddily buried in a wood where wild boar had already started to eat his feet . . .

Now it was Monsignor Sercambi's turn. Then it would be over. Bordelli hoped he would never again have to live through such an ordeal, but for now he had to see it through to the end . . . The monsignor would be the final effort. After him, the whole terrible crime would be buried for ever. Giacomo Pellissari could rest in peace . . .

He went home about two o'clock, pleased not to have smoked any cigarettes. He had a leisurely lunch, and after coffee he went and sat in the armchair with his book. A busy afternoon at the cooker awaited him. He lit his first cigarette of the day. Blisk's bowl was still in its place and would remain there. While reading he very nearly fell asleep to the sound of the wind blowing across the fields . . .

At five o'clock he got up from the armchair, determined to get busy. He took his purchases out of the fridge and opened the gospel of Botta:

*This version comes from my Zia Maria. Everyone has their own recipe, but after trying a good ten of them (essentially those of all my aunts – we're a big family), I've come to the conclusion that this one gets first prize.*

*There's not much to say about it, Inspector: the secret is entirely in the beans. You have to find the right beans: good, tasty beans, with plenty of pulp. Which shouldn't be very hard to find in our city. Anyway, you know better than I: the Florentine eats beans . . . and licks plates and tureens . . .*

*The Peposo is a dish typical of Impruneta, Inspector. And since you live there now, I think it's not a bad idea for you to learn how to make it. This recipe also comes from way back, apparently from the time they were building Florence Cathedral. It was invented by the craftsmen from the brickworks. In order to have a hot meal, they would cook the meat – which probably wasn't top-notch – in the kilns they cooked the clay in, obviously as far as possible from the flames. And they would let it cook for hours and hours, until it became extremely tender . . .*

For the rabbit recipe, Ennio had taken a roundabout approach, going into great detail, explaining where and when he'd learned it.

*Once, when I was at La Rufina for a little job (nothing illegal, mind you, one mustn't always imagine the worst, Inspector!), I went out to eat at a trattoria. Usually I don't set foot in a restaurant until I've 'studied' it first, and I'll walk around outside the place for a while, trying not to attract attention, to see what kind of people frequent it. I also do this, quite frankly, to avoid any nasty surprises when the bill arrives . . . Normally, however, I'm more interested in examining the customers' faces and expressions. You have no idea how many fascinating things you can discover about a restaurant. And my conclusions are usually right on target.*

    *That time, however, I was hungry as a wolf. I had in mind a nice dish of* pappardelle alla lepre,[23] *and so I took the plunge and sat down at a table right beside the door . . . in case it turned out I had to run away without paying – that is, if the price was exorbitant or the cooking abysmal.*

    *But, to continue, my blood froze when I realised I was the only customer! And, on top of that, it was one o'clock sharp!*

*Unbelievable! But by this point I was already inside, and I couldn't very well have got up and left, especially since the cook (who at that moment I took for the waiter) was approaching my table. I immediately noticed his cowboy-like swagger . . . He reminded me of Tex Willer,*[24] *the comic-book character. I was expecting him to pull out his six-shooter at any moment, and I could even hear the music . . . Anyway, now he was right beside me, but all he pulled out was a pencil he'd been keeping behind his ear. Without saying a word, he put a piece of paper on the table and wrote:* Table one, rabbit stew, *and left. It was probably the only dish they had available that day. A bit disconcerted, I resigned myself, knocking back a full glass of red wine, which, to tell you the truth, wasn't all that bad. I heard the cowboy fussing about at the cooker, and a few minutes later he returned with a steaming plate in his hands. He had a strange smile that wasn't a real smile, but a sort of ironic sneer. He went back into the kitchen, but I knew he would keep spying on me without ever changing his expression. Would you believe, Inspector, that that rabbit was the best I've eaten in all my life? After sucking every little bone and cleaning the plate with bread until it looked as if it had been washed, I went to the kitchen door and asked Tex for the recipe. It was only because I'd drunk almost a whole flask of wine that I had the courage to do this. He looked at me as if I was crazy, and so I had to insist. I told him I was a cook myself, and so I suggested we have an exchange: his rabbit recipe for one of my specialities (don't ask me which, I don't remember). Anyway, in the end he accepted. I ask you only not to give anyone the recipe, because I swore to keep it secret . . .*

Bordelli of course would respect this oath, another secret to take with him to the grave . . .

*This is not the classic apple tart, but a more 'chic' version, if that's the right word. It's the perfect conclusion to a romantic little dinner. The ideal accompaniment for the tart would be a lukewarm custard . . . It makes my mouth water just thinking about it! You must be very careful with the proportions. With puddings it's best not to improvise; the results will be disastrous . . .*

It wasn't going to be a romantic little dinner, not in the usual sense of the term. No women. Just five men at the table, by the fire . . .

As expected, Piras was the first to show up. They shook hands in the doorway, and as soon as the young man entered the kitchen, he looked around for the dog.

'He's gone,' said Bordelli.

'How'd that happen?'

'One morning he went out like every other morning, and he never came back.'

He remembered the sort of goodbye that Blisk had barked at him before leaving, and felt a twist in his gut.

'I'm sorry . . .'

'He chose his own path.'

To change the subject, he gestured with his eyes towards the table, which was set in grand fashion, with a brand new table-cloth, silver cutlery, crystal goblets, and a bottle of wine in the middle. Another five bottles were lined up on a shelf, ready for decapitation. The fire was lit, a big log of oak burning slowly between the andirons. The rest of the kitchen was in a state of chaos. Dirty pots and pans, wooden spoons, ladles, lettuce leaves on the floor, greasy dishtowels, bloodstained cutting boards . . .

'Happy birthday, Inspector,' said Piras, digging around in his pocket.

Against orders, he'd brought a present, a rather original one at that: a sheet of paper folded in four, with a report, handwritten in pen, of Monsignor Sercambi's habits, from when they'd had him tailed during the investigation into the boy's murder.

'This might come in handy,' he said allusively, as Bordelli scanned the page, pretending not to understand.

'For what?'

'You never know . . .' the Sardinian muttered.

Bordelli had no need of those notes. He remembered everything quite well. Piras knew this. His birthday present was simply a way of broaching the subject. He snatched the page out of Bordelli's hands and threw it into the fire.

'Let's enjoy the evening, Piras . . . I'd like to forget that I've just turned fifty-seven.'

'Another three years and you'll be officially retired.'

'I'm already retired, Piras.'

'I'm more likely to believe that pigs can fly, Inspector.'

'I did all the cooking myself . . . Aren't you surprised?' Bordelli said to change the subject, and he started to sweep the floor cursorily.

'You are one continuous surprise, Inspector,' Piras said suggestively.

Bordelli ignored the provocation, set the broom aside, and started putting the kitchen in some sort of order, just so it didn't look like a galley. Lifting the lid on the *Peposo*, he gave it a final stir and at that moment heard the sound of a scooter arriving outside. Botta came in carrying a case of champagne, as promised.

'Don't worry, I didn't steal it,' he said, winking at Bordelli. After greeting Piras he set the case down in a corner and went and put one bottle in the fridge. He, too, was surprised not to see the dog, and Bordelli explained that Blisk had departed.

'Too bad, he was a great dog . . .'

'It was his decision.'

'Apparently he didn't like the cooking.'

'Shut up and eat first, Ennio. Only then can you say anything.'

'I can hardly wait . . .'

'That sounds like a threat.'

'Oh, go on, I'm just really hungry,' said Ennio, going over to the cooker to peek into the pots.

'Monsignor Della Casa[25] advises you not to speak of wanting food; it's like talking about poo at the table,' said Bordelli, noticing that Piras had screwed up his mouth at the sound of the word *monsignor*.

'Who cares what some priest says? This is me talking here . . .'

'Never mind, Ennio. Pour us some wine,' said Bordelli, stirring the *Peposo* in a terracotta stewpot.

A rumbling motor outside announced Dante's arrival on a magnificent red Moto Guzzi Falcone. Entering the house, he took off his goggles and helmet, releasing a burst of long white hair. For some strange reason Bordelli had expected him to come on foot.

'I didn't know you had a motorcycle,' he said, shaking his hand.

'I didn't know I did, either,' said Dante.

Bordelli couldn't help but approve, and as he was about to close the door, he saw the lights of a car coming down the dirt road. A shiny black Fiat 1100 pulled up alongside the Beetle, the driver's-side door opened like a coffin-lid, and out came Diotivede, as elegant as usual. He came towards Bordelli holding a rather large, cubical box, hastily wrapped and tied with red ribbon.

'Happy birthday, caveman.'

'I said no presents . . .'

'You said it, not me.'

'Bloody hell, Peppino . . .'

'Wait before you thank me; you may not like it.'

'I wouldn't put it past you to give me a skull as a present . . .'

'How'd you guess?'

'We'll open it when we drink the champagne,' Bordelli said, smiling, and went and laid the box on the sideboard. There was another exchange of greetings with the new arrival, and Bordelli had to get another bottle from the shelf. Dante came up to him, holding a strange metal object in his hand.

'The sacred moment for bequeathing you this jewel of science is upon us. It's not a birthday present; I would have given it to you anyway.'

'Lovely . . . What is it?'

'A corkscrew, of course . . . Of my own invention . . .' said Dante, handing him the gift.

'How does it work?' Bordelli asked aloud, turning the object round and round in his hand, trying to understand the mechanism.

'It's quite simple, really. Here, I'll show you.'

Dante took the bottle from him and, manipulating the device, managed to pop the cork in seconds.

'Fantastic . . .' said Bordelli, sincerely surprised, eyeing the instrument. Dante's inventions didn't always make sense, at least not to normal people.

'I have a confession to make,' said Dante.

'And what's that?'

'Actually I found this remarkable device at the open-air market at I Ciompi, but whoever designed it must certainly have been a past incarnation of mine,' said Dante, laughing.

'From now on it will be my only corkscrew,' said Bordelli, immediately opening another bottle, for the thrill of it. He filled their glasses and they made a first toast. The atmosphere was warming up, and the four guests began talking loudly. After a last round of wine, Bordelli asked everyone please to sit down, and brought a large tray of *crostini* to the table . . .

'I have to confess, Inspector, I hadn't expected it,' Botta said in admiration, tasting the incarnation of the apple tart made according to his gospel. Bordelli concealed his own satisfaction behind an ironic smile. He felt weightless. At that moment no thought of lost loves could darken his spirits.

His other tablemates were also, quite frankly, astonished, and they never stopped complimenting the chef throughout the meal. Perhaps it was thanks to the wine, which never stopped flowing. Now they were on the *vin santo*, and as usual Piras seemed the most sober of the lot. The empty bottles remained on the table, like ninepins waiting to be knocked down.

Dante was in one of his pensive moods, smoking his cigar in silence. He didn't look uninvolved, however, but was observing the others and listening with great interest as Piras did his best to ignore the clouds of smoke enveloping him. The log of oak in the fireplace was still slowly burning . . . It was time to open the champagne.

Bordelli decided the time had come to open Diotivede's present, and he went to get it. Sitting back down with the others, he untied the red ribbon and unwrapped the package. Lifting the lid to look inside the box, he smiled and shook his head.

'So you weren't joking . . .'

'Obviously not,' said the doctor.

'Thank you, Peppino . . . Words fail me . . .'

'Since you don't read philosophy books, I brought you the most concise summary I could think of,' said the doctor.

The others stared at the box, curious to know what was inside. At last Bordelli lowered his hands into the box and pulled out the present . . . A human skull, which he placed at the centre of the table.

'Magnificent . . .' Dante muttered with loving eyes.

There wasn't much light in the room, and Botta leaned forward for a better look.

'But is it real?'

'Of course,' said Diotivede, almost offended. He would never have given a fake as a gift. Bordelli left the skull on the table, turning it towards the fire. Thanks to Diotivede, he had a new friend.

'Do you know who it was?' asked Bordelli.

'A criminal. But I can't say any more.'

'How did you get your hands on it?'

'You're looking a gift horse in the mouth . . .'

'Sorry . . .'

The champagne was excellent, and with the second round they emptied the bottle. Bordelli stood up to get a bottle of grappa and five small glasses, then sat back down. He lit a cigarette, his second of the day. He poured everyone some grappa, and taking advantage of a moment of silence, suggested that they each tell a story, as they'd done on other similar occasions . . .

'Who goes first?' asked Botta, pleased to volunteer. The fire popping in the hearth, the big kitchen immersed in shadow, all the hands clasping the little glasses, reminded him of certain evenings when he was a little boy, when he would listen in amazement to his grandfather telling stories of the Great War.

The oak log hissed, the flame tinting the five men's faces red as the death's-head sat quietly watching the fire.

'Could I have a cigarette?' asked Diotivede, who normally didn't smoke. He lit it and blew the smoke upwards, looking pensive. He wasn't one who liked to talk about his personal experiences, but the dinners at Bordelli's were a sort of pleasant anomaly. The others looked at him, waiting for him to begin his story. The doctor remained silent for a few minutes, as if to put his thoughts in order, then grinned . . .

'It must have been in '52 or '53; I was around sixty. I still had the smell of the war in my nose, and I paid close attention to the country's excitement about the future. I was living in Via Masaccio at the time, in a penthouse apartment. A young engineer moved into the flat on the floor below with his wife and their beautiful little girl, called Cosetta. The first time I met the girl it was on the staircase, and she was with her mother. I stopped to introduce myself. The little girl was eight years old at the time. She had a dark complexion and the blackest hair I'd ever seen, and she was very quiet and always looking mysteriously out at the world with her dark, deep eyes. I was quite struck by her beauty, and by those eyes. Her gaze was like the moon, luminous and nocturnal . . . You'll have to forgive me for all the second-rate poetic imagery, but I don't know how else to describe her.'

'I can see her in my mind . . .' Ennio whispered, staring into space. Dante's eyes were closed, and he was grinning faintly behind a cloud of smoke. Piras poured himself another grappa, quiet as a cat. Bordelli was the only one gazing at the skull. The doctor waited for a few seconds, to make sure he had the floor again.

'I remember saying something nice to the girl, to be polite, and when I reached out to stroke her cheek, Cosetta stepped back. I felt rather bad about it, worse than I would have imagined. I immediately withdrew my hand and masked my embarrassment and disappointment behind a wizened smile. The mother noticed my unease and made excuses . . . *Pay no mind, she's very shy . . . At home, though, she's quite the chatterbox . . .* I bowed and took leave of the lady and went on my way, crushed by the little girl's hostile rejection. I crossed paths with the mother and daughter numerous other times after that, but the little girl would never deign to look at me. Her mistrust hurt me; it was as if she had struck me from the lists of the living, and I promised myself I would win her over. I tried using smiles, making little jokes, even feigning indifference. But Cosetta was unreachable. One morning when I was feeling particularly bold, I tried again to stroke her cheek . . . and she stepped back like the first time, making me blush all over . . . That time, too, her mother noticed my embarrassment and had to stifle a laugh. She quickly said hello and kept going, pulling her daughter along by the arm. I just stood there like a fool, furious at myself. I felt naked, stupid, ridiculous. All the self-importance of the old doctor who spent his days cutting up corpses had been swept away by the eyes of a little girl, eight-year-old Cosetta. I felt like a complete nothing in front of her; it was as if the pure beauty of a freshly blossomed flower could not stand any contact with old age and ugliness. It was a painful, unbearable feeling. A few weeks later I decided to try again, one last time. Early that morning I waited on the landing until I heard them coming out of their door, and then I hurried down the stairs to catch up with them. After greeting her mother, I bent down towards the girl and put a chocolate in her pocket, then held out my hand to stroke her hair . . . She recoiled and shot me a glance that burned a hole through me. Was I really so horrific? So monstrous? And so, muttering goodbye, I ran away, and from that day on I avoided crossing paths with them. I would slow down on the stairs to avoid catching up with them, and when we were about to cross on the staircase, I would quietly tiptoe backwards. A year later the engineer's family moved out, and by chance I found out they'd gone to live on the far bank of the Arno. I was unlikely ever to meet Cosetta, my tormentor, again. And so, little by little, I forgot about her and my humiliation . . . Until the day when, a couple of years ago, while walking through the centre of town, I saw her sitting at a café with a young man. It was her, there was no mistaking that. She'd turned into a beautiful young woman. She had the same deep, lunar eyes as before, and at that moment she was smiling. I'd never seen her smile before. I kept on walking, feeling confused, but after taking a few steps I stopped. I didn't think I had it in me to do what what I had in mind, but I summoned the courage. So I turned back and went up to the table where the two young people were sitting.

"'You're Cosetta . . .' I said with a smile.

"'How did you know my name?' she asked me, a little astonished. But she didn't seem shocked. The lad looked on in silence, apparently amused.

"'Don't you rembember me? I used to live in Via Masaccio, on the top floor . . . When you were a little girl . . .'

"'Oh, yes, I do remember . . . The man with the black bag . . .'

"'Is that what you called me?'

"'I must confess I was afraid of you . . .'

"'You were? Why?'

"'I don't know . . . You looked like an ogre from a fairy tale . . .' she said, laughing.

"'How are your parents?' I asked, to change the subject.

"'They're fine, thanks . . .'

"'Please give them my best . . .'

"'Of course.'

"'Could I ask a favour of you, Cosetta?'

"'Yes, of course . . .' she said, seeming curious.

"'When you were a little girl, I tried several times to stroke your hair, but you always recoiled . . . Could I . . . now?' I felt like a madman, and I was sure she was going to tell me to go to hell or laugh in my face . . . But, instead, she said yes. The lad just watched us, wrinkling his brow. So I reached out and caressed her hair ever so lightly, as she looked at me with the sweetest of smiles. I muttered thanks and, after vaguely gesturing goodbye, I dashed away. As I was running off, I heard them burst out laughing and felt my face turn red and my ears burn. I had never felt so ridiculous in all my life . . . But I had, finally, succeeded in caressing her. I'd slain the monster, one of the many . . .'

The doctor downed his glass in one gulp and noticed that the others were silently expecting him to continue.

'That's it. I'm done. It may be a silly little story, but I enjoyed telling it,' he said by way of conclusion, giving a slight shrug. Piras was silent, his dark Sardinian eyes glistening in the penumbra. Bordelli refilled the doctor's glass.

'I'm truly amazed,' he said, in all sincerity.

'At what?'

'I didn't realise you were so sensitive . . .'

'It depends on the circumstances,' said Diotivede.

'You certainly never caressed my hair "ever so lightly".'

'I didn't want to upset you . . .'

'So, who's turn is it now?' Ennio asked impatiently, interrupting the skirmish.

'I'm going last . . . Is that all right with you?' said Bordelli, caressing the skull.

Dante was staring at the fire, a majestic smile on his face, pulling on his cigar, as Botta invited him to take the floor. The others supported the suggestion, and at last Dante stood up. He went and shook his ash into the fireplace, then turned to face the table, taking a big drag on his cigar.

'I was about ten years old. The Spanish flu had just finished making its way around the world, killing more people than the war. Our family survived, but the scourge struck down some of our relatives, including a cousin of mine, a little girl of eight, whom I was forced to witness laid out in a little white coffin. My parents didn't want their children to grow up unfamiliar with the hard facts of life, and I thank them for that. One night in August my mother woke my sister and me up with tears in her eyes and told us that Nonno Alfonso was feeling bad and about to leave this world. Nonno Alfonso was her father. It was Nonna Nerina who'd called, saying that Nonno was about to die and wanted to see us all. Mamma told us to wash our faces and comb our hair, and she dressed us as if we were going to school. My father was already waiting for us by the door, and we all went out of the house together and into the warm night. In summertime we lived in a villa at Radda in Chianti, and so we headed off for Florence in my father's magnificent car, a Fiat 505 that emitted a great deal of smoke. My mother was whispering prayers, saying the rosary. She wanted to stop at the church of San Domenico, where we used to go to mass every Sunday before having lunch at our grandparents' villa in Fiesole, and she ordered my father to wake up the priest, Don Camillo, who, aside from the name, was nothing like the Guareschi character. He was skinny, old, always serious, and seemed always to be wandering through the sins of the world in search of his own holiness. My father didn't want to disturb him, adding that it was better that we get to Nonno's place as quickly as possible, because he might leave the world of the living at any moment.

But my mother wasn't in any mood for argument. In the end my father obeyed, and after knocking for a long time, he found the sacristan in front of him in his pyjamas. He apologised, explained the situation, and asked whether Don Camillo might be so kind as to accompany them to the dying man's bedside. But they had to move fast, very fast. A few minutes later we saw the priest come out, sleepy eyed and unsteady on his feet. In his hand was a small briefcase with the holy oil. My mother got out of the car to greet him, thanking him with all her heart, and gave him her place beside the driver. The priest got in the car, smelling strongly of candles and mildew, and before long we arrived at our grandparents' house. The old housekeeper was waiting for us, sobbing in the doorway, pressing a handkerchief to her eyes. She said the signora was waiting for us at the master's bedside. We went up the stairs together with the priest, in silence. When we came to my grandfather's bedroom, we found the door closed with a piece of cardboard on it, hanging from a string, with a message on it, written in his hand, which I've kept all these years. We later learned that it was his wife, on his orders, who'd hung it there. Every so often I reread it, just to amuse myself, and by now I know its contents by heart.

*By my wish and command*
*THE PRIEST BEGONE*

*I will die with God. He alone is quite enough for me. He who can create worlds will find a way to forgive my sins, while you, hypocrite priest, lying impostor, and worse, you should stay home. He needs no middlemen. Your prayers are self-interested prayers that come from no deeper than the lips, while my prayers come straight from the heart. Forgive me, Lord. This you can do, because you are all powerful.*

Don Camillo turned pale and bit his lips, while my mother felt herself withering with embarrassment. Neither of the two had even noticed that in the lower right corner of the sheet was the word: *Over*. And so my father turned it over.

> *I am dying.*
> *My beliefs to all were known.*
> *Come, O Death, I feel you near, and fear you not,*
> *I go serene to the unknown.*

When the priest headed down the stairs muttering between his teeth, my mother burst into tears and ran after him, begging him to stay, but Don Camillo was offended and wouldn't hear of it. My mother kept insisting, to no avail. My father, my sister and I watched the scene from the top of the stairs, not knowing what to do. The upshot was that Nonno Alfonso got to die the way he wanted, without a priest and with a crucifix in his hands. He said goodbye to us one by one, calling us each by his name, and after breathing his last, his eyes remained wide open. I remember well those lifeless eyes; it looked as if he was thinking of something funny. He'd always been a jokester, and remained true to himself even in death. A few days later, when we all went to the notary to discuss the will, we learned that in it, in addition to allotting his possessions, he'd left a note containing what he wanted for his epitaph: *Pray for yourselves. I am already dead.'*

Dante laughed, and after tossing his cigar butt into the fire, he sat back down at his place. Botta raised his glass and proposed a toast to Nonno Alfonso, who must certainly be watching them from the beyond. They clinked glasses, and after taking a sip, Dante revealed to everyone that he, too, had already written his own epitaph: *Here lies Dante, who devoted his life to not knowing anything*.

Ennio was not to be outdone.

'I want mine to say: *Burglars and con men/are all fine gentlemen*. And after my funeral I want there to be a sumptuous banquet, paid for by me, where everyone should stuff themselves like pigs and get drunk,' he said, to the others' approval.

'Peppino, what do you want want for an epitaph?' Bordelli asked the doctor. By this point the game had begun, and each had to say his bit. Diotivede thought it over for a moment.

'*The scalpel was powerless against the sickle,*' he said, smiling coldly. Bordelli turned to Piras.

'How about you?'

'I've never given it any thought,' said Piras, who was barely more than twenty years old. Ennio then passed the question on to Bordelli, who finally thought he'd found the right statement.

'*He loved women above all else.*'

'You're such a romantic,' said Diotivede.

'It depends on the circumstances,' Bordelli retorted, looking over at the skull.

They all sat there in silence, while the wind outside could be heard tossing the boughs of the trees. The log burned slowly in the fireplace, enveloped by a thin veil of fire. All that was missing was a howling wolf in the distance . . .

'Your turn, Ennio,' said Bordelli, calmly lighting another cigarette.

The night was still young and seemed made for telling stories. Botta put his elbows on the table and, heaving a sigh, started talking . . .

'Nowadays I don't do this kind of thing any more – the inspector knows that . . . But once upon a time I used to break into villas and steal a few things. I did it to get by, and there are even some priests who say that to steal out of hunger is not a sin. If only there was a little more justice in the world . . . But let's forget about that – sometimes, when we talk about certain things, all that comes out is hot air. Anyway, one night, many years ago, in winter, I broke into a villa in Pian dei Giullari, where a party seemed to be going on. There were several fancy cars parked outside, the most modest one being a Mercedes as long as a train. When the rich throw a party, they drink like fish, especially in the wee hours after the servants have all been dismissed to their quarters. In other words, it becomes very easy to steal. I'd climbed up a big wisteria plant and came in through a first-floor window . . . I went out into the hallway and looked down into the staircase. I pricked up my ears, but couldn't hear anything. Before rifling through any drawers it's usually a good idea to figure out what's happening in the house. So I tiptoed down the stairs with the help of my torch, to go and listen at the various doors. It was an enormous villa, full of corridors and dimly lit by a few weak hall-lights. I remember seeing scary portraits hanging on the walls in the shadows. I made my way along the carpets, making as little noise as possible.

You could have heard a pin drop. After peering through the keyholes of a number of doors, I found the right one . . . and I couldn't believe my eyes. There, in a dim salon illuminated by the light of a single candle, I saw about fifteen people seated at a large round table. They all had their eyes closed and their hands open and resting on a dark tablecloth, pinkies linked to form a chain . . .'

Botta paused to take a sip of grappa, and nobody breathed a word . . .

'In short, it was a séance. I could steal whatever I wanted without anyone knowing, but I was unable to take my eye off that keyhole. I was too curious to know what would happen next. I'd never seen anything like it with my own eyes, though my uncle Rolando, who said he'd taken part in many séances, used to tell me about them and said some things that were pretty hard to believe . . . Drawers opening by themselves, doors slamming, cold gusts of wind, even ghosts appearing in a corner of the room and answering questions . . . My uncle swore it was all true, and so now I had a chance to witness one of these miracles myself. I wasn't going to miss the show for anything, even though I felt a little nervous. Actually, I was really afraid, I have to admit, but my curiosity wouldn't let me go. The table was pretty far from the door, and so, to get a better look, I opened it slightly. The hallway was almost completely dark, so nobody could see me. And, anyway, they all had their eyes closed. I was struck by the presence of a rather thin lady, with black, sort of ruffled hair, who was sitting bolt upright and seemed to be muttering something. She must have been the one my uncle called *the medium*, the person who established contact with the spirit world, who "goes into a trance", as he put it. Everyone else sat there in silence without moving. The minutes went by, but nothing happened. Every so often the medium would seem to grow impatient, as if she felt frustrated and unable to communicate with the world of the dead . . . I was starting to think it was all nonsense and that my uncle had been pulling my leg. I even got the idea I would come forward and pretend I was a ghost, just to make them all happy. I was thinking I could say – in my best ghostly voice – that if they wanted to save their souls they had to give me all the gold they had on their persons . . . I was laughing inside, imagining the scene . . . But then I suddenly heard a noise behind me, and I turned round and my hair stood on end. In the shadows I saw a little girl in a nightgown coming down the stairs, and so I hid behind a piece of furniture and watched her. The girl headed straight for the séance room, walking slowly but with determination. I realised she had her eyes closed. She looked like she was sleeping. She was a very pretty little girl, about five or six years old, with long, curly blond hair. She looked like a cherub, but she had a string of spittle hanging from her lips, which were half open. Without a sound she pushed open the door and went into the deathly silent room. The curiosity was eating me alive, so I came out from my hiding place and went to spy on the scene. The little girl had stopped a few steps away from the table, but everyone seated at the table had their eyes closed and nobody was aware of her presence yet. A few seconds later the child raised her arm and pointed at one of them.

"'You . . .' she said, startling everyone at the table.

"'Costanza! What are you doing up at this hour?' one of the women said affectionately to her. She must certainly have been her mother, because they looked alike. The chain had been broken, and everyone was looking at the little girl, who was still pointing at a man in the group.

"'You . . . Tomorrow you will die . . .' she said in her squeaky little voice, making the hairs on my arm stand on end. A moment later she peed herself and it dripped on to the rug.

"'Costanza! What are you saying?' her mother shouted, and went over to her.

"'Can't you see she's asleep?' said someone.

"'She's in a trance . . .' someone else whispered, and was immediately hushed by the others. The man the girl had pointed at stood up. He was skinny as a beanpole, with a goatee and round spectacles. He tried to smile, but looked around with a terrified expression. The mother took the child in her arms and headed for the door. I barely managed to hide in time, and I watched them go upstairs. The girl's feet were swinging in the air; she hadn't even woken up. The woman returned a few minutes later and went back into the salon, leaving the door open, probably so she could hear her daughter calling.

"'Count Anselmo, I'm so sorry . . .' I heard her saying. Anyway, I resumed my spying and saw that they were all rather confused. The count had sat back down, with a doltish smile on his face. He was terrified but was doing all he could to appear untroubled.

"'Good heavens, Count . . . You're not going to believe the words of a sleepwalking little girl, are you?' said an old woman.

"'She was just dreaming . . .' a man said, quite sure of himself, but you could see he was pleased not to have been the one who was singled out.

"'Would you like a glass of water, Count?' the girl's mother asked him. The man shook his head and kept on smiling. All he did was smile. Everyone else kept downplaying the whole thing and trying to reassure him. Only the medium had remained silent all the while, staring into space with a worried look on her face. Every so often the count stole a glance at her, ignoring what the others were saying. Moments later a few people stood up and someone turned on the ceiling lamp. I realised the gathering was about to break up. I disappeared the same way I'd come, and a minute later I was flying down the hill on my bicycle, happy to be back out in the open air. The moment I got home I buried myself under the covers. I couldn't get that girl out of my head, and her squeaky voice, saying, *Tomorrow you will die* . . . It took me a long time to fall asleep, but when I woke up the following morning, I felt fine. It was a nice sunny day and I soon stopped thinking about the whole episode. I had other problems, and you can never tell your stomach to wait. I spent the afternoon looking for another villa to visit, and that night I went and did what I had to do. The next day, as I was reading the newspaper, I very nearly cried out . . . There was a photo of Count Anselmo Belforte Rovatti de Marina, with his goatee and little glasses. I felt like I'd been run over by a bus. His three surnames hadn't prevented him dying just as the little girl had predicted. And, I can tell you, if I hadn't seen it with my own eyes . . . Anyway, it really starts you thinking that everything is preordained, and there really is such a thing as fate. And from time to time, someone is born who can know things before they happen . . .' Botta concluded, shrugging.

Bordelli smiled, remembering that he'd thought the same thing a few days earlier. Fate again . . . Lately the subject just wouldn't leave him alone, not even on his birthday . . .

In the general silence, Dante stuck two fingers into the skull's eye sockets and pulled it gently towards him.

'Apparently the little girl had occult powers even greater than those of the medium, and nobody knew,' he murmured.

'I would never want to know my future, not even what will happen five minutes from now,' said Botta, shaking his head.

'There are times when it could be quite useful,' said Diotivede, though it was anyone's guess what he was alluding to.

'Do you believe in destiny, Piras?' asked Bordelli. The Sardinian had pushed his chair a bit away from the table, to distance himself slightly from the cloud of smoke in the air. He half smiled.

'When I was a little boy, there was a sorceress who lived in our town, an old, toothless woman who could tell you the future by standing on your feet and looking into your eyes. She used to say she'd never been wrong, and I was able to attest to this a few times in person. The priest couldn't stand her. During mass he would call her a crazy old hag and say it was a sin to frequent her. But nobody listened to him. So one day he decided to confront her, and went to see her wearing a giant crucifix round his neck. "Since you know everything," he said, "why don't you tell me when you will die?" The old woman smiled and said: "If I could look into my eyes with my own eyes, and stand on my feet with my own feet, I could do that. But I could tell you when you will die." The priest said angrily that he would die when God wanted him to die, and then he challenged her to tell him his fortune. The old woman sat him down in front of her, put her feet on top of his, looked him in the eye, and said: "You will die in seven years, struck by lightning." And, making the sign of the cross, she added: "This is the Lord's decision. I see only his Divine Will . . .'"

'I bet the priest died seven years later,' said Botta, his finger suspended in air.

'Struck by lightning,' Piras confirmed.

'What did I say? Fate is real. Man, is it ever real.'

'And what happened to the old sorceress? Is she still alive?' asked Bordelli.

'She disappeared one day, and that was the last that was seen of her.'

Everyone fell silent again, but you could almost hear their thoughts filling the room. The sound of the wind in the trees outside made their symposium even more intimate.

'Why don't we have our own séance and try to call forth her spirit?' said Ennio, but nobody paid any attention. Bordelli served another round of grappa, then turned again to Piras.

'Don't think you're going to get off easy just telling us about the sorceress . . . Now it's your turn to tell a story . . .'

'One morning in Bonacardo when I was ten years old, we heard gunshots. A few minutes later, out of the classroom window, we saw Salvatore, a kid from town, limping along the road with blood pouring out of one of his legs and leaving a red trail on the ground. We all ran outside, including the schoolmistress. Salvatore was howling in pain, saying he'd been shot by Fidele Marra, a thirty-year-old shepherd who lived in a shack up the hill. Nobody would believe him, because they all knew Fidele was a gentle man. The Carabinieri arrived, and after turning the lad over to the medical team, they climbed up the hill to go and talk with Fidele. They were greeted by gunfire, and the sergeant very nearly got killed. A bullet grazed his ear, and he had to keep a handkerchief pressed up against it to stanch the bleeding. A few centimetres to the other side and the buckshot would have hit him right in the face. Fidele kept firing away, taking long pauses to recharge the shotgun, and every so often he cried out a woman's name: *Bibina* . . . followed by some decidedly rude adjectives. Bibina was a beautiful girl from Millis, who just the day before had married a lad from my town. The Carabinieri kept trying to persuade him to come out with his hands up, but the shepherd only answered with more gunfire. The whole town gathered at the top of the hill to see what was happening, ignoring the Carabinieri's orders to stay away. The schoolteacher had come running behind us children, unable to stop us. We were hiding behind some boulders sticking out of the ground, excited but frightened, trying to see if we could see the shepherd's silhouette in the dark space of the window. But all we could see, and not very well at that, was the barrel of his *lupara*. Everyone was wondering why Fidele Marra was calling Bibina a slut, a trollop and a whore. No one had ever seen her so much as talk to him. All the same, everyone in town started gossiping about it, questioning the girl's morals. The ones that came down on her hardest were the ugly girls, the ones who hadn't found husbands. They'd always been jealous of her and finally had an opportunity to give vent to their feelings. And meanwhile Fidele kept shooting. After every two shots, there was a few seconds of silence, the time needed to change cartridges, and then the shooting started up again. During one pause, a friend of Fidele's stood up and started approaching the shack without fear, yelling at him not to shoot. By way of reply he took a blast in the shoulder, circling round twice in place and then falling to the ground, screaming in pain. He was carried away, and the marshal said that if anyone tried another stunt like that he would shoot them himself. Everyone was wondering how many cartridges Fidele had left. The only way to get him out of there was to wait until he ran out. Still more people came to watch, and they brought news that Bibina herself was on her way with Giacobbe, her husband. And in fact a few minutes later we saw her climbing up the slope, dragged along by her husband. Giacobbe was frowning angrily, and she seemed furious. Another two shots ricocheted off the ground, raising clouds of dust. The Carabinieri went to meet the young couple, telling them not even to try to come closer. Bibina was disgusted and swearing she had nothing whatsoever to do with that madman. Giacobbe was clenching his teeth and glaring at her as though looking in her eyes for proof that she was lying. Then she suddenly broke free from her husband and started running towards Fidele's shack, shouting at him to come out and have the courage to call her a whore to her face. Giacobbe started running after her, but a rifle shot persuaded him to lie down on the ground. The marshal ran after the woman, but got some buckshot in his leg for his trouble and rolled to the ground without a sound. Bibina kept advancing, furious, and stopped about fifteen feet outside Fidele's window, still screaming her rage at the shepherd: *I don't know you, I've never even seen your face! If you're a man, come out!* And other things like that . . . Her honour was at stake, and she didn't want to lose the husband she'd just married. We were all waiting with bated breath, expecting to see Bibina's head explode like a melon. Fidele had just fired two shots and was surely reloading. The girl was out of breath and started crying. Her wailing sounded like a young lamb's before its throat is slashed. Her husband looked on from a distance, feeling desperate and tormenting himself with doubts, but didn't have the courage to get any closer. Suddenly there was another gunshot, but Bibina's head remained in its place. And all felt silent. Bibina stopped crying, and then started slowly walking towards the shack. As soon as she went up to the window, she let out a scream and ran away in terror, yelling that the madman had killed himself. We all went to look, even us little kids. Fidele's face was almost all gone, and floating on top of all the blood was a faded photograph of Bibina when she was a little girl, returning from the well with a jug on her head. When they showed her the picture, Bibina said her cousin had taken it many years ago, and she swore on the Blessed Virgin of Bonacatu that she had no idea how it had ended up in Fidele's hands. Her husband, in the end, believed her, and embraced her in front of everyone and tried to kiss her, but she spat in his face and told him it was too late. She went back home to her parents, creating a scandal that finally forced her to move to the mainland, and nobody ever saw her again.'

'A courageous woman,' said Bordelli.

'I hope she's in Paris with a rich and fascinating man,' Botta said solemnly.

After they all toasted Bibina and made a few more admiring statements, Bordelli went to tweak the fire a little. When he turned round again to go back to the table, he noticed that the others were all looking at him. Now it was his turn. He dropped into his chair, lit a cigarette, and blew the smoke up towards the ceiling. All evening long he'd been undecided as to whether he should tell the crowd a fairy tale of ogres who ravish children. He'd even imagined the opening: *Once upon a time there was a little boy named Giacomo, who lived a quiet life with his family. One terrible day he vanished into thin air, and a short while later his corpse was found buried in the woods . . .*

He wouldn't have minded submitting the whole affair to the court of his friends and hearing their verdict . . . Even if only in an attempt to understand whether what he was doing was right only for him, or had instead a universal ethical value. It would have been a little like consulting the Pythia at Delphi . . . But deep down he knew that he would not tell the story of Giacomo, at least not that evening. He didn't want to foist his responsibilities, or his crimes, on to others. He'd started out alone on this path, and he had to reach the end without involving anyone else . . .

Searching his memory, he remembered an episode from his days in the San Marco Battalion, a story he'd never told anyone. In the first years right after the war he'd thought about it a lot, almost every night before falling asleep, curled up under the covers. He'd kept it jealously to himself, almost to the point of forgetting it. Taking a sip of grappa, he began to speak, hoping he could elicit in his listeners the same emotions he'd felt himself . . .

*It was late May 1944; they'd broken through the lines at Cassino a couple of weeks earlier, and the Germans were fleeing northwards. The Duce at this point was merely a puppet in Hitler's hands, and clearly had no hope left. All anyone talked about was the forthcoming Allied landing in France, but nobody knew where they would arrive along the coast. By now it was clear to all that the Nazis and Fascists would lose the war, but it was hard to tell at what cost in human lives. It would not be a walk in the park, that much was certain. Italians would have to pay for Mussolini's idiocy and the cowardice of the king and Marshal Badoglio.*

*The battalion had struck camp in the hills of Narni for the night, after a tortuous trek that had taken them from the Abruzzi to Umbria. At dawn that morning, some patrols had left camp to reconnoitre the area. They needed to find out how much distance there was between them and the retreating Germans and to blaze a trail for the bulk of the Allied troops, with whom they were in constant radio contact. The German back lines were seeking to slow down the enemy advance, to allow their army to consolidate a new line of defence. It was the harshest, cruellest moment of the whole conflict.*

*There were four men in Bordelli's patrol. Aside from him, there was the giant Molin from the Veneto and young Cuco from Potenza, both released from prison in Brindisi in exchange for enlisting in the San Marco. The fourth man was Gavino, young Piras's father . . . Surely he, too, remembered that day. The other two could not remember it, since they died a few months thereafter while clearing a field of mines.*

*There was a glorious sun that day, it was quite hot, and they preferred walking in the shade of the woods. It had been a few days since they'd heard any gunfire. In the darkness of the underbrush grew flowers of every colour, and there was a strong scent of tree-bark in the air. It seemed like one of those peaceful days on which nothing could possibly happen. But they were dead wrong.*

*They pushed several miles northward, more carefree than ever. Every so often they would exchange a few words on sundry subjects ranging from women to family memories. Sometimes they would indulge in fantasies of roast pork or a plate of pasta. If not for their sweat-drenched uniforms and the weapons they were carrying, they could have been on a country outing.*

*They stopped to eat, sitting on a bare patch of rock emerging from the moss. They ate a few biscuits and a bit of Allied tinned meat, washed it down with a swig of disgusting coffee, then resumed their march.*

*Climbing one hillside they spotted a farmhouse at the top and approached somewhat cautiously. Aside from the clucking of a few chickens, everything was quiet, a fact that seemed to promise nothing good.*

*'I don't like the look of this, bloody German hell,' Molin muttered.*

*When they reached the house, a spectacle of horror lay before their eyes. Gavino started cursing in Sardinian. In the middle of the threshing floor lay an old peasant with arms outstretched, his head smashed open like a watermelon. Three or four chickens scratched around the body, pecking the blood-spattered ground, surrounded by a cloud of flies whose buzzing made the scene all the more macabre. Cuco, who'd gone over to the stables, called to them from the doorway, and they all went to have a look. Lying on the straw was the corpse of a little boy with a pitchfork still jammed into his chest. He had not died instantly, to judge from the furrows he'd made in the straw with his kicking feet. They pulled out the pitchfork and tossed it angrily aside. The killers hadn't fired a single shot, to avoid making any noise. Had it been the Germans, or only some mad wretches brutalised by hunger and poverty?*

*Inside the house they found an old woman with her throat slashed. Her eyes were still open, staring at the ceiling, her fingers intertwined with a rosary. Bordelli tried to close her eyes with his hand, but the eyelids immediately reopened halfway, making her look like a witch. He noticed she was holding something in her hands and, opening them, found a small SS insignia, torn off a uniform. It was the last thing she'd done before dying. There was no longer any doubt who the culprits had been.*

*The men exchanged silent glances, biting their lips. Bordelli couldn't help but imagine the scene in his head, the terror that had descended upon that house. Since the boy could not have been the elderly couple's son, they started looking for his mother. First inside the house, then in the surrounding land, but they found no body. They wondered whether the woman had, perhaps, managed to escape.*

*The bodies were not yet stiff, and the puddles of blood seemed still rather fresh. The Germans could not be very far away. The men decided to try and go after them. They headed north, letting their restlessness guide them. They kept their ears pricked and said not a word, fingers on the triggers of their machine guns.*

*About an hour later they heard some men's voices laughing and hit the ground. Bordelli grabbed his binoculars and spotted some Germans bivouacked amid the trees on the hill opposite them. He told the others, and they continued advancing, heads down and hiding in the dense vegetation. Cuco was sweating like a hog and drawing flies. Taking a long detour, they descended into the valley and came back up on the hill in front, managing to get quite close to the Germans. They lay down in the bushes to spy on them. Five SS were sitting on the ground, leaning back against trees, their machine guns lying to one side. Some dead chickens and a headless goose had been thrown on to the grass. A skinny cow was tied to a tree and eating whatever she could find, unaware that her fate was to be transformed into steaks . . . Molin mimed the gestures of cooking her on a grill, and kissed his fingertips in appreciation. Even at such moments as these, he couldn't resisting thinking of such things.*

*The Nazis were bantering and laughing, smoking and drinking from small flasks. They were enjoying a moment of rest after their massacre. Only one of them was not taking part in the merriment, a sort of giant with a grim face who sat in silence, casting menacing glances around him. His SS helmet made him look like a real ogre. Every so often the others would toss a pebble or dry pine cone at him and burst out laughing. The one goading him most was a small, angelic-looking blond lad with eyes a pale blue like fresh stream water, as one could see even from afar.*

*All they had to do was come out shooting, and they could have killed them all without effort. They were waiting only for the right moment, but then they noticed that a bit farther away there was a young woman lying on the ground with her wrists and ankles bound. Her clothes were torn and her face soiled with dirt. She was trembling slightly, and keeping her eyes closed. They didn't want to risk her life in a shoot-out, and so they crouched in wait behind the shrubs.*

*The blond guy took a long swig from his flask and stood up. He started walking towards the woman, unbuckling his belt, and the giant yelled something at him. The blond guy ignored him, encouraged by the other men's laughter. After pulling down his trousers, he untied the woman's ankles and mounted her, whispering sweet nothings in German. Gavino became restless, biting his lips till they bled.*

*Suddenly the giant Nazi leapt to his feet, cursing, and ran towards the blond guy. He pulled him violently off the woman, and with a single thrust sent him rolling on the ground. The woman had opened her eyes and was watching the scene with an absent expression. The blond angel's comrades rushed to his defence, still laughing. The giant shook his fists in the air, inviting them to take him on, but no one dared meet the challenge. The woman looked at him in disbelief, seeming hopeful. In the meantime the little blond had got back up and was furious. Pulling up his trousers and clenching his jaw, he approached the giant, pointing his pistol at his face. He said something harsh, and when the giant threw himself at him, he shot him in the head. The gorilla fell to the ground, gushing blood, as the blond angel calmly put his pistol back in its holster, turning round in a circle as if to follow the echo of the report. His anger had made him careless, but he didn't look too worried. Their camp was probably not very far away, and he felt safe. The others were stammering, staring at the corpse of their dead mate in stupefaction. When the woman's eyes met those of the blond lad, she looked away and curled up until her knees touched her lips. They all burst out laughing again, and the blond guy dropped his trousers again. He refused to give up his quarry. He bent over the woman, trying to spread her legs. She moved away, which only made the young German start slapping her. In the end she spread her legs and froze, resigned, blood dripping from her mouth. The others formed a circle round the blond guy to egg him on, and they even lit cigarettes, turning their backs on the San Marco patrol.*

*Bordelli traded glances with his comrades, who were trembling as much as he was. By this point they were convinced they had to risk it; they couldn't stand to wait any longer. He made one slight gesture with his fingers, indicating they should aim high, so as not to hit the woman. At his signal, they jumped out of the bushes and ran straight ahead, firing, strafing the three standing Germans, who fell like sacks of potatoes before they even realised what was happening. The blond kid had jumped to one side with his bum in the air, not daring to reach for his pistol. The woman was in a daze, trying to get away by propelling herself along the grass with her bare feet. When the blond guy tried to stand up, he stumbled over his trousers and fell backwards. They disarmed him without any difficulty, and Molin put one of his giant shoes on the young man's* naked belly. The barrel of Bordelli's machine gun was mere inches from his face. The blond angel asked permission to pull up his trousers, like a prudish schoolboy. Bordelli nodded, but before the German had even finished buckling his belt, he squeezed the trigger, and in an instant the burst of fire erased the young man's delicate face.

There was no more grappa. Bordelli tossed his cigarette butt into the flames and got up to get another bottle. Nobody breathed a word, awaiting the end of the story. After refilling everyone's glass, Bordelli went and sat on the bench in the fireplace, bringing his grappa along. On that occasion, too, he'd killed to settle accounts. Staring at the burning log, he resumed his story . . .

*As Cuco, on Bordelli's orders, was freeing the cow, they untied the woman's wrists and helped her to her feet. She was still trembling, dripping with sweat, and her clothes smelled of fear. Someone passed her a canteen and she drank avidly, letting the water spill on to her chest. They wiped the blood from her face with a wet handkerchief, and she started in pain. At one point the body of the blond soldier was shaken by a spasm, and the woman grabbed Bordelli's arm.*

*'It's all right . . .' he said, having often seen dead bodies start that way. The woman sighed and went over to the giant who had died for her, looking at him with boundless sadness. Kneeling down in front of the body, she ran her hand gently over his forehead. But it was no time to tarry. After stuffing the chickens and the headless goose into their backpacks, they led the woman away with them, making it clear to her that it was best they vacated the area in a hurry. They moved through the woods in silence, keeping their ears pricked for the slightest sound. The woman walked between them, turning round and looking back every few seconds, as if she feared being followed. Bordelli was looking at her out of the corner of his eye, and realised just how beautiful she was. With her torn clothes, her*

*face smeared with dirt, her body bruised, her black hair a mess,
she was the very image of suffering . . . Still, she was
beautiful.*

*After half an hour of walking, they were back near the site
of the massacre, and the woman started running up the hill.
They had trouble keeping up with her. When they got to the
top, they found her in the stable, clutching the child to her
breast. She was kissing his brow and whispering his name
without tears . . . Nicola . . . Nicola . . . Nicola . . .*

*They left her alone, and after finding a couple of hoes and
a spade they started digging three graves. The woman came
out of the stable with the boy in her arms and laid him down
on the ground. She went up to the old man but didn't have
the courage to touch him.*

*'Is he your father?' Bordelli asked her. The woman nodded
and ran into the house. They heard her going from room to
room, calling, 'Maria.' When she came out, they asked her who
Maria was. She said she was her little five-year-old daughter.
When the Germans arrived she'd been playing and chasing
the chickens around but had disappeared when they were
beating Nonno to death . . . Hopefully she'd hidden somewhere
and was safe . . . The woman was desperate, and Bordelli took
her hands . . .*

*'Your daughter is alive, I'm sure of it . . . We'll find her
presently . . .' he said, without actually believing it. He just
wanted to the give the poor woman, who'd lost everything, a
little hope.*

*They finished digging the graves and lowered the bodies into
them, before the survivor's bewildered eyes. Molin and Cuco
laid the bodies down carefully and respectfully. The warm air
was redolent with new life, bumblebees buzzed happily about,
birds zigzagged in the blue sky, all of it making the macabre
ceremony even sadder.*

*They waited for the woman to throw some flowers over the
bodies of her parents and little boy, then began quickly refilling
the graves, first pushing the dirt back in with their hands, then*

*using the spades. Meanwhile Gavino had fashioned three crosses, tying together with string some branches he'd found in a nearby thicket, and planted these in the mounds of dirt. There was no time to write their names.*

*They resumed their march without saying a word. Molin stared fiercely ahead of himself, muttering curses through clenched teeth. Gavino was stony faced, walking as if he could crash through a wall with his head. Cuco kept stealing glances at the woman's bare legs, which looked wild and beautiful. Nobody felt like talking.*

*After a while the woman began weeping in silence, and took hold of Bordelli's arm again. He embraced her, and felt almost guilty for it. She kept on crying and holding him tight.*

*'What's your name?' Bordelli asked her.*

*'Amelia . . .' she said, sobbing.*

*'I'm Franco . . . He's Gavino . . . That's Cuco . . . and that gorilla is Molin.'*

*The woman eventually calmed down, and a light of stubborn determination appeared in her eyes. She looked like a little girl who thought she could strike people down with her thoughts alone. She dried her eyes with her hands, without letting go of Bordelli. He put his arm round her back and let her rest her head on his shoulder. He couldn't help wishing he could kiss her. He would never have dared, of course, but there was no point pretending it was otherwise. She was as dirty as a fencepost in a chicken coop and smelled of sweat, but he nevertheless wished he could hug and kiss her. He wished he could caress her, make her feel safe and as beloved as a princess . . . He wished he could give her pleasure, make her feel better . . . Fall asleep with her in his arms, whispering a lullaby in her ear . . . Whereas they were actually in the wooded hills of Umbria, having just slaughtered a group of Nazis and buried three corpses, an elderly couple and a little boy . . . It would just be improper . . . Still, you can't stop your brain thinking, and Bordelli kept on imagining . . . In his mind the memory of those fantasies was as powerful as if they had actually happened . . .*

*They reached the camp an hour before sunset, and as the others were going to lie down in their cots, Bordelli accompanied Amelia to the mess tent, before the curious eyes of the entire battalion. As soon as they entered, the woman stopped short in shock . . . It was like witnessing a scene from a tragedy of Aeschylus . . . Amelia ran up to a little girl half asleep on a blanket in a corner of the tent, and hugged her so hard you could almost hear her bones cracking. The little girl returned the embrace, hugging her mother with dirty little hands. Both kept their eyes closed and did not cry, desperate smiles playing on their lips.*

*'Where's Nicolino?' asked the girl.*

*'He'll be along soon . . . He'll be along . . .'*

*'And Grandma and Grandpa?'*

*'They're fine . . . they're fine . . .'*

*After nodding to the cook in greeting, Bordelli left Amelia and her daughter, who were still embracing as if to form a single being, and went to talk to Captain Spiazzi, the camp commander. He reported what had happened that day, concluding with the story of Amelia, who'd been reunited with her daughter in the mess tent. Captain Spiazzi told him it was Bardini's patrol that had found the girl running through the woods with her feet all bloodied and her face all scratched from brambles. They'd had some trouble catching her, as she was terrified and ran in all directions like a hare. When they were able to calm her down, they asked her what had happened, but the child wouldn't speak. The moment they took her in their arms, she fell asleep, and so they decided to bring her at once to the camp.*

*'The woman and the girl should be transferred to the Allied camp as soon as possible . . . You take care of it, Bordelli . . .' the commander ordered. Amelia and her daughter could not stay there. They needed a real medic, some warm showers and decent food.*

*'I'll send three men and a van tomorrow morning,' said Bordelli, sketching a military salute and leaving. Going back*

to the mess tent, he found the mother and daughter alone, sitting on the blanket and eating a bowl of hot soup. The girl was as pretty as her mother, and had that same wild look about her. Amelia set down her bowl, got up and came over to Bordelli.

'You were right,' she whispered, alluding to the child.

'I just felt it,' Bordelli lied, stroking her cheek. She took his hand and raised it to her lips.

'Thank you . . .'

'I'm going to free up a tent for you tonight, and tomorrow morning someone will take you to the Allied camp,' said Bordelli, resisting the desire to put his arms around her.

Amelia nodded and went back to the girl and kissed her on the head before resuming her eating. Bordelli left with his gut in a knot. An oppressive sadness had come over him. It was chow time, and in spite of everything, he managed to eat. He couldn't get Amelia out of his head, and thought it was best if he didn't see her again.

He gave the order for a tent to be made available, and selected three men to make the next day's journey in the van. Then he retired to his tent. Sitting on his cot, he carved another notch in the butt of his machine gun. He registered only Nazis he'd killed personally, to be sure that the count was exact. It was now up to nineteen. He didn't know yet that he would end up carving eight more notches and return home from the war alive.

He slept like a log. At dawn Gavino shook his shoulder to wake him up.

'The woman is about to leave. She wants to see you.'

'Where is she?'

'Right here, outside . . .'

'Give me just a minute, then bring her in,' said Bordelli, getting out of bed. He quickly put on a clean jersey, rubbed the sleep from his eyes, and ran his fingers through his hair. Amelia entered the tent, holding the little girl by the hand.

'How are you, Maria?' said Bordelli, stroking the little girl's head.

At the edge of the camp, a van already had its engine running, and one could hear the rumble of aeroplanes in the distance. Amelia went up to Bordelli, ran her fingers over his stubbled cheek and kissed him lightly on the lips.

'Good luck,' he said, out of breath.

'Farewell . . .' she whispered, and she went out without turning around, pulling the child behind her.

Moments later Bordelli heard the van drive off. He never saw them again. Who knew where they were now, what they were doing . . . Who knew whether every so often they remembered the San Marco commander who'd correctly guessed fate's plan without really believing it . . .

'We always end up talking about women . . .' said Bordelli, mildly moved. The log burned in the half-light, smoking like some underworld deity. Botta managed to recline even in a wicker chair.

'If I had to choose one single word to describe women,' he said, 'I would say . . . *Beautiful* . . .'

'I would say . . . *Noble* . . .' said Dante, as though inspired.

'*Crazy* . . .' whispered Diotivede.

'What about you, Piras?' Bordelli prodded him again.

'*Dangerous* . . .' said the Sardinian, lost in thought.

'Your turn, Inspector,' Botta pressed him.

'I think I'd say . . . *Mythic* . . .' said Bordelli, raising his glass imperceptibly. They made a last, somewhat muted toast. The party was over, and it was time to go beddy-bye. They all went out on to the threshing floor to exchange goodbyes, their hair tossed by the wind. A silent owl watched them from afar, perched on a branch. The car motors started up one by one, and the white dirt road was lit up by their headlights. Dante had put on his helmet and goggles, and started singing as he pulled away.

Bordelli waited for the last tail-light to disappear over the hilltop, and went into the olive grove, which was bathed in the moon's muted glow, still thinking of beautiful Amelia and little Maria, who must now be almost thirty years old . . . If he ever crossed paths with them, would he recognise them? Perhaps he had already done so, and each had continued on his or her way . . .

A strong wind was blowing, his hair swirling over his head. The warm gusts of sirocco smelled of the sea and of sulphur, and seemed to stick to one's skin. From the woods came the sound of thousands of birds singing wildly, as usually happened at dawn. Love made them do strange things, too.

He walked at a leisurely pace along the path that led to the wood. By now he knew it well and could follow it with his eyes closed . . . All at once, amid the olive trees, he saw the silhouette of a large animal looming in the darkness, some twenty yards ahead, and he stopped. It must have been a stag. Its great horns glistened in the dark, as it moved its head slowly, majestically, sniffing the air.

He stood there watching it, spellbound by its beauty. The great deer wouldn't leave, and so eventually Bordelli started slowly edging forward. He got within a few yards of the animal, and when their eyes met he had a vague feeling he was being judged. A moment later the animal shook its head in the air and trotted lazily off towards the wood, still brandishing its horns. Bordelli watched it disappear through the trees and felt envious . . . He wished he were a beautiful animal running through the woods at night in pursuit of females, coupling in accordance with the call of nature, not having to waste away in human affairs, oblivious to good and evil, far from the perfidy and perversion of the chosen species . . .

Continuing his walk through the olive grove, numbed by the wind and his own thoughts, he tried to forget the world and all its disappointments and sorrows. It was a special night. He no longer felt the way he had the night before, though he could never have said exactly why. It couldn't possibly be only because of his birthday. He felt a profound transformation occurring. An era was ending, and another was about to begin . . . A long shudder of joy combined with terror confirmed that something inside him was changing. It was something to do with him alone; nobody else could understand it, and even he didn't really know what it meant. He was aware only that his way of seeing things had changed, as had happened to him many times before. Nothing drastic, just a slight shift in the visual angle . . . Just the pleasure of discovering that life is in constant motion . . .

He woke up quite late and spent the afternoon working in the garden and reading in the armchair. He'd put Diotivede's present carefully on top of the cupboard . . . *Memento mori* . . . It was as if the death's-head had always been up there, looking down on the worries of common mortals. It was part of the decor. Soon he wouldn't even notice it any longer . . .

He calmly prepared dinner. At half past eight, he turned on the telly and sat down at the table, filling his glass to the brim with wine, head full of disagreeable thoughts . . . The world was a disgusting place, that was certain. Man was basically a monster, and the worst of the lot were those cultured individuals, capable of choosing, who out of self-interest did not hesitate to act in the service of evil. The world was a disgusting place, who could possibly think otherwise? You had only to look around. As he blithely ate and drank in front of the TV news report, listening to useless information on the lively Italian political situation, millions of people were dying of privation just so that a handful of very rich people could cover themselves in gold. Of course everybody knew that; it was even a cliché. But it wasn't easy to change things. Nobody was in a position to tamper with the diabolical machinery governing human affairs . . .

Should he feel somehow at fault at that moment for enjoying the flavours of a simple dish of pasta with tomato sauce? How could he help it? Was it somehow a crime not to love power? The few who gave the orders were the ones who'd devoted their lives to bullying others. Greed and selfishness were the fuel that made the engine of violence run, but every epoch had its own tools for sanctifying that violence. The clever ones were those who could find the most effortless route, and the one most fitting at that moment, to achieving the same goals. To change everything so that nothing would change, as someone had written.[26] It had always been this way. Nowadays there was no longer any need to spill blood, just to milk the poor. The wealth of a few could come only from the poverty of many. Once you understood this simple equation, there was no longer any need for blood. Sweat was the new blood; violence had a new face, but the upshot was the same as before. How many people had to die to pay for the villa of an oil magnate in Capri? How was this different from Nazism? And yet everything continued just as before, but in a different form. So where were the culprits? What did they look like? And were they really guilty of anything? Every epoch had its monsters and its saints. Ever since the birth of the world, the nature of guilt had been defined by the language of power. Whoever did not agree had two choices: keep quiet or die. Schopenhauer was right: the foundation of morality was compassion, identification with the suffering of others. Failing that, horror was inevitable . . . And compassion was a rarer thing in this world than a five-legged dog . . .

He poured himself another glass, sighing. If Panerai the butcher, Beccaroni the lawyer, Monsignor Sercambi the prelate and Signorini the rich boy had put themselves even for an instant in the shoes of little Giacomo Pellissari, if they could have identified with him, imagined what he was feeling . . . But they hadn't, and Giacomo died. Once again the powerful had toyed with the life of an innocent, thinking they could get away with it . . .

The world was a disgusting place, and thinking one could set it right was an illusion. All one could do was patch up a few small rents in the fabric, though the whole thing was rotten. It was just a way not to resign oneself to defeat, not to succumb, not to leave the rule without any exceptions. Every so often the untouchables had to pay for their crimes, in full. Whosoever toys with life puts his own at risk, however unawares . . .

He smiled, imagining himself as David with the sling in his

hand. He'd struck the giant Goliath square in the forehead and watched him fall to the ground. Now he had only to stick his sword in his heart. It was Monsignor Sercambi's turn. He was the heart of Goliath.

The days went by, but Bordelli couldn't make up his mind to take action. He was waiting for a sign. He sometimes smiled to himself, feeling like those ancient soothsayers who searched through animals' entrails. By this point, however, he could no longer afford not to consult the fates, he thought, exchanging long glances with the skull.

He kept watering the garden, walking in the woods, reading novels . . . and waiting for a sign. One morning he transplanted the tomatoes, following Botta's instructions. Three weeks later he would have to start fertilising them with *pollina*, and when he counted the days he realised it would fall on the anniversary of the Liberation.

He was proud of his plants. Just a few months earlier he would never have thought it possible. Lately many things had happened that he would never have thought possible. Such as the fact that he now spent a lot of time cooking, and enjoying it more and more.

He would go to bed late at night and wake up early in the morning. The days were long, but he never got bored. Even just sitting in the armchair by the fire was pleasurable. He never felt that he was wasting his time. Eleonora and Adele floated around his head like ghosts, and melancholia was a faithful, caring companion that never abandoned him . . . How could he possibly feel lonely?

One morning he woke up at dawn when he heard a strange sound, like someone tapping at the window. It certainly couldn't have been the postman, since it was on the first floor. He got out of bed, and as soon as he opened the inside shutters, he saw a magpie take off from the windowsill. Was that what had woken him up? What could a magpie want from him? He hadn't even managed to leave the room before the magpie returned and started pecking the windowpane again. Every so often it would start singing like a nightingale and imitating the calls of other birds, twisting its head and hopping about. After a few more pecks on the glass, it flew away. Bordelli waited a few minutes, but the magpie didn't come back. Maybe it was Giacomo Pellissari's soul come to tell him the day had arrived. The idea made him smile, but perhaps this was the sign he'd been waiting for. Actually, he was certain it was. Or he wanted to be certain. That same evening he would go and exchange a few words with the monsignor. It was do or die, like the other times . . .

He spent the morning vaguely trying to think up a plan, without ever leaving off any of his rustic chores. He knew very little about Monsignor Sercambi, aside from the bits of information that had emerged from the police surveillance of him in November, the same stuff that had been in Piras's 'birthday present' to him. Monsignor lived in a beautiful villa in Viale Michelangelo, he employed an assistant who also served as his chauffeur, and his days, at least until suppertime, were cadenced by a rather unvarying routine.

He could have procured a high-precision rifle and shot him from a distance, as he'd sometimes imagined. But the idea didn't sit well with him. He wanted the prelate to look him in the eye; he wanted him to *know*. It was no longer necessary to simulate a suicide. Monsignor was the last sentence in a fairy tale. Once accounts were settled with him, the whole affair would be closed and buried. There would be no more danger . . .

When he parked in Piazza Tasso, it was a little after six. He'd brought gloves, the torch and a pistol in the holster under his armpit. That was all he would need.

He went into the bar and, after greeting Fosco, headed straight into the billiards room. At lunchtime he'd managed to speak with Botta, and they'd agreed to meet there. Ennio was in the midst of a game of eight-ball with a bald bloke Bordelli knew by sight, a cigarette smuggler reputed to be an excellent billiards player. Some ten or so idlers were standing around watching the match. Botta, concentrating intensely, made a shot that sank two balls and elicited shouts of amazement from the audience. When he spotted Bordelli he signalled to him that he wouldn't be tied up much longer. And so it was. The smuggler lost handily and, after a handshake, paid up. Ennio laid his cue down and left the bar with Bordelli.

'There's just no two ways about it, Inspector . . . I'm the best . . .'

'How much did you win?'

'Five thousand.'

'That's just spare change, now that you're rich.'

'After a life of poverty, even a hundred lire has its charm.'

'You haven't mentioned that property in Borgo dei Greci that you were going to look at . . .'

'Forget about it . . . It was a pigsty.'

'I need you to lend me a hand,' Bordelli said bluntly.

'Whenever you like, Inspector . . .'

'I need you right now, if that's all right with you.'

'Some locks again?'

'Good guess.'

They got into the Beetle and drove off.

'What's this about?' asked Botta.

'I'm trying to write the ending to a nasty fairy tale.'

'From the look on your face it seems like something serious.'

'More serious than you could ever imagine . . .'

'I'll do my best, Inspector.'

'Me, too . . .'

They went up as far as Piazzale Michelangelo and then came down Viale Michelangelo. They parked along the service road at the corner of Via San Bernardino, and Bordelli gestured towards the great villa of Monsignor Sercambi towering behind the trees.

'That's the one . . .'

'Who lives there?'

'Please don't ask any questions, Ennio.'

'Why not?'

'That's another question . . .'

'Life is made up of questions, Inspector.'

They started making small talk, clouds of smoke floating out of the Beetle's windows. Cars and motorbikes streamed past on the boulevard, but the pavements were deserted.

As the daylight began to fade, they saw the white Peugeot 404 come out of the gate, with the chauffeur at the wheel. It was almost eight o'clock. They waited for the chauffeur to lock the gate and drive off down the *viale* towards Piazza Ferrucci. Bordelli started up the car, and they sped off quicky and parked at the end of Via Tacca. Setting off casually on foot, they came at last to the *viale*, walked along the pavement and passed Sercambi's gate without stopping. Ennio, however, had a look at the lock and said it was child's play. They glanced around to make sure nobody was approaching on foot. It was almost dark out now, especially under the lush trees, and the faint light of the street lamps wasn't enough to conquer the shadows. They quickly turned round and came back at a fast pace. Just to be sure, Bordelli rang the doorbell, but nobody answered.

'Let's go . . .' he said.

Botta opened the gate in just a few seconds, closed it behind him, and they hastened towards the villa. The windows were all dark, the garden barely illuminated by a lamp over the main door. Through the trees one could see the house next door, which had only one window lit up.

'This one's trouble,' Botta whispered after seeing the lock.

'Try to be quick, we haven't got much time.'

'Let me concentrate . . .' He got down to work with a twisted piece of iron wire, biting his lip. In the meantime Bordelli circled round behind the villa, as the sky was shedding its last veil of light. He discovered a small outbuilding not visible from the street. He went up to one window and cast the beam of his torch inside. He saw an unmade bed, a nightstand with a bottle of water on it, some clothes piled up on a chair. It must have been where Monsignor's chauffeur slept; therefore he did not sleep in the villa. Good. That would make it all easier. On his way back he almost ran into Botta.

'Success, Inspector . . .'

'Thanks, Ennio. And now you'd better leave . . . Sorry to make you go on foot . . .'

'I'm happy to have a little walk. Break a leg, Inspector.'

'Thanks . . .'

They nodded goodbye outside the half-open front door, and Botta vanished outside the gate. Bordelli put on his gloves and, using a handkerchief, wiped Botta's fingerprints from the lock, assuming there were any. He went inside and locked the door behind him.

He lit the torch and aimed the cone of light into the darkness of the vestibule, feeling the same sort of thrill he used to feel when, as a boy, he would break into abandoned houses with his friends. The first thing he saw was a beautiful wooden sculpture, in warm colours, of a woman. To judge from the long hair, it must have been a Mary Magdalen. He stopped to look at it, fascinated by the sorrowful expression on her face.

Walking on magnificent carpets, he kept slicing through the darkness with his beam of light, admiring the fine furnishings, the austere oil portraits of cardinals and popes, the beauty in the details. It seemed that all he'd been doing lately was visiting villas and castles.

He knew he didn't have much time, but curiosity led him into various rooms to get a glimpse of Monsignor's soul through his abode. Salons with frescoed ceilings, monumental bookcases, highly precious art objects, a large kitchen that smelled good . . . A magical, luxurious world where the stench of survival could never enter.

He went into what must have been the prelate's study. A sober but elegant desk placed slantwise in front of the window, the walls lined with ancient tomes in Latin and Greek . . . Seneca, Julius Caesar, Tertullian, Epictetus, Aristotle, Sophocles, Euripides, Herodotus, Pliny, St Augustine, the *Vulgata* of St Jerome, the *Summa* of St Thomas . . . But there was also Petronius, Apuleius, Horace, Ovid's *Ars amandi*, the epigrams of Martial, the poems of Sappho . . . Monsignor clearly had a keen interest in the lustful works of pagans as well . . .

In the middle of the desk was a modern, electric Olivetti

typewriter, with several typewritten pages beside it. On the first page was the title: *Saint Ambrose: Charity and Firmness*. The language teemed with learning, but was at the same time clean and fluent. Monsignor Sercambi's knowledge seemed boundless, yet to all appearances it hadn't been enough to keep the demon of perversion away. Was it possible for a love of knowledge and a taste for depravity to coexist in one and the same person? Could good and evil cohabit the same soul? This brought to mind the stories of Curzio Malaparte that told of Nazi salons in Poland where high officials would expound upon the Renaissance, sublime music and great literature while their fat blonde wives stuck knives into the roast goose with delicate ferocity to the accompaniment of girlish little cries . . . While at the same moment, children in the Warsaw ghetto were freezing to death and starving. He also recalled a story he'd once heard about Rudolf Höss, the commandant of Auschwitz. One winter morning, Höss saw a Jewish child trembling in the snow and immediately phoned his wife, saying, 'It's very cold outside today; be sure to bundle up the little ones, my dear . . .'

He went upstairs to the first floor and had a quick look at all the rooms, which were austere but noble and rather welcoming. Three bathrooms with sober mirrors, silver soap dishes, immaculate bathmats, conferring on those spaces a sense of intimacy that made one want to stay there . . . In one of them, a white bathrobe hung from a fancy hook, and on a chair lay some clean, folded undergarments.

He found the prelate's bedroom, the only one that showed any signs of being lived in. An antique canopy bed, and one picture, on the wall opposite, an oil painting of the Blessed Virgin crushing the serpent's head. Lying on the blanket was a light, pale blue housecoat, which looked as if it hung loose on the body, like a frock. On the bedside table were more books, all with bookmarks sticking out from the pages. A few ancient works, a book of medieval history, a novel by Tolstoy . . .

He went back into one of the rooms that gave on to the front garden and partly opened one of the inside shutters, so that he could keep an eye on the gate through the slats on the blinds.

He didn't have to wait long. Soon a car's headlights lit up the garden, the chauffeur got out to open the gate and then ferried Monsignor out of his public life and into his private one. He stopped the Peugeot outside the front door, got out again to open his master's door, and then went and parked the car behind the villa.

Bordelli heard the front door open and close, then some footsteps coming up the stairs. He went to eavesdrop from the door he'd left ajar. Monsignor had shut himself up in the bathroom and started running a bath. Moments later the front door opened and closed again, this time with less authority. It must have been the chauffeur.

Although Bordelli wasn't familiar with the household routines, he felt he could grasp everything that was happening as well as if he could see it. Monsignor was bathing, as the chauffeur was getting supper ready. Clearly he was setting the table in the dining room for the master alone, while he would eat in the kitchen.

Some twenty minutes later, Monsignor came out of the bathroom and went downstairs. Bordelli stole out of the room, careful not to make the slightest sound, and crossed the penumbra to the balustrade. There was a bit of light coming from below. Amid the silence he could hear the driver's footsteps as he went from the kitchen to the dining room, and every so often the sound of a voice. The city seemed quite far away . . .

When, about an hour later, the ground-floor light came on, Bordelli stepped back to hide round the corner of the wall. Monsignor had finished dining and seemed to have retired to his study. Perhaps he wanted to work a little on his text on St Ambrose. Was he planning later to go out in search of human flesh? Or would he keep writing late into the night on the charity and firmness of the bishop of Milan? Whatever his intention, he didn't know yet that fate had other plans for him.

Bordelli could hear the muffled sounds of the chauffeur bustling about in the kitchen behind the closed door. Water running in the sink, clattering dishes, cupboard doors shutting . . . Aside from this, silence reigned.

Half an hour later, the chauffeur came out of the kitchen and went down the corridor, probably to tell his master that he was retiring to his cottage. There was the distant sound of a voice, then the chauffeur came back through the vestibule, went out of the house and locked the door behind him with several turns of the key. Bordelli continued listening, hidden in the first-floor darkness. What was Monsignor Sercambi doing? It was time to go and say hello . . .

He descended the stairs slowly, pistol in hand. A soft light filtered out of the half-closed door of the study. He drew near, treading softly on the carpets and, even before he saw him, he imagined the prelate bent over his books, his gold-framed glasses sitting on his nose, his expression one of concentration.

The telephone rang, and Monsignor answered with his customary severity. Bordelli stopped to listen, catching only a few harshly uttered phrases . . .

'Yes, I'd heard . . . I have to think about it . . . No, not at the moment . . . If need be . . . Never . . . I really don't think so . . . An important decision . . . Nobody . . . Absolutely . . . No, it's impossible . . . Tomorrow, yes . . . Goodnight . . .'

He hung up, and a few seconds later there was the sound of the typewriter. The high prelate of the Episcopal Curia could at last turn his efforts to the creation of his work, and had he been able to finish it, it would certainly have been published by a prestigious publishing house . . . But was there, in some corner of his conscience, any guilt over the murder of Giacomo Pellissari clamouring to be heard? Or had he succeeded, with divine intercession, in rendering the memory of that night harmless? And in what corner of that immortal soul was the rape of Eleonora hiding?

Bordelli peered into the study and found before him the same scene he'd imagined . . . It was like seeing a Nazi official discussing art and literature while the children in the ghetto . . .

He walked into the room with the pistol pointed.

'Nice to see you again, Monsignor,' he said, approaching the desk. The prelate remained motionless in his chair, like a marble bust. He stared at Bordelli with his mouth half open, and as soon as he realised this, he shut it.

'How did you get in here?'

The surprise had shaken him up, and his hands were trembling slightly. His elegant pale blue housecoat fell from his shoulders in soft folds. Bordelli sat down in front of him, always keeping the pistol pointed at him.

'Aren't you going to say hello?' he said calmly.

'How did you get in here?' Monsignor repeated.

'I passed through the walls, the way ghosts do.'

'What do you want from me?' the priest stammered, turning pale.

'Do you always treat your guests this way?' said Bordelli, smiling faintly.

'Have the decency to explain what you want from me . . .'

His bald head glistened like a peach in the sun.

'Don't you feel the need to confess?'

'To confess what?'

'I'm sure you know better than I . . .'

'God already knows my sins.'

'And that's enough to clear your conscience?'

He could have put an end to things at once, instead of wasting time chatting, but he couldn't resist the desire to make the man admit to his crimes . . .

'I don't know what you're talking about,' said Monsignor Sercambi, seeming confused. With the barrel of a pistol aimed at him, he couldn't decide whether to act tough or docile. He was trying to understand what could be going through the mind of this barbarian who surely was unable to translate Ovid and had never read the correspondence between Heloise and Abelard . . .

'This is no time to play innocent, Monsignor.'

'I don't understand . . .'

'Before throwing himself out of the window, Italo Signorini

told me everything, which I'm sure you realised straight away.'

'I still don't understand . . . I'm sorry . . . I don't know any Signorini . . .'

'And your other playmates, Panerai and Beccaroni, also killed themselves in remorse.'

'You must forgive me, I don't know any of these people . . . May they rest in peace . . .' said the priest, hands folded as though he wanted to pray for their sinning souls.

'Amen . . .' said Bordelli, miming the sign of the cross in the air with the pistol barrel.

'And what can I do for you, Signor Bordelli?'

'Finally, someone who doesn't call me *inspector* . . .'

'Would you please be good enough to put your weapon away? And explain why you should want to torment me?' He was trying to appear untroubled, but behind his fine gold spectacles his pupils seemed to be drowning in fear.

'I suggest we play a game, since you like games so much . . . If, by the count of ten, you don't start confessing your sins to me and to God, I shall release your mortal soul from the prison of the flesh . . . One . . . Two . . . Three . . . Four . . . Five . . . Six . . . Seven . . . Eight . . . Nine . . . Ten . . .'

'No . . . All right . . . All right . . .' said Monsignor, raising his hands slightly. It must have been truly appalling, for someone like him, not to be able to dominate the situation.

'Thank you . . . So, tell me . . .'

'It was a misfortune . . . A tragic misfortune . . .' A large drop of sweat streaked his cheek.

'Of course . . .' said Bordelli, as though bored.

'You must believe me . . .'

'Was it also a tragic misfortune when you raped a little boy?'

'I have repented . . . Profoundly . . . As God is my witness . . .' the prelate said, in more or less the same terms as Beccaroni.

'Perjurors go to hell – I learned that in catechism,' said Bordelli.

'Then you must also have learned about Christian charity . . . The joy of forgiveness . . .'

He was panting lightly, and Bordelli read in his eyes a profound unease at having to humble himself.

'The only one who could have enjoyed any forgiveness was strangled.'

'I didn't do it . . .' the prelate was quick to say.

'All you did was rape him, is that it?' said Bordelli, thinking of the horror the boy had been subjected to. Monsignor lowered his eyes contritely, but quickly looked up again.

'I pray for him every day, and I shall pray for him to the end of my days . . .'

'Let him rest in peace,' said Bordelli, yearning for a cigarette. For no precise reason he kept postponing the moment, pretending that Monsignor Sercambi had a future. Maybe he simply wanted to look him in the eye for a little while longer, to try to understand . . .

'You cannot imagine how sorry I am,' said Monsignor.

'God will reward you for it . . . I imagine you're also sorry for having ordered two gentlemen to rape a young woman . . .'

'The devil clouds the mind . . . I was no longer myself . . .' the priest said in a whisper, looking away.

'Interesting . . .'

He finally had proof that it had indeed been the prelate who had ordered the rape, and with a tingling in his forearms he again saw Eleonora curled up under the covers, her face covered with bruises.

'Man is half angel, half beast, said Pascal,' the prelate continued, in a submissive tone that must have cost him a great deal. In spite of everything he seemed calmer now. Perhaps he thought it was only a matter of finding the right words . . . If the matter took a seriously bad turn, he could always count on his 'friends'. The Masons knew no obstacles.

'On your feet . . .' said Bordelli, standing up.

'What's that?'

'Stand up.'

'What do you intend to do?'

'I said stand up.'

'Yes . . .'

Monsignor got up, gently pushing the chair away. He was shorter than Bordelli had imagined and, if one took a good look at him, rather delicate. The imposing air he often communicated came entirely from his eyes, and an awareness of his own power . . . Whereas now he simply looked like a poor, frightened priest.

'Go and stand over there,' Bordelli ordered him, pointing to the centre of the rug. Monsignor obeyed, not understanding what his 'guest' had in mind. Bordelli took a few steps towards him. 'Take off your clothes,' he said.

'You can't be serious . . .' the prelate muttered, goggling his eyes, standing stiff as a tree trunk.

'Take off your clothes,' Bordelli repeated darkly.

Monsignor waited for a few more seconds, dazed by the strange command, then took off his housecoat and tossed it on to the back of a chair. That left him in underpants and undershirt, both with his initials embroidered on them. His naked legs were streaked with blue veins, and his knees were shaking.

'What do you intend to do?' he said in terror.

'Take off the rest as well.'

'I beg you . . .'

'Don't make me repeat it,' Bordelli said with a harshness that made the prelate give a start.

'Be merciful . . .'

'I'm about to shoot you.'

'No . . .'

Monsignor Sercambi took off his undershirt, shaking like a leaf. He had narrow shoulders, and his ribs were visible. Bordelli, with a gesture, ordered him to take off the underpants as well. He wanted to make him suffer the same humiliation the Nazis inflicted on the new arrivals to the extermination camps. Monsignor let his drawers fall to the floor and then covered himself with his hands, gasping in shame. Bordelli, disgusted, smiled.

'If you're looking for the devil, you'll find him between your legs,' he said, thinking of Giacomo Pellissari's last half-hour of life.

'Why all this?' the prelate stammered in despair.

'The little boy you raped wondered the same thing.'

'God, please help me . . .' Monsignor wailed, collapsing to his knees. He fell forward almost to the point of touching his forehead to the rug, then burst into sobs. 'I have repented . . . I have sinned . . . I repent, I repent again . . . God forgive me . . . God forgive me . . .'

He had crossed the threshold of dignity and was falling lower and lower.

'I'm a monster . . . I did the demon's bidding . . .'

Until a few minutes ago he'd been a high prelate in the Curia, feared and respected, a Freemason, a scholar writing an important treatise on the thought of St Ambrose . . . He'd fallen from the lofty heights of power and into the mire . . . Now he was just a naked man crying, kneeling before a pistol . . .

'Repentance . . . Repentance . . .'

He raved without restraint, and his pain seemed genuine. It wasn't hard to repent *in articulo mortis*. As Bordelli watched him he remembered Italo Signorini's words about the evening the four friends had spent with Giacomo: *After a long groan, Monsignor Sercambi collapsed on top of him* . . .

All of a sudden he felt endless compassion for this minister of God who'd been unable to resist the call of his basest instincts, unable to distinguish good from evil, pleasure from the abuse of power . . . And as had also happened with the lawyer, he thought perhaps he wouldn't kill him. He could force him to write a detailed confession and then drag him into court . . . But then what if, in spite of everything, he still got off scot free? The humiliation he'd suffered would make him even fiercer, and he would avenge himself. No scandal could ever bring him down. With his wealth and power he would be back on his feet in no time . . . He might even emigrate to some poor country where he could live like a nabob and buy the children's misery . . .

He stuck his pistol back in its holster, then straddled the prelate's body, grabbed his neck and started squeezing with all his might. It was harder with gloves on than with one's bare hands, but he would manage just the same. Sercambi struggled but was unable to break free, and his gold-framed glasses went flying to one side.

'Panerai and Beccaroni did not commit suicide: I killed them myself, and I wanted you to know that,' said Bordelli, panting from the effort. After a minute that seemed it would never end, Monsignor Sercambi collapsed lengthwise, rattling and weakly thrashing, scratching his fingernails on the carpet . . . Bordelli kept on squeezing, to avoid the risk of having him recover. Before his eyes the man's bald head turned all red, then purple, almost black . . . When he was sure that Monsignor's soul had left his body, he let go.

God! What an effort, he thought, getting to his feet. His brow was drenched in sweat, and he wiped it with the back of his gloved hand. The flaccid white carcass of his victim lay at his feet, open mouthed and goggle eyed. He would no longer harm anyone. Goliath the giant had been slain again . . .

Bordelli fell into a chair to catch his breath. He looked at the clock: almost eleven. Monsignor had suffered the same horror as Giacomo: so it was written. He, Bordelli, had merely been the secular arm, like the men-at-arms who used to burn heretics in the days of the Inquisition. He hadn't taken revenge; he'd merely restored order. The justice of the courts didn't always function properly, and in such cases another solution was needed. The ogre had been slain, but the outcome was not like the ending of a fairy tale. Nobody would live happily ever after . . .

It occurred to him that he should do something to mislead the investigation into the murder of the respectable Monsignor Sercambi. It had to be something very odd, to create confusion in the minds of the investigators. He had to use his imagination . . . What might best muddy the waters and induce them to make the most complicated conjectures? What was needed was an inexplicable mystery, something completely fake and useless . . .

At last the right idea came to him. He took a pen from the desk and drew a large swastika on the dead prelate's back. A war vendetta . . . The poor detective assigned the case could bang his head against the wall till kingdom come . . .

Before leaving, he made a final, risky bet with destiny: he decided he would take no precautions when exiting the villa. If there were no snags, he would have the final confirmation that he had merely followed the dictates of fate. He looked one last time at the corpse on the carpet . . . Adieu, Monsignor . . .

He calmly went down the stairs, lighting his way with the torch. Casting one last glance at the sorrowful sculpture of the Magdalen, he turned the knob of the lock and went out through the front door, closing it behind him and heading for the gate. The garden was in semi-darkness, immersed in a fable-like atmosphere. One window of the villa next door was faintly lit by the flickering glow of a television set, and he imagined husband and wife sitting on the sofa, watching the conclusion of a film on the National channel.

He hadn't given any thought to how he would exit the gate, but wasn't worried. He was ready to clamber over the grille, or even climb the trees . . . But there was no need. He felt around inside the ivy covering the pillars and found a button. Clicking open the lock, he stepped out on to the pavement. He looked around but saw no one. The boulevard was deserted. As he approached his car he removed the gloves and stuffed them into his pocket. He felt weightless, and perhaps a bit shaken. He couldn't work out in his own mind whether the world really did now seem a little less dirty, as he'd hoped. There was also a feeling of emptiness, as when one finishes a major undertaking and leaves it behind . . . Most of all, he felt very hungry . . .

He went up Via Tacca, encountered not a living soul, and got into his car. Puffing on a cigarette, he turned on to Viale Michelangelo in the direction of the Arno. Nobody had seen him. It was as if he'd never set foot in that magnificent villa. The swastika on the prelate's back would trigger a pointless hunt. It challenged everyone to try to understand, and to seek a motive.

He crossed the bridge and while driving through Piazza Beccaria he looked up, as usual, at the thick black band making its way entirely around the medieval gate, several metres above the ground. For those who hadn't witnessed the spectacle, it must have been hard to imagine that one November morning the *viale* was a river of stinking mud. But the traces of the past were not easily erased.

He tried not to think of Eleonora, but failed. The death of Monsignor Sercambi marked the end of a chapter, and the next one might even include her. Now he could tell her that the guilty party had paid. He shook his head, realising he hadn't asked him for the names of the two thugs who'd raped her . . . But maybe it was better this way. He was tired of hunting down sons of bitches like some solitary gunslinger. And killing those two would have been a purely personal vendetta.

He pulled up outside the Trattoria da Cesare with a hole in his stomach. Getting out of the car, he tossed his cigarette butt aside. The air was warm and lightly tossed by a breeze that rustled the young leaves on the plane trees. He entered the restaurant, which was nearly deserted, nodded to Cesare in greeting, and went into Totò's realm.

'Inspector, I'm glad to see that you deign to come down from your mountain every now and then,' said the cook, coming towards him.

'It's a long and lonely road . . .'

'And what are you doing at home? Eating out of tins?'

'I've learned how to cook . . .'

'But what's happened to you? You should see your face . . .'

'I'm just a little tired, Totò.'

'No, I meant you look younger.'

'It must be the country air.'

'You still haven't had any dinner, I can read it in your eyes.'

'Good guess . . .' said Bordelli, sitting down on his stool.

'You can't hide hunger, Inspector. What do you feel like eating?'

'If it's not any trouble, I'd like a nice steak, blood rare.'

'Trouble? I'll have it ready for you in one minute . . . Would you like a few beans on the side, or would you rather have some broccoli rabe sautéed in garlic?'

'The beans sound good, thanks,' said Bordelli, pouring himself a glass of wine.

'Beans it is . . .' said the cook. After stirring the embers with a poker, he took a beautiful steak from the fridge and dropped it on the red-hot grill.

'How are things with your lady-love Nina?' Bordelli asked as the steak sizzled.

'Women are funny, Inspector. Just to be up to date, Nina's family bought a washing machine, and do you know what she and her mother do now? They spend all their time sitting in front of the washing machine, watching the clothes go round and round behind the glass . . .'

'Maybe it's better than television.'

'At any rate I'm going to marry her sooner or later.'

'The washing machine?'

'That's probably already happened in America. Those guys are capable of anything,' said Totò, as one familiar with the peoples of the world. Sticking the steak with a meat-fork, he flipped it over, as the beans were warming in a pan. Bordelli poured himself his third glass of wine. Every so often he remembered that scarcely half an hour earlier he'd strangled a monsignor of the Curia, and this seemed quite strange to him.

At last the steak and beans arrived, and Totò cut three slices of bread for him. Bordelli was as hungry as a wolf and immediately started devouring the bloody meat. The cook as usual started telling a macabre story about his home town . . . This one involved a chemist, a rather respected family man who led an honest, quiet life . . .

' . . . then one fine day he was found out in the country, completely naked, murdered, with a knife stuck in his chest and a mouse stuffed in his mouth . . . Nobody could ever make head or tail of it, and they never found the killer . . .'

'Maybe the esteemed pharmacist had done some terrible thing, and somebody decided to avenge himself.'

'They needed you there, Inspector . . . After just a few days, the culprit would have been behind bars . . .'

'Not everyone who kills deserves to end up behind bars, my dear Totò,' said Bordelli. Who knew what the cook would have said if he'd told him how he'd just spent the evening . . .

'Have I ever told you the one about the woman who was cut in two?'

'I don't think so . . .'

'She was a schoolteacher, young and pretty . . . The whole town came to her funeral . . . The little children cried like fountains . . .' That time, they found the killer. He was one of the children's fathers. He confessed in tears. For several months he'd been meeting secretly with the pretty teacher, and when she got tired of him, he cut her open like a calf . . .

'Why don't we talk about women who are still in one piece?' said Bordelli, who didn't feel much like spending the rest of the evening talking about murders. He wanted to savour his steak in peace, and kept refilling his wine glass. He seemed unable to get drunk, feeling only a slight euphoria that would later turn to sadness. A bit the way it always happened with Rosa . . .

They started talking about women and politics, spicy salami

and the new Fiat 500, which Totò wanted to buy for himself . . .
The time passed placidly, like a peaceful river.

Bordelli finished his steak and beans and complimented the chef.

'You can't refuse a little dessert, Inspector.'

'I think I'd better . . .'

'I have a *crostata* that can wake the dead.'

'All right, but only a little sliver, just for a taste.'

'I made it with Nina's jam . . .' said Totò, seeming almost offended.

'Well, all right, then, make it a whole slice.'

'That's what I like to hear, Inspector.' He set a quarter of the pie down in front of Bordelli.

'Starting tomorrow I'm going on a diet . . .'

He washed the tart down with two small glasses of grappa while the cook tidied up the kitchen.

'This tart is a masterpiece, Totò.'

'You flatter me, Inspector . . .'

Cesare's head appeared through the service hatch, telling them he was going to bed. Moments later they heard the screech of the rolling metal shutter being lowered. It was almost one o'clock.

Bordelli finished his *crostata*, and honoured it with one last grappa. When he got up from the stool he swore he wouldn't eat another crumb for a week.

'Already going to bed, Inspector?'

'I've had a busy day.'

'Well, try and come back before Christmas . . .'

'Never fear, Totò, I'll be back soon . . .'

Driving along the Imprunetana through Pozzolatico, he felt like a medieval knight returning to his castle after slaying monsters in the dark wood. During the stretches where the stone walls were lowest, the moon's bloodless glow cast a silvery light over the olive groves. The wooded hills in the distance were blacker than the night, concealing their primordial mysteries. A sight Giacomo, and his killers, would never see again. If there was an afterlife, the victim and his tormentors would never meet. An infinity separated heaven and hell . . .

He tossed his cigarette butt out the window, curbing the impulse to light another one immediately. How nice it would have been to have Eleonora, or even Adele, waiting for him at home. He tried to pretend this was really the case, and for a second he felt butterflies in his stomach. Men really were quite silly at times. When jilted by a woman, they felt ugly and mean and thought: *Nobody wants me.* But when the object of a woman's love, they soared to seventh heaven, thinking they were the cat's whiskers. They were entirely dependent on women and felt a kind of sacred terror in their regard, and maybe that was why they had always tried to subdue them. But women were not the way they used to be, and now pawed the ground in their enclosures, wanting to gallop far afield . . .

While passing through Mezzomonte he felt the desire to exchange a few words with Dante. He was tired, extremely tired, but didn't feel the least bit like going straight to bed. He turned and went through the gate, pulling up in front of the house. It was almost 2 a.m., but Dante was sure to be still in his underground laboratory.

He went down the stairs and pushed the door open, smelling the unmistakable odour of the place, a blend of melted wax and cigar smoke. The suffuse, wavering light of the candles was as calming as the dusk. Dante was at the back of the laboratory, pacing back and forth in front of his workbench, looking pensive. The whiteness of his smock and leonine mane stood out in the penumbra, suggesting a ghost. Upon seeing Bordelli he smiled and grabbed a bottle of grappa.

'I wasn't expecting you so early, Inspector,' he said, filling the glasses.

'Forgive me, I didn't want to interrupt your thought processes.'

'It's good you did; I was getting confused.'

'If you don't mind, I'm happy just sitting here in silence . . . Just pretend I'm not here . . .'

'*If you're alone, you'll be all yours; if you're with someone, you'll be only half yours*,'[27] said Dante, handing him a glass.

'You're right; what I said was silly.'

'Then we should toast.'

'Every excuse is good . . .'

They lightly clinked glasses and took a sip.

'Are you going to stand there all night?' asked the inventor.

Bordelli collapsed into an armchair. He was so tired, he risked falling asleep. Dante, on the other hand, did not sit down; he seemed full of energy. He downed his glass, and after lighting a cigar stub he'd recovered from an ashtray, he resumed pacing back and forth. Bordelli followed him with his eyes, hypnotised by the fat snakes of smoke twisting in the air over his head.

'Have you ever been in love with two women at the same time?' asked Bordelli, immediately realising that he'd never heard Dante speak of women before.

'Even three or four, when I was a lad,' said Dante, stopping in front of him.

'Sheer hell . . .'

'Then one fine day I met Maddalena, and in one second all the others were swept out of the picture, all the present and future women. It may sound like the usual romantic refrain, but it's the simple truth. We lived together for almost ten years, loving each other and quarrelling in the most wonderful ways. But one terrible day she left me – or, more precisely, she left this world . . . She died, in short. Since then I have never found another woman capable of making me forget her, and since then I have been quite happily alone . . . Or, rather, by her side. I feel her hovering around me every second of my life, and sometimes I talk to her . . . So, to conclude, I'm a raving old madman, and proud of it,' said Dante, smiling sadly.

'What a beautiful love story,' Bordelli commented, charmed.

'And so you're in love with two women?'

'Maybe – but neither of them wants me any more.'

'*Il faut la troisième . . .*' said Dante, emitting smoke from his mouth.

'I'd welcome her with open arms, if she could sweep away the other two,' said Bordelli, eyes drooping with fatigue.

'And if one day they both came back, would you be able to choose?'

'Of course. I'd choose both.'

'So you see very clearly on this matter . . .' said Dante, laughing.

'Maybe . . . Or maybe not . . . I don't know . . . I . . . Maybe . . .'

'The truth of the matter is that you have killed three innocent people! Three men loved and respected by everyone! Only to follow your delirious vision of destiny! And now you feel crushed by remorse!'

'That's not true . . . not true . . .' Bordelli stammered, waking up.

Dante was standing before him, looking at him with curiosity.

'What's not true? That you fell asleep?'

'I'm sorry, I was dreaming . . .'

'Would you like to spend the night here?'

'Thanks, but I'll be going home now,' said Bordelli, standing up. He needed his own bed, the smells of his own house.

'Are you sure you can drive? Shall I give you a lift?'

'No, thanks, don't worry, my horse knows the way home.'

They said goodbye with a handshake, and Bordelli headed for the stairs, trying to wake up.

'If you're alone, you'll be all yours . . .' Dante said aloud.

Before going up the stairs, Bordelli turned round and waved goodbye again. Outside, the cool night air cleared his brain a little. He got in his car and let it drive him home.

Before going to bed, he glanced over at the death's-head, as if checking to see that it was still there. By now it was a familiar presence, and if he wasn't careful, he would end up talking to it, too.

Sticking a few small logs into the stove, he remembered the gloves and threw them in as well, then watched them contort over the embers. He staggered on his feet while undressing and then got under the covers. He felt sleep grab him and overwhelm him, as when he was a child and would suddenly collapse . . . Mamma would take him to bed and undress him, tossing him around like a puppet, while he took immense pleasure in the feeling of being in her hands . . .

In the distance he heard a frog croaking obsessively. His bed had never felt so big, and for a moment he thought he smelled Adele's scent in the sheets.

He put the espresso pot on the burner, thinking that there were three things he had to do that day. He'd slept like a rock, feeling more rested than he had in a very long time. It was almost eleven. Monsignor Sercambi's chauffeur had surely discovered the body by now, probably a few hours earlier. It was anyone's guess who would be investigating the murder. He pictured Diotivede grappling with the initial findings, with his ironic smile and his black bag set down on the ground . . . the assistant prosecutor biting his lips, thrown for a loop by the swastika drawn on the prelate's back . . . while the newsmen pressed to get inside with their cameras round their necks . . . The usual stuff . . .

He heard a rumbling car engine draw near and, peering out the window, saw a fire-red Alfa Romeo pull up on the threshing floor. He couldn't work out who it was at the wheel because of the daylight reflecting off the vehicle's windows. The car door opened, and out came Ennio. He hadn't given in and bought a Porsche, but, to all appearances, his new wealth was beginning to bear fruit . . .

Bordelli went and opened the front door and noticed immediately that Botta had a strange look on his face.

'Weren't you going to squirrel it all away, Ennio?'

'When I woke up this morning I felt more like a fox, and so I went and bought this old heap.'

'So you finally got yourself a present.' They shook hands.

'You only live once, Inspector . . .'

'You did the right thing,' Bordelli said in all sincerity.

He went out to get a closer look at the Alfa and started

circling round it, running a finger over the body. Botta kept his hands in his pockets, jangling the keys.

'What do you think?'

'You've got yourself a very fine car.'

'It's a Giulia Sprint, it can go almost a hundred and eighty kilometres an hour,' said Botta, but you could tell he had something else on his mind. Bordelli opened the door and got in behind the wheel. He started it up, just to hear the sound of the engine. He revved it twice, then turned it off.

'I feel like it's a little mine, too,' he said, getting out.

'You can borrow it whenever you like, Inspector.'

'Feel like a coffee?' He headed for the door, with Botta at his side.

'I'll only stay a minute . . . I need to help a friend move house . . .'

Ennio made the coffee, and they sat down at the kitchen table in front of the steaming little cups.

'Nice new housemate you've got there,' said Ennio, indicating the death's-head spying on them from above.

'He's very wise; he never talks . . .'

'But he makes himself understood.'

Botta smiled, but his eyes remained pensive.

'Do you want to tell me something, Ennio?'

'No . . . I mean . . .'

'Out with it.'

'Nothing important . . . I just wanted to say . . . Half an hour ago, as I was trying out my car on the Viale San Domenico, I heard a news report on the radio . . .'

'It must have been a thrilling experience.'

'They said that last night an important priest of the Curia was strangled in his villa.'

'Ah . . .'

'And do you know where this priest's villa is?'

'No, where?'

'In Viale Michelangelo.'

'Get to the point, Ennio.'

'Well, we were outside a villa on Viale Michelangelo when we said goodbye last night . . .'

'Quite a coincidence, don't you think?'

'Yeah . . .'

'Is that all?' said Bordelli, fiddling with his demitasse.

Botta shook his head. 'So you really don't what to tell me what happened?'

'What are you talking about?'

'You know what I'm talking about, Inspector . . .'

'Have you seen my garden? It's become quite a marvel . . .' said Bordelli, yawning as he stood up.

They finished their coffee and went out the back door. The tomatoes and chilli peppers were thriving, and all the artichokes but one had taken.

'I was expecting worse,' said Botta, studying the young plants with a clinical eye.

'I should start using the *pollina* in two weeks, right?'

'Right . . .'

'Can you imagine it, Ennio? For the first time in my life I'll be eating the fruits of my own labours.'

'Wait before you say that. If we get one of those hailstorms . . .'

'There won't be any hailstorms, and I'm going to have tomatoes this big,' said Bordelli, miming the size of a watermelon with his hands.

'So you really don't want to tell me anything, Inspector?'

'What would I want to tell you?'

'About last night . . .'

'Well, let's see . . . I had a good sleep, how about you?'

'Okay, okay, I get it . . . I'll leave you to your mysteries, Inspector. At any rate, I'm not one who talks,' said Botta, looking at his watch.

Bordelli walked with him out to the threshing floor and watched him drive off in his red Alfa. The sky was covered with big dark clouds, and the thunder in the distance sounded like kettle-drum rolls. But there was no guarantee it would actually rain. Just to be safe, he went back to the garden and started watering the plants, thinking that Ennio would never betray him.

Back inside the house, he ran a bath and carefully shaved while waiting for the tub to fill up. He remained immersed in the hot water for a long time, feeling as if he was removing the filth of a bloody battle from his body. Then he got dressed and went into the kitchen. He set the table, and in a variation on the gospel of Ennio, he prepared himself a dish of spaghetti with butter and parmesan cheese. An apparently simple dish that was actually very difficult. He ate it slowly, complimenting himself in his solitude. After his coffee, he went and looked up the telephone number of the Pellissaris in the phone book.

'Hello?'

'Signor Pellissari?'

'This is he, who is this?'

'Inspector Bordelli . . .'

'Hello . . . How are you?' said Pellissari, surprised and upset.

'Not too bad, and you?'

'Have you found anything out, Inspector?' His voice was trembling a little.

'If it's all right with you, I'd like to come and see you.'

'Yes, of course . . . Have you got some news?'

'If you'll just be patient, we can talk when I get there.'

'As you wish . . .' said the lawyer, seeming more and more worried.

'Half past two all right?'

'Yes . . .'

'It's probably better if your wife is present as well.'

'She's right here. We'll be waiting for you.'

'See you in a bit . . .'

As soon he set down the receiver, he left the house and got into his Beetle under a blanket of low clouds.

It was a long journey through time, during which he relived those awful days in October and November . . . The boy's disappearance, the discovery of the body in the woods, the frantic investigation . . . The incessant rain . . . The flood . . .

He pulled up outside the cemetery of San Domenico and went in through the gate. There was nobody there, as he'd hoped. He calmly searched the graves until he found Giacomo's. There was a photo of the boy on the tombstone with a gap-toothed smile and a cyclist's cap on backwards.

'Ciao, Giacomo . . .'

'Ciao, Inspector . . .'

'Do you know who I am?'

'Of course . . . Even though we've never met . . .'

'I did what I could.'

'I know . . . I saw everything . . . The dead see everything . . .'

'I had to do it . . .'

'Are you so sure?'

'There was no other way. Either that, or forget about the whole thing.'

'I would have rested in peace just the same . . .'

'But I wouldn't have, Giacomo. You're on the other side, but I'm still here. I just couldn't tolerate . . .'

'You did it for yourself, Inspector . . . For yourself alone . . .'

'I don't know, and I don't want to know . . .'

'Farewell, Inspector . . .'

'Farewell, Giacomo . . . Remember me from time to time . . .'

He waved goodbye and headed for the exit. A woman in black stood motionless in front of a grave, arms dangling at her sides. She must have come in while he was chatting with Giacomo. He walked past her, but she didn't move. Perhaps she, too, was speaking with the dead . . .

He left the cemetery and, driving slowly, steered on to Via della Piazzuola. He didn't want to get there early. Turning on to Via Barbacane, he advanced a few hundred metres and then parked along the street where the road surface widened, near the Pellissaris' villa. He rang the buzzer at the gate, and seconds later the lawyer and his wife appeared in the garden and came towards him. They greeted him with trepidation and showed him into the house, where chaos reigned. The entrance hall was cluttered with large boxes, parcels and suitcases.

'We've sold the house,' said the lawyer, glancing over at his wife. 'We're moving to Rome.'

They showed him into a sitting room and sat down opposite him, on the sofa.

'Rosalba is expecting . . . And we thought it would be best to leave Florence . . .'

'I understand . . .'

'If it's a boy, we'll call him Giacomo,' the woman said with tears in her eyes. Bordelli looked away, thinking it was a noble, courageous idea. One son was dead, and another was about to be born . . . Would they eventually tell him what had happened to his brother?

'What did you have to tell us, Inspector?' Signora Pellissari asked with a furrow in her brow, twisting her fingers. Bordelli took his time, searching for the right words. He heaved a long sigh . . .

'I've found out who your son's killers are.'

'Ah . . .' said the woman, blanching. The lawyer sprang to his feet.

'I've known for a few months, but I had no proof . . . And so I didn't want . . .'

'How many are there? Who are they?' the lawyer asked breathlessly.

'Please sit down . . .' said Bordelli.

Signor Pellissari sat down heavily on the sofa.

'Who are they?' he repeated, trying to control himself. Bordelli was tempted to tell them the whole truth, but immediately decided against it. It would have been careless.

'Fate has evened the score. Three committed suicide, and the fourth was killed last night.'

'I want the names!' the lawyer pressed him, as his wife tried to catch her breath.

'They're dead now . . . All four of them . . . Are you sure you want to know?'

'Yes . . .' said Rosalba, leaning forward.

Bordelli nodded, even though he knew that it would not be very pleasant for them. Over those past few months they'd shut themselves up inside their suffering and managed to find a sort of resigned balance in it . . . Now they would have to turn it all upside down and start all over again.

'Italo Signorini, the youngest of the group. He was the one who kidnapped Giacomo. He confessed this only to me, with no other witnesses around . . . He told me everything, even the names of the others . . . But then, as we were getting ready to go to police headquarters, he threw himself out of the window, destroying any chance of incriminating his friends.'

The lady squeezed her husband's arm, biting her lips.

'Livio Panerai, the butcher from the shop in Viale dei Mille. He was the one who actually murdered your son. He shot himself in the mouth with his double-barrel shotgun last February.'

The lawyer seemed to have trouble breathing and was rotating his head like a bull in the arena.

'Moreno Beccaroni, the lawyer . . .'

'No!' the woman cried, standing up, her hand over her mouth.

'Oh my God . . . We went to his funeral . . . He was a collegue of mine . . .' the husband muttered, upset. Giacomo's mother sat back down and buried her face in her hands, barely managing, with great difficulty, to suppress her sobs, while her husband delicately caressed the back of her neck.

Bordelli waited patiently, seeing the corpses of the four play-mates file past in his mind's eye . . .

'And who was the fourth?' asked the lawyer, trying to control himself. His wife looked up, eyes like two charred chestnuts.

'Monsignor Sercambi, a high prelate of the Curia . . . He's dead now, too . . . Strangled last night in his own home . . . I heard it on the radio . . .' Bordelli concluded.

Signora Pellissari looked around as though lost, and a moment later started whimpering like a puppy. Her husband put his arm around her waist, managing to make her stand up, and accompanied her out of the room. He returned about fifteen minutes later, and Bordelli stood up. The lawyer had recovered a certain composure, though it could not have been easy.

'I imagine it's not worth the trouble of making this horror story public . . . To expose the killers anyway . . .' he said, trying to appeal to legalistic reasoning.

'Nobody would believe us . . . There's no proof . . .'

'I think you're right, though it's hard to swallow.'

'I'm sorry . . .'

'I'm very grateful to you, Inspector. Nobody can give us our son back, but at least we know now that his killers are not living out their lives undisturbed . . . I don't like being happy over the death of another person, but in this case I can't help it.'

'That's not hard to understand . . .'

'Thank you again.'

'I'm just the messenger.'

'At last it's all over . . . Now we can try to carry on.'

'You'll find peace again, I'm sure of it,' said Bordelli, smiling with difficulty.

'Let me show you out . . .'

They went out of the villa in silence, walked through a garden full of flowers and bumblebees buzzing, and stopped at the gate.

'Have a good journey, Signor Pellissari. And please give my regards to your wife.'

'Goodbye, Inspector.'

'Goodbye . . .' said Bordelli, shaking his hand firmly.

As he headed down the street he heard the gate close behind him. He got into the Beetle and continued down Via Barbacane, shouldering a melancholy feeling of death. Coming out into Viale Volta, he turned right.

As he drove past the house in which he was born he remembered a spring afternoon from some fifty years earlier . . . He was six or seven and had just discovered the thrill of death . . . He would pretend to have been hit with a bullet, or stabbed in the back, run through with a sword, poisoned . . . It was crazy, insane fun, pretending to die . . . He would fall on the ground, start kicking wildly, breathe his last breath . . . He was very good at dying, and his mother used to say that he would be an actor when he grew up . . .

There was one last thing he had to do, and he realised he'd been waiting for this moment for a very long time. Crossing the overpass of Le Cure, he turned on to Viale Don Minzoni and a few minutes later pulled his car up outside the guard booth of the police station. Mugnai ran out to greet him and came up to the car window.

'Inspector! How are you?'

'Hello, Mugnai, I missed you.'

'You look good, sir, years younger . . .'

'I guess tending a garden is good for you.'

'Makes me sweat just thinking of it . . .'

'Need any help with the crossword puzzle?'

'I've stopped doing that stuff, Inspector.'

'So what do you do now?'

'I read *Diabolik*, it's a lot more fun.'

'I don't doubt it . . .'

'Have you heard about last night's murder?'

'I heard it on the radio . . . Is Commissioner Inzipone in?'

'I think so, I haven't seen him go out.'

'I'm going upstairs for a minute.'

He said goodbye to Mugnai and parked in the courtyard, as he had done for so many years. While climbing the stairs he said hello to a few former colleagues, and even stopped to exchange a few words. The uniformed cops he crossed paths with saluted him as if he were still in service. When he got to the second floor, he knocked at the commissioner's door and went in without waiting.

'Good afternoon, sir . . .' he said, approaching the desk.

344

Inzipone welcomed him with a look of astonishment that quickly turned into a sort of smile.

'It's not's a good afternoon, Bordelli; in fact, it's a bloody awful day all round . . .'

He stood up to shake his hand and then immediately sat back down, putting his elbows up on the desk.

'Yes, I know, I heard it on the radio,' said Bordelli, who remained standing. He didn't intend to stay long.

'Just what we needed. Jesus bloody Christ!' the commissioner cursed.

'Life is full of surprises . . .'

'But what are you doing here, anyway, Inspe— Mr Bordelli?' asked Inzipone, as if he'd just woken up.

'If I may . . . I've come to tell you something.'

'Then tell me . . .'

'I'm ready to return to duty – if you want me, that is.'

'Are you serious?' said the commissioner, wide eyed.

'I'm afraid so.'

'I knew it . . . I knew it all along . . .' Inzipone muttered. He opened a drawer, took out Bordelli's badge and pistol and laid them on the desk.

'Thank you,' said the inspector, gathering up the tools of his trade.

'I shall inform Rome at once of your return to service.'

'Starting tomorrow, if you don't mind.'

'Immediately would be better . . .'

'Who's in charge of last night's murder?'

'Inspector Del Lama . . . You don't know him, he hasn't been here long . . . Young, but on the ball . . .'

'Any leads yet?'

'Del Lama spent the entire morning questioning the monsignor's chauffeur, but nothing came of it . . . Clearly the poor bastard's got nothing to do with it . . . All he's been doing is crying . . . He worshipped his boss . . . As for everything else, total darkness . . . Nobody saw anything, no fingerprints . . . And, as if that wasn't enough, there was even a swastika . . .'

'A swastika? What do you mean?'

'Listen, Bordelli – *Inspector* Bordelli, that is . . . Why don't you handle this dreadful affair?'

'Thanks for thinking of me, but I'd rather wait for the next murder. I don't want to deprive Del Lama of the thrill of arresting the killer.'

'This is a difficult case – we need someone with experience.'

'If you like I could give Del Lama a few pointers . . .'

'Such as?' asked the commissioner, staring at him.

'First of all, he should probe deep into the victim's private life. Usually a murder of this kind masks something unexpected. It might come out, for example, that the prelate lived a double life. Maybe he lent money at usurious rates, or sold indulgences under the table, or was some sort of perverted child-rapist . . . And, you know what? I've changed my mind: if you want, I *will* take the case . . .'

'No, no, no . . . If you put it that way, it's out of the question. Do you want to create a scandal? I've already got a call from a big fish at the Vatican, and have even heard from Minister Taviani. I'm supposed to report daily on the progress of the investigation . . . I'm under orders to proceed with extreme sensitivity, so you can forget about digging into the priest's private life . . .' said Inzipone, nervously bending a pen as if wanting to break it.

'All right, then, sir.'

'All we needed was that damned swastika. Bloody hell . . .' the commissioner muttered, biting his lips.

'I'm sorry, but what office should I use?'

'You can take your own back; nobody else has moved in.'

'That's excellent news. I'm a creature of habit . . . Have a very good day, sir . . .'

'See you later, Bordelli.'

'Break a leg on that sensitive case . . .'

'Oh, to hell with it all!' said Inzipone, almost yelling.

The inspector gave a slight bow and left, ignoring the

commissioner's embittered mutterings. He went down to the first floor and pushed open the door to his office. It smelled stale in there, and he threw open the windows. A golden, almost blinding light was filtering through a break in the clouds. Less than six months had passed since he'd left his gun and badge on the commissioner's desk, but he felt as if he was returning after a decades-long voyage. How many times had he looked out of that window, trying to put his thoughts in order? How many paces taken back and forth across the room . . . How many cigarettes smoked while watching a moribund fly crash against the walls . . .

He left the window open and sat down at *his* desk . . . Other memories surfaced in his mind . . . Depositions . . . Interrogations . . . Confessions . . . He ran a finger over the dust and smiled. Nothing represented time better than dust.

He shut his pistol up in the bottom drawer, where he had always kept it. Three more years, and they would put him out to pasture. Now that he lived in the country, however, the idea no longer scared him.

He picked up the phone and called Mugnai, to find out whether Piras was on duty.

'He's out on patrol, Inspector. But his shift is almost over, so he should be back shortly.'

'Could you please tell him to come up and see me as soon as he gets in?'

'Where are you, exactly, Inspector?' Mugnai asked, unsure.

'In my office . . . Consider this my official announcement that, as of tomorrow morning, I'm back on the job.'

'Nooooh! This is a great day, Inspector . . . I won't tell a soul, sir . . .'

They said goodbye, and Bordelli lit his first cigarette of the day. He started staring at the wall before him, realising he remembered every single crack in the plaster. He could only imagine how much hair poor Inspector Del Lama must be pulling out of his head at that moment, in his struggle with his 'sensitive' case. You had to stick your nose everywhere to make any progress at all on any case, and the murder of Monsignor Sercambi was a particularly hard nut to crack . . . What was the motive? Nobody had any idea. And the murder weapon? A pair of gloved hands. Witnesses? None. Even the best detective in the world could never make head or tail of it. Against fate, they were all powerless . . .

He forgot about Monsignor Sercambi and continued his aimless journey through his memories, as the office slowly filled with ghosts. How many people had sat there before him, to answer his questions? And what if he'd been wrong once, and sent an innocent to jail? He certainly had done the opposite once, letting the killer of a loan shark go free . . . And now he was letting himself go free as well . . .

There was a knock at the door, it opened and Piras appeared.

'Inspector . . . Don't tell me you're . . .'

'I'm back, Piras.'

'I'm glad to hear it . . .' said the Sardinian, waving away the smoke with his hand.

'I was hoping at least for some sort of Tarzan yell.'

'I'm yelling inside, Inspector.'

'The famous silent yell of the Sardinians . . .'

'Can I ask you a question?'

'Go right ahead . . . Why don't you sit down?'

'Was it you who killed Giacomo's three killers?' Piras asked point blank, still standing. He stared hard at Bordelli, as though trying to discover the truth in his eyes.

'What's got into you, Piras?'

'I just wanted to say that if it was you, you did the right thing.'

'It wasn't me, Piras . . . It was clearly fated to happen . . .' said Bordelli.

'I'd gladly have lent you a hand, if you'd asked,' the Sardinian persisted.

'I haven't done anything, Piras. I've merely been patient, and my patience has paid off . . .'

He sat down at the table in front of a plate of pasta but did not turn on the telly. He'd spent the remainder of the afternoon wandering about the back streets in the centre of Florence, turning around to look at the girls' bare legs.

Once back at home, he'd lit a big fire. Now and then he turned to watch the flames twisting up into the flue. One vein in a still-fresh log was emitting a tongue of smoke that hissed like a snake. Blisk's bowl was still in its customary place. Just looking at it was enough to make him see the white bear running through the woods again . . .

Now he was certain he would never tell the fable of the four ogres to anyone. Now that it was all over, he could grasp in full the enormity of what he'd done. He alone would bear the burden of the whole nasty affair; and that was only right. The responsibility was his alone; he mustn't share it with anyone. He couldn't quite work out whether he actually felt guilty or not. But he'd acted with conviction, and if he could go back in time, he would do it again. And you certainly couldn't say it had been a walk in the park . . .

An era had ended, and another was beginning. Who knew what surprises awaited him? The following morning he would resume working with the police, and after the first murder he would set out to find the culprit . . . What was it, really, that drove him to hunt down killers? Was it only a simple desire for justice? Or was he driven by some dark motive that had found an outlet in his profession? Perhaps it was some kind of psychic flaw, an obsessive need to set shattered balances right again, to close circles. When he was a little boy he used to have trouble falling asleep when his father was in a bad mood for no apparent reason, or if he'd seen his mother furtively wipe away a tear.

He finished his supper and went and sat by the fire, with a glass in hand. He even lit a cigarette . . . All that was missing was Venus, to reduce him to ash . . .[28] The death's-head watched him, smiling, from atop the cupboard. Was it trying to tell him something? Perhaps what he was already thinking: now that it was all over, perhaps he could see Eleonora again. He could tell her the terrible fable was over, the ogre had been defeated . . . *And they all lived happily ever after* . . . Why couldn't it actually be that way? He tossed his cigarette butt into the flames and stood up, feeling impatient. He grabbed a pen and paper and sat down at the table.

*Dear Eleonora,*

*I have never once stopped thinking of you, but only now have I found the courage to write to you. What happened has weighed as heavy as a boulder on my conscience, but I cannot resign myself to the idea that evil could ever destroy something so beautiful. I have so many things to tell you, if you're willing to listen. I'm not very good at expressing what I feel; only poets can find the right words. All I can say is that I wish I had you here with me now, in my arms. I've moved house, and now live in the country. I include here my new telephone number. If you want to call me, know that it would make me very happy.*

*Franco*

He'd managed at last to write something acceptable, perhaps because he hadn't worried about finding the right words. He'd wanted only to be sincere. Carefully folding the letter, he smoothed it out with one hand. The following morning he would buy an envelope, and after licking it shut, he would write Eleonora's address on it . . . He pictured the moment when he would post it, imagining the metal hatch of the mailbox swallowing it up . . .

Shaking his head, he got up, went over to the fireplace and tossed the letter into the fire. Watching the flames devour it, he thought he would once again let fate decide.

He went out for a short walk, cutting through the olive grove. Although it was night, from the valley below came a great din of twittering birds in love . . . Every male was desperately seeking his female . . .

'Do you, Marianna Salimbeni, take Peppino Diotivede to be your lawfully wedded husband, to love and to cherish, for richer, for poorer, in sickness and in health, till death do you part?'

'I do,' said Marianna, as Rosa wiped a tear from her eye, looking over at Bordelli.

'And do you, Peppino Diotivede, take Marianna Salimbeni to be your lawfully wedded wife, to love and to cherish, for richer, for poorer, in sickness and in health, till death do you part?'

'Of course, that's why I'm here . . .'

'You're supposed to say "*I do*",' the priest whispered, as the people laughed.

'Yes, I do . . .'

# Acknowledgements

Laura and Enneli . . . *Semper* . . .

Neri Torrigiani: On the door of his bedroom in his country house he hung the handwritten sign of his great-great-great grandfather Davide, father of the poet Renato Fucini, the full text of which was quoted by Dante Pedretti at Bordelli's birthday dinner party, as part of the story of the death of his grandfather Alfonso.

Stella Viera and Vania Dionisi, for their help with French.

Domenico Antonioli, for his help with Massese dialect.

Piera Biagi and Cesare Rinaldi, for their advice in farming matters.

Carlo Zucconi, for his long and profitable talks with me in the woods.

Laura Nosenzo, for giving me the Parker pen with which I corrected this novel. A Parker is always a Parker.

Inspector Franco Bordelli, for having generously told me one of the most harrowing stories of his life.

# NOTES

## by Stephen Sartarelli

1. – A Tuscan term for a sort of itinerant pedlar.
2. – Roughly the equivalent of several thousand pounds, which at the time amounted to a considerable sum.
3. – Giacomo Leopardi (1798–1837), 'Il tramonto della luna', XXXIII, *Canti*.
4. – The famous Fascist 'battle cry', invented during the First World War by the poet Gabriele D'Annunzio, who claimed it was once the battle cry of the ancient Greeks. The latter part of the cry, *alalà*, derived from the Greek verb ἀλαλάζω (*alalázo*), is found in Pindar and Euripides and appears in the work of nineteenth-century Italian poets Giovanni Pascoli and Giosuè Carducci as well. Mussolini later adopted the *eja eja alalà!* as the vocal equivalent of the Fascist salute, itself derived from the Roman era.
5. – A comical Italian caper film from 1958 (*I soliti ignoti* in the original, released as *Big Deal on Madonna Street* in the US), by Mario Monicelli, starring Totò, Vittorio Gassmann, Marcello Mastroianni and Claudia Cardinale, among others, in which a carefully planned burglary comes to naught.
6. – The Carbonari ('charcoal-burners') were a widely scattered secret society of revolutionaries in early nineteenth-century Italy who fomented a number of uprisings.
7. – Primo Carnera (1906–1967) was a famous Italian boxer who was world heavyweight champion for 1933/34 and known for his tremendous size.

8. – By Italian custom, the offspring of titled nobility can use diminutive forms of the titles of their parents. Thus the daughter of a count or countess becomes a *contessina*.

9. – In Florence, the Lungarno is the avenue running above the banks of the Arno.

10. – *Questo matrimonio non si ha da fare*. A famous line from Alessandro Manzoni's nineteenth-century novel *The Betrothed*, in which the marriage between the book's young protagonists is opposed by a local feudal lord, who wants the bride for himself.

11. – In 1959 Socialist MP Lina Merlin passed the law that bears her name, outlawing organised prostitution, including brothels, while keeping prostitution – that is, the exchange of sexual services for money – technically legal. The upshot was to drive most prostitutes into the streets.

12. – A much-quoted phrase ('*corrispondenza d'amorosi sensi*') from the famous 1807 poem by the pre-Romantic poet Ugo Foscolo (1778–1827), "I sepocri." It refers to the communication, through love, between the living and the souls of the dead.

13. – That is, the red star of communism. The Case del Popolo were social centres established and run by the Italian Communist Party.

14. – In 1565, at the behest of Duke Cosimo I de' Medici, Giorgio Vasari, famed author of the *Lives of the Artists* but also a painter and architect in his own right, designed an elevated corridor connecting the Palazzo Vecchio to the Palazzo Pitti on the other side of the river, passing by way of the Ponte Vecchio, where it can be seen as an upper storey above the sundry structures lining the bridge.

15. – That is because the March on Rome, when about thirty thousand Fascist militants marched upon the capital city, demanding that their party be handed the reins of power if the country wished to avoid a violent coup, occurred on 8 October 1922.

16. – That is, after Mussolini's Fascist government fell, the Nazis

occupied Italy, and the country had to be wrested back from German hands.

17. – In Italy the number 17 is believed to bring the same bad luck as the number 13 in the English-speaking world; hence Friday the 17th has the same connotation as our Friday the 13th.

18. – Lire, that is. Roughly equivalent to twelve thousand pounds at the time.

19. – In keeping with a fine Italian tradition, Botta prays to the Blessed Virgin to make his criminal endeavour a success. The exhortation means: 'O my beautiful little Madonna, make it all go well.'

20. – That is, Bordelli was conscripted and sent off to war when Italy, as a member of the Axis and ally of Nazi Germany, joined the German war effort; but he ended up shooting at Nazis as a volunteer member of those Italian brigades which, after the fall of Mussolini's government on 8 September 1943, joined the Allied effort to reconquer Italy from the Nazis – who had occupied the country after Mussolini's initial fall, only to prop him back up as the puppet head of the quisling Republic of Salò in the north of Italy – often serving as an advance guard and taking on the risky responsibilities of reconnaissance and de-mining.

21. – A Latin saying. The full phrase is *ubi major minor cessat*, which means, roughly, 'where [there is] the greater, the lesser gives way'.

22. – A series of untranslatable puns based on Ennio Bottarini's nickname, 'Botta', which means, variously, 'blast', 'burst', 'blow' and so on. The play on words could be said to mean, roughly, and respectively, 'Quip-counter-quip' (or 'Blow-counter-blow'), 'A blast and then off', 'Sucker punch' and 'Chez Outburst'.

23. – A traditional dish of broad egg noodles (*pappardelle*) in a sauce of stewed hare (*lepre*).

24. – The protagonist of *Tex*, an internationally popular Italian

Wild West serial comic book first created in 1948 by Gian Luigi Bonelli and Aurelio Galleppini and still published today.

25. – Giovanni Della Casa (1503–1556) was a writer and Roman Catholic prelate (who rose to the rank of archbishop) known above all for his book on good manners, the *Galateo overo de' costumi*, known in English as *Galateo: The Rules of Polite Behaviour*, which was published posthumously, in Venice, in 1558.

26. – The actual quote is 'Everything must change, so that everything can stay the same', a bon mot uttered by Tancredi Falconeri, the beloved nephew of the Prince of Salina, Fabrizio, main protagonist of Giuseppe Tomasi di Lampedusa's 1958 novel *Il Gattopardo* (The Leopard), when trying to convince his conservative uncle why he must support the Garibaldian unification of Italy, which would purportedly bring about a bourgeois-liberal order, as opposed to the old aristocratic one.

27. – An Italian aphorism attributed to Leonardo da Vinci.

28. – In Italian there is a saying that *Bacco, tabacco e venere, riducono l'uomo in cenere*, which loses its sonority, and therefore its charm and purpose, in English translation ("Bacchus, tobacco, and Venus will reduce man to ashes"). As Bordelli has just poured himself a glass of wine and lit up a cigarette, his conclusion is that all that is missing is the goddess of love to finish him off.

# Death in Florence

Marco Vichi

Florence, October 1966. The rain is never-ending. When a young boy vanishes on his way home from school the police fear the worst, and Inspector Bordelli begins an increasingly desperate investigation.

Then the flood hits. During the night of 4th November the swollen River Arno, already lapping the arches of the Ponte Vecchio, breaks its banks and overwhelms the city. Streets become rushing torrents, the force of the water sweeping away cars and trees, doors, shutters and anything else in its wake.

In the aftermath of this unimaginable tragedy the mystery of the child's disappearance seems destined to go unsolved. But obstinate as ever, Bordelli is not prepared to give up.

Out now in paperback and ebook

HODDER

Shortlisted for the Crime Writers' Association
International Dagger 2013

# Death in Sardinia

Marco Vichi

Florence, 1965. A man is found murdered, a pair of scissors stuck
through his throat. Only one thing is known about him – he was a
loan shark, who ruined and blackmailed the vulnerable men and
women who would come to him for help.

Inspector Bordelli prepares to launch a murder investigation. But
the case will be a tough one for him, arousing mixed emotions:
the desire for justice conflicting with a deep hostility for the
victim. And he is missing his young police sidekick, Piras, who is
convalescing at his parents' home in Sardinia.

But Piras hasn't been recuperating for long before he too has a
mysterious death to deal with . . .

Out now in paperback and ebook

**HODDER**

# Death and the Olive Grove

## Marco Vichi

April 1964, but spring hasn't quite sprung. The bad weather seems suited to nothing but bad news. And bad news is coming to the police station.

First, Bordelli's friend Casimiro, who insists he's discovered the body of a man in a field above Fiesole. Bordelli races to the scene, but doesn't find any sign of a corpse.

Only a couple of days later, a little girl is found at Villa Ventaglio. She has been strangled, and there is a horrible bite mark on her belly. Then another little girl is found murdered, with the same macabre signature.

And meanwhile Casimiro has disappeared without a trace.

The investigation marks the start of one of the darkest periods of Bordelli's life: a nightmare without end, as black as the sky above Florence.

Out now in paperback and ebook

**HODDER**